Sword of Cho Nisi

Book 1

Rise of the Tobian Princess

D. L. Gardner

Sword of Cho Nisi
Book 1

This story is the sole work of
D. L. Gardner.
No portion may be copied or used in any form without the consent of the author except for small portions in a review.
@ 2021 D. L. Gardner

Information may be obtained by contacting
Dianne L Gardner at gardnersart.com

All characters are fictitious and any resemblance to any place or person is purely coincidental.

More works by the author as well as video and audio are listed on the author's website. https://gardnersart.com

Cover design Mario Teodosio
marioteodosioart.com

"(Sword of Cho Nisi book 1) is a nicely packaged fantasy adventure with a good secondary romance. There's never a dull moment in here; it's jam-packed with monumental events and action to look forward to. Princess Erika is one hero that readers are going to be thrilled to discover."
 - *The Independent Book Review*

"A masterful painter of words, D.L. Gardner's brush strokes of prose bring to life a compelling fantasy tale that demonstrates the power of forgiveness and redemption in the aftermath of tragedy."

 - *Award-winning author Stephen Zimmer of the Fires In Eden Series and the Rayden Valkyrie and Ragnar Stormbringer Tales.*

*This story is dedicated to my sons and daughters.
It's my hope that you find your strength in the storm.*

Contents

Erika	12
Skotádi	17
Cho Nisi's Magic	20
Lord Garion	29
Beasts of Mount Ream	36
Kairos the Wizard	47
Barin and the King	52
New Magic	61
The Sisters	66
Erika's Plea	70
The Wharf	74
A Spy	82
The Castle at Cho Nisi	85
They're Coming	89
Erika's Landing	94
King Tobias	98
Arell's Tactics	102
Erika the conqueror	108
Failed Query	117
Kairos' Answer	123
Relent	128
Misgivings	135
Olinda and Rhea	138
Dark Lord at Fairmistle	143
The Ride	148
Aftermath	153
Silas and Kairos	159

A King's Tears	165
Mourning	171
A Skura Spy	174
Erika's trial	176
Erika and Sylvia	183
Homecoming	188
Captured	194
Osage	204
Despondency	217
Rory	222
The Dark Lord's Prisoner	230
Barin and Skotádi	235
Journey Home	251
Invasion of Cho Nisi	260
Rory Visits Fairmistle	267
Siege	273
Kairos' escape	280
Arell's letter	288
A Wounded King	293
Witnesses	300
The King's Son	303
The Curse	311
Father's Wisdom	315
Truth	319
Return	330
Acknowledgments	337

Erika

Erika's woolen cowl hung over her forehead, veiling her pale complexion so she didn't glow when the moon rose. Crouched in a crevice, bow in hand, she guarded the men-at-arms as they hurried down the ridge of the canyon.

"By the might of my father's gods, keep them safe," she prayed as they dashed into the shadows. They weren't just soldiers, they were the men she'd sparred with and who taught her what she knew concerning warfare. Men she admired. Men whose characters she respected—powerful men. She'd be joining them for the first time in action against the opponent. A chill of excitement rushed through her, but a knot formed in her stomach when she caught wind of their foe.

"Barin, these skura smell worse than boar's hair in a sty!" she uttered. Her brother slid into the cranny alongside her. His warm breath against her ear reinforced her confidence, and a smile crossed her face. He rested a hand on her shoulder and pointed to the hillside. "Look! There's one across the way. See it?"

The bright of the setting sun blinded her but for the silhouette of an olive tree and the lone skura that perched on its limb. The beast—tall as a man—unfolded a featherless wing twice the size of its height. When it did, it blocked out the sun, allowing her to see its features. She shrank at its size and the ugliness of its body, owl eyes, a squat nose, and fangs that protruded from its human mouth.

"They're horrid. How could anyone live around them?" she asked, sinking further onto her knees and staring at the creature. Barin had described them to her at home, in the comfort of the grand hall over a chalice of wine. How much more daunting they were in the flesh!

"It's not as though Lord Garion has a choice."

She took her eyes off the skura to study Barin. "Tell me. Is it true this wizard bonded with the emperor of Casdamia to gain power to control these creatures?"

Barin hadn't admitted to believing in the Vouchsaver named Skotádi. The legends came from country folk who lived in the southern villages along the River Ream. Even Erika thought the tale far-fetched. According to legend, the wizard Skotádi had taken on the properties of his magic rather than wielding it, and bonded himself to the emperor Bahldi in a conspiracy to conquer the world.

"Someone assassinated Bahldi the Great years ago," Erika whispered. "If this Skotádi still lives, did he bond to Bahldi's grandson, Barte, son of Moshere, as well? Are these skura a leg of the Casdamia's army? Or is Skotádi acting on his own?"

"You're assuming the legends are true."

"Well, if they were true, what would Skotádi want with these vineyards?"

"Revenge, they say," Barin replied.

She peeked at him. His smile had disappeared, replaced by a set jaw.

"Our grandfather fought these beasts, Erika. Same enemy. Same war."

"Then it's ours to end." She lifted her bow.

"Not yet." He stayed her hand. "Patience. We'll have plenty of opportunities to kill these beasts. Wait for the ambush." He surveyed the terrain. "A band of foreign warriors is coming to aid us. I'm not sure when they'll be here, but we can't wait too much longer. We need to attack before dark."

Erika took her focus off the skura and regarded the landscape. Limestone cliffs grew dim as the sun sank behind the crest of the mountain. Nothing stirred. No sound, not even the chirp of a cricket. The breeze itself held its breath—no sign of any foreign army.

"When Commander Neal and I reach the olive grove, we'll strike. Shouldn't be more than a hundred of these beasts, and then we'll dodge for cover. You and these men will pick off the ones that fly out of the gorge."

Erika wet her lips and glanced at the men hunkered along the rim. They had crossbows, a Casdamian weapon so new to their kingdom Barin hadn't yet trained her with one.

You'll do well." Barin patted her on the back. His smile reassured her. "After this, you won't need to petition Father to come with me. I have faith in you, Princess Erika."

"Thank you, Prince Barin," she uttered with a grin. Nothing pleased her more than her brother's trust.

Silence cloaked the landscape as Barin joined his men-at-arms, now swallowed in shadow. Erika blew a curl from her forehead. Today held her chance to prove to her father she could be a warrior.

She switched hands holding her longbow, and then brushed the dampness off her palms onto her leather leg guards, taking a deep breath to quiet her racing heart. The few men on the ridge crouched by her side with their poisoned bolts loaded, waiting for her brother's wave—young men and less experienced than Barin's men—but zealous.

The breeze from the mountain summit picked up again as dusk encroached, dropping the temperature. She hadn't grown accustomed to the bitter cold, but at least snow had not yet covered the ground.

Samuel, the soldier next to her, nudged her.

"That skura—the one you were watching—I think he's seen your brother."

As soon as Erika sighted the beast, it took to flight and glided above the canyon, circling over Barin. Her brother glanced her way, pointed at it, and then dove behind a rock. Taking that as a signal, Erika aimed, but it didn't attack. Instead, it landed somewhere to the right of her in the brush just as the sun fell below the horizon. The world gave way to the darkness she felt more than saw. She blinked hard—the fading landscape played tricks on her. Because the skura was so large, it should have been visible, and yet she saw nothing, only the rustling of sward where no other grass stirred.

A heavy breath helped to steady her hands as she drew her bowstring. Samuel waved at the other men and they slipped out of her line of fire. Her target moved.

Something stirred behind the tree limbs, and images of her brother being devoured by these horrid beasts flashed in her mind. More rustling in the bushes and the sound of wings flapping quickened her reflexes, and then a deafening howl, so brash Erika winced.

She let loose her arrow.

Someone screamed.

With what rumbled like headwaters rushing into a canyon, a dark cloud of flying beasts tore out of the trees below, soaring in formation like a plump of geese.

"Draw bow and sword!" Barin's order echoed through the ravine as the enemy stormed upon them too soon. The other soldiers scattered, dropping into the valley to fight with Barin's men. Erika swallowed her fear and slipped over more rocky terrain to join them. She skidded down the hill, dodged behind a tree, and released her arrows in rapid succession.

No sooner had she reached the basin when an opened-mouth skura flailed at her, its bloody tongue flapping in the wind. Before she could shoot, its talons snatched her by the shoulders and dragged her through the brush. As it dug into her leather armor, she dropped her bow and clenched her dagger. She slashed the beast's scabby legs. Its talons dug deeper as it dragged her over rocks, stripping her baldric free, crushing her quiver, and breaking the pack off her back. She thrust her dagger into its body. Blood splattered. The skura released her, and she plummeted to the ground. The wounded beast fell beside her. She rolled away from the skura's body, staggered to her feet, and picked up a sword lying next to a fallen soldier, then charged into combat swinging and hacking at scaly forms and ghastly faces that screeched until her ears hurt. Her arms grew heavy. Her fingers cramped around the hilt of the weapon, but she could not stop lest she die.

Louder than the skura's screeches, drums beat.

Drums?

A force unseen sucked the beast she had been fighting into the sky and a whirlwind took shape, spinning it and hundreds of other winged beasts into the heavens. The faster the drums beat, the wilder the wind reeled until the entire legion hovered overhead.

Just as the pounding had started, the drumming ceased, and the horde of skura tumbled. Soldiers dodged out of the way as the skura crashed against the earth one after another, dust billowing into the air. When the grime settled, a pile of dead skura remained.

Silence followed.

Erika swayed, blinked sweat out of her eyes, and wiped the blood from her face. Her shoulder ached. She abandoned the sword letting it drop into the same dust that will bury its keeper. Soldiers rose from the debris, stumbling among the fallen, treading over the limp bodies of men and beasts. There must have been twenty Potamian soldiers fallen. Many more skura than Barin had estimated lay scattered among them.

Barin ran up the slope and met with his commander and several other men who hid in the shadows. She followed and paused when Barin, his face pale in shock, fell on his knees at the feet of a white-haired man lying in the grass. The stranger wore attire she had never seen. Leather pants, red bands adorned his ankles, turtle shells covered his calves, beads laced his neck, and black feathers fastened dangled from his arms and in his hair. Armor made of woven grass had shielded him but now collapsed, broken apart, an arrow embedded in his chest.

Her arrow.

She stepped back as Barin dropped the dead man's wrist, leapt to his feet, and marched toward her. His cheeks flushed.

Erika's blood ran cold.

She stumbled over the stony field as Barin grabbed her arm and pulled her away from the others.

"Don't let those people know you did this!"

"I—," she stuttered as she watched Commander Neal and a group of dark-skinned men approach the body. Dressed identically to the fallen—feathers in their long dark hair—drums strapped to their backs, the foreigners carried the dead man up the hillside, making a somber procession against the last light of the day. They sang a low, mournful chant.

Neal hurried toward Barin.

Thoughts flew through Erika's mind, but no words formed. She tried to recall what had happened, how she had mistaken those men for the enemy, but found no excuse. She'd been a fool, a mindless, unintelligent fool!

"Who was he?" she muttered.

Barin let go of her arm as Neal moved between the two.

"It's over," Neal said. "They're going home."

Barin gave Neal a nod. "Not a word," he reminded Erika with a look so forbidding the impact drilled a hole in her heart. He pivoted and walked away.

Erika's unanswered question loomed.

"The Cho Nisi King. He and his warriors came to help us." Neal's voice lacked the fierceness of Barin's, yet his continence displayed the gravity of the man's death. He followed Barin.

Stripped of dignity, Erika's heart sank as shame devoured her. Her hands shook, her throat tightened. Had they abandoned her on a raft in the middle of the ocean, she would not have felt more alone.

Skotádi.

The Reign of Bahldi the Great during the time of The Eastern Conquest. Ninety years prior to the reign of Barte Son of Moshere. In the desert plains of Lativia. Summer months.

Skotádi hurled the curse across the valley while his voice echoed off the buttes surrounding the river basin.

"This is the decree of Bahldi the Great, conqueror of Lativia's kingdom," he announced.

A brilliant burst of light swallowed the sun for a crushing moment and then, like a sheet of ice, the Vouchsaver's spell crystalized. Sharp fragments of rime fell on the enemy's army. Horses reared and froze, forelegs stretched, stiffened in mid-air. Men's arms froze above their heads, swords suspended, glistening in the sun. Every fighting man in the Lativian army—mounted or on foot—solidified. Bahldi charged, his cavalry thundered from the foothills, their battle cry rang in Skotádi's ears. A bloody massacre took place before him as the enemy shattered like fragile glass with the swipe of Casdamian blades.

Skotádi once gloated in this magical mastery, but today a cynical smile thinned his lips. The death of the Lativian soldiers didn't bother him. He drooled at the sight of their dying bodies when their pathetic souls drifted above their corpses as tiny yellow clouds of pain and defeat. If he were in the fields, he would consume those vapors of death, a savory lunch for a Vouchsaver. The tasty morsels would have given him strength, confidence, and even more power, which would eventually benefit his bondmaster, the emperor.

What a waste!

For three battles the emperor sent him atop a hill or mesa to wield his curse, far enough from killing fields that Skotádi could not reap the harvest of souls. He'd been brewing over this oppression all morning, and now that he saw what a huge in-gathering he could have devoured, he clenched his fist. Hot air streamed from his nostrils. And to think of all the boasting the emperor did the night before.

Bahldi's conquest of the northeastern kingdoms lasted over three moons' time. They traveled over mountains and plains, conquering cities and villages, and gathering bounty as their victory allotted them. Bahldi took the glory for himself even though without the Vouchsaver he would have fallen a long time ago. What did Skotádi get as a reward? Not the satisfaction of tribute, nor the tang of men's spirits, but a mere mage's pittance. Didn't he and the emperor have a bond that sealed their psyches as one body? Was being a Vouchsaver to Bahldi worth nothing more than enough coin to buy a bowl of stew?

Today marked the ultimate victory, the final subjugation before the Great Rivers prohibited their crossing to further conquest. After plundering the city of Lativia, Bahldi would travel south and return to Casdamia as the Grand Lord of all that lay east of Casa de Moor and southeast of Ream River. 'The Mighty One', Skotádi heard the emperor call himself while boasting to his confidants. Not a mention of the Vouchsaver and the magic that put his enemies in their hands. Not a word about Skotádi.

"You must give me reign to wander the killing fields and reap the bounty." The taste in Skotádi's mouth turned bitter as the emperor chuckled when the wizard visited him in his grand marquis. The tent swayed in the desert breeze—tapestries that hung as walls rustled—the lantern flickered. Bahldi lay against the embroidered pillows piled on the sheepskins. He had a parchment bound in leather on his lap, and a quill in his hand, sucking the tip. He did not bother to look up at Skotádi.

The Vouchsaver's lust for souls burned hot in his gut and hotter even more now that the emperor ignored him.

"Your incessant soul-sucking would warn our enemy of our tactics. I don't care to have you seen, nor even rumored. No, Skotádi, you must remain anonymous at all times." The bald man looked up at Skotádi and squinted his dark beady eyes. His long mustache rippled when he sneered. "Better no one but our men know you even exist. You're not a pretty picture, Skotádi, most of our men would rather not see you at all."

Skotádi's appearance frightened people, but did he care? His potions boiled over and splattered on more than one occasion, pitting his face. Long nights of conjuring magic deepened the hollows of his eyes. Still, appearances had nothing to do with the bargain the emperor made.

"And take the glory for yourself?"

Bahldi shrugged. "What is glory? You wanted half the kingdom, didn't you?"

Skotádi would have no power if he were only owner and not ruler of the kingdom.

He'd grown tired of Bahldi. One could not break a Vouchsaver bond, but if he made more power for himself than he made for Bahldi, the tables would turn, and Bahldi would beg him for mercy. That very night, Skotádi vowed he'd retreat into the caves of Mount Ream and create mayhem for the emperor.

Cho Nisi's Magic

Stars glimmered in the heavens—their reflections sparkled in the sea as jewels would if they were submerged in pools of dark waters. A ribbon of silver from the moon rise outlined where the earth ended, and firmament began. The western shore of the Island of Cho Nisi blushed, beckoning breakers to grind its shells and stones to powder. Crabs scrambled about sideways, scavenging for whatever menu the tide served.

Arell rested on driftwood, his bare feet buried in the cool sand, his dark hair tied back over his shoulders. He wore his embroidered gambeson, more to stay warm than to boast his princely status. The plume on his hat quaked and his cloak rustled with his movements as he carved an arrowhead from a fine specimen of jade he'd found that afternoon.

Chief Silas—dressed in his ceremonial tunic, beads adorning his neck—beat quietly on a cottonwood drum with other members of the tribe. They chanted an incantation that provided a protective spell around the island, making it invisible to foreign eyes. Tradition mandated the vigil whenever the Cho Nisi faced danger. Arell's father, King Rolland, and many of the island's warriors left a little over a week ago to aide their neighbors to the North in a battle against a dark lord. They would return soon. Tonight. Arell lifted his head often, watching the sea. With the return of his father's ship, Silas would have to lift the spell to let them in.

A warm breeze shifted sands along the beach, sweeping a lock of hair into Arell's eyes. He brushed it back and breathed in the sea's fragrance, satisfied in the choice he made to help Silas keep watch tonight. Just as the wind carried the sand, so too, rumors floated in the air, and some had reached him earlier today. Whisperings from the city of Moaton that he should be more princely and enjoy the wealth of the palace. To Arell, the night skies along the shore dwarfed the majestic halls in the castle. White sands were more lovely than silken pillows and gilded furniture. No incense brought to him in royal bronze burners could match the fragrance of the ocean. No, on these beaches lay his sanctuary. The rumors didn't bother him.

A soft tap hit his cloak and laughter came from the cliffs above. Arell peered over his shoulder at Silas's two daughters tossing pebbles at him. He waved at Serena and her younger sister Bena, both wearing white chitons that caught the moon's rays and made them glow like angels.

They blew kisses. He shook his head and turned back to face the sea.

"What would you do if you ever had to take on the responsibility of the crown?" Silas asked him as he glanced back at the girls and chuckled.

"The Moaton Crown? King of Cho Nisi?" Arell shrugged. He never gave the idea much thought since his father showed little sign of aging. He would worry about succeeding him in due time. His grandfather and several hundred immigrants came from the Casdamian Empire on the mainland to the island, seeking refuge years ago. Their treaty with the Cho Nisi chiefs granted them their own village and gave them power as envoys with foreign nations, as long as they lived in harmony and respected the native's way of life. When his grandfather died, his father took the throne and ruled peacefully for decades. Arell, having a Cho Nisi mother, preferred living with the tribal people and spent little time in the palace. The Cho Nisi taught him to hunt and fish and build canoes and many other crafts. Fresh air and white shores lured him away from the rigid stone castle, built high on a hill overlooking the entire island and all the sea. Equally dark and cold nested the immigrant village of Moaton where his father's people lived.

Arell opened his mouth to respond to Silas when the chief moved away from him. Two soft hands covered Arell's eyes from behind, and girlish laughter warmed his ears. He placed his carving down on the driftwood, reached back, and took Serena's arms. She wiggled away. He stubbed his toe on driftwood as he leapt over the log and chased her. Bena tossed another pebble at him when he caught Serena, who hadn't tried to escape. He lifted Serena, cradling her in his arms, and swung her around. The fabric of her silken dress wafted in the breeze. She weighed next to nothing compared to his strength. He marveled at her smooth dark skin and her catching smile. Holy Idols! What a pretty woman! As he set her down, she grabbed his hair, her dark eyes tempting. "Let go," he laughed, trying to free himself.

Bena threw another pebble.

"Oh, so you want attention too?" he asked the younger child. Serena released his hair and Arell caught the little one in his arms and tossed her into the air. She screamed. When she could barely catch her breath from laughing so hard, he set her in the sand. Serena grasped onto his arm, pulled him to her, and kissed his cheek. He would have liked her kiss to last longer and on the lips, but being a tease, Serena slipped away. The two girls hurried back up the hill.

Arell sighed, not in the mood for running up the hill barefoot. He glanced at their father. "What would I do if I were king? Why I would bring your daughters into the castle and have them wait on me!" He laughed, sat down, and rubbed his sore toe.

Silas shook his head and took a seat on the driftwood. "You would make an interesting king," he chuckled. "My daughters are fond of you, Arell. Perhaps you'll marry one someday."

Arell shook his head in protest. Too soon for him to marry, he gently rebuked the Chief's attempts to couple him with Serena. Her father didn't need to find a husband for her. As lovely as any jewel, with her silky black hair, doe-like eyes, and bronze skin, her compassion surpassed her beauty. She cared about people, cooked better than any native on the island, and knew the healing remedies of the tribe. She could wed any warrior she chose. Arell wondered why she flirted with him so much. His right as a Moaton prince shouldn't impress her. With her father, the Cho Nisi chief, she already held the title of princess.

"There are too many attractive girls on the island, Silas. I'm not ready to settle on anyone in particular. You know that."

The chief nodded. "No. You're too flirtatious to have my daughter. Someday you'll take life more seriously, and then maybe I'll consent."

"Me flirtatious?" Arell laughed and glanced back at Serena. Who flirted with whom? His smile bent slightly, and he chuckled as he resumed carving.

Silas tapped on his drum softly and Arell regarded the sea. Had the sun been up and the sky clear, the tips of Mount Ream and Casda de Moor would peek over the horizon. Even then, one had to look hard to see them. Tonight, nothing but a dark vista suggested an endless ocean.

"Your father would be hard to replace. He's a righteous king, wise and kind. I told him not to be a part of this battle, but his good heart carried him away to help those people."

Arell nodded and considered Silas's frown. For a moment, the chief's doubt quickened his heart. He didn't expect something to go wrong, did he?

"Father, look!" Serena called out from the hill behind them. She pointed toward a shadowy mass in the sky, moving at rapid speed, blotting out the stars and darkening the moon.

The chief stood and waved to the drummers. "Skura! Shadows of evil," he announced.

The warriors, seeing the encroaching danger, picked up their instruments and ran down the beach, positioning themselves at key points along the way, until the last few men vanished into a nearby cove. Their chant immediately stirred the elements. A strong wind and ocean spray blinded Arell. The shoreline rippled, whirlpools formed in the sea, and a waterspout rose to the sky, climbing higher and higher until it reached the stream of darkness. As the cyclone swallowed the skura, they formed an ominous cloud that spun for a moment and then stopped. Arell held his breath as the earth stilled. A flash of lightning, a roar of thunder and the waterspout imploded. With a blood-curdling shriek, the entire body of skura fell and disappeared into a turbulent sea.

Arell watched through his spyglass and then focused on something in the water. "Silas!" He tucked the scope into a pocket in his gambeson. "Those skura were chasing a boat with our standard. The dingy is coming this way."

Silas whistled and waved to the drummers. The chanting ceased as the men signaled each other, and soon the wind died down, allowing quiet waters for the skiff to enter.

"It's Father," Arell announced. He splashed into the surf but stopped before he reached the dinghy. He had expected to see his father at the bow. "Where is he?" Arell asked the men on board as the hoy drifted ashore.

King Rolland should have been greeting him by now. Several men slipped out of the dinghy and into the gently rolling waves, guiding the craft to the beach. There were no happy words that met Arell's ears. No cheers of triumph. Arell waded further and helped pull the boat in, his cloak drenched—his hat flew into the breakers, but he didn't retrieve it. He asked again, but no one answered.

"I command you to tell me. Where is my father!"

"I'm sorry, Vasil. The king has fallen," one warrior said. "He's in the boat."

Reflections of stars glistened in the sea and cast a dim light on the people on board. The men ambled somberly—the wet boards of the skiff's deck creaked under their feet. The moment lasted for eternity as they beached. Arell climbed into the dinghy, his heart in his throat, afraid to face the reality that waited. Lying on the wet deck, hands folded across his chest, face peaceful in the moonlight, rested his father. Arell knelt next to him.

"He can't be."

Breathless, cold, and pale as the moon, his father's eyes were closed, his soul gone.

Disbelief stunned Arell like the sting of a centipede, and thrust him into another space and time, numbing his senses.

No one spoke.

Once the men had secured the hoy, someone touched Arell on the shoulder.

"Come," the chief said.

The warriors carried the king ashore and laid him on the sand. Arell stood over his father, too stunned to speak, too dazed to weep. He shook his head. His heart screamed, but not a sound escaped his lips.

"Arell," Chief Silas spoke. "What are your orders?"

Arell had no orders. He had nothing. Nothing!

"How did he die?" Chief Silas asked the men.

"An arrow through his heart," one warrior whispered.

Their voices resonated like iron against iron as Arell gazed upon the lifeless body. His father couldn't be dead. This didn't happen! He felt Silas's stare.

"Arell?" Silas said.

The shock had consumed Arell.

The chief turned to the men. "Keep vigil tonight. Watch for ships. Have sentries secure the castle," Chief Silas waved to the others. "Drummers!"

Several men ran quietly up the hill while the other warriors encircled Arell and his father's body. They chanted a dirge—the Cho Nisi Farewell Song.

The sea brings life as it trundles ashore
A heartbeat rolling like yours and mine
Milling sand from rock and stone.
Forever tumbling down life's gravel path
Swaying, singing, reeling
Until the last of days, we see
At rest our soul slumbers
Like the Sea of Nisi, soaking the sun with eyes closed
Farewell, my king.

Arell's grieving soul found solace in the gentle rumble of calm breakers rolling on silvery shores. He spent his days sitting next to his father's grave on the grassy slope overlooking the sea, refusing to return to the castle where memories were too painful to bear. He chose instead to spend his time outside. Alone. He thought it not fitting for a man, much less a prince to weep, and so Arell composed songs in his head and sang them to the wind, to the seagulls, to the starfish that clung to tide pools near the cliffs. He walked the coastline during the day and lay in the graveyard under the stars at night. How many moons lulled him to sleep he never counted, but if he had spent the rest of his life in melancholy by his father's grave, he would have been content.

After the seventh day of solitude, Arell returned from his walk along the coast to the burial grounds and found Chief Silas waiting for him. The older man stood solemnly as Arell trudged through the sand and up the hill. He avoided looking at Silas. The man no doubt would lecture him on being a chief—insist that he had a responsibility to lead the people of Cho Nisi and keep the island peaceable from the violent world that surrounded them—to hold fast to tradition and ceremony. Yes, Arell knew the native way of life. He learned the integrity and honor of the Cho Nisi. However, if Silas wanted a king to live in the castle, Silas should be that king, not Arell. His legacy died with his father. Arell wanted nothing more than to live humbly on the beach.

Arell walked past Silas, hoping the chief wouldn't say aloud what they were both thinking. Silas grabbed his arm gently but firmly. "You need to eat."

"Eat?"

"My daughters have brought you food."

Arell looked beyond the chief and saw that Serena and the chief's other daughters, not too much younger than himself, had spread a blanket on the grass near his father's grave. On the blanket were clay pots filled with cooked food, fruits, and a flask of wine.

Arell shook his head. His hunger had left him after the third day of fasting. He had no desire to eat. "I can't."

"No. You must. We'll eat with you."

"Silas—" His voice tapered. Refusing the natives' kindness would be offensive, but how do you forget your troubles? With food? With companionship? He'd be dishonoring his father to overlook his sorrow. "I can't just quit grieving, Silas. My heart won't let me."

Silas shook his head solemnly. "Grieve as you must. But your father left you his throne. You must rule from it."

Arell shook his head, looked at the sea, and breathed the salty air. Like life itself, the ocean was a never-ending sway of waves, faithful in the rocking of the breakers—eternally the same. He had no desire to rule anyone. Why couldn't they leave him alone?

"There is much trouble in this world, Arell. You saw the skura swarm when our warriors came home. That won't be the last we see of them. We're in a dangerous position. Our enemies know that our king died. They may plan an invasion. Who will lead us out of danger?"

"I'm no leader, Silas.".

"When your grandfather came to settle here, we had a truce. He and his heirs were to be our ambassadors, keep us safe from invading nations. That contract has come to you, Arell. You are the holder of that scepter."

His father had educated Arell enough to know that Silas spoke the truth. After the assassination of the emperor of Casdamia, his grandparents immigrated from Casdamia. They had a choice—flee or become slaves. They fled, and Cho Nisi took them in. In trade, the foreigners offered new skills that made the islanders' life simpler by helping them build sturdier homes that the winds could not blow over. They had made a road through the forested part of the island where the natives fetched fresh water and constructed carts and brought horses from the mainland. Everyone benefited from the trade, so much so that the Cho Nisi appointed the Moatons as mediators to foreign nations and allowed them to appoint their leader as King of Cho Nisi. The immigrants built a castle and the surrounding village high on the tallest hill of the island, which they called Moaton—a tribute to the lake they created which encircled the castle.

"Arell, the same danger in which your father's people fled hovers over this island. Should the Potamians attack the island, there is nowhere for us to flee. We have no other choice but to fight. When a ruler falls, it leaves a void on his throne. The king's heir or the king's enemy will fill that emptiness. Which is your will for us?" the chief asked, his face dour.

Arell sighed heavily. Silas spoke the truth.

"His heir," Arell whispered.

The chief nodded slightly, not only in agreement with Arell's answer but in approval. Arell would step into his father's place.

"It's destiny then, I suppose, isn't it? Very well." He observed the individuals who had gathered and the brilliant party that had begun. "It'll be hard to live in the castle alone. I'm not sure I can do it, Silas. Those walls are permeated with the essence of my father and my grandfather. I am not near the man they were. I'm inexperienced."

Chief Silas didn't respond to Arell's excuses or musings. He simply waited for Arell to talk it through. "You'll see me here on the beach more often than not. Fresh air and the sea are what I love. This is my existence. I cannot renounce any of this, Silas."

"I know. And I'll visit you in the castle, as well."

"Be my advisor?"

Silas nodded. "My family will go with you. My daughters, my sons."

His sons? That may not be so easy. Silas's two sons. Bejal and Ross were proud Cho Nisi warriors and despised everything about the Moatons, the castle, and even him. Arell chose not to press the matter.

"You're a good friend, Silas." Arell smiled at the girls. Their beauty and cheerfulness comforted him. Even during native funerals, they celebrated life, like today, with a feast spread out before him.

Though Silas's sons were not in attendance, other young Cho Nisi men brought their drums and lyres, already playing music. More people appeared on the hillside, laying more woven blankets, more food. More wine. Many of his father's people from Moaton mingled with the natives.

"Your father's spirit is here with you, celebrating. Join him," Silas took his arm and led him to the feast. Serena handed him a chalice of wine.

Silas waved his arm. "Choose which one of us you want to serve in the castle. All these people have offered to move into the palace with you if you so desired. Even my daughters."

Arell nodded and broke into a smile. "No one would live on the beaches then Silas."

How could he not accept this amity? He beamed at Serena and her sisters and the other young women who, dressed in white linen chitons with flowers braided into their hair, and beaded armbands around their silky bronze skin, giggled flirtatiously.

He could make do, he supposed.

Lord Garion

Shadowed by the mountain, the graveyard rested on a foothill overlooking the valley and one of Lord Garion's lush vineyards. Those who had survived the battle against the skura worked alongside Felix, Lord Garion's son. For five days they dug the ultimate resting place for those who had died at the hand of Skotádi's demons. Lord Garion had provided his finest hospitality during that time, affording ample food, shelter, and tents pitched in the soft soil of his tilled farmland.

Erika assisted in grave digging, working alongside soldiers she had fought with, and those with whom she sparred at home. Hearts were heavy and voices low. Men, whom they buried, had been friends and so laying them to rest became a solemn ceremony. Several times she had to step away from the scene to gain inner strength.

During those days she wandered into the gardens and the vineyards seeking solitude. Barin had warned her frequently about the aftermath of battle, and until now she'd never experienced such trauma.

"You must grow callouses, Erika," he had advised her. "War is not about glory. War is about death and seeing wounded people that you cannot help. It's about counting bodies and digging graves."

Part of her training entailed preparing to see death and experience sorrow. But how does one ready themselves to see friends die? She wished this battle had not been so lethal and that she hadn't caused the death of so many good men. Their kingdom had been under constant attack. That Lord Garion and his estate lived in such conflict made no sense. Tellwater residents wanted to till, plant, prune, harvest, and live a humble and honorable life. Even as a princess, Erika had yearned for a simpler life.

When the time came for the Potamians to return home, Lord Garion invited the troops to a feast in his manor. Every bit a castle in its own right, though not as adorned as her father's palace, the stonework and thatched roof encased a grand and beautiful interior with enormous rooms for both Lord Garion's family and some of his domestics. The large oak table filled the dining area, as extensive as any of her father's. Spread before them were savory loaves of bread, meat pies, and bowls of fruit paired with wines harvested from the vineyard awaited them. Erika's stomach stirred at aroma of such wholesome food. She waited until the men sat down and then she took a seat next to Neal.

Her brother sat across the table from her, taking the role of spokesperson for the group, as he should. "I and my men thank you for this hospitality, Lord Garion. We weren't expecting such cordiality."

Erika avoided eye contact with anyone while at the table. Only a few soldiers were aware she had killed the king of the island, and they had said nothing to her. But the burden weighed on her heart, and with everyone eating together she gritted her teeth, hoping no one would mention the slain king. Hungry, yet feeling ill, she picked at her food and none of it reached her lips. She spent a long-time spreading butter on her bread, listening to the men.

"It's the least I can offer for what you've done for us." A thin man, Lord Garion, stood tall, but with an honest stature. He dressed well for someone living in a valley so far from Prasa Potama. Clothes made from the sheep he raised: wool layered upon wool in natural hues. All his serfs dressed as he did, their simple vests and trousers in browns and blacks with the same musty smell as the lambs they fostered. Tellwater Valley had its own culture unlike the more fanciful sophistication of Prasa Potama. Lord Garion's hands were unlike the hands of a nobleman. Their coarseness, along with his weathered facial features, disclosed the work in the field he did, tilling the ground alongside his serfs. His manor offered an informal, comfortable and non-pretentious home, despite its size.

"I'm not sure we eradicated the problem," Barin admitted. He took another bite of turnips and paused his dialog to chew.

Garion frowned.

All the men knew the truth. Barin spoke it. "We've eliminated the prevailing threat, but the demons will return."

Lord Garion poured a chalice of wine and offered it to Barin. They passed the decanter around the table. When Neal poured wine in Erika's cup he smiled at her but she only nodded a solemn thank you.

"I have to agree with you, Vasil," Lord Garion said. "It's a never-ending battle, and our enemy grows stronger rather than meeker. I'm afraid I may run out of men. The serfs have lost many sons in these attacks and are hesitant to have those who are coming of age join the militia. We have fields to work in the spring. There's no sense defending a valley in which no one is alive to till."

"I'm aware of your lack and have made note. I can't speak for my father, but I'll request more troops and better weapons. We can bring crossbows, the plans of which we've recently gained and have consigned smiths in Prasa Potama to build. If you have housing for reserves, they can fight under Felix's command this winter."

"That would be a much-needed relief, Vasil. What we don't have for housing now, we'll build." Lord Garion breathed easier hearing Barin's pledge.

"My father may want to construct a fortification for his men-at-arms here, and a place wherein your people can find shelter. Let it be so."

"Thank you." Lord Garion stood when the door opened, and a group of young men entered. They didn't wear uniforms, but they had fought with Barin and still wore their leather armor.

"Felix!" Lord Garion greeted.

"Good evening, Father," he said. "My apologies for being late for supper." He addressed Barin. "We've constructed a simple memorial for your men, Vasil," Felix bowed. Barin acknowledged the gesture and stood.

No stranger to Erika's family, Rhea and Olinda, her twin sisters, talked often about the handsome young man who led the militia in the valley. Olinda had fallen foolishly in love with Felix—swooning and carrying on though they lived so far apart. The relationship had potential heartbreak, and Erika had often reminded her sister of that fact. Felix led his father's soldiers in a never-ending battle against the dark lord's skura. How long the young man would survive she couldn't guess, but Erika suspected that his days were numbered. No one soldier would outlive so many horrendous battles. Olinda should put him out of her mind, or else come to Tellwater and fight alongside him—and die with him.

"Thank you, Felix. My father, and all of us in his kingdom, are grateful for what you do." Barin offered his hand as Felix came to the table.

"It's good to see you, Barin." Felix took his hands, and the two embraced.

"It will thrill Olinda to know we fought alongside each other and that you are alive and healthy," Barin said, patting his shoulder.

"Tell her I miss her. When this is over, I will come and see her." Felix hung his coat on a peg and stepped aside for his friends still filing in the door. Their energy comforted Erika. Surrounded by many, and committed to none, the more men who came to the table, the easier to slip into obscurity.

"Felix, everyone, come join us. Let us feast together and enjoy this time before Prince Barin and his men-at-arms depart," Lord Garion offered. Felix sat next to Barin, and the others found their place at the table. Lord Garion addressed Barin. "The journey to Prasa Potama will be difficult. As winter approaches, the more dangerous your travels will be. Even now there are dark clouds to the north."

"Which is the reason we're leaving tonight."

Barin regarded his men, focusing on Erika. She bowed her head lower. They'd be facing dangers going home, and Barin had already said he wanted to leave that night. He had great faith in his abilities, Erika thought. Demons come out at night—the mysterious mountain men, or another crude puppet of the evil mastermind. She kept her concerns to herself, trusting Barin.

The conversation grew light as the men drank. Lord Garion's vineyard made the best wine in the Tobian kingdom, and so these weary soldiers feasted.

"Barin offered to send troops to us, perhaps to spend the winter," Lord Garion briefed his son.

Felix's face lit up, and he turned to Barin. "You'll return?"

"We'll bring reinforcements. All that Prasa Potama can spare. Armory. There's a new crossbow invented that may help you."

"Excellent! I'm eager to appraise your new weapons." Felix served himself a ladle of carrots and cabbage, passing the stew pot to the man next to him.

"We find them better than a longbow. Easy to use. Even a woman can draw one with a good amount of accuracy. We should train our female soldiers to shoot the crossbow. It might simplify things." Barin's words burned.

Erika glared at him.

"You should. We have a few women here in Tellwater who can shoot straighter than our men! They have to be as good, at least.

They're at as much risk as anyone else." Felix added.

Barin nodded, took another swill of his wine, and ignored Erika's stare.

"That fascinates me, Felix. The women in this valley are beautiful and worthwhile soldiers as well? I should think I may settle here myself and marry one," Barin said.

"The women are handsome, but the skura are ugly as sin. You'd be looking at both if you lived here," Felix advised, and everyone laughed.

Erika chuckled to hear Barin talk in that manner. Barin would no sooner live in Tellwater than he would give up his horses.

"True. You just decided for me."

They passed the plate of food around again. Erika shook her head and refused. She doubted she'd be able to eat for days.

"I'd leave myself but for these farms and this fertile soil, and father." Felix adopted a faraway look and his eyes glazed over, if only for a moment. "I'd move to Prasa Potama and marry your sister. Lead a quiet life, one free from battle."

Barin seemed sympathetic to Felix's penchants. Erika felt for him too, poor man. She couldn't imagine living in such a remote valley, wrestling demons for months at a time.

"The kingdom needs this valley occupied. I'm sorry for your sacrifice," Barin said.

"Silly fantasies!" Felix shrugged. "Pay no mind to my musings. King Tobias has his allies, I must admit. If it weren't for him, I'd have left already. He's a righteous monarch. His people love him. Even your neighbors on the island respect him, don't they? It's a pity about the Cho Nisi ruler."

The men around the table mumbled low, agreeing with Felix. Erika cringed, wishing she could shut her ears.

"Cho Nisi's magic is inspiring. I would build them all homes and ask them to stay here forever," Felix commented. "How they slaughtered the skura amazed me.."

"I think their illusion would not be as effective if they lived anywhere else besides the island," Barin noted. "They seem to draw their charm from their lifestyle and their drums."

"I need to learn about these people," Lord Garion interjected. "I keep hearing tales, but I have met none of them. They departed soon after the battle, didn't they?"

"Directly after, yes. The Cho Nisi only lost one man, but a great one. They brought their king back to the island for a ceremonial burial. They had little to say when they left," Neal relayed.

"I would think they departed with misgivings. It sounds like a touchy situation if their king died from friendly fire," Lord Garion suggested.

A stony silence followed. Samuel peeked at Erika from across the table. Her face heated. When she caught Barin's stare she wanted to slam her cup down and run out of the house into the cold misty air. Maybe she'd run up to the mountain and offer herself as a sacrifice to the skura. Something! Several of the other men glanced at her.

"Yes. King Tobias will know what to do," Neal breathed.

"And so, we will take the Norberry trail home," Barin announced as a change of subject, much to Erika's relief. "It seems a safer route."

"Longer," Lord Garion cautioned. "There are more switchbacks and a canyon that could ensnare you should the spirits follow. Once you reach the western ridge of the canyon, though, it's straightforward and easy rambling."

"What spirits?" one man asked.

Lord Garion shrugged. "There are many on that mountain. Some more evil than the apparition of Lord Skotádi. Some that shape-shift and take on the body of a hydra. Some whose fidelities are a mystery. Some change their allegiances on a whim."

"What do you suggest?" Neal asked.

"All a matter of preference who you're best adapted to fight." Lord Garion held his cup up and grinned. "Choose your demise. Winged brutes, shape-shifters, fire breathers. I'm surprised you didn't encounter any of them on your way here."

"Aside from a few false alarms, we had a safe journey," Barin informed him.

"Good! Though, because your army just slew a horde of skura, I doubt you'll be as lucky on your return trip," Lord Garion concluded with a leery eye at Barin. "Perhaps it will be us rescuing you next."

"Our scouts saw a flock of skura follow the Cho Nisi," Felix commented.

"That's not good news."

"The islanders have the power to conceal themselves. Let's hope they were aware they were being followed." Felix looked to Barin for confirmation.

"They're cautious people. I am surmising, they were aware." Barin raised his cup. "Peace and prosperity to you and yours, Lord Garion."

"And a safe journey home to you!" Lord Garion lifted his cup. The men at the table met the toast. Erika lifted her chalice and whispered the goodwill of her father's gods for them all.

Beasts of Mount Ream

The sun melted into the eastern mountains, illuminating the snowcapped summit with golden hues, and sending a cool breeze over the valley. Clouds in the north gathered and darkened the horizon. If the company didn't start soon, they'd be navigating the steepest part of the trail in the dark and cresting the mountain in a storm. Erika slipped her bow over her shoulder and strolled to where her brother and Neal were deep in conversation. They stooped, hovering over a map spread on the ground in front of them.

"You said we were taking the mountain trail." Neal seemed exasperated.

"I've changed my mind. There's snow on the mountain already and a blizzard on its way." Barin glanced at the sky and Erika followed his gaze.

"It's the shortest distance," Neal argued, folding open a corner of the map that had curled.

"How accurate is this map?" Barin asked.

"It's one of your father's."

"Ancient, most like," Barin replied.

Erika stretched her neck to see the chart as Barin brushed the creases out of the torn and mildewed parchment. He set rocks on each corner of the map. Inverted V-shapes showed Mount Ream, the northernmost point of the Potamian empire, and the mountain range that made up the western side of the valley. Barin drew an invisible line through the valley with his finger south to the flood plains of Bowmont and then back north again where a thin squiggle showed a junction.

"Here is Canyon Gia?"

Neal scratched his stubble and let a low grunt escape his lips. Erika leaned in closer.

"What's all that?" she asked, pointing to an unmarked section of the map east of the mountain range.

"That, my dear sister, is the Casdamian Empire."

"Isn't the phantom Vouchsaver supposed to live on that other mountain?" she asked. "The mountain named Casda de Moor?"

"Allegedly," Barin answered. "And according to legend, Mount Ream is the sacred grounds of the mountain giants."

"They're seldom seen," Neil argued. "Except by the simpletons in Fairmistle."

"…Who claim they guard Mount Ream." Barin rolled the map and tucked it in a leather case hanging from his belt. "I would rather tackle the skura in the canyon than the giants and the snow on the mountain." He looked at Neal and rose. With a whistle and a wave, he called the men.

Erika followed well behind her brother, the pack on her back and her bow and quiver strapped on her baldric. Once they were well into the forest, Barin led them to a grassy clearing by a creek and dropped his pack.

"Let's rest," he breathed. Thirty-nine men had left King Tobias' court and ventured on this mission a week ago. Only nineteen were returning.

Erika wandered away from the men a short distance. Though old-growth forest surrounded them, she could still see the stars. A creek gurgled nearby. Frogs and crickets sang. She sat on the mossy ground and leaned against an old cedar tree, hoping to clear her mind.

All her life she had rejected the ways of royalty—nobility seemed so self-centered, and yet here she worried about how the murder she had committed would influence people's sentiments toward her. She hadn't once thought about the poor man who died by her hand. How callous that her reputation bothered her more than the effect it had on the people he knew.

What about the man's family? His kingdom? What would become of the island? She closed her eyes and could still hear the mournful lamentation of the native people who had carried him away. A king. A beloved king. An entire nation grieved because of her.

"I'm so sorry," she whispered. "If I could take back those moments, I would." The deaths of the soldiers were also her fault, for her arrow startled the flock of skura before Barin and his men had been ready. To think she had so much blood on her hands!

Erika knelt by the creek and splashed water on her face, hoping the cold would wake her from despondency. With the moonlight behind her, she gazed at her reflection for a long moment. Why? Why had she come to fight when she could have stayed home safe, like her sisters? What made her so eccentric? So abnormal? Even her grandfather had seen an oddity in her. What had he told her?

The night he died, she sat in candlelight by his bedside. He spoke in a whisper, his lips hidden under his gray beard. He squeezed her hand as if to drive the very meaning of each utterance into her heart. Tonight, as she gazed in the quiet pool, she saw his face in the reflection and heard his words in the creek's babble.

"You must win, Erika. Princely matters distract your brother, but you have the fortitude. Your father sees the little girl in you. I see an empress. The land is for ploughing. For growing crops to feed our families. Not for breeding humongous cockroaches with faces of horror and tongues of fire that creep over the countryside, devouring everything in their path. No. We wiped them clean from our lands, but they must never gain a foothold again, and neither should their cousins, the skura, or the goblins. Keep the valley safe from anything evil and self-serving."

She had promised him she would. All her life she had trained for that day and now she had foiled everything.

Would he have given up on her after she killed an allied king?

She held her breath, hoping to hear something from him, a word of either admonishment or encouragement, but of course, she heard nothing except the sound of the creek.

"No one in our family ever gave up. I have Potamian blood running through my veins," she told the worried image staring back at her. "This mistake cannot destroy me. Though I committed a horrible transgression, it's over. Somehow good must come from this!" The pool had ceased rippling, tinted blue from the moonlight, her youthful reflection staring back at her.

She dried her face with the hem of her tunic and returned to her place by the cedar tree. With eyes closed, she tried to think of a way to overcome her misdeed. Her thoughts wandered until she fell asleep.

Erika woke to the sound of men snoring. A few men-at-arms were awake and had made a campfire. She could hear Barin discussing tactics with Neal somewhere in the shadows.

Mist rose from the valley and into the hills and with it, a chill. She shivered and wrapped her cloak tighter around her. When she heard a branch break behind her, she started. It could have been someone collecting firewood. She listened. Something moved, but not a person. It could have been a badger or a raccoon. She peered into the shadows, letting her eyes adjust to the dense darkness of the forest. Fog settled among the trees. The mist parted into fingers which crept over the land like the hand of a giant man tapping on a table. Closer and closer it came until she saw the shape of a man, but a man without substance, only mist, and huge. A mountain giant? Her eyes followed the arm until she saw its shoulders bent over and then his face above the treetops, back-lit by the half moon. She jumped up and gasped. "What's that?" she asked.

"What?" someone asked. She had garnered several soldiers' attention, and they had drawn their swords and hurried to her.

Barin also came to her side and squinted into the dark forest where she stood, but the mist had disappeared, the arm, the shoulders, the face—gone.

"Did you see it?" she asked.

"What, Erika?" he asked, his inquiry cold and accusing. Barin must think she's gone daft seeing shapes in the woods. The stress of this journey had affected her mind.

"The mist. It had fingers and looked just like an enormous man."

Their eyes met. He nodded, but only slightly, as though he wanted to keep a rein on any panic her sighting might cause.

"I saw nothing." Barin turned to his men. "Pack up. Let's go. We have a long hike ahead of us. I want to be in Prasa Potama by the sun's zenith tomorrow."

Someone kicked dirt on the fire while the rest of the men gathered their knapsacks, satchels, and quivers, and others rolled up their blankets.

Erika knew she saw something, but of course, it disappeared when Barin looked, making her out to be a fool.

"I saw it. A mountain giant t'was," Rory, a fair-haired young soldier from Fairmistle, a river town to the south, whispered in her ear.

"Don't let them fool you. They saw it too—they're just not confessin'." He nodded and gave her a smile which she returned, soothed by his soft country dialect.

Not long after they began their ascent did the trail steepen to a vertical incline. The forest thinned as she hiked and instead of dense firs now needle-less saplings scattered the landscape, their twisted branches grasped for the stars. Leafless underbrush exposed bare ground, and massive boulders glowed like lantern globes, casting shadows that could have been goblins waiting to ambush them. Erika's lungs grew hot from the thin air and heavy breathing. She walked with eyes wide, flinching at every unfamiliar sound, regarding the others to see if they too showed alarm. If so, she couldn't tell, but Rory kept looking at her as if he sensed something strange in the air. The discomfiting foliage, the whistle of the wind, the perilous climb all added to the discordance of this mountainside. But something worse hovered over them.

"Do you sense anything?" Erika asked Rory.

"Aye, I do, Fairest. But we be on Mount Ream and there're legends rooted here. We'd be fools not to suspect the spirits. Take guard of yerself, if you know what I mean. Be leery."

"Is there a difference between being mistrustful and being afraid?" she asked, half laughing, though she felt no gaiety. Fear had tightened every muscle in her body.

"Two in the same," Rory answered, scanning their surroundings. "I would not trust a single creature livin' here. Man, nor beast alike."

She wondered if men lived on this mountain, and what sort of human they'd be?

Well into the night at an hour when she should be asleep under the stars wrapped in a woolen blanket, the company reached the canyon of which Lord Garion had warned them. The gorge wasn't just a dip in the ground where one skips down to the bottom and then climbs up again. A huge fracture in the earth defined Canyon Gia, dark and foreboding—a bottomless pit—and to descend into its domain would summon one's doom.

"Why did we come this way?" she asked under her breath.

Only Rory and Samuel heard her. Rory shook his head. "A fool's challenge?" He eyed Barin. Erika's brother had been surveying the canyon, pacing along the rim, no doubt looking for a fitting way down. Neal trailed behind and at one point he and several other soldiers gathered sagebrush and wrapped the dried leaves around branches. Neal stooped on the ground and struck his dagger with flint, nursing an ember. When the kindling ignited, he shared his flame with soldiers holding the other two torches, and then walked with Barin, lighting the way. They stopped at an incline.

"If we had taken the northern trail, we would have had to pass the caves," Samuel interjected. "Strange beings occupy the caves."

"Dragons, they say," Rory agreed.

"Who's saying dragons are wicked?" Erika asked. "No one knows their allegiance. Maybe they're allies."

The young men looked at her with surprise. "Nary a man in his right mind confronts a dragon askin' who his king is, save those wishin' for death."

"I'm just saying our chances may have been better traveling that route than this one."

"Maybe you'll get to lead the next expedition," Samuel laughed. Erika frowned and hushed him, anxious that her brother might hear and suspect insubordination. Erika seldom questioned Barin's decisions, but stepping into this ominous chasm gave her pause, reminded of Lord Garion's warnings.

"Pick up your things. We're going in," Barin told the group, and without hesitation, he started down the cliff. With tired legs and sore shoulders, Erika lifted her heavy satchel onto her back again and followed the others.

Barin had not found an actual trail into the gorge, but a steep creek bed filled with snow and ice. Erika slipped as soon as she stepped down, and Rory grabbed her hand from above.

"Slowly, Fairest. We don't want to be losin' a princess."

His words surprised her. She hadn't felt like a princess—not now, not after all that had happened. If he had called her a murderer, she would have deemed it more fitting.

She appreciated Samuel and Rory staying with her. They could have walked with the prince and foot soldiers who were halfway down the bank already.

"You don't need to stay behind with me. I can make it," she said.

The men looked at each other. Rory shrugged. "No, bother."

Rory led, treading cautiously from one stone to the next, avoiding the frozen snow in between the rocks. "Mind you for this one, Fairest, it's icy," he advised her.

Barin and Neal were far below them, their torches gleaming like lightning bugs against the darkness. The other men-at-arms, their dark profiles barely distinguishable from the shadows, made their way after them, helping each other just as Samuel and Rory were helping her, each at their own pace.

Soon Erika could not feel her nose or her earlobes because of the cold, and she kept her hands tucked in her cloak unless she had to grab onto frozen limbs to keep from falling. Without Rory and

Samuel, she'd be struggling to find her way alone. The other men had already reached the basin.

Halfway down the embankment, she heard rushing water.

"Almost to the bottom," Rory announced.

"Where are the others?"

"Upstream."

Unusual vegetation fringed the flowing river at the nethermost part of the canyon. Thorny trunks of neither trees nor bushes entangled one another, making it impossible to determine where one began, and another ended. The closer to the riverbank, the denser the muddle, so that if she were to leave the trail she'd have crawled through a labyrinth of branches.

A long way from Barin and his soldiers she could see their torches flickering in the distance until they disappeared.

"Call my brother," Erika asked of Samuel. He gave her a puzzled look. "Call him," she repeated. "You have a more thunderous voice. He'll hear you."

The soldier took a deep breath and sent his bid echoing against the canyon walls. "Sir Barin!"

"Just a little way forward from you. We'll wait at the river!" came the reply.

"No fear. We'll catch up to them soon," Rory assured her.

Unlike her skittish sisters, Erika spent her youth climbing trees, swimming rivers, and sparring with the men. She learned a bit of nursing and the sight of blood didn't make her sick. But the cliffs closed in on her as the chiseled rock walls of a dungeon. Tree limbs hugged each other with crippled arms. The ground, lumpy with roots and stones, made it difficult to walk, and the smell reeked like a musty old cave, choking out any fresh air the river might have brought. Walking stealthily with nothing but twisted tunnels commanding her movements.

"Are we on the same trail as my brother?" she asked. Neither Samuel nor Rory answered.

After trudging through the darkness with no end in sight, no flames of her brother's torch nor a hint that an outside world still existed, she stopped and touched Samuel's arm.

"Call them again, please." Again, Samuel's voice echoed. They waited longer than they should have. No response.

He called again louder. This time his voice seemed muffled by the surrounding growth. She heard no echo, neither did Barin answer.

"Perhaps they're too close to the river to hear us. Come, let's keep movin'," Rory said.

"I suppose we'll meet up with them eventually," Erika agreed.

Regardless of how long they walked, the landscape didn't change but for the wet air that now formed around them. A fog seeped through the trees, filling the tunnel with fingers of mist.

Fingers, yes. Just as she had seen on the mountain. Long knobby fingers with sharp fingernails. When a vivid and vaporous finger pointed at her from up ahead, she grabbed both Samuel and Rory's arms.

"Holy Idols!" Samuel whispered through clenched teeth as he drew his sword.

"That weapon will do no good against the mountain giants, Samuel," Rory whispered nodding toward Samuel's sword, though he drew his own.

"What will, then?" Erika asked, pulling an arrow from her quiver.

Samuel shook his head. "If we cannot see him, perhaps he cannot see us, either," Samuel whispered. "Or hear. Avoid his touch."

As the misty finger moved toward them, they crouched low and moved aside to let it pass. But more fingers were making their way along the trail toward them.

"What do they do when they touch you?" Erika asked, wondering if these mountain giants had ever caught anyone.

For an answer, they heard a scream coming from further up the trail. Barin! The mist changed course, melting into the darkness up ahead. Erika broke into a run after it, Samuel, and Rory at her side.

The vapor now appeared as the feet of a giant. Like lightning, the mountain ogre sped through the canyon toward the cries they had heard. Erika and the soldiers followed jogging, and out of breath. The tunnel widened, and before them, a thick blanket of haze covered the forest. Muffled groans of human beings came from the center of the fog. Erika would have hurried in, but Samuel held her back.

"Careful," he whispered. "Something's happening. Something's in there."

Rory stepped ahead of her and a misty hand grabbed his foot. He hit the ground, and the vapor rolled over him, thickening until Erika could barely see him.

"Help," Rory cried as he tossed in the dirt. "I'm being crushed."

Even as he spoke the mist took form and like a sponge, grew. From the white vapor, it darkened until it became a broad-chested being. His arms were as large as a horse's body, his head the size of a castle gate. Limb by horrid limb, he materialized as he planted his knees on Rory's back and pushed the young man against the earth with his huge cloudy hands, laughing as he pressed Rory into the ground.

The harder the mountain giant pushed, the stronger he became until his hands turned to stone and the rest of him unfolded. Behind him, hovering over the giant, encouraging him, stood a figure in a dark cloak. The form knelt, sucking in the air around Rory, breathing deeper and deeper as the soldier's screams became muffled. Erika dove forward, reaching for Rory's hand. The giant slapped her away, and she fell backward. Samuel scrambled and grabbed Rory's arm. The giant growled, swiping out at Samuel. The cloaked figure had inched near enough to Rory's face, as if stealing his breath.

Erika jumped back up, catching her wind. Samuel still had hold of their friend, and so she lunged for Rory's other arm. The giant let up, his weight no longer holding Rory, and took a swing at Erika. Much quicker than the slow-moving ogre, Erika dodged his iron fist. Samuel pulled, moving Rory away from the giant. Erika waved her arms to distract the giant long enough for Samuel to pull Rory into the tangled web of trees nearby. Erika sped into the brush and joined them as the giant dissipated into mist again, his fingers chased them, but with a body too large to slink in-between the folds of the forest.

Rory panted—his face covered with bruises. He bent over, gasping for air. Had he not been wearing armor, he would have been dead. "They come alive as they kill," he said. "I felt my life being sucked away."

"By the figure in the robe?"

Rory nodded, still gasping. "Yes. It felt odd as if the devil stole the life out of me before I died."

"Did you see him, Samuel?" Erika asked.

"I did."

"The dark spirit," Rory remarked in-between breaths.

"Lord Skotádi?" Erika asked.

Rory shrugged. "I'm not sure if it be the same. There's a dark lord who steals the life out of people dyin'. It's an old legend in Fairmistle, but my people have seen it and know it's more than a folktale, sure as the stars come out at night. Now I've seen it too."

Erika brushed the dirt and grime off the young man's face. "Will you be all right?" she asked.

"Better than if you hadn't dragged me away."

"The giants are running to where we heard those cries. We've got to find Barin," Samuel urged.

Erika and Rory followed Samuel, weaving in and out of roots and low growing branches while the mass of mountain giants rolled like a wave of fog on the road. The monsters had the appearance of translucent warriors shifting in and out of one another, half vapor, half form heading toward a thicker more ominous mass. The cries of men grew louder. When the mountain giants reached their destination, they piled themselves atop one another until their bodies fused in one thick and eerie cloud.

"There's a heavier mass under them," Rory whispered, his voice trembling.

"Enjoying their kill as if at a feast."

Erika saw arms and legs of stone and iron moving over what she presumed were their victims. Hurrying toward the mass, she stumbled over a sword. Weapons lay strewn in the surrounding dirt, satchels, boots, remnants of her brother's army. Her heart stood still. The screams coming from the center of the haze were unbearable.

"No!" She rushed toward the fog, her arm snatched by Rory.

"They'll slaughter you," he pleaded. "We don't want that."

"We need to do something!"

Samuel had dashed ahead and finding a torch Barin's troops had carried, he returned, blowing on the embers until a flame ignited. As he walked back to her, led by the flame, the mist recoiled from it.

"The fire! The giants are dodging the fire. Light another!" She and Rory broke branches from the vines and lit the tips from Samuel's torch. Erika stepped into the mist, swinging her torch in a broad circle, stomping at the giants, angry and determined.

"Go away, you beasts! Leave this place!" she commanded. The mist flinched wherever the torch touched it. Though it tried to return, with the three of them wielding fire, the giants had no recourse but to leave.

In the thinning mist, a fleeting cloaked figure disappeared among the trees.

The giants that had materialized diminished back into vapor.

One by one they peeled off each other like an onion shedding its skin, leaving a wretched pile of human beings uncovered.

Erika moaned when she saw her brother's army. Mangled armor, crushed helmets, and clothing strewn across the ground. She stepped over the remains searching for life. Samuel knelt next to a soldier and lifted him into his arms. Rory helped a wounded man remove a bent cuirass. Because of their armor, most of the men were still alive, rising, catching their breath, and removing damaged armor.

"He's here, Fairest. He's alive. A might muddled but breathin'," Rory answered.

Erika rushed to her brother as Barin sat upright, in better shape than Rory had given him credit. She helped him remove his helm and then threw her arms around him. "Thank Pólemos you're alive," she whispered as she hugged him.

"We were dead men. What did you do? Why did they flee?" Barin asked Rory.

"The torches, Vasil," Rory answered.

Barin rose and took command again, gathering his army, helping to revive the rest of his troops. Of all nineteen men, one had died and one crushed so brutally that his leg needed a splint.

"Now that we know how to keep mountain giants away, we can move on. We have a river to cross, and a canyon wall to climb. Let's pick up our weary bones. Gather what is usable and begin our journey home. We'll bury Richard, and then two of you will take this man as your charge," he nodded toward the soldier with the broken bones. "From now on we stay close together."

Barin's eyes rested on her, and he smiled. What a sight she must have been with her hair no longer tied but hanging in knotted streams over her shoulder guards. Sweat had mixed with tears and when she wiped her face, she removed a handful of mud.

Neal returned from scouting upstream. "There's a way across the river I think we can handle well enough if some men will help the wounded and others carry twice the load. It's no more than waist high for any of us."

"Good news, at last!" Barin said. "Then let's leave this place!"

No one would question that command. Barin limped toward the river and Erika and the men followed.

Kairos the Wizard

Kairos paced across his tiny room inside the highest tower, his hands clasped behind his back, deep in thought, struggling with the king's words rattling his brain.

"Find a spell to obliterate these skura, Kairos. It's your duty to the kingdom. Do not fail me!"

Kairos had a reputation to live up to—his father's—and he would probably fail miserably. He usually did. Had he his mother's magical abilities, he might come up with a solution. She'd been a nature-wielder who swallowed tinctures of minerals and herbs that, when blended with the magic flowing in her veins, could influence the surrounding atmosphere. That probably wouldn't help the Potamian war against the skura. She could influence artesian wells during a drought, aid anglers by commanding the tides, and assist women with their monthly cycles, but he highly doubted her magic would stop a skura attack.

He glanced at his profile in the mirror. His prominent nose rivaled his father's, long with a notable hook. Good old Father! Lord Rincon! Had the man lived longer, he'd be King Tobias' Vouchsaver, entitling him to half the spoils in battle and a manor of his own. Lord Rincon could control both heat and air. His power might have had more influence on the skura than his mother's. In his day, his father could send flames of unimaginable distances, setting fires and explosions wherever needed. Kairos had some of that same alchemy running in his veins, but he hadn't yet learned to dominate it. He'd been procrastinating a few years too long, and for good reason!

He grunted at the thought of how talented his parents were. If his father had not been such an accomplished sorcerer, Kairos probably wouldn't be in the palace at all, but performing stunts at the ghetto pubs in East Prasa Potama. Who else hires wizards these days but high political figures or squalid innkeepers? A Lord but lords under Potamian rule were skittish about acquiring magic. If you had a wizard in the house, you would attract demons. Kings had no fear of evil if a wonderful wizard followed him around. Hence, the palace held the only legitimate proprietor of sorcery in the kingdom. Kairos needed to accommodate the king, or he'd be on the dole. His livelihood depended on his performance.

Once again, he would dig up his father's and mother's formulas and see if he could find anything new. They had written a discourse on Countering Malevolent Creative Activities of the Phantom Lord Skotádi. Though neither of his parents could prove the existence of the legendary apparition, the dark lord's beasts were real. His parents believed that if they could somehow destroy the mastermind of these creatures, they would eliminate the threat to humanity. First, they had to prove him real.

The two never finished proving their thesis. Kairos had, in the past, attempted to continue the work but got distracted. Reading a five thousand page manual of dry, uninteresting data discouraged him. Worse, the manner of his father's death left him traumatized. His father died while fighting a hydra. The battle had been a horrendous event. Worse, the beast did not kill his father. An overload of magic in Lord Rincon's body triggered heart failure during the battle. He died an unnatural natural death.

Kairos frowned as he recollected that day. The trauma left him too paranoid to achieve his true potential.

The wizard wet his lips, his heart racing a bit.

"I'll be fine," he whispered to himself, a cold sweat forming, as it always did when he thought about his father's death. "I will avoid using extreme amounts of magic." His hands shook. He knew he'd have to overcome this fear if he were ever to please the king. Until now, Kairos hadn't cared. Fame didn't appeal to him, as long as he had a job and could stay in the palace performing remedial tricks to entertain the court. But Lord Garion's call for help against skura put him in a precarious situation. The king needed more power from him. Kairos did everything he could to counter his phobia, to the point of begging King Tobias to hire lesser wizards as apprentices, which the king did. Still, Kairos had to invent the magic.

He found the sought-after papers, pulled them out of the drawer, and sat at his desk, contemplating over his charts and graphs by candlelight. Each formula written seemed workable. Each formula demanded some physical exertion from him. Not so workable. Kairos by nature had a slothful streak. After reviewing the last procedure, he slapped his hand on his desk and sighed, pushing his dark locks out of his face.

Springing out of his chair, he opened the shutters to his study high in the tower and looked out over the castle walls. The fresh air helped his thinking and kept him awake. In the daylight, beyond the township of Prasa Potama, clay roads ribboned through the grasslands to the sea, to the farmlands, and the forests. Tonight, he could see as far as the moat, the bridge, and a few alleys lined with stone-wall apartments.

He donned his midnight blue cloak, the one lined with gold embroidery. It made him feel a bit more magical. His father wore this same cloak when he had cast spells. The colors matched the astrological charts on the walls now rustling in the breeze.

Someone tapped at his door. Rhea! How could he have forgotten her visit tonight? He brushed the wrinkles from his cloak and fixed his collar as he rushed to let the most beautiful woman in the kingdom enter his humble abode.

"Rhea," he whispered and took her hands, pulling her into the room and holding the door open for the train of her dress to slip by. "Quickly! Did anyone follow you here?"

"I'm not a fool, Kairos. I know how to avoid my father."

"Of course, you do."

Their conversation ceased as they drew close to each other. She smelled like lilacs. Her topaz hair glowed gold and orange in the candlelight. The fabric of her bodice felt soft, and the warmth of her body under all that clothing made him tingle and his blood run hot. He held her tight as they kissed. She touched his cheek, played with his hair, and smiled when she pulled away.

"You've been hiding in this tower way too long. I've missed you."

"I'm afraid your father is making unreasonable demands of me. I wonder if you could persuade him to give me more time." He nodded toward his desk. "I haven't come up with anything powerful enough to take down a swarm of skura."

"Father won't listen to me. Only Barin may counsel him about military strategies. Would you like me to talk to my brother?"

"No, my princess! Your brother is more demanding than your father. Besides, Barin doesn't like me all that much. Is he back yet?"

"Barin and his troops arrived this evening. We're waiting to hear how he fared."

"I'd be curious as well. Maybe they slaughtered all the skura and they don't need me."

"Are you shirking your duties?" she asked with a chuckle, and then she shook her head, causing Kairos to frown.

"No. No, of course not." He couldn't show his cowardliness, though disguising it proved difficult. "No, but if they won this battle, then it would be over, and no one would have to return to that horrid valley. It's a long trip over that mountain, you know. With many dangers on the way."

"And I wouldn't want you away that long," she assured him. "Not when you could be here with me. I'm against all this violence as well." She took his hand and pulled him closer to her. "I love you."

Kairos smiled at those words, but when he looked, his smile disappeared. King Tobias stood on the threshold, hands on his hips, and an angry scowl across his face.

"Rhea, go to your room," the bearded king commanded.

Rhea jumped back and wrung her hands, her eyes wide. "Father! I didn't know," she started.

"Of course, you didn't know I followed you. How could you?"

Rhea opened her mouth to protest, but her father stopped her with a raised hand. "Go to your room. Now."

Kairos' pulse went into overload when he caught King Tobias' glaring at him.

"Go! I have words to speak with this young man and you don't need to hear them."

She left, but not without a fleeting look of pity at Kairos as she stepped out the door. Kairos pursed his lips and gave her a sullen wave.

King Tobias shut the ingress after her, flinging his cloak behind him as he turned to face the wizard. Kairos stepped back and bowed, not knowing what else to do. Perhaps King Tobias didn't know what he should do either, for he paced to the window and looked out, breathing deeply. The embroidery on his tunic glimmered in the candlelight. Kairos monitored the man's dagger sheathed in his belt, hoping the king wouldn't use it.

"Your father was a powerful magician," the king's voice shook the tower, or maybe those were Kairos' weak knees trembling.

"Yes, Vasil."

"A man of honor and courage. He gave his all to the throne."

"Yes, Vasil."

"What happened to you?"

Kairos swallowed. "I...don't know."

"Neither do I. But I am just as much a man of honor as your father. That's why I will not dismiss you. I could you know. You'd be nothing more than a street vendor if I did." The king pointed his finger at Kairos. He wore many rings—silver and gold, and some were brass. They glimmered with priceless stones. Large stones. Stones that could knock a man senseless were they thrust in his face with the force of a king's fist. Kairos gulped again.

"I'm convincing myself that the reason you have not created the right sort of power for us to win against these beasts is..." he inhaled and nodded toward the door. "Is because of my daughter!"

"Rhea? Vasil?"

"Your flirtatious relationship is distracting you."

"Yes, Vasil." He swallowed. He couldn't deny that Rhea distracted him.

"Therefore, I am forbidding you to see her."

"But..."

"By threat of imprisonment. For now. Or something." The king waved away the thought. "Find us what we need to rid Tellwater of the skura and anything else the dark lord is brewing in that iron pot of his. Maybe then I'll let you two see each other." He moved toward the door. Sweat seeped down Kairos' forehead. The king turned around. "Imprisonment, mind you!"

Kairos bowed.

With that, the king made a royal exit. His cloak caught the air behind him, the sound of his boots resounded through the hall.

Kairos collapsed at his desk and buried his head in his hands.

Barin and the King

The young valet's elegant blue tunic caught the sun as light filtered through the curtains. A single beam landed on his matching felt hat and yellow hair. Moving in and out of the morning ray, the boy quietly draped Barin's cloak over his shoulders and fastened it with confident hands. Barin stared past the boy. Emotionally unable to make eye contact with anyone from the palace—certainly not a youthful domestic who had never seen combat. The bloody memories in Barin's mind were too vivid still. Not only the death of his men during their encounter with the skura, but the terrifying mountain giants that had taken his squire's life and left the rest of his troops traumatized. He had no desire for this royal protocol.

Still weary from the trudge over the mountain with a shattered and bleeding militia, he considered himself emotionally, mentally, and physically drained. The battle brought him in touch with his humanity. He felt for his men. His heart went out to the common folk of the valley, and the poor souls who took that journey with him. His soldiers, and the farmers who worked the fields, were foremost on his mind.

He had buried his disappointment toward Erika. For now. He would not speak of the murder of King Rolland. Another time. If he were to tell his father tonight what happened, all the anger and shame rooted inside of him would rise to the surface. Barin needed to temper those emotions if he were to act like a prince, a son, and a brother.

At least his sister hadn't whimpered or carried on during their venture home. She had made him proud of her response to the terror in the canyon.

He bit his lip as the valet strapped the royal sword around his waist. A beautiful tool made for formality rather than for use. A heavy piece of steel with a gilded hilt and etching of a destrier, the Potamian symbol for honor. He didn't deserve such honor. He pushed the belt away.

"My Liege, it's required of a prince returning from battle, otherwise it would discredit your Father."

Barin looked into the boy's innocent blue eyes. Correct. Protocol required him to wear the sword. He cleared his throat and muttered.

"They say a prince who has honor will not wear it around his waist to flaunt it but will instead bow his knee to the servants who gained it for him."

"And if the prince gained the honor for himself, my Liege?" the valet asked.

"No one gains honor for himself save those who died in its name."

The servant hesitated. "Yes, Vasil" he whispered and bowed, backing away to return the sword to its mount.

The death of the Cho Nisi King brought not honor, but dishonor. The image of Rolland bleeding at his feet haunted Barin more than the evil giants that later attacked him. He would have mourned for the king's death regardless, but that his sister had slain the man devastated him. Barin should have taught Erika better.

All his life he had wished the best for his younger sister. He'd been training her, hoping that she would gain the skills she needed to be a warrior simply because she wanted the challenge so badly. He hoped she would overcome her gloom. A sadder person he had not known, always wishing for something just beyond her reach. Eventually Father would learn that she had killed their ally, and then what would happen to her? A soldier's punishment? He doubted their father would admonish her too severely.

Father had a soft spot in his heart for Erika. Their mother had sacrificed her life to bring Erika into this world. And if rumor does not become public, there will be no repercussions from the kingdom's citizens. Finding a tactful way to deal with the island will be another matter.

Barin sighed when the valet stepped back and bowed.

"You are ready, Vasil."

Barin nodded, allowed the valet to open his door, and walked into the hallway. Cold air greeted him as his eyes rested on the marble statue of Pólemos, the God of War holding a bolt of lightning in his right hand, and a sword in the other, a chiseled robe draped over his shoulders. Barin didn't believe in his father's gods. There is no such thing as glory in war, nor is there a god that offers men a portion of that glory. Barin breathed deeply and proceeded to the grand hall.

The castle held the chill this time of year. The ceilings were high, the walls cold stone. Every tap of his boot heels echoed down the chamber to the throne room. He struggled with forming the words he should say to his father as the majestic doors swung open to the king waiting on his throne for him.

Morning light seeped through the stained glass, accenting more statues. Eidy, the goddess of love and her lover Eroto. Father had moved these deities to his throne room after their mother had died, to keep the love they had shared burning.

Busts of his ancestors lined the walls in between the gods. Grandfathers and uncles who, for centuries, had kept this kingdom united. The wars they saw, the celebrations, the deaths were folklores now. Their heritage bore legends of heroes and mighty deeds, and still the threat of annihilation haunted the empire. Barin did not consider himself a hero among them.

He bowed before his father.

"Son." A gentle sigh came from King Tobias. "It hurts my heart when you do that."

"It's protocol, Father."

"Rise." Tobias stepped off his throne and as soon as Barin stood, they embraced. "Your soldiers tell me the battle didn't go as expected."

"No. It didn't."

"Well, sometimes we expect too much." Tobias kept his arm around Barin's shoulder, a warmth that only his father could give. Barin needed reassurance, not just for losing good men in a conundrum, but for losing faith in his capabilities. He should have trained Erika better, or have prevented her from coming. Barin was responsible, in part, for the death of King Rolland.

"At least you and your sister came home alive. Are you hungry?"

Barin shook his head. "I'll wait for dinner."

"Tell me what you've learned. What happened?" King Tobias ushered Barin to a table while a servant placed two chalices and a decanter before them. The king nodded for the servant's dismissal.

"I learned there are way too many skura in this world. It seems no matter how many we kill, twice as many reappear. We slew hundreds. The most impressive fighters were those from Cho Nisi. Their magic did remarkable things. The surviving skura fled. To where I don't know. They're back in the valley already. I'm certain whatever good we did will not be the end. They'll return, possibly in threefold. Or hundredfold."

"What do you propose?"

"I promised Lord Garion we'd dispatch troops and that they would stay in the valley with him. They'll be under Felix's command. We can't leave Tellwater unprotected. Felix lost more men than we did."

"Very well. We'll prepare to send him men. Supplies maybe. Anything he needs. This will take time. How many men did we lose?"

"Twenty in the valley and my squire in Canyon Gia on the way home. He fell to mountain giants!"

The king's eyes widened. He moaned. "Squire Richard? I'm sorry."

Barin ran his finger over the rim of his chalice. He hated losing men, and Richard had been but a boy. He grieved silently, but a prince must quell his own suffering. Otherwise, he would shrink from battle, and there were many more to come.

"The other men made it back safely, though worn and disheartened. We had a long and grueling journey. I suggest we return by the southern route and with a mounted army."

King Tobias nodded and fell silent, as though struggling for words. He poured wine into Barin's cup, and then into his own. Barin stared at the dark red liquid before taking a sip.

"The best from Lord Garion's vineyard." King Tobias offered a toast. Barin tapped his chalice to his father's. The king frowned. "It's my hope there will be more wine after this. And crops. Whatever mastermind is behind those demons will seek revenge. I'm believing the legends. If what they say is true, this Skotádi's hand is swift and vehement. I fear the loss."

"Skotádi. The phantom demon," Barin whispered with a nod, remembering the cloaked figure in Canyon Gia who vanished with the mountain giants.

"Perhaps. I'm not one to believe in ghosts. Nevertheless, Lord Garion will need a good-sized army…"

The king looked up from his chalice. "I heard that the Cho Nisi King died."

Barin took a sip without looking at his father. "How did you hear?"

"Your sister told me."

Shocked that Erika had already told their father, Barin met his eyes.

"Yes. She told me she accidentally released the first arrow that began the battle and killed our friend. She is suffering remorse over the matter. As much sorrow for his death as for your rejection of her."

"I don't snub her. I am equally guilty. I didn't know the Cho Nisi had already arrived, but I should have. My negligence caused the Cho Nisi king's death."

"And you will have a price to pay, I'm sure. We lose many men in war, and many still in friendly fire. This accident could have been avoided, but perhaps we're all to blame," the king replied.

Barin shook his head and set his cup down. "What if they find out whose arrow shot their king? Neal spoke with the warriors. He apologized, but they seemed not to accept. I'm afraid they'll seek revenge."

"Yes, I fear that as well." King Tobias leaned back and cleared his throat with a concerned frown. "They may deem us enemies now. If that's the case, we will take the offensive. Do you know if King Rolland had children? An heir?"

"I have no way of knowing. The warriors never mingled. I barely spoke to any of them. You spoke to King Rolland, didn't you?"

"Only politics. I didn't inquire about his family life. He mentioned no children. I had heard enough reports of his magic, and I'd have been a fool to refuse his offer of help. Because no son or daughter fought with him, I am going to assume there is no heir. I'm thinking it's time we move to secure that island."

Barin stared at his father in disbelief. "An invasion at a time like this? After we caused the loss of their king? Father! That would guarantee a war!"

"We must take our chances. Negotiate! An island without a ruler is fodder in the hands of our enemy. The island rests in our seas. Should the Vouchsaver's army conquer Cho Nisi, our own kingdom will fall."

"Too soon. They'll think we assassinated their king intentionally."

"Don't they already?" King Tobias' face flushed, and he clenched his fists when he rose. "My intention is to protect the people of Prasa Potama and the Potamian kingdom. That is our charge! Let this island become part of our kingdom and we'll protect it."

Barin stood as well. Normally a quiet man, when Tobias raged, the entire room vibrated.

"They have called me soft-hearted many times, Barin, but for the welfare of my subjects, I will not relent. They are priority. Do not forget that."

"Yes, Father."

Tobias grunted and slammed his chalice on the table. "Blessed idols, son! I didn't mean to become so irate. It seems I'm having to raise my voice too often as of late."

"I'm sorry."

"It's not just you. I had to speak to Kairos again."

"And Rhea?"

Tobias shook his head and grabbed the linen napkin from the table. He wiped the wine off his beard. "I haven't talked to your sister yet, but yes. If Kairos doesn't come up with some kind of solution, I fear the enemy will get the best of us regardless if we conquer the island or not. But the boy keeps…" he waved his hand in disgust.

"They're in love."

"Yes, well, that matter can wait for times of peace. We can't afford to be in love. Not now. None of us."

Barin observed his father with concern—his quickness to anger, his gestures. If there were comforting words to offer, Barin would utter them, but tonight he himself wondered how fruitful all these battles and quests could be. "The worst we can do is let our emotions decide for us."

His father looked wide-eyed at him. "Are you suggesting my fears are unfounded? I lose men every day to evil. Lord Garion has lost crops, livestock. His people cringe in fear. They're afraid to step outside at night. Are you suggesting that's tenuous?"

"No, Father."

"Whoever is behind this evil has an agenda, son. If the devil meant to kill us, he could have done that by now. He must have a more devious plan. And yes, it scares me!"

"What do you suppose is his plan?"

"If I knew, I wouldn't be sitting here begging a worthless magician to come up with some kind of magic potion to destroy a flock of skura. It's all we have right now." He sighed heavily and calmed himself. "I digress in this conversation. You expressed concern about Cho Nisi, and I gave you my solution. They've been loyal to our cause and we've returned it with a grave injustice. The island is without a king now. It seems to me we must visit them. One of us. You have more pressing matters, so perhaps we'll send an ambassador. There needn't be any bloodshed. Perhaps offer some coin, some trade, a treaty. They would receive our protection in return. They need our protection. They have magic, but how much magic? Can they hold off all of Skotádi's demons indefinitely?"

"They did a remarkable job the other day."

"What I want to know is how long can they last? There are limits to all magic, son."

Barin leaned on the table and rubbed his eyes. "I don't know. There's no guarantee they will agree to becoming part of our kingdom. If our offer angers them, who knows what they would do. The Cho Nisi would be just as powerful an enemy as the ones we face now. Do you really want to be on the receiving end of their magic?"

"Son, I have never been to Cho Nisi, but I have been to similar islands. Native people live humbly. They work with their hands. Forage for food. They have no access to weapons such as ours. I don't doubt Skotádi has more powerful spells than the Cho Nisi. He could destroy their island in a wink of an eye. With no place to run to, all the inhabitants there would die a callous and tragic death. They need our protection."

"It seems they can take care of themselves?" Barin said.

"Did these natives that fought with you have swords and bucklers on them?"

"No." Barin glanced past his father. Erika stood at the door. He didn't acknowledge her presence, not with words. He couldn't help looking at her, though. No longer the rag doll in a man's armor, she had cleaned up and donned a dark frock. A simple cut, the dress could have been a mourning gown. Her thick red braid fell stylishly over her shoulder. The resemblance to his mother stopped his heart.

Barin looked away. "I'm not sure conquering Cho Nisi would be as effortless as you suppose, Father. They may live humbly, but from what I've seen, they're a proud people. When King Rolland died, they communicated with Neal only, and even then with strained interaction. I fear them, father. We have nothing to counter their necromancy. And with our arrow having killed their king, I doubt they would negotiate." Barin dreaded another battle against insurmountable odds. Fatigued, his men were worn and wounded. They were distressed and frightened, if not from the skura, then from the ordeal in Canyon Gia.

"Speak sense, son." The king sat down again. He, too, saw Erika and said nothing, but his eyes lingered on her form for a moment. Perhaps the ghostly resemblance of his beloved wife kept his glance.

Barin took a seat across from him, blocking the king's view of Erika with his back to the door. He handled his chalice thoughtfully, running his fingers along the etched design. "I don't think you've ever seen this kind of magic before, Father. I never have. It's ...strange."

"All magic is strange."

"The Cho Nisi commanded a cyclone to take the skura into the air and drop them, so that every last one fell with a broken neck or shattered bones. I have heard rumors of similar spells transpiring along the shores of their island. The land will mysteriously disappear or turn to treacherous sandbars. Whirlpools seize shape so fast and so deep that ships sink in them. The tide will rise inexplicably or fall and send boats adrift. Those waters are dangerous. Sailors avoid them. Anglers will steer clear. I don't see how we can invade."

"I'm not afraid. I will go," Erika said.

King Tobias looked up. Barin peered over his shoulder at his sister.

"Give me sailors and I will go to Cho Nisi and offer myself as hostage. I owe it to you. To them."

"No, Erika," Barin faced his father again, snickering and shaking his head. "And make another fatal error? You've already killed their king. What kind of reception do you think they'd give you? They'd hang, draw and quarter you as soon as you got near. If you could get near."

"I can get near. They wouldn't hang me. My father's reign on that island would be for their favor."

"No, Erika. That's nonsense. If they viewed our fleet approaching their island as an invasion, we'd have no means to counter their magic," Barin said.

"I'll take Kairos with me."

Barin laughed, choking on his wine.

Tobias scowled at him but spoke to Erika with his fatherly voice. "Barin needs Kairos with him, Erika, my lovely daughter. When preparations are in order, he'll return to Tellwater and take the magician. Besides, I don't want you as a hostage on some remote island."

"I must make amends for what I did."

She took a breath when Barin faced her. There were more to her words than what she said. He could read it in her eyes, and the way she stood.

"You will have time to make amends," King Tobias assured her. "Lord Garion will need shelter for the troops we send him and so I have scheduled a two day-trip into the city tomorrow to discuss tent-making with an old friend of mine. The three of us will talk more when I return."

Barin turned away and sipped his wine, avoiding eye contact with his father, hoping the king did not intend to give Erika another assignment with him. He set his chalice on the table, shuddering at the thought of returning to battle with his sister in tow. He had hoped Erika had learned her lesson and would stay home from now on.

The silence stiffened until she finally spoke. "Very well."

The door closed before Barin finally looked over his shoulder to where she had stood.

"You'll watch after her while I'm gone, I trust?"

"Yes, of course, Father."

New Magic

"I'm not bad looking," Kairos mumbled to himself while studying the young, dark featured man in the mirror—not bad looking at all with his long black hair pulled tight and tied. The white collar on his robe accented his dark complexion and emphasized the whites of his eyes. He contorted his face in a series of peculiar expressions. Delivery meant everything when one practices wizardry—a snap of the fingers, the roll of his eyes, a snarl—the way he spat out his words could determine the effect of his spells. He rubbed his chin, hoping for signs of stubble and finding none. A beard would be beneficial, but his father had also lacked suitable facial hair for a wizard. Perhaps destiny kept him clean-faced. He shrugged. Rhea didn't like beards, or so she swore. She had complemented him more than once on his dark "mysterious" eyes though. He moved closer to his image to take a better look, but his breath fogged over his likeness.

"I don't see it," he whispered and wiped the dampness with his sleeve. "No, but if she likes my mysterious eyes, that's good enough for me."

He inhaled and stepped away. Time to work. All his analysis of his father's notes and charts and books and journals had to make a difference. King Tobias meant what he said. Being caged in this tower without Rhea wouldn't be any better than being sealed in the dungeon without food—an inhumane punishment which would be his demise! He sighed, shaking his head clear of her image.

Rolling up his sleeves, he strolled to the chest-tall table overcrowded with vials and decanters. Flasks filled with fluid metals, oils, and vapors—substances he himself had conjured. Recipes passed down from his great grandfather. The secret to Alchemy did not lie wholly in the mixture of gold and tinctures as most people thought, but in the mind of he who blended them. A sensitive balance of energies co-mingling with one another to create the perfect result.

In this case, killing a flying demon.

He'd been working days on this concoction. Sleepless nights triggered fatigue, frustration prompted weariness, yet he pressed on. Alas, days of not seeing Rhea added to his despondency. He set a vial down and closed his eyes. Golden hair flashed through his mind, eyelashes tickling his nose, soft skin under his fingers. The vial in his hand heated. Startled, he woke himself from his daydream and inhaled deeply.

"Work, Kairos," he scolded himself. "Work first and then your reward." He gathered his notebook and his potions and laid them on the table. "Yes!" he exclaimed. "The spell is ready to test!"

Kairos took off his robe and hung it on a hook by the door. He slipped on a pair of leather gloves. Dusting off an ancient bamboo bird cage, a net he had borrowed from an old fisher some years past, and a lantern, he slipped out of the room into the dark stairwell. With only the flickering flame of a burning wick to see by, he ascended the stairs to the hoarding. The higher he climbed, the narrower the passage, and the mustier the air. The last tapered rung ended at a low oak door, sealed with an iron bolt. Kairos set his tools on the step below him, fixed the lantern on a hook on the wall, and released the lock. The door creaked as it opened and cold, moldy air immediately chilled his whisker-less face. He coughed, and when he caught his breath, he retrieved his things and entered.

The soldiers had built the hoarding during the siege of Menhaden, a border township on the river between Casdamian and the Potamian dominion. In retribution of Potama's victory, the devils came for the castle near a hundred years ago with their hordes of goblins. The invasion had been short-lived, and King Tobias' great grandfather defeated the onslaught.

Weathered from storms that blew in from the coast, they should have dismantled the rotten wood which once protected the castle from enemy fire. However, no one felt the urgency to do the work since no one has stormed the castle for a full generation. Should an enemy arise and attack King Tobias' palace, they'd build a new one. This one, ah yes, this one provided a perfect breeding ground for Kairos' specimens.

He crawled through the oak ingress onto the platform, checking the planks vigilantly. If they were completely rotten and gave way under his weight, he'd fall to a brutal death. He needn't go far, though. Just above him in the rafters hung his prey. Kairos set the bird cage near the supporting beams by the door, stepped onto the first two planks and bent his body around the timbers. He reached into a cleft between the boards with both of his hands and grabbed the warm body of a bat, pulling the creature from its nesting place. The creature fought, biting at his gloves, but Kairos, though he lost his balance and nearly fell, tossed the bat into the cage without incident. He scrambled for his footing and again saved himself from plummeting into the courtyard below. With the cage door securely shut, he collapsed on the floor, panting.

"All right," he said to the bat. "I have chosen you to be the great sacrifice for humankind, little fellow."

The creature flapped in panic from side to side of the cage, beating itself against the bamboo bars. Kairos spoke softly to the bat while sliding through the door. He set his newly captured varmint down on the rung and bolted the hoarding door shut. With the cage and net in hand, he lifted the lantern off the hook and descended the narrow hallway back to his study.

Kairos hated to sacrifice animals, but in this case, since there were no skura to work on, the bat would have to do. . Were his spell to work, it would save many people and a sheep or two as well. Back in his quarters, he pouted as he placed the cage on the table and bent over to study his captive.

"I really don't enjoy doing this, you know?" he whispered to the bat as he pulled off his gloves. "But the King asked me to come up with something that would put an end to the demons. The only way I can find out if it works is by...." He bit his lip, pulled a hankie from his pocket, and blew his nose. "Is by testing it out on you. If you're lucky, it won't work."

Kairos put on his robe, still talking to the bat which had crawled to the top of the cage and hung upside down.

"And judging from my track record, the odds are in your favor." He picked up a vial of bubbling liquid which had been brewing on his desk just as a gentle tap at his door interrupted him.

"Come in, come in." He glanced at Erika as she entered the room. "I'm about ready to perform some sort of, I don't know, some sort of miracle," he informed her, still busying himself. "If it works, that would be the miracle."

"The magic that my father needs for Tellwater?"

"Yes, yes, that's what I'm trying to do. Trying, mind you." He held up the vial for her to see and set it on his desk. He cleared a space in the middle of the room, moving a heavy wooden chair, several leather-bound journals, a broomstick, and an end table. "You may come in, find yourself a corner." He looked up. "How is your sister?"

"Rhea? She's fine."

"Has she asked about me? At all?"

Erika shrugged. "I don't know. I didn't much talk to her. If she wanted to see you, she'd be here, wouldn't she?"

"Your father won't let her. Not until I'm done."

"Makes sense."

Kairos scowled at her.

"Well, we need this…this whatever you're doing. There's a war going on, Kairos. People are dying. You wouldn't believe the horror we experienced. Not just the skura, but the mountain giants. You're so sheltered here at the castle. Have you ever seen a skura, Kairos?"

Kairos heard her talking but paid little attention, too busy hanging the poor bat's cage from a beam in the center of the room. Erika stepped back while Kairos stood on a stool and tied the cage to the rafters. He hurriedly stepped down, removed the stool, and then pick up the vial. Making a face, he dropped a dollop on his tongue, spread his arms and closed his eyes.

"Take this," he said with a trembling voice and shaking hands. Erika grabbed the vial from him.

The floor to his study vibrated as his fingers shook. He sensed the power rising inside of him. Yes! Control. Easy now. Not too much. Remember poor Father. He opened one eye, his fingers glowed. He stepped forward and opened the door to the cage. The bat didn't move. Kairos shook the cage a little. "Come on, fly, you wretched beast," he growled.

Kairos tipped the bottom to the coop. The bat clenched its perch tighter. More frustrated than angry, Kairos shook the bird cage harder and finally the bat swooped out into the room. With a quick incantation Kairos flicked his wrist in the air, a vapor emitted from his fingers, formed a cloud that swallowed the bat, and with a minor explosion, the cloud and bat disappeared.

A moment of silence followed.

Kairos held his breath, mouth open. His heart raced. No, his heart burned. No! He couldn't be having heart failure. Excitement triggered the rapid beating in his chest. He did it?

The fear subsided when Erika set the vial down and applauded. "You did it!"

Kairos shook his head, exhaling. "Yes! Poor devil, I did, didn't I?" He had his notes, the potions, the magic, a witness, to present to the king. "Rhea, my love, I am yours!"

The Sisters

While Kairos trotted away down the stairs to see the king, Erika walked through the halls and stopped in the drawing room where her sisters sat at a table by the hearth sipping rose soda. She stood in the doorway, hands folded across her chest, watching them giggle and fan themselves and talk about niceties. Did they not know how dangerous things had become in this world? They lived in a powder puff reality while soldiers and serfs sacrificed their lives to keep them safe. Having returned from battle where she watched men torn apart by wild beasts and crushed by ghostly spirits, the sight of her sisters enjoying their fineries repulsed her. It broke her heart that these were her siblings. Worse, the pain and torment she had experienced on the battlefield still raged within her. She wanted to lash out, tear the jewels off of her sister's clothes and rough up their hair. As daughters of the king, they should at least care.

"Erika, come sit with us," Rhea offered. Rhea and Olinda were identical twins, though few people had difficulty distinguishing them from one another. Both were blond and blue eyed, their hair fell in curls pressed in place from the tight braids they wore at night. Yet they never dressed the same. Rhea liked earthy colors, greens, and browns, whereas Olinda favored pastel pinks and lavenders. Olinda wore her hair up and pinned with flowers when she could, but Rhea preferred to wear her hair down. They held themselves differently too. Rhea stood straight, which made her seem taller than Olinda and more aggressive for a girl.

Erika stepped into the room cautiously, anxious that the twins would reprimand her for the mistake she made. Being older than her, they often criticized her, and at the moment Erika didn't need their judgment. Still, she couldn't hide from family forever. Erika kept an invisible wall around herself.

"What sort of infusion today, ladies?" she asked.

"Rose soda, Eri." Olinda loved to give people short names. Erika hated it. Olinda poured green liquid from a silver pot into a finely etched silver teacup.

"Why wear black today, Erika?" Rhea asked. "You look like you're in mourning." Her curls drifted gently as she fanned herself with her colorful silk fan and munched on a cracker.

What's this? Rhea digging for unspoken guilt? A technique she often tried to get Erika to apologize.

"I am in mourning." Erika squinted at her when she answered, chugging her tea with one swallow.

"You're supposed to sip rose soda, Erika."

"Who says?"

"Who are you mourning?"

"Squire Richard." Erika replied curtly. Rhea straightened in her chair with a look of indignation.

"I'm sorry about your soldier." Olinda offered as consolation.

"Twenty-one. There were twenty-one soldiers who died."

"And you mourn just for Squire Richard?" Rhea asked.

"I mourn for all of them. But Richard shouldn't have perished. We were on our way home."

"No doubt there were others who shouldn't have died as well." Rhea stabbed.

"No one should die in war, Rhea. But they do. And everyone makes mistakes. I know you two have been talking about me. I can see it in your faces."

"I'm sorry," Olinda repeated.

Erika looked Olinda in the eye. "Sorry?"

"About Richard,"

"It would have been nice if you apologized for gossiping about me."

"Talk among sisters is hardly gossip," Rhea muttered.

"Why are you sorry about Richard, Olinda? I've heard you talk about our servants. You never had concern for errand boys."

"Come, now, Erika, there's no reason to be hostile toward Olinda. She's only offering you condolences because she sympathizes with you."

"Olinda?"

Olinda had been staring into her chalice. She set the cup down and wiped her mouth with a linen napkin. "Actually, I have no sympathy for you. I think you were foolish to have accompanied Barin. You muddled matters with your charades. Slaying a king who offered his army to help us! Shame on you," Olinda said.

"I've made a mistake and regret it. I don't need either of you to rub salt on my wounds."

"We're not rubbing salt." Rhea stood.

Erika, cheeks burning, slammed her chalice on the table, splashing tea on the tablecloth.

"Whether you know it, you are. And it hurts. Neither of you should judge what I do. I didn't see you offering to help our men." Erika struck back. "Perhaps you don't care for the soldiers who went with Barin, but you claim you love Felix. Felix endangers himself daily, battling the same monsters our grandfather fought. And look at you! You sit here with your silver chalice and sweets and discuss the weather and what dresses you'll wear tomorrow when you have no notion if there will be a tomorrow. You have even less knowledge whether Felix is going to be alive tomorrow. You say you care, but you don't. You're the fool, Olinda. And yes. I made a mistake. But at least I tried, and I fought alongside our men enduring war. Watching people die. Rescuing some and burying the others. You're a fine one to criticize. How will you feel if next time I come home I tell you I buried Felix?"

A dead silence followed. Erika poured another cup of tea and drank it.

"Now, Erika," Rhea uttered softly. "That's no way to talk to your older sister."

"And as for you!" Erika turned on Rhea. "Where is your courage?"

"What do you mean?"

"You and Kairos are passionately in love with each other, but neither one of you will confess. You tiptoe in the shadows, caressing and carrying on. I can't say I sympathize with you, but if you two are lovers, why slink away to dark places like a couple of thieves? When are you going to tell Father how you feel? He already knows. Maybe he'd appreciate hearing it from the both of you." Erika leaned on the door post with her arms crossed.

Rhea stuttered, unable to answer.

"You're both cowards and that's the reason the dark lord can invade our kingdom, kill good men, and make slaves out of our nations. Too many of our people are just like you. You're afraid of your reputation or that you might get in harm's way, or that you'll make an error, so you shroud away in your regal curules, pretending everything is just splendid, secretly coveting something you'll never own because you refuse to fight for it!"

Erika enjoyed their silent outrage for a moment before she stormed out of the room.

Erika's Plea

The steward closed the door to the king's study just as Erika came to the top of the stairs. He started down the hall toward her with quick, confident steps. His silver tray bore an empty decanter and scraps of teacake on a pottery platter.

"Fairest." The thin man, well dressed in his blue-velvet doublet and matching hat, bowed with a nod as he approached.

"Is my father in his study?" Erika asked.

"He is."

"Is he alone?"

"He is alone and tending to paperwork." The steward nodded when she thanked him and went on. Erika took a deep breath, patted stray ends that had escaped from her braid during her confrontation with her sisters, and fixed the laces on her bodice. Dressing in woman's attire never appealed to her, and this black gown had a morbidity about it. She felt melancholic, though—sorrowful, remorseful, depressed— yet black represented strength also, and she felt strong.

She mustered her courage as she walked the dimly lit halls. She had no fear of speaking to her father directly, but she worried that she would falter with her words and so he wouldn't understand. She had only so many chances to explain herself to the king before he would consider her a nuisance. After that, no one would ever take what she had to say seriously again. Her aspirations would fade to nothingness. They'd keep her from fighting and make her sit idly about the halls, fanning herself like her sisters did, making excuses for her indifference, doing nothing to help anyone, sipping rose soda, and changing gowns. There she'd remain until a lord married her and stuffed her away in some castle or manor where she'd have to curtsy and smile at his house guests.

She knocked boldly on her father's door.

"Enter," came a muffled voice.

Candles lit the room, and myrrh smoldered in a brass burner

on her father's desk. King Tobias enjoyed his incense. It calmed his nerves, he once told her—kept him focused when he had work to do. He glanced over his shoulder and stood when she stepped inside.

"My dear Erika."

She curtsied. "Father. Are you too busy? Might I have a word with you?"

"Of course, my child."

Offering her a chair by his desk, he waited, and when she sat down, he fell back into his own chair.

"Are you well, Father?"

"Dizzy for a moment, but I'm fine now. Tell me what's on your mind."

"I came to make a request."

"Does it concern fighting?"

"No. I mean, hopefully not."

He held his hand up for her to stop. "Before you make your request, and I think I know what it is, let me speak. I'm concerned for you, Erika. Barin tells me things that I can scarcely believe."

Erika sat upright in her chair. "What sorts of things? "

"Calm yourself, dear. Nothing detrimental to your reputation. Barin loves you and wishes the best for you."

"If he loves me, he should tell me himself. He's barely talked to me since we came home. I'm afraid he will not forgive me for what I did."

"Give him time. He's a commanding officer. He has responsibilities to his men, and to our allies. He's going to have to answer for what happened."

She cringed. "He shouldn't bear any of the responsibility. Because of me the Cho Nisi king is dead, and I'm willing to be liable and bear all the consequences. Let me answer for my error. Allow me ships to travel to the island and offer myself as hostage for our kingdom. Perhaps while there I could persuade the commoners to allow you to rule the island until they find another king."

"They would hang you." King Tobias breathed.

"Send me there with soldiers."

"Erika, understand that this is a sensitive undertaking. I must work out our strategy not only for the issues of a dead king, but for the attacks in Tellwater and these giant creatures on Mount Ream. If this

Vouchsaver is real, and I'm thinking he is, he'll discover soon enough that the island has no monarch, no forces to counter an attack. He will easily invade them. Cho Nisi is too short a distance from us. Can you imagine what would happen if this same evil in the north takes over the isle? Our enemies would have surrounded us."

"I don't think you're hearing what I'm saying, Father. Let me go there with soldiers and offer our help. I could do it peacefully. They could hold me hostage until you signed a treaty. We could station troops there to protect them."

King Tobias studied his daughter and then shook his head.

"Why not?"

Her father only grunted, and Erika flushed. "It's Barin isn't it. He told you I'm incompetent because of what happened."

"No, it's not that."

"Then what if not that?"

"Erika—"

"What then?"

"You're my daughter. You're a beautiful woman. Look at you! You've grown into the image of your mother." He sighed, regarding her with dismay.

"Why would you want to dress like a man, and fight like a soldier? You should court men, not act like them. I approved your venture to Tellwater with Barin. Foolishness on my part. I'm not sending you anywhere else."

"Father! Let me right the wrong I did. I beg of you! If something happens to that island—to those people—I will be beside myself with grief. I wronged them!"

Her father shook his head. "I sympathize with your feelings and I'm sorry, but I've decided. Someone else will go."

"Father—"

"Erika, do not beg."

She took a breath and watched him, hoping for another chance to present her case. He focused on the ledger he'd been entering.

"I have something I want you to do. It will keep you busy and get your mind off of all of this."

Erika sighed. Nothing would keep her mind off the fate of the poor islanders after she killed their king.

"What is it, Father?"

"I'd like you to visit a particular vendor in Prasa Potama. A fisher. They make the best smoked cod in all the country. Get us some, and order three months' supply for Barin to take on his journey." He scribbled a note of order on another ledger. "I've written the name of the merchant. "Bring an escort or two. Kairos. He deserves a brief vacation away from your sister."

King Tobias handed her the ledger and when she received it, he took her chin in his hand and sighed, his eyes gentle.

"I love you, my precious daughter. Don't fret so. Things will work out."

The Wharf

It seemed odd to Kairos that King Tobias would send him with Erika to Prasa Potama on horseback. Why didn't the king have Rhea do the errands? The two of them could have taken a carriage and made a day of it. Instead, Tobias had Rhea working with the gardeners. After finding the magic to do away with skura, the king should have rewarded him by allowing more time with her! Alas, Kairos knew not to question the king over such matters.

Unfortunately for him, Erika rode horseback, explaining that she didn't care for carriages. Kairos had no fondness for being on the back of an animal. Before he knew he'd be in a saddle, he had chosen his finest red and gold brocade jerkin to wear over his doublet and of course his billowy sleeved chemise. Because the weather had cooled, he chose wool Hosen and black venetians. He topped his outfit with a black velvet beret and let a curl drop onto his forehead. A wizard must look his best when accompanying a princess!

He followed behind Erika and her escort, a young, red-haired soldier as they rode down the hill into the bustling city. Tents and cabanas stretched from the pier along the cobblestone streets into the allies amid high-rise flats and stone cottages. As the sun laced the sky with colorful hues, merchants had already swung open their tent flaps, and hung their wares. The sausages looked exceptionally savory and as he wiped drool from his chin, he checked his purse and pulled out several copper coins. The sausage vendor would be the first booth he visited.

When they reached the livery, Erika dismounted. Kairos zealously slid off his horse and almost fell. His legs were so rubbery.

"We should rent a carriage for the ride back," he muttered.

Erika laughed.

"What? I'm serious, Fairest."

"You'll be fine riding home, Wizard."

He waited with Erika's soldier outside the stable, guarding the hoofed beasts while Erika went in. The soldier, dressed in his uniform with the king's emblem on his tunic and a shining sword strapped to his side, stood upright and proud. The lad nodded a greeting.

"Your name?" Kairos asked.

"Rory, sir, and you be the wizard Fairest holds high." He offered his hand and Kairos shook it.

"My name is Kairos. You have an accent. You're not from around here?"

"Fairmistle's my home."

"Ah yes, the river township."

"Now, where to begin!" Erika returned from the livery with a groom. He took the reins of the horses and, with a formal bow, led the animals to the stables while Erika pulled out her ledger and began reading.

"I don't know about you, but I'm hungry. The aroma of those sausages is too tempting. How about you, Rory? Can I get you a bite to eat?"

"Don't mind if I do, if it's all right with the princess?"

"Go ahead, you two. I'll look for my fisher," Erika replied, regarding the busy street vendors.

"We'll find you," Kairos assured her and nodded for Rory to follow him. Kairos strolled past an oxen cart loaded with pots and pans, headed for the booth he'd seen earlier. Sausages hung from ropes stretched above his head. Thin brown links, some reddish next to thick gray liver sausages, dangled temptingly. They smelled of garlic and peppers and a variety of spices, some aromas with which he had no familiarity. How would he decide since they all made his mouth water and his stomach growl? He stared at the lineup of meats that hung from one end of the tent to the other. The merchant, a plump little woman with a rosy smile, missing a tooth or two, approached him.

"And that one is?" Kairos pointed to one savory looking tube of meat.

"Metworst," the woman grinned. She had an accent, though Kairos couldn't tell her ethnicity. "Smoked. Serve with stamppot."

"Oh, you need to cook it?"

"Yes."

"Perhaps you have something I could eat now?"

The woman laughed and cut a link from another sausage and handed it to him.

"Ready now. Lucanian." Kairos broke off a morsel and tasted it, offering a bit to Rory.

"Very good, we'll take this one." Kairos handed her his coin to seal the transaction. He turned to Rory and broke off a larger chunk of meat for him.

"Now let's get to our business," Kairos said with a mouthful.

"Fairest went that way."

Kairos stuffed a chunk of meat in his mouth and moaned with pleasure. Delicious. The two hurried through the market, which had come alive with people, donkeys, and a few chickens. They dodged a pig running toward them, and then again, the boy chasing it. The smells were captivating. Food everywhere—pastries, tiny meat pies, exotic fruits all mixed with the fragrance of hickory smoke.

As they searched for Erika, they came to the fishing wharf where the scent of smoked fish filled the air. There they found the princess speaking to a couple of merchants, a father and son it seemed, with her ledger out. Under the canopy were rows and rows of smoked fish, tubs filled with salt water where astakos crawled on top of one another looking for escape, and another barrel filled with shellfish. Kairos, fascinated by the spotted, clawed sea monsters, leaned over. He'd seen lobster on a dinner platter, but never alive like this.

"Can I help you?" a woman asked. Kairos shook his head. "I'm with the princess," he said, still with eyes keen on the shifting mass of crustaceans.

"And we need three months' supply. Is that possible?" Erika asked the oldest of the two men.

"Yes, Fairest. It will take time, but we can get the King's order to him before the end of the month."

"That will do. Sooner if possible."

"What do you do with those?" Kairos asked the woman who had approached him. "You sell them alive?"

"Tastes best when cooked fresh. Just throw them live in a kettle of boiling water."

Kairos looked up. "Throw them live in a pot of boiling water?"

She grinned at him as he shuddered and stepped away, glad not to be a lobster. As Erika chatted with the fish merchant, Kairos regarded the booths behind her on the other side of the road. A milliner and tailor booth where hung rows and rows of brightly colored berets, jerkins, doublets, and capotains, the newest fashion of hat Lord

Sylvester had worn at dinner the other night. Everyone had admired how tall and handsome he looked in it.

"Excuse me, Fairest," Kairos whispered to Erika. "I'll be right over there." He pointed, and she looked over her shoulder briefly, nodded, and continued to barter prices with the merchant.

"Goin' to grab one of those sugar loafs?" Rory asked with a grin. Kairos merely winked at him and strode away to the hatter.

Though he'd coveted the capotains from afar, once in the merchant's tent, the colors, textures, and scent of all the wares distracted him. What a fine tailor! The hats had elegant design and texture. He took one down and set it on his head—a bit large! A middle-aged merchant with a salt and pepper beard, deep blue eyes and furry brows nodded came to him.

"Does you well, sir!" he said.

"Wouldn't you say it's too big?"

"It is. I have a smaller size in my wagon if you 'd like to try another."

"Yes, please."

While Kairos waited for the man to return, he sorted through the jerkins. So many rich colors—blues, greens, wine reds mixed with gold in intricate patterns of paisley and Fleur-di-lis.

"Kairos," Rory stepped into the tent.

"Rory! Did you see these jerkins? You ought to get one of these. You don't always wear that uniform, do you?"

Rory laughed as he wandered into the thick of clothing. "When I'm not servin' the king, I'm in my galligaskins. Not much need for a soldier to be wearing these fancies."

"Oh, but surely you'll want to dress up occasionally."

Rory shook his head, laughing. "Fairest has settled with the fish merchant. I think she's ready to move on."

"Oh, very well." Kairos left without the hat, and the two of them waited as a crowd of people passed by before they crossed the street. He did not see the princess once they returned to the fish merchant. Expecting Erika to be waiting for him, he grimaced.

"Where did she go?"

The fishing merchant overheard and pointed behind him. "Curious about our rig," he told them.

Kairos scurried past the barrels of lobster and shellfish, nets and buoys stacked up on the side of the wharf, Rory at his heels. He hurried past pilings where seagulls nested. The floating pier wavered when he stepped on it, and Kairos got his balance. He despised being on the water and sauntered with extreme caution past several row boats tied along the dock. At the end of the pier rocked the merchant's fishing rig with nets piled high on their deck. Erika stood near the rig, speaking to three men standing by a small skiff.

"Since I am the king's daughter making this request, I don't see where you have a choice. We'll pay you well." Erika said.

"Erika?" Kairos cleared his throat. She had an especially cheerful smile when she looked at him. The blue cloak she wore seemed to make her eyes sparkle as it radiated the color of the sky. He hadn't noticed the armor she wore under her cloak before. Why, he wondered. Women are a mysterious lot, and all of King Tobias' daughters more so than most. He breathed deeply and waited to hear more of the conversation as a gentle sea breeze blew on him. Indeed, fresh sea air had its appeal.

"Whatever is the king's command." An older angler said, his face weathered by the sea with dark skin and an unkempt beard. "But if we take your horses home, how will your father know we didn't just steal them?"

Erika pulled a dagger from her sheath.

Kairos opened his eyes wide and stepped back.

"What are you doing, Fairest?" the wizard asked, his heart skipping a beat. She continued to grin, cut a small curl from her hair, and handed it to a sailor.

"Bring this to my father. He'll know it's from me and he'll pay you well for your boat."

The man stared at the lock of red hair glistening in the palm of his hand.

"Then it's settled. Is it not?" she asked the fisher. "You may keep that, if you like," she added.

He clenched the lock in his fist, nodded to his two friends, and handed Rory the line that held the bow of the boat.

"Tight lines, to you, Fairest," he said, and the three hurried down the dock.

When they had gone, Erika exhaled joyfully. "Well, Wizard, it appears as though you don't have to ride horseback to the castle after all."

"What?" Kairos asked.

"Fairest," Rory interrupted, wearing a frown.

"You can return if you like, Rory, Kairos. I have money to give you for a carriage."

"Where are you goin'?" Rory turned to the boat, inspecting it, his nervousness clearly more productive than Kairos who stood silently gawking.

"I'm taking care of matters in Cho Nisi. I couldn't feel better about this."

"You know how to be mannin' the sails?" Rory stepped into the skiff, checking the lines, the helm.

"I've never done it before, but I'm sure I can learn."

"Pardon my saying so but goin' out ta sea by yourself isn't the safest way to learn."

"What in the name of our King's gods are you doing?" Kairos heart had already skipped three beats. He couldn't let her go afloat by herself. Unspeakable!

"Kairos, I have to make things right. I will offer myself hostage to these people as they negotiate with my father for his army's protection. Many people of inferior status have offered the same ransom. How can they refuse?"

"They'll hang you."

"No, I don't think so. I'm King Tobias' daughter."

"I'm sure that means nothing to them. In fact, it might make matters worse. The king's daughter kills their king? No, Erika, you're not thinking. They'll lynch you."

"I'm going in peace, Kairos. This act is for their benefit."

"I won't have it! I'm taking you back to the castle," Kairos took her arm, but she pushed him away.

"I'm doing this, Kairos. You can't stop me."

"I'm going to try."

"I order you to silence, in the name of my Father." She spoke with authority, and Kairos had to obey. He shut his mouth and bit his tongue, trying to keep it closed, all the while his cheeks burned hot and swelled with anger and fear for her.

"Fairest, if that's what you're going to do, I can't be letting you go alone. Not in a boat with no sea knowledge," Rory interjected.

"You know how to sail?"

"My grandfather had a skiff not unlike this one here. Fished the Fairmistle River, we did. Perch and sturgeon. Made some plump, merry meals! I can get you across the sea to where you're goin' if you're swearin' to go."

"You'll attend me, then?" She clapped her hands and her face lit up. "Kairos? And you?" She turned to him.

Holy idols! She wanted him to sail to Cho Nisi with her? Without the king knowing. Without Rhea? Preposterous! Yet he couldn't let Erika go alone, not with just one lone soldier. He promised King Tobias he'd watch after his daughter, but this is ridiculous—tenacious and willful Erika who, unfortunately, held authority over him.

"Will they see this as an invasion?" Rory asked as he loosened a line from the jib.

"I don't mean it to be, Rory. We'll see what sort of reception they award us."

"And when we arrive? What plans do you have?" Kairos asked leeringly. "Before I step into this snare?"

"The perfect scenario would be to apologize for the death of their king and offer my father's protection by claiming the empty throne. They may keep me as hostage if they fear an advance, in which case you and Rory can return and tell my father. From there Father can negotiate. Or perhaps I can negotiate for their allegiance. If I'm successful, Father will have an island as a fortress."

Kairos raised one brow.

"Are you coming? Please."

Rory had already untied the boat, and the bow bounced gently in the water, veering away from the dock. Kairos growled and then climbed in, holding his nose with one hand to ward off the fishy smell. He squinted at Erika, angry that she could make him do something against his will.

"I never agreed with what your sister said about you. Until now—" he said. "Now I'm seeing she's fairly accurate with her assessment."

"Rhea knows nothing about me, Kairos." She lifted her chin and stepped in the skiff, Rory giving her a hand. "If you must know, the reason I'm traveling to Cho Nisi is because I killed their king. I'm heartsick over it. I've left them vulnerable and open to many perils. I've seen skura attacks firsthand. Yes, the Cho Nisi have magic, but no one knows how long they can hold their own. There are thousands of skura, and the island now has no leader. My father can remedy that by offering protection under our kingdom. And you, the King's Wizard, have magic against skura as well."

"Tested only on one lone bat!"

"I have faith in you, Kairos. This is the least I can do, even if it puts my life in jeopardy."

"And if the Cho Nisi decide to hang you?"

"You can help me with that."

"I'm to stop them?"

"You wouldn't?" she asked.

Kairos' cheeks heated, and he held onto the side of the boat. "I would do my best to see that you're safe, Fairest. But I'm not exactly sure how capable my powers are. That's a magical island, Fairest. They have spells…"

"Oh, the Cho Nisi won't be hangin' our princess, Sir Kairos." Rory assured him. "We won't be lettin' them touch her," Rory picked up an oar and pushed the skiff from the dock. "I think it's an honorable deed, Fairest, and I'll be supportin' you best I can as a soldier for King Tobias. Makin' the island safe from the dark lord. Helping the natives. Honorable, indeed!"

Kairos settled himself in the boat without saying another word. After drifting to deeper water, Rory lifted the halyard and set the skiff to sail. By mid-morning they sailed.

"Perfect weather for being on the water, feel that crisp breeze?"

"Cold," Kairos mumbled, wrapping his cloak tighter around himself.

"The sun is warm."

"The sun is warm." Erika seated herself at the prow while Kairos huddled at the stern, Rory in the center with the oars.

Cottony clouds adorned the heavens, and the boat drifted quietly under them, boosted by the wind.

Kairos had to admit, the sun warmed his back.

They traveled the entire day, drifted in the moonlight at night, and by sunrise drew near enough to see the island.

A Spy

Taking on the characteristics of the monsters he created, a scaly skinned Skotádi perched on his private watch tower outside his cave—a jagged cliff on the peak of Casda de Moor—staring at the large dark cavern that burrowed into the hollow of Mount Ream. Skotádi longed to enter the chamber where he first created his power, now guarded by a dragon that would consume him should he come near. Into the darkest of tunnels, the spell of eternity beckoned him— an incantation written on the walls of the cave that would give him an ever-lasting life.

Below, in between the two mountain ranges, lay the fertile valley of Tellwater. Spread out in a patterned landscape, Tellwater had proven the most valued property in all of Prasa Potama. Nestled in the mountain shadows, yet low enough for a more temperate climate, canals fed by the Ream River irrigated Lord Garion's vineyard. Two days' ride from King Tobias' army, Skotádi found it perfect hunting grounds for his skura who raided livestock and brought the animals to his cave on Casda de Moor. From these creatures, he crafted the mountain giants. Meat for meat, any animal would do. The Vouchsaver preferred humans, but skura had not had luck capturing them yet, so sheep and turkey would have to do.

Skotádi regarded the vineyards of Lord Garion in the distance with a disgusted sneer. The valley should have been a dusty killing field filled with bodies of men whose souls he could have reaped, but for King Tobias' new allies! Those magic wielding foreigners destroyed his entire northern flock. He would need to make more immediately.

His pet skura, Demetri, clung to the slated rock with his talons to keep from sliding on the ice. Skotádi paced along the cliff edge.

"They think they won the battle, but they didn't." Skotádi scoffed.

"They killed hundreds of my brothers," Demitri complained.

"Pawns, Demitri. Throwaways. Those skura were unintelligent beasts."

"You made them," the skura squawked and then recoiled when

Skotádi pointed a bony finger at him.

"To raid, pillage, and kill. Do you think I can't make more?"

Demitri hung low his vulture-like neck and scooted up against the slate walls. A brief snowstorm had dusted the mountain top the night before and left an icy wind that whistled through the cavern. The cold didn't bother Skotádi. He'd spent too many years leaning over kettles of bubbling potions that rearranged flesh, formed scales, and restructured bodies. Breathing in the fumes of such mixtures left his skin like a lizard's. His blood ran hot.

"Your brothers would have killed all those men, were it not for those power-wielding magicians. But for them I would have reaped souls and gained more strength and captured humans for my brew. Think how many mountain giants I could have created! Who were those men? Why hadn't my scouts returned with news of the ones who left?"

"You have too many foes. I say rekindle your bond with Bahldi's grandson. He's ready. He would be a benefit to you."

"In time, Demitri."

Soon he would have the Potamian kingdom crumbling into a land of chaos. He would carry out his plans of conquest, and the world would turn against itself and succumb to him. When it does, with an army of men, he can approach the caves on Mount Ream and pursue his immortality.

"What if King Tobias is creating a new alliance with those strangers who wielded the magic?" Demitri challenged.

"It will end soon. Didn't you see? The king's daughter killed one of them. An important one, I think." Skotádi smiled at the thought. War will soon stir in the west. "If my scouts would bring me word of where they live, I'll make sure they end the alliance between King Tobias and these foreigners."

"They live on an island."

"You know this?"

Demitri squawked and moved nervously. "We've been near it. We're afraid of the magic of that place. They command the elements. They make the sky dark, the wind to spin, and the sea to swell. It probably destroyed the skura you sent."

"You go, then. Alone."

"My Liege!" the skura begged. "Please, it's a dangerous mission."

"When have my missions not been dangerous?"

"What am I to do there? I can tell you where it is, in the middle of the sea."

"Very well, since you know where it is, be my spy. Bring me word of who rules there, what their defenses are, and if there's any sign of King Tobias' soldiers."

"They'll surely see me," the skura protested.

Skotádi snatched a vial from the sash around his waist and pulled the cork. The skura flapped its wings in protest and would have taken flight had not the wizard grasped its feet with his other hand. He jerked the beast upside down by its legs and let the potion drip into its mouth. Demetri's body relaxed, its wings fell limp.

"Don't question me again. Tell me if they declare war with Tobias. Find out who the princess killed, and what they'll do to her should they get their hands on her. I'll give you a disguise. No one will know you're the enemy."

With that, Skotádi placed his palm over the creature's head and muttered a spell. The skura's plates on its chest fizzled, as if melting and slowly each scale changed form, elongating, softening, breaking apart and diminishing into fine fluffy feathers. The skura's man-head tightened. His nose and mouth grew together and hardened to a beak, and then its entire body shrank to the size of an overgrown raven.

"There!" Skotádi huffed, pleased with himself, turning the bird right-side up and pushing it away from him.

The bird opened its mouth and called out, but its voice had changed. No longer could it speak in man's language. Skotádi chuckled.

"Yes, you'll go to the island and observe their rituals. Learn their drumbeats and tell me all you see. Stay far enough away and unseen. I want you to observe. Tell me how they make the sky dark, the wind to spin, and the sea to swell. Do that, and I'll reward you."

Demitri may have complained if he could still talk. Skotádi took the bird with both hands and walked to the edge of his cavern.

"Go!"

He released his spy, tossing it out over the valley. The bird flailed over the chasm having to learn how to fly anew. Skotádi snickered over its struggle.

He would wait until Demitri returned with news. Perhaps it would be wise to attack the island if a war between the foreigners and King Tobias doesn't break out.

The Castle at Cho Nisi

Amid a village of high-rise flats pinned together tightly along narrow alleyways, the settlement surrounding King Arell's castle contrasted against the quiet beaches. The Moatons who inhabited the city were as dissimilar to the natives as their abodes were from the native villages. While a child, Arell never got comfortable among the closed-mouthed Moatons, perhaps because his mother raised him as a Cho Nisi rather than a prince. Even after she died, Arell often felt ill at ease in the palace when people from Moaton were around.

Since his grandfather's day, the Cho Nisi elders had worked in collaboration with the king, but Arell wanted nothing to do with politics. The sea, the tide pools, canoeing and spear fishing pulled on his heartstrings. He spent evenings in the warm sun and lingered on the white sands long after daylight dimmed, and shadows chilled the villages.

Before his father died, there had been gossip about the prince living with the Cho Nisi, but his father's counselors advised the king to let him be. Some said a boy half-native could never rise to be a monarch. Arell hadn't cared. He had no ambition to be a ruler. The small island and introverted residents needed little governing. Perhaps boredom and search for adventure prompted his parent to go to the aid of King Tobias.

Now Arell, more somber than he had ever been, donned his father's fur-lined robe, gilded with gold and silver threads, and sat on the throne. The time had come for him to query the men who had seen his father die.

Serena, Bena, and three other native maidens fixed his mantle in a perfect circle at his feet. Such graceful women, slim, dark, sleek black hair bouncing over their shoulders. Dressed in chitons, they wore anklets and gold bands on their arms, gifts Arell had given them.

Had they been home, they would wear beads, but he liked the way the gold contrasted against their skin. The fragrance of ginger blossoms calmed his temperament. How could he be anxious amid their charm?

"Is there anything else, Vasil?" Serena asked.

"When this meeting is over, yes. I will have you fix my bath for me." He took her hand and kissed it.

"As you wish." She curtsied.

Blood crept into his cheeks as he watched her leave.

"I didn't realize my father enjoyed so many amenities," he told the chief sitting by his side. "Your daughters know how to soothe a nervous king."

Silas grunted.

A valet opened the door to the throne room and four Cho Nisi warriors entered, bowing before him. They wore the after-battle ceremonial garb of their sect, the Bombadons. Blue tunics, crow feathers on their belts, and a string of Umbonium shells around their necks.

"Vasil, you wanted to speak with us?"

"Yes," Arell rose, shed his robe, stepped off his pedestal, and ushered the men to a table nearby.

"Wine?" he offered. The natives looked at each other. They seemed intimidated, to Arell's disappointment. He hadn't meant to discourage them from speaking their hearts.

"Come, sit. I'll have the servants bring fruit." He nodded at an attendant who left the room. "Let's not be formal, soldiers. You fought with my father and I respect what you've done. Thank you for bringing him back home. The journey must have been long and difficult for you."

They sat at his table silently.

"I have some questions." Arell waited in silence until the servant returned and set plates of fresh vegetables and shellfish before them. So rigid were the fellows that Arell gave Silas a puzzled look, and immediately the chief spoke in their native language. They nodded and served themselves. No one poured themselves a chalice of wine, though.

"Please, tell me how my father died."

"An arrow," a man responded, looking at his plate.

Arell knew that. Who? How? He would have to construct his questions differently.

"What is your name?"

"Tema," he answered. He had long hair tied neatly in back, his frown seemed fixed, as if life had not treated him generously.

"I appreciate what you and your friends have done." When Tema looked up at him, Arell placed his fist over his heart, the Cho Nisi sign of honor. "Please talk to me. Tell me exactly what happened? What point in the battle did my father fall? Were there human volunteers of Skotádi's in among the skura? An enemy our warriors should know?"

"No. No men."

"No?" That surprised him. "Possibly another form of demon who can fight like a man, use a man's weapon. Or a new breed of monsters?" he asked.

"No. Just skura."

Arell sat back in his chair and watched them eat.

"Are you suggesting that the enemy didn't kill my father?"

"We only fought against the skura. We saw no other enemy. Only beasts from the sky, the Potamian knights and Lord Garion's militia. No others."

"But King Rolland died from an arrow wound."

"Yes. To his heart."

Arell sipped his wine while digesting this news. Who would have killed the king of Cho Nisi if not Skotádi? Surely not any of King Tobias' soldiers. Never had there been any trouble with the mainland. Never! His father trusted King Tobias. Lord Garion, he had never met, but why would a nobleman kill an ally? He clenched his fists and then opened them, breathing deeply to control his angst.

"Then my father's death was an accident. Had he been in the way of Potamian crossfire?"

Tema said something to Chief Silas. The two exchanged words in their language. Silas kept nodding toward Arell, and then Tema stood and looked straight into Arell's eyes. The other men stopped eating.

Arell held his cup to his lips without drinking as his eye's met the warrior's. His heart raced.

"Our king, your father, died before the battle began."

"Before?" Arell stuttered, the shock sinking into his soul as if someone had plunged a sword into his heart and kept it there. "Before?"

An assassination?

He bolted from his chair and dropped his chalice. Wine splashed on the floor, the goblet reeled in a circle, and tottered at his feet. Its gold rim, brilliant from the sun, blinded him. He said nothing. Words wouldn't form, nor could he move. The light that leached into the throne room glowed brilliantly, seizing him from reality. He stared at the herald but did not see him.

Silence.

"King Arell?" Silas sighed.

The world may have ceased rotation, it mattered not. His mind spun away from reality. Chief Silas said something to the men. The people in the room stood and one by one they bowed, moved away as if disappearing into space.

"Vasil," someone whispered. A hand took his shoulder and shook him gently. "Arell, my king. The elders will confer. There is much to discuss."

In the radiance, his father's pale and lifeless body lay on the deck of a boat.

Assassinated?

Time passed. Eternity.

Another voice sounded in his mind. A woman's tone. Sweet, melodious.

"Vasil. Come to your quarters. Your bath is ready."

They're Coming

Arell greeted the morning as solemnly as he had addressed the night. Reality slowly came into focus and with it, a responsibility that weighed heavily on his shoulders. Added to the grief of losing his father, his nation tottered on the brink of war.

Chief Silas sat in Arell's room. Cho Nisi sentries stood at his door. The chief stared out the window while Arell sat on the end of his bed, half of the covers spread carelessly on the floor. He hadn't slept.

"I don't know what to do, Silas," Arell confessed. "I'm at a total loss."

Silas didn't answer, but his sympathetic eyes and grave expression offered no solution for him either. Arell looked up, his hair disheveled from pulling at it. His eyes puffed with misery. Worry had tormented him as he grazed over the tragedy that might happen should the island take arms against the legendary King Tobias. The foreign ruler would have allies. Perhaps the empire Casdamia would stand by the king's side. Hundreds of fully armored soldiers with state-of-the-art weapons and a fleet of battleships might invade them. Cannons perhaps, and magicians who could more than match the feeble charms of their remote island.

Were the chant-induced spells powerful enough to ward off such an onslaught? Could they disguise their isle from the human eye and hide their homeland from the rest of the world undetected? For how long?

One truth stood out concerning the magic of Cho Nisi. Spells would last only as long as the strength and passion of the men who chanted. Should any of the champions who chanted become tired, or doubt, or lose interest, the spell would falter. Others could stand in the gap, and that has happened before. But a doubter could also influence those in his circle. So, war with a kingdom such as Potamia proved as risky as if the Cho Nisi had no magic.

"How do we discover the truth? How do we find out if King

Tobias ordered the murder of my father?"

"The warriors believe he did. They're waiting for you to retaliate."

"Retaliate? How? Declare war?"

Silas shrugged. "I understand your hesitancy. It would be difficult."

Arell let out a cynical laugh. "Difficult? Our barefoot warriors against the king's multitude of armed soldiers? And while there's a war with demons burning hot over all of us?"

"We have powers which the king does not have," Silas reminded him.

Arell studied his friend, puzzled. "Do we know the capacity of those powers? Have we ever tested them to their end?"

Silas shook his head.

"You're advocating war against the greatest nation on the mainland? King Tobias has been our ally for years. Father trusted him. What happened? What if my father's death were an accident?"

Silas glared at him. "The first shot killed your father. It was no accident."

Arell rubbed his head again. He couldn't think anymore. He hurt inside. The ache of betrayal battered his heart and wrenched his gut, becoming a physical throbbing he couldn't escape.

Silas gazed outside again as if the answer to their trouble hung in the air above the castle. "Your father stood brave and strong. He loved you, your people, and our people. You will be strong like he was, I have no doubt. Understand this, though. Cho Nisi are proud. They do not take being wronged well. They expect you to stand up and demand justice. There must be retaliation. How you do it, that is for you to decide. You're king now."

What a mandate! "I need time to think about this, Silas."

The chief nodded and rose. "I sent warriors to watch over you when they brought your father home. They still keep watch. I will send more if it eases your mind. When an heir sits on the throne after one assassination, there is often another. Be wary."

Silas slipped out the door. Arell took off his nightclothes and dressed carelessly, leaving his shirt unlaced, the tail hanging over his trousers. He slipped into his doublet, more for warmth than for show, and left it unbuttoned. The need for fresh air beckoned him outside. He needed to be alone in the elements. If only he could feel the physical world. An icy wind, a warm sun, salty sea air—something besides this numbness.

He made his way down the corridor and slipped out a side entry that opened to a stony trail. As sincere as Silas's intentions were to keep him guarded, Arell sought solitude in order to consider the dilemma.

A war with King Tobias? Arell had never met the man, but he had heard stories regarding the Potamian family and how they stormed after the dark lord years ago and chased profane beasts from their borders. How they conquered creatures of inscrutable abilities. King Tobias doesn't have Cho Nisi magic, but he has powers of his own—wizardry, sorcery. He is a rich man and can order any catalogue of spells he needs. It would be foolish for the island to declare war against him.

As a new king, he couldn't lose favor with his people at such an early period in his career. It was the elders' job to impart wisdom. Many of them witnessed his father's death and wanted to avenge him. What sort of son would Arell be if he didn't also want reprisal?

"Well?" he charged himself as he jogged a mountain trail to an overlook. The morning air filled his lungs and calmed him as he inhaled. "What sort of son are you?" he asked himself aloud. He stopped, closed his eyes, and faced the sun, arms outstretched, absorbing its warmth, petitioning its powerful rays for healing from the pain within.

Atop the tallest hill on the island, from the castle he could see the entire span of ocean and the continent that bordered it. Far to the north, across the sea, stood Mount Ream and Casda de Moor, two snowcapped peaks facing each other, and where Tellwater Valley stretched. That mountain range bore witness to his parent's death.

Arell breathed deeply as he looked at those mountains, only tiny white dots in a field of blue. Betrayal? Vengeance? How had the fate of the island so suddenly come to rest on his shoulders? The wise thing to do for the welfare of everyone would be to let it go. That's what he wanted to do. Just let it pass. Bury his father and all the ills attached to his death. End the violence.

Across the sea, coming from the north, sailed a ship. Arell

pulled the spyglass from his doublet and focused on the skiff. His heart skipped a beat. A banner, red and gold, a destrier as the insignia—King Tobias' standard.

The Potamians would not let him bury his father in peace. How many more ships had stolen to their shores in the night? Perhaps King Tobias had already raided and pilfered his shores. This legendary king might have ordered his execution, and these ships carried men to kill him and claim his throne. Arell quickly tapped the spyglass closed and raced back to the castle. Opening the door, he hurried past the scullions, the servants in the hall, and glanced briefly at the young chamberlain whose duty it was to dress him.

"Sire," the chamberlain called out after him.

"I know," Arell answered and grabbed at his doublet buttons to close them on the run. "Where is Silas?"

"On the study balcony," the young man answered. "Let me…"

Arell pushed open the doors to the balcony. Chief Silas recoiled in surprise. Arell halted, panting. "They…they're coming. King Tobias' soldiers."

Arell needn't say anything else. Silas grabbed his coat and growled at him as he left. "Tuck your shirt in. Button your doublet." The chamberlain met him in the hall and handed him his hat as Arell rushed out after the chief.

Arell raced to catch Silas, pushing his shirt into his trousers, and brushing the creases out of his doublet. By the time they reached the pathway to the beach, his feathered hat crowned his head. Silas signaled to every warrior they met on the way—the sentries, the guards, the Cho Nisi singers.

"Get your drums," he ordered. "Gather the weapons. Prepare the catapult."

When they arrived at the beach, the men there, having seen the boat nearing shore, were already beating their drums and manifesting a spell. The warriors who had followed Arell and Silas skipped down the hill to the sand and joined them. Other warriors ran up the shoreline, the throb of their song resonating loudly. The wind stirred and blew sand into the air, which slapped against Arell's cheeks and into his eyes. A twister appeared offshore, lifting sea water as it rose, becoming a dark tornado swirling over the waters.

"Don't destroy their boat," Arell cautioned. "Not yet. See if there are more vessels than this skiff that heads our way. If so, shift their bearings, get them lost. Make them retreat. Drive them away, but don't kill them." Arell said, his temper rising the nearer the boat came.

"We see no others, Vasil," a warrior called out.

"What is this they're doing? Only one skiff? I don't believe it," Arell asked Silas.

"A parlay perhaps?" Silas replied.

"Maybe." Arell paced up and down the shore watching everything—the tempest, the ship rocking, the darkening of the skies, the warriors drumming. Who are they to approach like this, waving the banner of Potama? Killing his father and now bringing one small fishing craft to parlay? What do they want? Do they mean to insult him?

"Bring the skiff ashore. Let them come. Have archers ready and don't let up the magic. Watch them closely."

Silas whistled to his men and held up one finger. A tunnel of calm appeared in front of the vessel. Silas took Arell's arm. "Go to the top of the hill. Do not be down here on the beach when they arrive." He tugged Arell away and up the trail to the cliff that overlooked the beach. Arell followed, stumbling—more captivated by what he saw approaching than concentrating on his footing. When Arell reached the higher embankment with Silas behind him, he dusted his clothes and fixed his hat. Pulling out his spyglass, he watched the banner-waving skiff as it reached the shallows.

"I see only one soldier and a magician." His frown slowly formed into a bewildered smile. "And that's a woman at the prow—a pretty red-head."

"Is it?" The chief nodded with a half-smile. "Then you will be more a threat to her than she to you." he whispered.

Erika's Landing

How soft the sound of the sail on a glassy sea as silky-smooth waters took them near the island. A slight breeze picked up and soon turned to a moderate wind, which rushed them through the waters.

"Time to pull the sail," Rory called out, his voice competing with the gust. "The currents will bring us to shore, but the wind's a spinning. Can't really work it." His voice tapered off as the skiff rocked and white caps spat into the hull. Erika held onto the guardrail with both hands.

"Whatever you need to do. You're the sailor." She trusted Rory knew how to handle a boat, even in turbulent waters.

"Can't you do anything about this insidious rockeen—?" Kairos' words turned into a choking sound. He leaned over the rail and emptied his stomach, and his hat blew into the water as he did. He grabbed for it but heaved again.

"Curses!" He muttered as his topper spun across the whitecaps and disappeared under a wave.

"Honestly, Kairos." Erika turned away from the sight to avoid getting sick herself.

The skiff pitched from side to side. The sea sent swells at them and Rory turned the keel, meeting the rising waves.

"I believe we've encountered a squall," Rory tied the sail, but could do no more in such a small craft and with such high winds.

"What have you done, Fairest?" Kairos asked.

"Me?"

"You knew these natives wielded sorcery. Why did you come here?"

"Because I must! As far as sorcery, you're the magician. Do something!" she commanded, amazed that he accused her of their predicament.

He heaved again.

"I cannot." He wiped his mouth with the hem of his robe.

"All we can do is hang on," Rory told her. "It's a wicked flurry, but I'm a powerful swimmer, Fairest, and if we capsize, I'll swim you ashore, sure as anyone's promise."

His offer did little to relieve her terror. The dark sea waters and wild skies pressed on, churning them in circles, thrusting them into the air and slamming them against the angry waves. Her hair clung to her face, wet from spray, and every time the skiff dipped into a swell she screamed, afraid the approaching surge drown them.

But they didn't die, and the waters grew calm.

"We're almost to shore," Rory mentioned.

Erika wiped the wet hair from her face and blinked her eyes dry. Seeing land and natives on the beach, she pushed back her cloak, adjusted her leather armor, and brushed her wet hair back over her shoulders.

"Have your weapon ready, Rory. We aren't sure what they'll do."

Stunned by an arrow that landed in the boat, she gasped. It could have been a warning for it simply dropped, doing no damage. Erika picked up her bow and nocked an arrow of her own.

"Kairos, are you with us?"

"What do you expect me to do, Erika? I'm a wizard, not a god."

"Shield us or something."

A spray of stones fell into their boat, slapping against her cloak, her arms, and if she hadn't turned her head, they would have hit her face. Rory ducked and Kairos raised his hands to protect himself. When the volley stopped, Kairos stood, fire flaming from his hands. He sent a streak of energy toward the group of natives. The fire would have burned them except the warriors weren't there any longer, but off to the right. Another volley bombarded them. The arrowheads embedded their skiff.

"You see?" Erika turned to Kairos, her heart thumping more from anger than fear. No allied nation should attack a craft with the King's standard. "Already they've gone lawless. They are in want of a king."

The skiff reached sand, so Rory jumped out of the boat and

pulled it ashore, ducking to avoid projectiles.

As he shoved the boat onto the sand, Erika unlocked the mast, pulled it down, and pushed it into the water. She jumped in after it, still holding her bow, and helped Rory to ground the craft on the beach.

"Kairos help turn this boat."

An arrow spun past her face, another grazed Kairos' cloak. They rocked the dinghy on its side and ducked behind it just as a row of arrows hit. Erika peeked over the top, aimed, and released her arrow, but the man she aimed at disappeared.

"Kairos, strike them with your magic again."

"I don't think I can do any damage." He rolled up his sleeves and pulled a vial from his belt pouch. Dripping a yellow ointment onto his fingers, he rubbed them together, stood up over the boat and threw liquid fire at the archers. The men ducked.

From up on the hill, an enormous stone soared at them. It twisted and turned in midair and came crashing down. Erika ran back into the water, Kairos and Rory followed. The rock landed on the bow of the skiff, crushing it.

"Wondrous thing I ever saw," Rory exclaimed. "They've got a catapult!"

"Who's running it?" Erika crept to the skiff, her skirt soaked. She pulled off her shoes, threw them on the sand and peered out from behind the guardrail of the upturned boat. A young man, taller than the others, stood on the hill with his hands on his hips. He wore a decorated doublet, a feather in his hat and a smile on his face. Who in the world is that?

"Hallo, there beautiful!" he called. "What brings you to our lovely island?"

"Restrain your archers!" Erika demanded.

"I already have," he said.

Another large rock came whirling at them. They ducked as it hit the boat, this time punching a hole in hull.

"Curses. Now we're trapped here," Kairos complained. "You'd better friend these people and negotiate passage home."

"Friend them? They're savages! And the man ordering them is a rogue. How can you make friends with insolence? Clearly these are rebels bent on taking the island themselves. They must be stopped if civilization is to have a foothold here."

"And you're going to stop them?" Kairos asked.

"No. But my father's name might awaken their senses. If they think King Tobias has come to claim the island, perhaps they'll end their coup." She stood.

"Erika!" Kairos tugged on her skirt, but she moved away from him.

"Stop your attack, I command in the name of King Tobias."

"King Tobias? Who's that?" the man asked.

"He's to be your king, you impertinent mutineer! I command you to stop by threat of death."

"Death?" The man's feather quivered as he laughed. "And who are you to command me?"

"I am Erika, daughter of the king, and your impending ruler, for I come to negotiate the throne of Cho Nisi for my father."

The man whispered to the native next to him. Kairos rolled his eyes and sunk further behind the boat. Rory crouched low.

"Well, you can't have the throne this day," the man said. He waved to the natives, who slung their bows over their backs and returned their arrows to their quivers. They climbed up the hill toward him.

"I will occupy this land until the Cho Nisi council negotiates with my father!" Erika repeated, blood rushing to her head. She'd never been so angry.

"You will occupy this land until you build another boat!" The man chuckled. He and his warriors walked away, laughing.

Erika growled.

King Tobias

Barin lingered at his father's table early in the morning, pressing a poultice packed in wet linen against his aching forehead. The skirmish against skura in the northern plains of Prasa Potama the day before had not only been a surprise but had been taxing. Still, his army returned whole after they had eliminated most of the enemy. That his sister had disappeared bothered him more than the sore on his head, or the weariness caused by a grueling confrontation with the enemy. He had no time to find her before Father discovered her absence. Neal waited with him, slowly swirling his cup of mulled wine.

"He's going to kill me," Barin groaned.

Neal grunted. "Royal Prince Barin and hero of the clamor! He who slays a thousand skura with one sweep of a blade and tackles mountain giants with his bare hands—who reclaims fertile valleys for the Crown and makes peace with the dark lord! But alas! Prince Barin, heir to the Potamian kingdom, dies at the hand of his father for not keeping track of a rebellious sister?"

"Making peace with the dark lord?"

Neal shrugged. "Seemed like a good rumor to spread."

"I had no idea Erika would sneak away."

"How could you? You brought her home from Tellwater in hopes she'd stay. She's a grown woman. She does what she wants."

"No, she's not a grown woman, she's a child."

"But she claims adulthood, and so how are you going to convince her otherwise? Your father's the king and even he can't make her obey."

The poultice had numbed his head. He set the rag on the table.

Neal gave him a sympathetic frown. "Listen, Barin, you have plenty to boast about to your father. Our mission has ended. In the last month we've brought a small army to Felix, and he can hold his own until spring. We vanquished a threat in Kevshire, and we returned home with no casualties while killing several skura as a gratuity.

Concentrate on that. King Tobias will be proud of you."

At that moment, a page opened the door and announced the monarch. Barin and Neal stood, bowing as King Tobias stormed into the hall.

"How did she get away?" The king's voice echoed off the walls.

Barin bowed again and stuttered.

"Oh, disregard my ranting, it's probably not your fault. The woman is impudent. I know where she is, and now she's in danger."

"You found her? How?" Barin should have guessed his father would be two steps ahead of him. King Tobias had a way of discovering the indiscoverable. That's what made him such a great king.

"Fishers, Barin. Fishers came to my door just now. On horseback. On our horses, mind you. The ones she gave them. She promised I'd pay them for their trouble. For their boat! Which she took!" King Tobias' face burned red. He paced the floor.

"What? She did what?"

"She traded our horses for a fish-harvester boat and directed the owners of the boat here with a message. Do you know what she told them to tell me?"

Barin shook his head. He couldn't imagine. His father's face swelled with rage, his eyes red. "She said she's going to claim the throne of Cho Nisi!"

"She's a fool! They'll kill her."

"That's what I said. And they just might. What happened with you?"

"An attack on Upper Potama. I lead a charge."

King Tobias took a breath and closed his eyes momentarily. When he opened them, a little calmer, he laid his hands on Barin's shoulders. "I'm sorry, son. I should have given you a father's welcome. I'm glad you made it home safely. You as well, Neal. We shouldn't let Erika's foolishness destroy this family."

Rhea appeared at the door, and both Barin and Neal acknowledged her with a bow.

"How could you be so inhumane as to let the man I love run off with our sister?"

"She took Kairos?" Barin shot a quick glance at Neal. He

needed Kairos on their next journey to Tellwater.

"You ruined my life!"

"Rhea," the king interrupted as he hurried to her and wrapped his arm around her shoulder. "I'm sure your fears are unjustified. There's nothing romantic between those two."

"No, there isn't," Barin interjected. "Erika cares for no one but herself. If she took Kairos, it would be simply for his spells. But I need Kairos. There's a war happening."

"She's a spoiled little horror," Rhea interrupted. "Why do you let her wear armor or carry a sword? She's proven herself unqualified."

A brother to three sisters, Barin spent many years teaching himself the art of family neutrality. Well-mannered Rhea caused a minor problem unless anger got the best of her. Then she could be a cannon ball. Better for him not to engage. Instead, even though his cheeks flushed, and a mild rage at her accusations stirred in his gut, he cleared his throat.

"I've no time for mulling over Erika. Father and I must discuss our plans for Tellwater." He would have to find Kairos before he returned to the valley, but he preferred not to chase after Erika.

"Rhea, please. Let your brother and I discuss affairs of the kingdom for now." King Tobias escorted her to the door. Rhea pulled away from him and left the room in a storm.

Barin's temperature had risen during the discourse, and he steamed as his father walked back to the table and poured a flask of wine. With a coaxing touch from Neal, Barin settled with him at the table.

"You'll be happy to know, Barin, that Kairos has had a breakthrough while you were away. He informed me—rather hesitantly—that he's ready for battle."

"I'm pleased with the news, and livid that he's not available. We can't return to Tellwater without him."

"I agree!" The king grimaced. He took another drink with shaking hands. "We leave Lord Garion to wrestle with Skotádi on his own, then?"

"Until Kairos returns. It's just as well. We can concentrate on securing other regions of our kingdom for now. We defeated the skura in Kevshire, but rumor is Fairmistle has been a target. Terror runs rampant, and no one had expected the skura attack in north Potama."

Barin tried to make eye contact with his father, but Tobias

stared into his mug. "I hate leaving the valley," the king said. "It's the most fertile region of our kingdom. And Lord Garion is a good friend."

Barin sighed. "Temporarily, Father. We can prepare now, but we can't leave until we have Kairos. Lord Garion has experienced and well-armed men. They'll be training the serfs in technique and they'll be recruiting the locals. There's not much more we can do for Lord Garion at the moment. The trip over the mountain is risky, and it's a long and dusty ride around the mountain. Winter will be here soon and when it comes, snow will bury the passes, if not already. It's a long journey and we need to make worth our while. Once we have Kairos, and his apprentices, we can bring supplies and workers to build a keep. Supplies will take time to gather, regardless."

"And now we have Cho Nisi to worry over. No telling what they'll do to Erika. Does Lord Garion know we won't be returning right away?"

"I'm sure he knows it will take time."

King Tobias nodded again and drank his wine in huge gulps. "And you mean what you said about your sister?"

"Don't ask me to go chase her down. Please, Father. She does nothing that I ask, but only devises ways to defy me. I've had enough. Her antics distract me."

"She loves you."

"Well, she has an astonishing way of exhibiting her affection. Just a short while ago, she sought my forgiveness. I see now she will not change. I cannot be around her."

The king set his chalice on the table. "Very well, I won't ask you."

King Tobias rose, and Neal and Barin stood as a courtesy. "I leave you in command of stratagem, son. I trust your decisions."

As he walked away Barin bowed, saddened to watch his father depart not as a regal and proud king, but as a tired old man.

Arell's Tactics

The Cho Nisi village of Nico stretched along the western coast where white sandstone cliffs provided homes carved directly into the bluffs. Harsh weather seldom plagued that part of the island, and so the residents never needed to seal windows closed, but kept them open for fresh sea air and sunlight. Atop the cliffs grew forests of pine, olive, and pomegranates. Wild salmon berries lavished the hillside. The islanders harvested fish, shellfish, wild fruit, millet, and olives. The natives traded for wool and linen from the Moatons, the immigrant village surrounding King of Cho Nisi's castle but unlike the modest immigrants who wore only browns, grays, and other natural hues, the Cho Nisi dyed their fabrics with stains made from mollusks, rose madder, and wild mignonette.

Arell enjoyed hunting with the elders. Occasionally men from Moaton would join him, but the immigrants hunted primarily on their own, choosing beasts from the forests rather than sea life.

On the same day of his escapade with the Potamian princess, Arell hiked to Nico with Silas and the tribal elders to discuss matters of his father's death, the war against the skura, and the threat of a war against King Tobias.

As he sauntered along the grassy trail, Arell pondered over the possibilities the small band of intruders presented. The appearance of the princess both complicated matters and provided potential solutions. A young and lovely princess, though gusty. It made no sense that her father sent her here without enough troops to back her assault. Was she simply a rebellious little firefly acting on her own? He smiled to himself as he walked, thinking how foolish she looked, and yet how… delightful. Perhaps she needed a good scare to teach her a lesson. If he kept her here, he'd ask Serena to give her a lesson on grace.

More seriously though, the murder of his father happened under the charge of King Tobias, and if the princess came under his instruction, Cho Nisi faced a grave threat. Despite a spirited daughter, no greater a king had reigned in Potamia than the Tobias family. Celebrated kings from a legendary dominance, their stories had spread even as far as a remote island in the Nisi Sea, leaving Arell puzzled over whether the princess was simply a warning, an omen, or a fluke.

Arell refused to act without the elder's wisdom and blessing. Silas called for this council, and so Arell followed the chief across the countryside from the castle to the beach.

The sweat lodge was located in a cove on the trail to the village. Here the elders often discussed the pressing matters that faced their people. Arell had attended a few of those assemblies with his father. Today they would meet in the sweat lodge. The chief believed purifying the body would create a healthy atmosphere and generate wise decisions.

Rocks were already roasting in the sand pit when they arrived, and heavy blankets sealed a driftwood hut. Burning sandalwood filled the cove with a thin haze of smoke as a gentle surf rolled onto the sandy beach, stopping at the sweat lodge's threshold.

"Our king!" Though he wore no smile, Abenda, an elder, met Arell and Silas with a bow as the two descended the rocky trail. "The lodge is ready for you. Lagan and Ral are inside." Abenda handed Arell a linen cloth like the one he wore around his waist and then dipped into the lodge. Chief Silas undressed and followed him. Arell unbuttoned his doublet and hung it carefully on the branches of a willow. He shivered, chilled in the cove's shade where the rocky bluffs absorbed the sea spray and cooled the air. He undressed completely and wrapped the linen around his waist. When he pulled the blanket that served as the lodge door aside, stepped in, and dropped the mantle, hot air hit his body. A strong incense mingled with the smell of sweat.

"Watch your feet," Silas warned as Arell stepped carefully around the pile of glowing rock in the center of the hut. He slid onto the bench against the adobe walls, blinking in response to the darkness. Before his eyes adjusted to the dark, someone ushered him onto the bench and other bodies moved aside for him. The beat of a drum claimed attention as a few men hummed quietly. Someone splattered drops of water on the rocks, filling the room with steam and accenting the delicate fragrance of myrrh.

"We invite the Creator of our world in this assembly," Silas chanted as he tossed more incense onto the glowing rocks. The men sang together. The drumbeat grew louder, and perspiration and condensation trickled down Arell's body. They stayed like this for well over an hour, chanting, singing, and sweating. When the rocks cooled, Abenda stepped outside for more.

"What is your decision, King Arell?" Silas asked. Though men older and wiser than Arell occupied the small enclosure, Silas reminded Arell that the burden of the island rested on his shoulders. Arell tried to see the chief's expression in the light of the glowing rocks, but either the man wore no emotion on his face, or the darkness of the sweat lodge prevented him from reading the chief's sentiment.

Arell thought for a moment, careful to form his words. "I must interrogate these invaders before I lead our people into a war we cannot win."

Someone grunted in disapproval. Another elder took a stick and rearranged the stones in the pit. Abenda entered the lodge with a spade piled high with scorching rocks. A breath of cool air followed him until the blanket dropped. Soon, heat saturated the small space once again. Arell wiped the sweat from his brow and someone passed him a cup of water.

"We don't have all the details and it's not honorable to begin a war on assumptions," Arell defended. He took a drink and splashed water on his face.

"Why did this woman come to claim your throne, Arell?" Abenda asked.

"Perhaps King Tobias wasn't aware that my father had a son." He handed the cup to Silas. "My father's affairs were not mine. The mistake would be understandable."

The chief grunted thoughtfully.

"I believe with the right questions this princess will provide us some answers. If she refuses to talk, perhaps her friends will. Let's not deduce for ourselves what King Tobias has intended, not if it means war."

"You sympathize with our enemy too much," Abenda mumbled.

A lull in the conversation suggested tension. The accusation didn't sit well with Arell. The drummer continued beating; the rocks cracked under the heat, and an occasional splatter of water touching the fire sizzled.

Abenda cleared his throat. "We have no concern for King Tobias' intentions. Cho Nisi Elders demand retaliation, Vasil King of Cho Nisi," Abenda reminded him. "King Tobias must deliver the murderer into our hands. We demand justice. That's the only way to satisfy Cho Nisi. Blood for blood."

Arell nodded, contemplating the man's words. The request did not sound unreasonable. He, himself, would like to lay eyes on the man who killed his father.

"And if the king had ordered it?" Arell asked.

"Then we declare war."

The pain of his father's death had not diminished, but his people wanted retribution. They would settle for nothing less. His heart also yearned for justice, but without innocent people paying the price. Still, how is it justified that a king of a great nation such as Potama order the death of his father? Where had King Tobias shown mercy? A powerful kingdom crushing a powerless crown seemed inexcusable. How could he pardon a rich and prideful nation who defeated a serene and humble people?

Arell loved the Cho Nisi people.

He loved his father.

"Very well. Until we deliver this message to King Tobias, and he responds, we will make captive of the people who invaded the island. No one is to harm them." Arell looked up. His vision had adjusted to the dark well enough that he noticed their faces and the whites of their eyes.

"We shall treat them as guests," Arell said.

Chief Silas cringed and shook his head.

"It's the only way they'll be truthful with us. Perhaps they have the answers we're looking for. Maybe they can give us the name of the man who killed the king. If we aren't fairly civil to them, we'll never find out."

The men grunted, but among their mumblings were sounds of agreement.

"It shall be so," Chief Silas said. "You can have your prisoners." He glanced at Arell. "You can be fairly civil to them." Silas added with a half-smile that suggested he understood Arell better than Arell knew himself.

Someone sprinkled more incense on the rocks, and the fragrance mixed with steam entered his lungs. Arell wiped sweat off his forehead and Abenda stepped through the door and pulled the blanket away. Cool air beckoned them outside. One by one they filed out of the sweat lodge naked and dove into the ocean. The shock of cold water after being so hot numbed Arell, and he laughed. Once bathed, the men dried themselves around the campfire and dressed.

"I would like to speak with you alone." Arell requested of the chief when they began up the trail. Silas nodded, and they walked side-by-side back to the castle. The late afternoon sun sparkled on the high plateau. Mountain flowers bloomed, and yellow monarch butterflies floated from one blossom to the next, gathering nectar. The island sparkled with beauty this morning. He couldn't ask for a more serene environment to live in. Though he'd been nowhere else, he had no desire to leave Cho Nisi.

"We'll need someone to return to the mainland and present a message to King Tobias," Arell said.

"Yes. We will. However, the warriors are angry," Chief Silas argued. "Also, we spotted the black demons on the horizon on the eastern shore. Skura. We'll need our warriors to keep vigil."

Arell kicked stones along the trail, eyeing the view of the hills and the sea beyond. Turquoise blue waters surrounded them in all directions, and where the sea wasn't visible, shimmering white leaves of olive groves patterned the hillside. "There are two men with the princess. One of them is a wizard. He stays. The man who pulled the boat ashore can bring a message to his king."

Silas grunted again.

"Or the Cho Nisi warriors might take him there. Let King Tobias figure out how to send us his answer. We'll keep his daughter hostage."

Silas nodded, pensively. "You're young. Too trusting."

"How so?"

"A wise king would imprison your messengers, or kill them, and send an army. This is not a wise choice."

"Then what is?"

"I can't tell you how to be king, Arell. I can only offer wisdom. But if you insist on my advice, give the young man one of our boats and send him back by himself. Give him the message to take to the king. Tell him we don't want violence, but we demand the murderer. If King Tobias did not order your father killed, he will bring the man forward. Otherwise, let him make the first move toward war if he wants his daughter. After that, wait. Be cautious, mindful, and patient."

"Splendid. Have a boat prepared immediately." Arell agreed.

"Arell," Silas stopped him and looked into his eyes as if something bothered him.

"What?"

"Be cautious."

"Of course."

"This young woman. She's attractive." Silas tapped a fist gently on Arell's chest. "Guard your heart. You don't know her. You have no understanding of her plan."

Arell, puzzled, nodded. "Of course, Silas. I'll be careful."

Silas grunted as if Arell didn't believe him. Arell sighed and walked on in silence.

The trail ended at the cobblestone road into Moaton. The streets were quiet, as they usually were late afternoon. Dinners were being cooked, families gathering for the evening. With the rumor of war and sightings of skura, shops closed early and most everyone slipped indoors before dusk. Even Arell hurried his steps toward the palace as if he had an unspoken warning. Chief Silas kept pace with him.

"Capture the visitors immediately and bring them to the palace. Inform the residents here that there are strangers wandering about. Make certain they keep their word do no harm." Arell instructed.

"I will see to it," Silas assured him.

Erika the conqueror

The late afternoon wind blew hard, shifting sands on the beach that spat at Erika's face and wedged into the corners of her lips. White caps dotted the sea and curled the surf, spraying salt into the air. The breakers clamored in harmony with the rustling branches of the wild olive trees and graceful willows.

Erika fought with the corners of the sail. If Kairos would fasten his end down and then come and help her, perhaps she could get the shelter finished. They had already tied driftwood poles together with line they salvaged from the ruined skiff. She thought to use the sail as a roof to secure their shelter better, but with this wind blowing and Kairos not cooperating, it seemed their efforts were fruitless.

"What are you doing, Kairos?" she demanded, glancing at him, and then up the hill at Rory gathering firewood.

"Exactly what you told me to, Fairest. Tying knots."

"And you can't tie any faster?"

"No, Fairest, I cannot. When you let go of your end, mine gets away from me as well."

How hopeless, she thought, at least until Rory returns. She depended on the young man from Fairmistle for everything. She should be stronger than this. Erika let go of the sail completely and walked away, leaving Kairos grappling with his end.

"It's unnecessary," he grumbled, tossing a log on the dithering canvas to keep it from blowing away. "I've slept under the stars more than once."

The skiff lay on its side with two large holes in the bottom where the rocks had catapulted through. Destroyed! She assessed the damage one more time, peeling away a sliver of the broken rib and swinging it into the sea.

"How dare he!" she grumbled.

High tide already threatened to wash the craft away, and so

Erika hurried to rescue her belongings, and anything else that seemed usable. Line, floats, nets in case they needed to do some fishing. After returning to the shelter with her pack, she strapped her quiver over her shoulder and picked up her bow.

"Aren't you going to help me finish this?" Kairos asked.

"Not now. Let's wait until Rory can help us. I'm foraging for food and exploring. Maybe I can get an excellent shot at the cheeky young hoodlum who had the audacity to insult me and ruin our skiff."

Kairos eyed her weapon. "You mean to kill him? What if he's beloved of those magical natives who best my spells? Then what?"

"I'll shoot them too. We're here for a purpose, Kairos, and it's not to homestead this beach, it's delivering the throne to my father."

"You said you were going to admit guilt and try to reason with these people."

She sighed and stared at the wizard. "I had intended to, yes. But wouldn't you declare it an act of war to destroy a king's boat?"

"Erika, think about what you're saying. Didn't you—," he looked up the hill and around him as he crossed the beach to where she stood, lowering his voice. "Didn't you kill their king?"

"They don't know that. And look at the reception they gave us. They saw our banner, so they knew who we were."

"They know their king died while fighting with our army. Perhaps they think someone assassinated him."

He made a point she couldn't deny. She sighed heavily and surveyed the hills.

"Let's find a spokesperson for these people. We can convince them that the king died an accidental death. Are you coming with me?"

"Does it look like I'm with anyone else?" Kairos dusted the sand off his hands and gathered his cloak, wrapping his potion belt around his doublet.

Rory appeared on the trail carrying an armload of wood. He dropped it next to the fire pit.

"We should have a nice warm fire tonight with the wind dyin' down. These sea breezes never last into the night. Did I hear the two of you were goin' somewhere?"

"Yes. You're welcome to come if you like. We're hoping to find the late king's castle."

"What would you do if you did?"

"I hope to find some intelligent human beings occupying it. Noblemen. Perhaps we'll do some negotiating and persuade the lords of this island that they need a leader, that they need King Tobias. No one wants to be weaponless against a dark lord. They need the king's blessing."

"Sure, they do," Rory agreed. "But I'm not much for bartering on behalf of a king, I'm just a peasant boy from Fairmistle. A soldier. You'd be better showin' your royal selves to noblemen without me. I'll stay here on the beach and keep our little shelter safe if you don't mind. I can fix that lean-to for you. I'm not bad with spear fishin' and there's plenty of driftwood I can whittle to a point. I'll have us a nice hot dinner ready for you when you get back."

"Thanks, Rory. I'll look forward to tasting your cookery. Let's go," she said to Kairos and tugged him gently on the arm.

True, she, the wizard, and the peasant-soldier from Fairmistle wouldn't be able to win any wars here, and not by themselves, but her idea of approaching an overseer of the late king's estate seemed workable, so long as it wasn't any of those vicious warriors who left them stranded, or their dark-skinned brigadier with the ridiculous feather in his hat.

"Are you still planning on apologizing for killing the king?" Kairos asked her as they hiked up the hill on a well-worn trail.

"No. I'm sorry for what happened and have brought penance before my Creator. With the attitude of the rogues we came across earlier, it might not be wise to divulge that piece of information just yet."

"Well, that's relieving!" Kairos exclaimed. "I worried that you'd apologize on your way to the gallows."

"I'm not a complete dizzard."

"You're getting better by the day," he agreed.

"Securing protection for this island is an honest atonement for what I've done. These islanders deserve a decent protector. There's none so fine as my father."

"There you go! Now if you can convince the nobles, we'll have what we need, a boat home, hopefully." Kairos pushed back an olive branch that hung low over the road, threatening to snag his silky cloak. The trail seemed to get narrower as they climbed with wild brush, scattered Olive trees, and bramble closing in on them.

"Why wouldn't I be able to convince them? King Tobias is

a legend. Even Casdamia acclaim his deeds, and the glory of his kingdom."

"That young brigadier with the feather didn't seem to know your father."

"Oh Kairos, do you believe everything you hear? That man lied through his teeth." When she reached a crossroads at the top of a hill, she stopped, took a deep breath of salty air, and admired the vista. A clear sky and a cerulean seascape surrounded the island. "It's really beautiful here, isn't it? Look, you can see our kingdom to the north, and the mountains we crossed recently. I wonder if Barin has returned home, or if the fishers reached the castle and delivered the message."

"What message? What did you tell your father?"

"Not much. Just that I would come here. Would secure the throne for him by the time he sees me again."

"That's quite a promise, Fairest."

Erika scratched her head and gave him a puzzled look.

"Not so much a promise as an end, Wizard," she responded. "Father will be angry. But once we have this island secure, he'll understand."

She started walking again, her spirits lifted by the view and the fresh air. The rugged passageway leveled to a well-worn trail. Westward saw olive groves and a steady downslope toward another shoreline. The eastward track rose over gently rolling hills. Assuming the western trail led back to the sea, Erika chose the hills.

The dirt trail that meandered through grassy fields adorned with flowers, and butterflies soon became a cobblestone road. Houses appeared, at first one or two on either side of road—small cottages similar to the whitewashed homes one would find outside the city in southern Prasa Potama where merchants and blacksmiths crafted their wares.

Further east blocking the sun, stood a city of houses stacked one on top of the other and joined their walls constructed of river rock, their roofs made with straw thatching. The city reminded Erika of Prasa Potama in some respects with the high-rise apartments, although much poorer in embellishments. Narrow cobblestone roads meandered through the settlement where tow-headed children played and women in long gray dresses chatted with one another. Erika brushed the sand off her cloak as she walked and combed through her thick auburn hair with her fingers.

"You look fine, Fairest," Kairos whispered and smiled at a gentleman nearby. The man looked at them, turned, and hurried up the road where he met a woman and her child. They disappeared into a house.

"You look exceedingly wizardly," Erika whispered back, sensing something was wrong. "And your hair is in disarray. You're scaring the villagers."

Kairos used the leather lacing he had borrowed from his shirt to tie his hair back.

"I'm devastated that I lost my hat." He complained.

Oddly, the street ahead of them had emptied but for one old, bearded man standing on a corner near a shop. He leaned heavily on a walking cane and chewed the end of a pipe. Thinking he might give her directions or tell her who ruled over the island at the moment, Erika approached him. Perhaps he could tell her something about the late king. She smiled, but he only scowled at her, his eyes a cagey blue shielded by bushy eyebrows as white as snow.

"Good evening, sir," she said.

He regarded her. His eyes scanned the sandy hem to her dress and her still-wet shoes. Her hair must be a mess. He glared at Kairos and then pointed the end of his pipe at her. "You the princess?"

Taken aback, she wondered how he knew. Erika stood upright and lifted her chin. "I am, good sir."

"Someone's looking for you."

"Who might that be?" Kairos asked.

"The king," he answered, squinting at them. The old man snickered, opened the door to the shop he'd been leaning against and quickly slipped inside, shutting the door behind him.

"What king?" Kairos asked in a whisper.

"My Father?"

"Yes, I imagine your father is looking for you. But I don't think that's who the old man was referring to. How did he guess you were a princess?"

Erika shivered, spooked by the encounter. When she turned around, the sight behind her shocked her more. A band of natives walked up the street with their spears held across their chests. They wore shells around their necks and beads in their hair, the same apparel the warriors in Tellwater had worn. She swallowed, remembering the horrid evening she killed the island king, and the solemn faces on the warriors who had carried him away. These were the same grave faces. Her heart raced, and she trembled. The lead man wore a bright blue tunic. He looked like the man who accosted them at the beach. Kairos took her arm and with his body shielding hers, turned her in the direction they had been walking.

"Just keep moving, Fairest," he whispered. "Make believe you don't see them. They're probably just headed for…the castle."

Erika let Kairos guide her and welcomed his body as a cushion between her and the warriors. They had nowhere to go but straight ahead. She held onto Kairos arm with one hand and the other clutched her bow hidden under her cloak.

The road led to the barbican, a gateway with two marvelous stone towers. A banner flew atop the battlements. She didn't recognize the insignia, but she assumed it belonged to the late king—white and blue with some kind of majestic bird. As they proceeded, the moat grew deeper the further they walked. Erika worried that, though she wanted to enter the palace, if she changed her mind she'd be unable to escape the armed men behind her. She shot a worried glance at Kairos and clung tighter to his arm.

"I have my weapon," she reminded him, eyeing the embankment that seemed to drop an immeasurable distance on either side of them.

"And do you have at least three dozen arrows you can project in a matter of seconds before one of these natives drives their spear through your heart? Fairest?"

"If that should happen, I trust the fire in your fingertips to help. Wizard."

"You overestimate me." He looked over his shoulder, smiled, and nodded at the warriors. "What you're asking for is a Vouchsaver's power. I'm afraid such force is not available at the moment," he whispered between clenched teeth. "I'm not a Vouchsaver, nor will I ever be."

The distance behind them shortened, and the warriors were so close on their heels that she could smell the incense they had been burning. Sandalwood, she thought.

The iron portcullis opened and before Erika could change her mind, turn around, parlay, or pretend a faint, the men had formed a half circle around her and Kairos.

"This way," the man in the blue tunic instructed them. He

walked in front now while the others surrounded them. He led them through an empty courtyard, through a heavy double oak door, and inside the palace down a marble hallway. The man stopped at an entryway and signaled for a guard to open it.

"For the wizard." He held out his hand to offer the accommodation to Kairos. Beads of sweat had formed on the wizard's forehead and he turned to the company behind him. "I…I have no words…."

"You'll have time to think about it," the chief said. He pushed Kairos into the room and shut the door, leaving a sentry standing guard.

"You, princess, come with me."

"Do I have a choice?" Erika asked sourly. The chief glared at her. Yes, he was the same man who'd been on the beach.

"No," the chief replied, tightening his grasp on his spear.

She followed the man—the horde of sentries behind her. They marched up a beautiful spiral stairwell to another room and shepherded her to the private quarters. When she stepped over the threshold, she turned around.

"My father will hear of this!" she exclaimed.

"That's the intent," the chief replied. He signaled four of the men to stand guard. They were rough-looking men, their spears long and deadly with spearheads the size of her fist having razor-sharp edges.

"One man watches the wizard, and you have four guarding me? I won't have this!" she protested as the chief closed the ingress. She beat on the solid oak door once it closed, but it did nothing but bruise her hand.

She spun around, grinding her teeth, nostrils flaring,

The chamber looked nothing like a prison. In fact, it had a huge, canopied bed, silky cream-colored sheets, and a glass door that looked out over the island. Ornate furniture adorned the room, gilded with gold. A dresser with a silver mirror faced the bed, and on it were a fresh hairbrush and several beaded necklaces, along with a pitcher of clean water and a washbasin. Next to that, the door of a closet hung open and several tunics of colorful linen hung. A table garnished with fruit bowls and a bottle of wine welcomed her, and on the table lay a note inked on parchment.

To the Beautiful Potamian Princess.

Welcome to our island of love. We are so honored to have you visit. I hope you find your stay here to your satisfaction. It will be my great joy and pleasure to dine with you this evening.

I take it my fine servants have seen you to your room by now. You may thank Chief Silas in person for his escort tonight, as he'll be feasting with us.

I am sending handmaidens to help you with your bath. Take a moment or two to nap. Rest well.

Arell of Rolland, the High King of Cho Nisi.

—post script um—The man with the feather in his hat.

—post, post script um—No need to bring your bow, I have my own.

She tore the note and threw it across the room. "That charlatan!"

A gentle knock at the door, and though Erika did not call out, nor did she open it, a young woman entered, and behind her several younger ladies. Beautifully attired in linen chitons, they carried hot steaming water, and bowed when Erika acknowledged them.

"Good evening, Fairest?" the oldest of the servants said. "My name is Serena, and I'm here as your personal servant. We have bath water for you."

Erika's mouth fell open. A bath sounded wonderful, for all she'd been through-traveling across the sea in a boat that stunk of fish, fighting insurgents, erecting a lean to in the wind—she must really smell.

One girl brought her a jar of cream and opened the lid. "Many herbs" she smiled. "It will make you soft."

"Soft?" Erika asked.

"She means the scent will calm you, and it's good for your skin. We can bathe you, or if you're shy, we can fix your tub and leave."

"Yes. That would be best. I prefer to be alone when I bathe, thank you."

The girls filled a copper tub in the corner of Erika's room and bowed on the way out. All except the older girl. She waited until the others left. "Is everything well with you?"

"No. Why? Will you help me escape?" Erika fashioned the girl wouldn't abet a flight, but what harm would come of trying?

The girl laughed. "I would never go against our king's wishes."

Touching the bath water with her fingers, Erika winced. She'd never be able to get in the tub with such scalding water. Perhaps this servant could provide information while Erika waited for the bath to cool.

"I heard your king had died."

"Yes. Arell's father. Such a good man as well. All the island grieves for him, as does Arell."

Erika hesitated for a moment—the guilt burned inside of her again. "I'm sorry for his loss," she whispered, and swallowed, meeting the girl's sympathetic eyes. "So, this Arell, you address him by his first name?"

"I've known him all my life. I grew up with him."

Erika raised brow. "And you're his servant?"

"Yes, Fairest, if that's what you wish to call me."

What else should she call her? But then she had no idea what their customs were. "And this man with the feather in his hat, he's not an impersonator? He's really a king?"

"Yes. He is King Rolland's son."

"I see. My father didn't know King Rolland had a son."

"Many do not. Arell grew up with us, the Cho Nisi. He didn't visit the castle often. He had no interest in politics. With his father's death, duty brought him home."

Well, that's a surprise. What an abrupt ending for all her aspirations! She could return home and let her father know that someone already sits on the throne. An arrogant and boorish young fellow, but someone, none the less. How will that help the war with Skotádi, she didn't know, nor could she assume anyone from her father's kingdom would be able to confer with such an arrogant monarch.

"I hear you are our king's prisoner."

Erika raised a brow. "Is that what he says? I hardly think so. We just haven't had time to negotiate yet, but I'm sure he'll release me and my friend as soon as we have a talk."

"Yes, of course." Serena smiled, bowed, and the left the room. The four guards still stood sentry outside her doorway.

Failed Query

Arell may only get one chance at this, so he went over the questions in his mind. Pacing the floor of his chamber, he stopped to glance in the mirror and fasten the top button of his doublet. The princess might not talk at all, so the situation with her needed tact. She had to feel comfortable and yet not enough to make her think she had the upper hand. A beautiful young woman. Still, the elders thought of her as an enemy. What suspicions he had, he can't reveal to her, though. All he wanted were details of his father's death. He toughened his look in front of the mirror, puffing his chest and practicing his frown—rehearsing his interrogation.

"Who shot the arrow that killed my father? Who commanded the attack? If he died accidentally, why hasn't anyone apologized?" He stared at his image for a moment. She might know nothing. She's just an adolescent daughter of a king. But why is she here? What are her father's intentions? Arell must learn her purpose.

He relaxed and looked away from the mirror, considering it better not to put on airs. He could just talk to her honestly. "Are Cho Nisi and King Tobias allies or not? If not, is your father planning an attack?" He shrugged. If her father were planning an attack, she wouldn't warn him ahead of time.

He needed the answers to all these questions without drilling her. "Let her know you're curious. Be cordial," he whispered. And yet, if too cordial, Chief Silas will contest him. A balance. There needs to be a balance.

Arell adjusted his dress doublet, the one his father once wore as a young man. Black and sky blue with gold cording and emerald buttons, tailored artfully against his body. This fine piece of clothing complemented his healthy physique. He chose the black felt hat with the ostrich feather. Ready as he'd ever be, he opened his chamber door where Chief Silas waited. The chief nodded when Arell stepped into the hall.

"You would think you're courting the princess rather than interrogating her, Arell."

"Too much?"

Silas shrugged. "It depends on your tactics."

"We'll see if this succeeds."

"She could be deceptive. Be alert, and careful that she doesn't take you by the horns."

"I enjoy a challenge." Arell winked at the chief. He desired to know more about this beautiful girl, despite Silas' warnings. The chief was his counselor for political matters, not personal ones. Perhaps Arell and the princess could negotiate on a more informal level and bring peace between their people. He didn't mind pluck in a woman. The native girls were charming and enticing, but extremely passive. The Moaton girls kept to themselves, having parents that betrothed them to their own. Besides, Moatons looked down on the dark skin people of the island. He wondered if Potamians did as well.

Enough of that! The girl came for his throne. The warriors saw her as an enemy to his people because of it. He must be cautious and diplomatic.

They entered the dining hall and, according to his wishes, the servants hadn't set the king's table, but a small round table near the windows. Intimate. Non-intrusive. A vase of flowers, enameled silver, all feminine. He thanked the servant as she set a flask next to the bouquet. "Perfect! Please send for her." The servant turned to leave. "But...we must have the sentries come with her."

"Yes, Vasil."

Arell paced nervously. Chief Silas stood against a pillar with his arms crossed, watching him. "Anxious?"

"Do I appear to be?"

"You appear as a young rooster caged next to a coop of hens."

Arell stopped pacing and took a breath. "Am I that obvious?"

"Keep in mind you are a king. This woman has threatened your throne. She is a hazard, Arell. One does not court threats, but rather eradicates them."

"You are correct. I will contain my natural instincts and ignore that she is stunning."

"Many things are stunning. A rose is beautiful but for the thorns."

"Keep me in check, Silas. I need all the help I can get. I'm not used to reigning as a king."

Silas smiled and patted him on the arm. "Keep your eyes and ears open. You'll know what to do."

A page swung the doors wide. Arell expected the princess to have changed into a dress he had the servants leave for her, so when Erika stormed through the door in her leather armor, shoulder guards and riding skirt, he raised his brow. She puffed into the center of the room, her arms folded over her chest, her bow visibly strapped over her shoulder. The sentries waited for Arell to dismiss them.

Arell waited as well. He bowed cordially, his plume shimmering grandly.

"Dismiss these men," the princess ordered.

"When I feel it is safe, I will," Arell replied. "Disarm yourself."

"I will not."

Arell took a breath and fought the temptation to look at Silas for instruction. "Very well. Guards, disarm the woman." Two of the guards stepped forward. Erika pushed one away with her elbow and, with the speed of an experienced archer, had her bow in hand and nocked, aiming an arrow at the other sentry. The warriors lowered their spears, pointing them at Erika. Had she shot one of them, they'd have killed her. They faced off. Arell waited with his arm raised.

"There is no necessity for violence," He kept his voice gentle, controlled. "Relinquish your weapon, Princess. You will not survive if you don't."

"You won't kill me. My father is King Tobias," she sneered.

"And your father, King Tobias, may well have ordered the murder of my father," Arell retorted angrily. She shot him a look he could not quite read and not one he expected. An answer perhaps to one of his most important questions, if only he could decipher what the look meant. "Relinquish your weapon and let's talk. Otherwise, I'll have you confined to your room."

She squinted at him, her face red. If she'd been a dragon, she would have spat fire, which brought him a chuckle inside, but he covered his mouth and looked away, glimpsing at an amused Silas. The chief shook his head.

She pointed her bow at Arell. The warriors stepped forward and grabbed her arms.

"Princess Erika, come, let's be reasonable. You can't fight all those warriors, even if you are a perfect shot." He ignored the arrow aimed at his heart and looked her in the eye. A frustrated and rebellious young woman, he almost pitied her. His voice softened. "Please. Let's dine. And talk."

She lowered her bow but refused to let anyone take it. Arell held out his hand. "Will you let me hold it for you? While we eat?"

"Where is my magician?"

"He's in a room as comfortable as yours."

"Bring him here."

"What? Now?"

"I'll let you hold my weapon."

This time Arell looked at the chief. The elder shrugged. Any of the Cho Nisi natives were more powerful than Erika's wizard. She should know that. We must terrify her.

"Very well."

Chief Silas said something to one warrior in their native language and the man left the room. The others maintained their positions. Arell waved at the page. "Have Serena bring another plate and a bit more food, please."

Erika did not move or soften until Kairos appeared among half a dozen warriors with a rather confused look on his face. "What's going on in here? Erika? What are you doing?" he asked, eyeing her bow. She ignored him.

"We've invited the princess to dinner and thought you might like to join us," Arell said, ushering him to the table with an outstretched arm which he then held up to Erika. He walked over to her.

She hesitated before she handed him the bow and quiver, brushed her hands on her skirt, and strolled to the table as a servant pulled the chair back for her. Arell seated himself across from her and laid the bow and quiver against his chair while Chief Silas and Kairos took the opposite chairs.

A stiff silence followed as Serena entered with trays of food. Kairos helped himself with generous portions, as did Silas. As Serena set a plate of food next to Arell, he stroked her hand.

"Thank you, Serena," he whispered. They exchanged a flirtatious smile. Seeing an affable face comforted him. When Serena left, both Erika and Arell spent more time eyeing each other than they did eating.

Arell took a drink of water and cleared his throat. "I'm curious. Why did you come to our island?"

"I had my reasons."

"No doubt. And I and the Cho Nisi people would like to know them."

"I told you."

"You did. You said you came to claim the throne."

"For my father."

"And how would that work? To kill me and take it by force?" Arell glanced at Silas, who subtly shook his head.

"That wasn't the original intent but the more I know of you the more I think it's a good idea."

"Fairest—" the wizard scolded.

She scowled and dropped her napkin on her plate. "Is this your idea of patronizing?" she asked Arell. "Silver etched with dainty flowers. Flowers? It's almost winter. Where do you get flowers? My sisters do better than this. At least they have flasks that hold more than a swallow and set a table according to the seasons."

"The food is simply scrumptious," Kairos commented rather loudly, chewing and nodding. "I wouldn't have suspected a little island like this could come up with such superb cookery."

Erika glared at him.

"Flowers grow all year long on our island. We have a much warmer climate—" Arell said.

"Your niceties do not impress me, King. And I'll not answer any more of your questions until you release me. Another comment about 'being confined to my room' and you'll have waged war against my father's kingdom."

"Your father would be foolish to wage war with us, especially over something so remedial as sending a princess to her room."

She glared at him. "You have no right to treat me in such a manner!"

Arell clenched his spoon. Any tighter and he'd break it. He had done his best to inhibit his rage. "Treat you how? My father went to your shores to help your father win a war, and he came back a corpse. Then you come here claiming my throne and refuse to satisfy my interrogation. Tell me who is treating whom unjustly."

Erika sat back in her chair, hands folded on her lap, her lips closed tight as a clam. Kairos also stopped eating and took a special interest in Erika's reaction.

"I did not want to conduct this dinner in such a manner!" Arell tossed his napkin on the table.

"Then conduct it however you see fit. I care not to have any part of your comely gathering nor of your interrogation."

Arell rose. He'd had enough. The woman was incorrigible. Silas rose with him. Arell addressed the page. "Call the sentries and have this woman imprisoned." He picked up the bow before Erika could reach for it and handed it to the guards as they entered and took the princess away. She fought, but to no avail.

"Kairos, stop them!" Erika cried. "I command you!"

Kairos stood, a sandwich in his hand and food in his mouth.

"Do nothing," Arell warned Kairos and nodded to Silas. The elder would know to counter any magic that might fly from the wizard.

When the sentries took Erika out of the room, Arell turned to the wizard. "Perhaps I could continue this dinner conversation with you?"

"Of course, of course," Kairos agreed, returning to the table yet looking anxiously at the door.

"They won't hurt her. They have orders not to. But I have questions that need answering and if she won't be cooperative, perhaps you will."

"Of course," the wizard said again.

Kairos' Answer

After Kairos had taken a seat at the table, Arell picked up a flask from the buffet and brought it and two chalices to his chair. He pushed one cup toward Kairos.

"Your name? So I might address you as something more than 'Wizard'?"

"Kairos, Vasil."

Arell held the flask up and offered to fill the cup for Kairos. "Tellwater Valley Vineyards," he announced. "The best wine in your kingdom. A fine commodity and a reason our regions have had such a lucrative commerce."

"Thank you. Vasil." Kairos' words came out slowly as he held his cup forward and Arell poured and then filled his own chalice. He took his seat at the table, giving Silas a cordial nod. The chief never drank. Arell lifted a toast to Kairos.

"May our profits continue."

Their flasks touched, their eyes met, but no friendly greeting transpired. No doubt the wizard mistrusted Arell as much as Arell suspected him. When Arell set his flask down, he cleared his throat, taking a petite sandwich from the platter and offering the tray to Kairos.

"You work for King Tobias?"

"Yes."

"And you've been his magician for a long while?" Arell tried to make his questioning sound like small talk, but Kairos' wary glances proved he was failing.

"Yes."

"What sort of…projects…if I may be so bold to ask."

Kairos' eyes searched Arell and Silas' both. He paused before he spoke, crumbs of his bread falling out of his hand. He brushed them off his lap. "King Tobias requested that I find a spell to kill the skura."

"Ah yes, the dark lord and his minions. Did you?"

"Yes."

Arell raised his brow in surprise and then nodded. Interesting. Perhaps the news would be helpful at a later date. He hesitated before asking his next question. Such a sensitive issue. He didn't want to rush the interrogation, and yet urgency drove him. He had already spoiled his chances with the princess.

"Skura were the beasts that my father and his warriors went to fight alongside your king's army. Were you there in the valley the day my father died?"

"No, I wasn't, Vasil."

Arell took a sip of wine to conceal his disappointment. He had hoped Kairos had been a witness.

"Maybe if I were there, I could have prevented some… things from happening," Kairos added, glancing up at Arell. He had a sympathetic look about him, and Arell frowned. The sun at that moment leaked into the room, shining on the flasks, and sending a ray of light across the table.

"You mean the death of my father?" Arell asked softly.

"Yes."

"Skura didn't kill him."

"No. They didn't."

Arell exchanged an anxious look with Silas. "Do you know what happened, then?"

"Only rumor."

"Which is?"

Kairos looked up from his food and shook his head. His hands trembled and so he dropped his cake on the plate and put them on his lap. "I want nothing to do with politics. I'm just a lowly wizard who barely knows a spell or two. I didn't mean to be here, but her highness had her mind set to come and so I had to follow to protect her. I'm in trouble with the king as it is. I have little to say that you don't know already. Please. Lend me a boat and let me go home. I'll deliver any missives you might have for King Tobias, or anyone else. If you're keeping Erika as ransom, I can tell her father. I can reason with him. Please?"

An unexpected response! In it, the wizard revealed more than he probably meant to. The princess came on her own free will. And because the wizard traveled with her, the king would punish him? That also interested Arell. Why did she decide to come and claim the throne for her father when she didn't have her father's permission? Arell thought for a moment, considering Kairos and how he might use the wizard's fragile character as leverage.

"So, you know what happened."

"No. Only rumors."

"What rumors are being spread in your kingdom?"

Kairos bit his lip and looked at Arell. Would he tell the truth or make something up on the spot? Arell waited while the wizard fidgeted with the crumbs on the table, sweeping them into a pile, brushing them into his hand and then onto his plate. Finally, the man spoke slowly, weighing each word.

"The rumor is that the king of Cho Nisi's death was an accident."

Arell breathed in deeply. "I see. I suppose I will have to accept that's all the information I am offered from anyone. Perhaps someday someone will tender me an apology."

His stomach churned, and his cheeks burned. Why did so many people know what happened, and no one had the courage to come forward and tell him?

This was his father, for bones' sake!

He looked out the window. Should he press the man further? Would he get the truth, or would this wizard play games, telling half-truths to disguise a conspiracy?

"So, you say that you're friends enough with King Tobias that you could return and speak on our behalf—even if we imprisoned the king's daughter? Even if the king will punish you for having come here with her?"

Kairos' eyes widened as he glanced at both he and Silas. The chief sat rigidly.

"I'm…" he paused, swallowed his food and wiped his mouth. Sweat dripped from his forehead. The confrontation bothered the wizard greatly, but Arell couldn't afford to relent.

"I'm …I have a relationship with his daughter. Erika's sister. Even if King Tobias were angry about Erika, he'd listen to me. I think. Perhaps."

"I see," Arell eyed Silas, who nodded. "I hold no hostilities toward you, Kairos, though I wish you'd be more transparent. I'm looking for truth. I don't want to start a war, but a war is an option if King Tobias does not meet my demands."

"What are your demands?" Kairos swallowed. "I mean, if you don't mind telling me."

"I demand to know what events led to my father's death. All details—who, how, and why."

Kairos paled and stared into his cup.

"I also would like to know more about this hot-headed young princess who's now in my charge. Why did she think she could rob my throne from me?"

"I'd like to know the answer to that question myself," Kairos sipped his wine, licked his lips, and took another sip.

Arell raised a brow. "Why is she so...violent?"

"She has problems. I don't know. A deprived child. Youngest of four. Mother died having her. Made a..." he stopped himself, striking Arell's curiosity. "She makes mistakes more often than not."

"What sort of mistakes?"

Kairos shook his head. "Coming here evidently." He set his chalice on the table and stared at it, perhaps to avoid looking at Arell.

"Why did she come here? Had her father banished her? Rebuked her somehow? Did she run away?" Considering her temperament, Arell would understand, though he never knew a king to exile his own daughter.

"No. She came on her own cheerfully. She wanted to prove herself." He threw up his arms. "You must ask her. I cannot speak for the woman. She's wild! No one can predict what she does or why."

"What do you think King Tobias will do when he finds out she's a prisoner?"

"He's a father. What else would a father do? He'd come with men-at-arms and try to rescue her. She's always causing trouble, that girl. I'm sorry this happened to you. Just her being here has put your island in jeopardy."

"Had Cho Nisi been in jeopardy before she came?" Arell asked. The wizard walked right into that. His answer would confirm whether Cho Nisi and the Potamian kingdom were still allies or not.

"Yes, I suppose."

Arell stood abruptly, knocking the table so that the chalices shook, and wine spilt. He walked to the window—the weight of Silas' gaze followed him. The room held the air captive as Arell struggled with whether to ask the last question. But he didn't ask it. He doubted

Kairos would give an honest answer.

"You're dismissed," he told the wizard. He crossed his arms and kept his gaze on the garden outside. How did this happen? His father had gone off to do a good deed and came back a corpse. War now brews between Cho Nisi and a kingdom known for great military power. What went wrong?

After the sentries led Kairos away, Silas approached Arell.

"He seemed to suggest that our nations are no longer allies."

"It sounded that way." Arell fingered a button on his doublet while still observing the garden. The elders would expect him to declare war. Arell had no desire to do so, nor did he think it wise.

"What are you going to do, Arell?"

The room had grown chilly. Arell rubbed his hands together and spun abruptly toward the chief.

"Why does one turn their back on a friend?"

Chief Silas held his gaze for a long moment.

"These things do not happen in Cho Nisi. You know that. Perhaps your father's people can answer. It is unheard of with us."

The confrontation with the princess, having to consider the mighty kingdom of Potama an enemy, and the death of his father still so raw inside—overwhelmed him.

"My father would never have done wrong to his allies. He learned Cho Nisi ways, Silas."

"I believe that, Arell. I'm sorry such questions haunt you. But you must remember the bargain you made with the elders. You must find this man who killed your father, and you must find out if he acted according to the king's orders."

Silas took hold of his arm with a firm hand as he looked into Arell's eyes.

"That is the only way you'll find freedom for your soul. And for your people."

Arell nodded solemnly. He could not back down now.

"I'm going to interrogate the princess again. Sing your chants for me, Silas. Ask for the Creator's help."

Relent

Arell set his hat on a stand in the dining hall, brushed his hair behind his ears, and gave Silas one last look.

"There is hope, Arell," the chief whispered as he turned toward the window, singing softly. The melody followed Arell to the door and played continually in his mind after he stepped outside into the starry night.

A Cho Nisi cradle song.

He could hear his mother's voice as if she were walking through the courtyard with him, and he hummed along. Why Silas chose that melody puzzled him unless the song gave him strength, or peace.

> *The stars and moon will bide the hour,*
> *Nesting in the shadowed bower.*
> *But night in time will fade away,*
> *Into the magic of a dawning day.*

Arell nodded to the sentry on watch. "Take me to the princess," he whispered. The guard quickly obeyed as if he, too, felt guilty he had locked the princess in a cell. A cold, dark stairwell led into the dungeon. The air smelled musty and rotten—a horror pit that when he descended he had to hunch over like an animal to avoid hitting his head on the ceiling. Arell hadn't visited this place since his childhood. As a curious young lad, he stole down here to explore, and the smell had been so bad, he left heaving his breakfast.

One could not cleanse a pit hole like this. No light ever seeped through these walls to dry it out, either. Stepping into its depths slammed him with self-reproach. He shouldn't have sent the daughter of King Tobias into this dismal hole. She did nothing deserving of confinement, especially not in a dungeon. She only sought to defend herself.

Had his father's death rendered him callous?

"We must release her," he told the sentry.

"Of course, Vasil," the soldier said and took the keys from a ring hanging near their heads.

Arell shivered from the dank air and the encroaching stone walls as the man unlocked the iron gate. A little farther and the jailer unlocked the gate to the cell.

The princess huddled in a dark corner, squatting on the damp floor, hugging her knees. He tried to touch her shoulder, but she flinched.

"You don't belong here," he whispered gently. "Come with me."

"You're an arrogant, condescending pig of a man," she stated simply, nestling farther into the shadows.

"Yes, I suppose you're right."

"First of all, why would you assume that I'm a dainty, fragile buttercup who likes floral covered chalices and shallow conversations?"

"I don't know. I suppose I assumed incorrectly. Come with me."

"Second, what audacity that you should send me to a room, as if I were a child who spilled milk on the throne."

"Another reckless conjecture."

"Who do you think you are? You just inherited a kingdom, and you have no inkling how to rule it. Yet you speak like a narcissistic superior to the daughter of the most famous king of this century."

Arell stooped to her height, holding on to his patience. He had to listen to her and not let her insults affect him. "I apologize for my imprudence."

She glared into his eyes—hers a deep, beautiful blue. He could look at them all evening, but not in this cold prison cell.

"And then you have me thrown into this rat hole of a dungeon. Who do you think you are?"

"No one, Fairest. Except a fool trying to fill the place of a great man who was prematurely and tragically taken away from us."

Her frown softened, and she looked away.

"I abused my power and I'm dreadfully sorry. Will you forgive me and come back to the palace? I believe we can work out our differences if I act according to my position."

It took a lot to admit his wrongs to her, especially after she came as a trespasser to his kingdom. She had some valid arguments, though.

"I'm willing to discuss our disagreements peacefully. Please?" He held out his hand again at the risk of her biting it.

Instead of hurling any more hostilities against him, she accepted his help. Holding her elbow, he escorted her slowly up the long stairwell. When they came to the castle, he thought quickly of a room wherein she would feel comfortable enough to converse, a place where they could be alone, a chamber where they could speak their hearts and perhaps come to some sort of truce. The second drawing room provided the perfect setting. An intimate chamber with a bookshelf, a fireplace and a chaise and chair, he the King of Cho Nisi and she, King Tobias' daughter——once allies and both great nations in their own right. Nighttime had darkened the palace, so he removed a lantern in the hall and guided her to the drawing room, shutting the door quietly behind him.

"Please. Make yourself comfortable."

She threw herself on the chaise, bent over, and buried her head in her hands. Arell sat on the end of the chair and waited, not sure what to say.

"You're like all the noblemen I've known. Are there any of you less taxing?" She wiped her cheeks with her hand and blinked tears from her eyes. "Except for my brother. My brother is a true gentleman."

Arell could do nothing but stare at her. Her rich auburn hair streaming off her shoulders in gentle waves, her rosy cheeks, and the dimple on her chin. Her beauty and her fortitude fascinated him.

"How are you so haughty? Are you like that with all women? Dominating all that they do and say?"

Arell shook his head. That's what she thought?

"You think I'll wear whatever you put in your guest closet? Directing strangers into my room to bathe me? Surely you jest!"

His cheeks grew warm. He hadn't considered her feelings on the matter, he merely thought she'd look pretty in the chiton's he had Serena deliver. He kept that to himself, though, so as not to give her more ammunition.

"And the note! How supercilious of you! Did you send a note like that to Kairos? No! You did not because you wouldn't insult him in such a manner. But you would insult me. Why?"

Arell opened his mouth to speak, but nothing came out.

"I'll have you know, I'm as good as any man. I deserve the same respect. Why are you staring at me?"

"I don't know, Erika. May I call you that? It's a beautiful name."

She looked into his eyes, searching. Something troubled her deeply, and he had an answer for her. Her voice softened.

"I suppose. It's my name. My brother calls me by my name." She sighed and looked away. "He always criticizes me. I love him more than anyone in my family. I look up to him. And yet I'm always…I don't know. Beneath him. My father's the same way. I'm a child unless I'm dressed in lace and finery. But that's just not me."

She looked up at him again as if expecting a response, but he had nothing to say to her. His mind spun. He had imprisoned her, and yet here they were talking to each other intimately. She poured her heart out about her family and looked at him as though he had counsel for her.

"In a way, I understand," he said.

"You do?"

"Yes. I'm not really a kingly sort of person. I prefer the beach to fineries. Spear fishing and canoeing. I can understand you not wanting to dress in frills if you'd rather wear …armor." Arell despised wearing armor. Perhaps he didn't understand.

She regarded his doublet and, with a look of disbelief, went on. "The dresses you gave me aren't really all that bad, not like those we have at home. This armor is the only corset I'll ever wear, just so you know. I'm not at all like my sisters."

"You have sisters?' He persuaded her to keep talking, though Kairos had already told him a little about her.

"Two. They're twins. Older than me. They're…courtly. Me, I'm…I don't know, a Tomboy I guess would be the proper term. I didn't know my mother. My father raised us, but I needed to prove myself to all of them. They grieved over the woman who died giving birth to me."

"I'm sorry–about your mother. You shouldn't have to prove yourself to anyone."

"Well, I do, and I have to."

"Is that why you came here? To prove you could conquer a kingdom?"

She glared at him.

"Just being yourself is virtuous enough. Your courage. Fighting for what you believe in, even if it's wrong," he smiled. She frowned. "Well, it was wrong, you know. You came here threatening me. I'm not sure how you expected me to react. What if someone you didn't know came to your castle and threatened to take your position away? Just on impulse?"

"I honestly didn't know about an heir to the Cho Nisi throne. I thought I would negotiate for my father."

"So, you were aware that no one sat on the throne. That our king was dead. How?"

"Everyone knew."

"How did he die?"

She focused on her hands, spinning a lace to her cloak in tight winding circles.

"How did my father die?" he asked again.

"By an arrow."

"By whom?"

She shut her lips tight, like a clam.

"Cho Nisi elders demand to know the name of his assassin. They've asked that your father send him to us so that we may serve justice for the king's blood. Do you know who this man is?"

She shook her head and wiped her face as if forcing tears back into the wells whence they came, but she didn't say a word. Perhaps he pressed too hard. Maybe she hadn't the courage she wanted people to think she had. Or maybe she had feelings for the man who killed his father. Or perhaps her brother is the murderer."

"One more question. Erika." He paused, taking in a breath. "Is your father, your King asking for war with us? Had your father ordered my father's murder?"

She started, opening her eyes wide with a strange, indecipherable look, almost as though the thought surprised her, and then she flushed, leaving Arell wondering why.

"No! No, not at all." She shifted in the chair. "My father is a gentleman and a righteous ruler. He had nothing to do with your father's death. Please believe that. My father is innocent of your father's blood." She paused. "The threat of the dark lord's minions coming against our kingdom is real. This threat will come to your island. You can't prevent it, it's only a matter of time. You need us and we need you."

"You need us enough to conquer us?" Arell studied her intensely.

"My father wants to protect your people. And our people need your magic."

She fidgeted with her cloak and so Arell scooted on the chair next to her and placed his hand on her fingers. To calm her perhaps, or to just feel her, to connect with her.

"I will ask nothing else. But you must stay here until we get this sorted."

"Am I a prisoner?"

"I wouldn't use that term. I'd rather call you our guest. Hopefully, you'll take advantage of your time here. The island is beautiful. The people are kind. You could enjoy yourself if you didn't think of yourself as a captive."

"But I am a captive. You've destroyed my skiff and separated me from my friends." She squinted at him, resentment coming from her eyes again. She moved to pull her hands away and he let her.

"Princess Erika, please remember that you've threatened my kingdom. Our nations were allies. My father died while fighting alongside your army. All I want is this mystery answered. I'm his heir. I'm entitled to know the truth!"

They stared at each other. What was it about her that enthralled him? Her beauty, her charisma, her fire. Or being the daughter of a king whom Cho Nisi needed to be allies with? What made his heart pound when he gazed into her eyes?

"All I ask is for cooperation." He took her hands again.

She stared at his hands on hers, and then gently touched his fingers with hers. He too watched their hands. She looked up at him. Her eyes sparkled like a pool of cool water shimmering in the sun. She might be feisty, but she seemed innocent, trembling, and afraid. He fought his instinct to comfort her. They had, after all, just met.

"Will you visit me?" she asked and added with a snicker, "while I'm confined to my room?"

He raised his brow in surprise. "I will not confine you to your room. The palace and the servants are at your disposal. Roam freely. If you like to ride, I thought I'd show you the island." he promised. They gazed at each other for a long while, and Arell fought the urge to not fall under her spell.

"Be alert, and careful that she doesn't take you by the horns."

Silas had misspoken this time. Princess Erika might know the answer to all his questions and be refusing to tell. With kindness, he might discover who killed his father, and with kindness he possibly could persuade her father to send the murderer to them. Chief Silas declared Erika an enemy, but Arell saw no adversary in her. He saw a passionate and confused young lady.

He offered her a hand. "Come. Today has been exhausting for the both of us. I'll take you to your room. We can speak politics another time."

Misgivings

Erika stood at her bedroom quarters and watched him walk away, tall, handsome, confident. The sentries followed, leaving her a free woman. Free as best she could be on an island with no way to get back home. Perhaps she'd been wrong about his insolence, his arrogance, and his lack of kindness. After all, the man just wanted to know how his father died. She'd be the same way if something had happened to her father. She'd probably be more aggressive.

She shut the door and locked it.

The irony is, she's the one who could tell him the truth and put his anxieties to rest. She caused his heart to ache. She killed his father. Why didn't she just tell him?

Because they are going to execute the murderer, and she doesn't want to die!

Home would be a good place to be right now. Home writing letters for her father, or helping Rhea in the garden, or sparring with her brother.

Erika swung open the balcony doors and looked out over the island. The rumble of the distant surf hummed quietly, and the night air blew gently against her cheeks, leaving a soft spray of mist that cooled her forehead. She leaned over to see if she could jump or climb down the cut-stone walls. Such a long way down! Chances were, she'd fall to her death. If she survived the drop, where would she go? Find Kairos and Rory and steal a boat? Foolish thoughts. She wouldn't have to risk her life to escape. Arell had allowed her to go as she pleased. She could just walk away in the morning.

"Fool!" Erika scoffed at herself. She had displayed none of the valor she believed in—the courage that she admired so much in her brother and the soldiers she trained with. Why not? Instead of performing heroic acts and fighting skura, she caused a king's death and grief to an entire island. Worse, she refused to admit it openly. Instead of being courageous, she proved herself a coward.

Erika bit her nails, trembling. She'd have to tell him. If she didn't, they could blame someone else for killing the Cho Nisi king, and then she'd have more guilt to bury.

She decided. She'd tell him now!

Erika opened the door to a silent hall. Not even a servant wandered through the corridor. She left her door open so she might find her room again and stepped into the foyer. Not sure which way to go, she drifted. Torches lit the aisle. A less elaborate castle than the one she'd been raised in. There were no statues of gods or goddesses lining the halls, nor were there great busts of conquerors or kings. Only stone, and hand woven tapestries with simple patterns and images of shells and low riding canoes with sails on them, and birds of the sea. Native art. Arell must have Cho Nisi blood, he didn't look Casdamian. She knew something of his legacy. His grandfather had killed the emperor of Casdamia and with several ships of insurgents fled the mainland, came here, and eventually his people were forgotten.

Curious, when she passed the ornate doors to the grand hall and found them open, she stepped inside to a large and empty room. Furnished only with a long table to her right, a smaller table to her left and a dais whereupon stood a simple throne. A chair not unlike her father's nested on the dais. Made of a slick hardwood and polished to a sheen, the lack of gilded decor didn't surprise her. Where would these people have gotten gold? Craftsmanship created the elegance of this castle, not riches. Two pillars bordered the throne, artfully carved with various animals she assumed lived on the island, some creatures she'd never seen before.

There were only a few windows in the hall, and moonlight shone through one of them. Odd that a lone crow sat upon a scraggly oak branch, its face tilted to the side, as if looking in. She stared at it for a moment. It opened its mouth to caw, but no sound came out. Crows didn't make themselves known at night. Erika shuddered and left the throne room.

Other doors in the hallway were closed, and she saw no sign of the king. She soon became discouraged and walked back to her room.

I'll tell him in the morning then, perhaps at breakfast. I won't hold back the truth, nor fear death. Death in the name of truth has honor.

That's what her brother had told her. Barin talked often about the soldier's sacrifice.

She snickered as she returned to her room and shut the door. Some sacrifice! More like a blunder. A mistake that costs a man's life.

Erika fell back on the bed and stared at the canopy, her thoughts drifting to their conversation and to Arell resting his hand on hers. *What wonderful eyes he has, she thought. Dark, kind. He has dimples when he smiles, and his touch sent tingles up my spine.*

She felt so good when he held her hand, like a washing of her soul had taken place. How gentle his stroke had been, his voice, the quietness in his eyes. He spoke as if he cared about her feelings. No one talked to her like that. Maybe her father, but no one outside her family. He had apologized for sending her to the dungeon after she had said all those horrid things to him. How could he do that? How could he be so kind?

She sat upright on the bed and shook her head, surprised at her thoughts. This sounded more like Olinda pining over Felix. Surely she couldn't be falling in love with him. Or could he be falling in love with her? Not under these circumstances! No!

No one falls in love with a man whose father they killed. That has never happened, nor will it ever. As soon as he finds out, he'll have her executed. She needs to get away from this island, soon. Her only hope is to find Kairos and Rory and steal a boat.

Olinda and Rhea

Changes in castle life had Olinda on edge. Her father spent more time alone in his study than talking to Barin about war matters. Sometimes she found him meandering in the garden alone and contemplative. She worried for him and wondered why Barin's soldiers no longer lingered in the courtyard. Nor had she witnessed men sparing in the fields near the castle grounds. It had only been a few days since Barin returned from Kevshire and news of Erika's disappearance had spread. Did her father and Barin change plans because of Erika? Did the men decide to no longer send soldiers to aid Lord Garion? If Barin were going to return soon, he'd be buying supplies, recruiting, and training, but none of those activities were taking place. With winter coming, the army would have to leave soon, yet there were no preparations being made.

If they didn't return to the Tellwater Valley, Olinda feared that Lord Garion's estate might not endure. If Felix had to fight daily to save the valley without her brother there to help, then indeed his days could be numbered. Erika might be right. Olinda tossed in her bed at night, unable to close her eyes, remembering Barin's stories about the skura and the mountain giants.

"When are you leaving for Tellwater Valley next, Barin?" she inquired at breakfast one morning, prodding for an answer other than the rumors being spread among the castle domestics.

Barin buttered his toast and poured himself a flask of mulled wine, seemingly unconcerned about the battle, or about anything at all.

"Not anytime soon."

"Don't you think that's a precarious decision? I mean, Lord Garion depends on our help."

"If you remember, we're lacking a wizard," he replied.

"You've been there without Kairos. You can't just leave Felix and his men to fight those skura all by themselves? What about the vineyards?"

Barin set his knife on his plate, his attitude more condescending than compassionate. He had always been a loving brother, but lately he'd been avoiding her and Rhea both. Ever since he came back from this last effort, he'd been irritable and pensive.

"Are you embracing the role of Erika now, nagging me about matters that don't concern you? Father and I have it under control. Our men-at-arms have more affairs than Tellwater Valley. I know how you feel about Felix, and I also have compassion for the man and his father. However, if you want private counsel on the difficulties of romance, talk to someone who knows more than I. Perhaps Rhea can serve you."

"That's a cold thing to say!" Olinda responded. "I care for someone and you make light of it!"

"War is about survival, not love. If Felix is a concern of yours, perhaps you should ask Father for a quiver of arrows, a bow, some armor, and an escort, and go to him."

Barin's answer neither comforted nor informed her. Olinda left the table without further conversation. She found Rhea in the drawing room.

Rhea, despondent over her little sister's betrayal, and the absence of Kairos, spent her days pining over the loss of the man she loved. She wandered aimlessly in the garden and wrote poetry in her journal to ease her mind. The girl hardly ever had a dry eye anymore. Worse, Father had been sympathetic toward her, but he had voiced no plans on chasing after Erika or Kairos.

Olinda sat on the chaise next to Rhea who once again penned in her journal and, after trying to read over her shoulder with no success, opened the conversation.

"They're abandoning Felix," she said.

Rhea looked up. "Who is abandoning Felix?"

"Both Father and Barin. They aren't going back to the Valley to help Lord Garion."

"Why?"

"You know how vague and extremely short Barin can be. Something about other concerns. How could they abandon Felix?" She lay her head on the back of the sofa and closed her eyes. "First Kairos and now Felix. Does Father want us to be old maids for the rest of our lives?"

"He can't want that," Rhea reminded her. "If neither you nor I marry, there will be no heir to the throne after Barin, unless of course Barin has a son."

"Barin has no love life."

"He will someday."

"Yes, if he ever stops fighting."

Rhea huffed in her direction.

"Regardless, if anyone is going to plan our role in our kingdom's future, it's going to be you and I."

"Well, here we are. Thinking, moaning, pining. Writing!" she tossed her journal on the cushion. "I'm tired and I'm angry," Rhea thumped her quill in the ink jar on the side table and stood. "I'm angry at Erika, yet her words are like a blacksmith's iron pounding against an anvil in my mind."

"She's an imp. Why would you listen to anything she says?"

"She might be an imp, but she made sense that day. Maybe the only time I ever heard her make any sense."

"When she said what?"

"She called us cowards. Look at us! Sitting around bleating like a couple of nanny goats, doing nothing! Which is why nothing is getting done!" Rhea picked up her book. "Olinda, don't you see. If we want change in our kingdom, we have to make the changes ourselves. I want Kairos here. He will not return as long as Erika commands him to stay with her. I have as much authority in this kingdom as she does. As an elder sibling, I have more. You and I will travel to Cho Nisi to bring him home."

Olinda studied Rhea as her twin paced across the room. "Me? Why do I have to go with you?" A fair plan—for Rhea. Olinda had no desire to embark on a sea voyage south while Felix is many miles to the northeast.

"If we bring Kairos back and then travel to Tellwater Valley with him, he can protect us, and you will be with Felix."

"I don't know, Rhea. That sounds dangerous. Tellwater Valley is a long ride away and from what Barin says, those skura are vicious." Olinda frowned at her sister.

"Kairos has the secret to fighting those skura. Barin wants Kairos to go with him to Tellwater Valley."

Olinda bit her fingernail and stared out the window. Could

they bring Kairos to Felix?

"You love him. You would die for him. Am I correct in saying so? Or at least you would fight at his side. If Erika can put on armor and ride horses and carry the king's banner, why can't we?"

Stunned by Rhea's suggestion, Olinda stared at her twin. "Have you gone daft?"

"Erika has gotten under my skin. I'm so angry at her I swear if I ever see her again, I'll challenge her to a duel."

Olinda laughed. "You couldn't win a duel against Erika."

"I could take lessons. There are plenty of men here who would teach me the sword. In due time I will, mark my words. But for now, I've been conspiring with the Constable. He's securing a ship for us. We'll sail to Cho Nisi and fetch Kairos forthwith."

Olinda's mouth hung open. "You *have* gone daft."

Rhea did not apologize, nor did she deny her plans. Olinda stood and strolled to the window. "I get seasick."

"A little wine and wormwood will cure your seasickness. Olinda, please? I need you."

"Oh!" Olinda eyed Barin at the drawing room entrance, leaning against the wall, arms crossed. He wore a twisted smile and bore a haughty stance. How much of their conversation had he heard?

"And what is this?" he asked. "What sort of collusion are my two lovely siblings going on about?"

"What did you hear" Rhea asked him.

Olinda flushed at his criticism but wondered why she worried about what Barin thought. Habit, perhaps. He walked with authority in the family, as if he were king. Someday he would be, but he didn't have to flaunt it now. Not around her, anyway.

"I don't want either of you near the battle in Tellwater Valley. You have no understanding of the peril there."

"Why would you stop us?" Olinda challenged. "You didn't stop Erika."

"I wish I had. If I could go back in time, I would have never let her come. I made a mistake and I'm not planning on repeating it. I will not let either of you go."

"We'll do what we want!" Olinda said.

"Do you know what you're asking, Olinda? Have you seen a mountain giant crush through steel armor and squash a human body?"

Olinda turned her head. "Must you be so vulgar?"

"Vulgar? Have you felt the heavy hands of an invisible ogre smash you against a rock and grind your face into gravel until all you can taste is blood?"

Olinda covered her mouth when bile rose from her stomach.

"Stop," Rhea insisted. "You don't have to be loutish!"

He moved into the room, walking closer and closer to Olinda as he talked. "Oh, but the enemy is vulgar, Olinda. You'll find out when you feel talons sharper than the point of a sword dig into you and tear your flesh apart, blood will drip from your body and stain your clothes, and then the beast will lift you into the air, and drop you onto the corpse of your best friend! Perhaps Felix."

"Stop it, Barin!" Olinda shrieked.

"And then it will dive at you with its grotesque mouth open wide, pointed teeth and face of a wild man, the flap of its scaly wings will beat against your head as it devours you one bite at a time?"

"Stop it, Barin," Rhea demanded.

"Pretty repulsive isn't it."

"Why are you doing this?"

"Because if you go to Tellwater Valley, I can assure you those are the horrors you will experience, and more. Every time we cross into that region, there is another adversary attacking us. The phantom himself has been sojourning the battle fields, sucking souls out of living bodies. You are fools to consider going there. My men have been training rigorously for years and it still challenges them. What makes you think you're better than they? And what makes you think Felix would be happy to see you, Olinda? He's told me more than once how glad he is that you are safe in Prasa Potama. Someday the two of you will be together, but not now. Not until we have victory. So, do not think on such things further. Either of you."

He pivoted like a knight, his face red with anger, and walked toward the door.

"We're still going to Cho Nisi to get Kairos," Rhea announced.

He turned and regarded them both. After a moment, he nodded.

"Good," he said.

Dark Lord at Fairmistle

No one from Fairmistle had ever felt the mountain shake like it had that night. The rumble began at Mount Ream and vibrated through the underground so violently that the villagers ran out of their earthen homes to watch. Fire bubbled from the peak of Mount Ream, and a dark, ash-covered mist floated from the hillside into the valley north east, blocking out the stars.

"The giants are waking," Grayson whispered to his band of Potamian guards keeping watch in the courtyard. In charge of the small militia and every bit a seasoned soldier, he ranked as one of King Tobias' captains, and had volunteered for this extension. He had a soft spot for the country people and had often complained that no one gave Fairmistle—and the river towns south of it—the protection they needed. Some of his grievances reached Prince Barin, and so the prince offered him the opportunity to lead a brigade and stand watch over the river folk.

At the edge of the plains, the quaint village of Fairmistle greeted visitors before they reached River Ream. No greater than perhaps a few hundred residents—enough to warrant a name and win an icon on King Tobias' maps—the adjacent structures of the village comprised of whitewashed adobe that shone in the moonlight. No two homes or shops were the same shape but built like cones and acorns, domes and boxes all interlocking to form a vast half circle surrounding a courtyard, a fountain, and vegetable gardens. They had built an inn on the road to the river where the visiting militia billeted.

Since Grayson's occupation several weeks ago, and because of the vulnerability of the village, the militia had dug ditches away from the village nearer the plains where they would fight from should the enemy attack.

For nights now men had patrolled the empty courtyard, keeping a keen eye out for skura and any other cruel puppets that threatened the land. Until now, there'd been no disturbance. Everyone in town suspected something would happen. That's why the curfew.

Even Grayson, an unbeliever in the apparition of Skotádi, feared the mountains. He took his hat off and scratched his bald head.

"Wonder what that means?" Jobin, a rather chunky enlistee from Prasa Potama muttered, as he pulled his dagger from his belt. His dirty uniform showed wear and his metal buttons were tarnished from being out in the elements too long. Tonight, he wore his jacket opened, a half-coat over his dusty shirt. Grayson, his captain, cared little what the soldiers looked like. No one did. Jobin could have been in peasant clothes for all it mattered in these parts. Jobin had served King Tobias for several years and requested to go to Fairmistle. "Less bloodshed and more women and wine," had been his reasoning. This assignment gave him the excuse.

So far, all the troops had plenty of wine as Tellwater's vineyards were a day's ride from Fairmistle. The river women loved the soldiers and their coin.

"Don't know what a rumble on the mountain means these days." Grayson regarded Jobin's dagger with a curious eye.

"Least wise mountain giants don't come off the mountain. Never had, won't never," Jobin picked his teeth with his knife blade.

"We don't know that. It's breedin' ill, that mountain is," red-haired Stormy cautioned. He was too young to enlist in the King's army—fifteen was all—but he had a heart for defending his country folk. "Nothing's right in these parts. Wish King Tobias would let my brother come here. He'd take care of skura and those mountain giants. Ole Rory would save us all."

Grayson patted the youth on his shoulder. "You'll see your brother again. Prince Barin will bring Rory here with more soldiers than you'd ever seen. We'll get rid of the menace. You'll see."

No sooner had he spoken when the dark cloud, the one everyone had expected coming, swooped in from the north, rising out across Casda de Moor. Shrill calls of winged demons spread out over the sky, making the night starless.

"Skura!" Grayson warned and signaled his troops to the ditches outside of the village. Others called men from the inn. Boys from inside houses flew out their doors, grabbing whatever they could use as a weapon, axes, pitchforks, shovels. The troops drew their bows, Jobin his flail, and Stormy the axe his father had made of forged steel.

Soon the entire Fairmistle army—enlisted Potamian soldiers, along with villagers who had volunteered—took position in the dugouts. If their plan succeeded, they would stop the entourage before it swept into the village.

Grayson ducked low, throwing the patch of grass over his head, and patted a patch on top of Stormy.

"Stay down until they're directly overhead," he told the others, his own heart beating hard. He'd been in battle with these beasts before, but he knew the younger villagers had only seen the destruction they do. He watched their faces closely, ready to offer an encouraging word if panic set in. "You won't like the looks of 'em, they're ugly as sin, so when they come, just kill 'em," he instructed. "Don't pause or think twice. Just shoot or flail. Get rid of 'em. Lay 'em down dead!"

"Don't need to be telling me twice, Grayson. I'm ready," Jobin assured him.

That's what they all say, Grayson thought to himself, before their bones are picked clean. He studied the volunteers of his forces somberly. They weren't all in armor like the troops he led from Prasa Potama. The volunteers from Fairmistle wore dirty linen trousers and knee-length boots tied by gaiters to keep the flaps up. Dusty earth-tone tunics torn and ragged for no other reason but that the boys were too poor to afford new clothing. What with skura raiding their lambs these last few years, wool had become scarce and expensive.

Grayson whispered a brief prayer asking for mercy of whatever god might hear—that if these young men died it'd be quick—and then he peered out over the bank.

The massive black cloud of winged beasts had disappeared. He squinted, focusing on the hills north of them, toward the mountain. The mist which had crept from the peaks now covered the foothills.

"Anyone got a spyglass?" he asked. One soldier offered the requested tool and Grayson pulled it open, focusing on the mist in the foothills. It validated his suspicions, for the creatures in the fog were devouring the skura. He grunted in satisfaction.

"Them are mountain giants," Stormy whispered.

"They're pulling the skura out of the sky and crushing them," Grayson stated with a smile on his face.

"Maybe so, but them killing the skura is giving them bodies of iron, and they're coming this way."

It didn't take long, either. Out of the creeping vapor, giants rose, their deadly stone bodies stomped across the plains toward Fairmistle. The earth shook with every footstep of every giant, and there were at least thirty.

"We're dead," someone exclaimed.

"Get inside," someone else hollered. The village soldiers dropped their bows and ran. Grayson didn't bother calling them back. They had just as much chance of survival running as if they fought. Their only hope would be to hide far away from town. He hardly blamed them for panicking. Adolescents who had only learned to shoot a bow a few days before. Grayson watched the boys skip away. Some dove into the river, some swam to the other side.

"Maybe they'll get away," Stormy squeezed into the ditch next to Grayson.

"Why aren't you running?"

"I'm a soldier" he answered. "Got a brother in the King's Army. How would it look for me to high tail across the river when Rory's servin' his Majesty? He faces these monsters regular. It's the least I can do."

Grayson had no time to respond. The earth rumbled as legs like pillars of stone kicked up dust. Giants were on them, mist rolled in torrents at their feet. The giants who had killed skura had already manifested, and others floated over the earth as misty fingers. Within minutes, the giants spotted the army. Those men who could, ran. Others fired their weapons, but arrows and axes did nothing to stop the foggy fingers from filling the ditches where the soldiers hid. The mist divided into sections, each fragment becoming a giant hungering to manifest. They grabbed soldiers, yanked them out in the open and spread them onto the ground. The fog hovered over them and pushed them flat with vaporous knees squeezing the life out of their bodies, A black-robed figure mingled in and out of the fog, leaning over the perishing men, sucking their souls as they died.

Grayson watched all this in horror when suddenly something grabbed his legs out from under him. Foggy fingers twisted around his ankles, and then his calves. He dropped his bow as his torso scraped against rocks. Pulled out of the ditch, he saw the wide eyes of the young man Stormy witnessing his ensnarement. As the giant's hands wrapped around Grayson's torso, Stormy's axe head went right through the fog, doing nothing.

Grayson moaned as the giant flipped him face down onto the ground, dirt mashed into his mouth. He gasped for air. A heavy weight pushed his body flat against the earth. He screamed until he heard bones snap and blood gush from his mouth. Darkness enveloped his face and with a whooshing sound something sucked the air out of him. Grayson's lungs caved as the apparition inhaled. The weight on his back pressed harder and his spine shattered. His life disintegrated with one final agonizing cry.

A sucking sound reverberated in Stormy's ears and then with a deafening scream, Grayson's body fell limp. Horrified, Stormy stared, his mouth wide, feeling the heavy beating of his own heart. The giant reached for him with granite hands. Stormy had no voice—numbed from fright—neither could he move. The ogre scooped him up into his fist. Its fingers closed around his body and entombed him. The giant moved. Stormy flew against one side of the ogre's fist and then banged against the other side. His head crashed against the rock again and all went black.

The Ride

Erika could not resist the exhilaration that came with riding a horse. The scent of the leather tack, the woolly wax of the saddle blanket, or the sweet fragrance of the animal, Erika loved riding. Add to that a beautiful island trail, crisp morning air, and a handsome princely escort, she could not have been more refreshed. Truly, she'd been seeking the day when her worries were vindicated, and happiness attained. That day had come. She laughed for no reason other than the joy which tickled her insides. Arell smiled at her with a puzzled look.

"You're in fine spirits this morning, Fairest."

"I am!" If she had tried to rid herself of her smile, she could not. The grin seemed to catch, for Arell's eyes sparkled with hers.

They descended to the beaches, and the sun warmed her back. She rode a dapple mare named Bonny, which had a quick response to her knees and a gentle amble. Once on the beach, they galloped along the shoreline on solid sand packed hard from pounding waves. The horses splashed blithely in the water as they cantered all the way from where she and Kairos had first set foot on the island, to the eastern shore, a full morning's travel along sandy beaches, in and out of hidden coves, and around tide pools.

"This is simply bliss," Erika said as they slowed to a walk. She ignored the promise she made to herself the night before. Politics could wait, as Arell had suggested. "I have never felt so good, nor so free."

He rode next to her, the late afternoon sun back lighting his strong bronze stature while his loose shirt blew freely against his form. His smile shone like the moon on a dark night, and whenever she caught his glance, she marveled at his dark eyes, which hinted of reds and browns.

I'm delighted you're enjoying your day," he said.

"Oh, I am. I had need of this."

"As did I. Come, I have something to show you." He dismounted when they came to a grassy coastline and helped her off Bonny. He held her waist as she slipped out of the saddle. The nearness sent chills through her body. Their eyes met when her feet touched the sand and the contact launched unfamiliar sensations inside of her—marvels that took her breath away—and then she realized how quickly her heart raced.

He blushed and then released her. She wished he hadn't. He touched her hair, his eyes vibrant. "Your curls shine like finely polished copper. You are the most beautiful woman I have ever seen."

A cold shiver raced through her. No one had ever told her she was beautiful. Sometimes her father and brother commented on her appearance, but only when she wore a dress, and only because she looked like her mother. Arell stared at her as though she were a precious jewel. She looked away, certain her face had turned red.

"We have to walk from here. It's up on the hill."

Arell took his boots off and stuck them in his saddlebags. Erika found a driftwood log to sit on and unlaced her boots. When she had taken them off, she rolled her stockings down and slipped out of them. She glanced at Arell, who'd been staring. He looked away quickly. Erika flushed, but inwardly she smiled. She'd never been prudish like her sisters who insisted ladies should be modest. Erika had shunned scruples. She'd been around men more than women all her life. There was no need to be ashamed to uncover her feet.

She wiggled her toes in the cool sand as she followed him over a stretch of dunes and climbed from the white seashore to a grassy hill. A hazy sun shone on endless turquoise waters and white gulls circled above them.

"Leave Bonny here. She won't go anywhere."

Not until they reached an olive grove, did Erika realize they were in a graveyard. She pulled back, but Arell didn't notice. Instead, he hurried to a freshly dug mound and knelt.

"Come," he said with a smile on his face—a pure, innocent, loving smile. Erika wanted to run away. It took all her courage to stay.

"It's my father."

Erika nodded.

"He's at peace, and I've come to terms with his parting, mostly. Sit by me. Please."

Her stomach twisted in a knot, and though she adored Arell's company, sitting at the grave of the man she killed sent a pain through her body.

"No one in the Potamian kingdom ever wanted your father

to die," Erika said. "Not King Tobias, nor any of his people. Please know that." Barin's warning reverberate in her head at that point. "Do not let those people know you did this!" She held her breath because everything inside of her wanted to blurt out a confession.

His gaze remained on the grave, as if churning her words into thoughts. He hesitated before he spoke, and when he did, he squeezed her hand.

"I need to know. The elders need to know. Who did this?"

For the love of her Father's idols, the words sizzled on the tip of her tongue but with an excruciating the struggle. She inhaled and looked at the sky. "What if I told you I did it?" she asked meekly.

"Did your brother kill my father?" he questioned softly, their hands still clasped together, his warm and strong.

She tried but couldn't repeat the confession. He heard and ignored her. She wanted to pull away, to run, and yet she didn't. Her pulse raced so quickly that she closed her eyes and tried to keep from fainting.

"No, my brother had nothing to do with your father's death." She needed to get home. Father had been right. She shouldn't be anywhere near this remote beach in the most beautiful place in the world, ready to lose her heart.

And her life.

Where is Kairos? Where is Rory?

"Could we go back to the castle? I'm feeling faint," she said. She gazed at the ocean, the gently rolling surf, the heron standing quietly on the sand. She felt his eyes on her.

"You think this a trap, and it's upsetting you, isn't it? Forgive me. I didn't mean to offend you." He stood and offered his hand to help her on her feet.

"A burial ground for the Cho Nisi is a comforting place. It's where we come and talk to our loved ones. Confide in them and they listen." He looked at the grave—pain radiated from his countenance—his grief buried deep. "Perhaps I shouldn't question you here. It is a dishonor to the departed. I didn't mean to cause distress."

Erika stepped away from him. She wanted to be angry that Arell brought her here, not hurt, not ashamed. Arell's love for his father matched the love she had for her father.

"He must have been a wonderful man," she whispered, biting her lip. How can she offer comfort to him other than admitting her guilt? And would that comfort him?

"If he were alive today, I would have you meet him. You would have liked each other."

Erika nodded, finding it difficult not to break down and cry. She looked away. "I'm sure I would have...loved him," she whispered. Her voice cracked.

"I shouldn't have brought you here."

He offered his hand again, but she didn't take it. She kept a distance between them as they returned to their horses. Her stomach churned, hating the lie she lived.

They walked their horses for a while along the coast. When they reached a lengthy stretch of shoreline, the tide surged. She followed Arell as he waded ankle deep.

Without warning, he spun around and splashed her. Cold, salty water hit her face. She screamed. He laughed. Again and again he splashed. Her anger roared to the surface. She bent low and slapped the water so hard with her hand that his face caught most of the spray. Knowing he'd retaliate, she sprinted away.

He chased her, and the horses trotted after them. She waded through the breakers and broke into a jog, feet slapping on the wet sand, the foamy surf spewing over her. She couldn't outrun him though, and so out of exhaustion she fell just as the surf broke over her and immersed her in saltwater. He dove next to her. She rolled over, dug a handful of sand from under the receding surf and smashed it into his hair.

She laughed—a wild abandoned roar, freeing all the sorrow she'd been harboring.

He shook the sand out of his hair and grinned. She tried the stunt again, but he grabbed her arms and held them down. He didn't hurt her. Fighting against him helped to release her anxiety. She grunted and growled at him. He loosened his hold and let her up as another wave washed over them.

When the water receded, she grabbed his arms, and they wrestled back and forth while the breakers rolled over them again and again, saturating their clothes, their hair, their bodies. She struggled against Arell's strength, her anger and frustrations struck out at him like the sea pounding on the shore. Drenched and laughing, they pulled themselves to their feet and jogged until Erika's knees buckled under her and she fell in the sand. When Arell fell next to her, they wrestled again until she emptied of every ounce of heartache.

Exhausted, she relented and lay on the wet beach watching clouds billow across the late afternoon sky. Foamy surf tickled her back, her legs, her toes as the breakers receded. Arell sat up and studied her for a moment. With a gentle sigh, he leaned over and kissed her.

Thrilled by his touch, she gasped. He tasted of saltwater—his warm body amazingly delicious. His tongue in her mouth pleasingly invasive. His skin glowed like fiery bronze, back-lit by the sun teasing the horizon. Bare-chested but for the wet shirt that had fallen open, she ran her fingers over his upper body, so solid, his arms so strong. He gently pulled her hips under his and kissed her neck. Though her wet clothes still covered her completely, he tenderly caressed her breast and put his lips to her nipple. He stopped and knelt over her. For a long time, they simply looked into each other's eyes.

"Fairest," he whispered. "I cannot violate you, but I cannot lie and tell you I don't want to." He inhaled and straightened. Water and sand dripped from his hair and trickled down his torso. He rose, offered his hand, and pulled her to her feet.

Erika adjusted her blouse and brushed sand from her hair as Arell left to get the horses. Her heart beat hard, her desire as strong as the ocean waves pounding the seashore.

This was the first time in her life she felt fulfilled. Surely, she had lost her heart to the king of Cho Nisi. If he had chosen to 'violate' her, she wouldn't have stopped him. She would have encouraged him.

Silver rays lined the clouds, the sand shimmered in the afternoon sun as Arell led the horses to her. He drew his cloak from his saddle and wrapped it around Erika's shoulders, taking a moment to hold her close as he did, his breath against her cheek, his hands tenderly touching her hair. His warm body took the chill away.

He helped her onto her horse.

Erika rode behind him, shivering slightly under his cloak, her eyes fixed on his strong back, his dark wet hair leaving stains on his shirt as it dripped dry.

Aftermath

Arell handed the reins to the groom once they returned to the courtyard. Once inside the castle they dripped water and sand all over the hall, but none of the servants seemed to notice, nor did anyone notice the closeness by which they walked. The servants were too respectful to meddle in the king's affairs, Arell's smile too wide as he nodded to a valet.

"I'll have Serena come and fix you a warm bath," he said when they got to her room. It had been the most pleasant day in his life. He'd lost his heart to this woman. No matter what happens now, he will fight to keep her. Erika opened her mouth to speak, but before she could say anything a page came running to them.

"King Arell, Chief Silas is asking for you. There are ships coming from the north. A fleet."

"I'll go with you." Erika whispered.

"No!"

The indignation he had seen in her before showed on her face. "I'm a warrior."

"This may be your father. If he has an army, he may not wait to talk before he strikes. Stay here and freshen up. I'll send for you. When it's time to take up arms, I'll let you know. You can fight alongside me anytime you want. But I have no intention of wielding a sword against your father."

He didn't give her time to answer but took her chin in his hand and kissed her. It was a simple kiss, but she pressed against his lips and then their tongues met, and she tasted sweet, her fragrance overpowering. Had not the Caller cleared his throat, Arell may have never stopped.

He pulled away, resisting his own urges more than hers. "I must go."

Several warriors waited for Arell and they hurried him out of the castle to the courtyard where Chief Silas had another horse saddled and spoke as soon as Arell mounted.

"You're all wet."

Arell held back a smile and changed the subject

"Did you see their banner?"

"A destrier. Red and gold."

"Tobias!" Perturbed, Arell looked over his shoulder at the castle. The king will want his daughter back, and Arell wasn't quite ready to give her up. Hopefully, Tobias will relinquish the name of his father's murderer without a battle.

"We didn't know how you wanted to proceed, so our men are shifting the sands, disguising the island. Several ships approach, and they may be familiar with our shores and able to navigate, regardless. We could call the winds…"

"No. We will destroy none of King Tobias' ships. If he's come for his daughter, we can settle this peacefully. Where is Kairos the Wizard? I want him down there with us."

Silas spoke in his language to one of his men who rode back to the castle.

"We'll parlay first. Perhaps we can convince Tobias to bring the murderer to us with no resistance."

"Yes. Trade the princess for the murderer. You think like a king, now."

Arell only nodded, his mind now on King Tobias' fleet. He hadn't any notion of trading Erika for the murderer. He would like to keep her on the island. At least until she said she wanted to leave. If ever she did. "I'll do the talking," he said, her kiss still moist on his lips, the taste of her still sharp in his mind.

They rode quietly after that. Kairos and the warrior who fetched him galloped to catch up just before they descended the hillside toward the beach.

A magical wind swirled along the coast, shifting the sands. Arell dismounted as soon as the drummers came into view. "No cyclones. Do not destroy any of their ships," he ordered. Silas relayed the message. The wind died slightly. Arell pulled out his spyglass, looking for the lead ship.

"That one," Arell pointed. The ship bore three masts: the tallest heralded the King's insignia beating forcefully in the breeze. Many people were aboard. Soldiers, sailors, and two women. "Let that one in only, but keep your guard up. There are soldiers. Chant a prayer."

The ship entered the calm and pulled down its sails, mooring in deep waters near shore. While the other ships turned about because the windstorm had blown them off course and away from the island, this one lowered a longboat. Soldiers climbed the rope ladders into it and then assisted a woman.

Arell tucked away his spyglass and called for Kairos and the warrior guarding him.

"What do you want of me?" Kairos asked.

"You're my leverage, Wizard. Say nothing. Do nothing." They watched together as the longboat made its way to shore. No one on the boat had a bow drawn, so Arell presumed he'd have time to talk.

"Holy idols, it's Rhea!" Kairos breathed. "It's my woman, my fiancé! She's come for me with her father's fleet! Do you know what this means? He approves. He approves of our love!" The wizard shook with excitement and would have jumped into the water to meet the boat had not the warriors held him back.

"Easy there, Kairos, not so fast. There's some negotiating to do first," Arell cautioned.

Natives took formation alongside Arell and held their spears on guard as Tobias' men-at-arms beached the longboat. A woman stepped out into the water, assisted by a soldier. She held her silk skirt up, though it skimmed the gentle breakers, anyway. She lifted her chin proudly as she strode up the beach. Her eyes lit when she saw Kairos, and then a frown crossed her face as she considered the warriors and Arell.

"I've come for my man," she announced.

"You saved us a trip, then." Arell signaled to Silas to call his warriors to stand down. Arell regarded this woman who garnered no resemblance to Erika, although equally pretty. She dressed as a royal princess and had the air of an elitist.

"Where is my sister? I have a score to settle with her," The woman asked. She surveyed the beach and her eyes lit up when she saw Kairos.

"And who is your sister?" Arell put on his cynical smile.

"You have Kairos, you ought to know who my sister is."

"Well, then, who are you?"

"Rhea, twin daughter of King Tobias. And if you don't return Kairos and Erika, our nation will declare war against yours."

"You're presuming a bit much, considering you haven't asked who I am." Arell enjoyed the dialogue and that the woman's face turned red.

She focused on him, her eyes meeting his. "Who are you?"

"Arell son of Rolland High King of Cho Nisi."

"Very well, Arell son of Rolland High King of Cho Nisi. Where is my sister Erika?"

"Indisposed."

She frowned.

"As far as your request regarding the release of 'your man', no one will leave this island without something in return. Something that rightfully belongs to us."

Kairos struggled with his guard and gained a few feet toward Rhea.

"Hold him back," Arell whispered to the sentry. Another warrior helped restrain Kairos.

"Vasil, you promised!" the wizard complained. "Release me!"

"I did not promise. I told you I would see. Now hold your tongue!"

Kairos grunted but stood quietly after that.

"What could we possibly have that belongs to you?" Rhea asked, somewhat muddled.

"The murderer of my father. The Cho Nisi elders demand to know his name and that your king release him into our hands. Should you meet that demand, I assure you that your wizard and your sister will go home with you, as will all of your sailors."

Rhea laughed. Not a joyous, amused laugh, but a bitter one. She wiped her eyes from the tears that came from her mirth. "You fool," she said. "She didn't tell you?"

Arell straightened, offended. Who is she to call him a fool? Kairos struggled to get away. "Rhea, don't."

"Why not, Kairos? He wants to know. It's in his best interest to know."

"Rhea, they want revenge."

Arell listened intently to their exchange. Perhaps in this struggle the Cho Nisi will finally get the truth.

"And why shouldn't they have their retribution?" Rhea asked.

"No, Rhea!" Kairos begged. "Think about what you're doing!"

Arell eyed Silas. He and the warriors remained calm, but their ears were sharp.

Rhea ignored the wizard. "King Arell of Cho Nisi, might I inform you that your murderer is already on your island. If it were a skura, it would have eaten you." Arell locked eyes with Silas and then glared at Kairos.

"Not me," the wizard argued.

"Who? Tell me who," Arell demanded of Kairos. Had someone stolen on shore while the princess had distracted Arell? Surely the warriors would have seen him. Unless he swam ashore before Erika's skiff beached. When the wizard wouldn't answer, Arell turned to Rhea.

"Release Kairos, it's not him," she demanded. "I'll be happy to tell you who killed your father."

"Let him go," Arell commanded his men. Kairos broke away and hurried to Rhea. She held out her hand, and he took it but stepped away from her embrace.

"Rhea, don't," he begged. "They'll execute her."

Rhea ignored him. Speaking to Arell with a grin, she answered. "The murderer of your father isn't a man at all. It's Erika!"

"You lie." Arell's body slowly froze. He could not accept this news.

Rhea shook her head. "Unfortunately, it's the truth."

A rumble of discontent came from the warriors as they exchanged angry glares. Rhea pulled Kairos toward her and led him back to the longboat. She waved at her soldiers to follow. The wizard looked over his shoulder at Arell with a sorrowful grimace.

Arell, stunned, watched as the Potamians pushed the longboat out of the shallows.

"It can't be," he whispered. He clenched his fist and dug his nails into his palms so that the pain kept him coherent.

"It can very well be," Chief Silas answered. "I did not trust her."

"No!" Arell turned to him. "She would have told me," And then he remembered she did. He backed away. "Remain here," he ordered the chief and his men. "Allow no other ships to come to shore. These people may attack regardless."

Other ships were not his concern. Confronting Erika before the warriors arrested her, was. He scrambled up the hill and took the reins from the man holding Honor. "Do not follow me," he ordered. "None of you."

Arell galloped Honor over the mountain trail, the horse kicking dust and working a sweat. He did not stop once, not even in Moaton. Lanterns in the village glowed against the twilight sky as the clatter of hoof beats on cobblestone brought villagers running to the walkways, asking questions of him as he raced on.

"What is it, Vasil?"

"Are we under attack?"

He sailed by them, answering none.

"Open the gate," he shouted well before he arrived at the iron portcullis. The gate flew open in time for him to lope into the courtyard. Stable boys ran to him as he dismounted. Panting, he raced into the castle and skipped up the stairs two at a time. He did not wait for Bena to announce his arrival, but threw open Erika's door. She jumped up, having been at her dresser combing her hair.

"Vasil," she said.

"You killed my father!"

She dropped the brush and stepped back. The moment before she answered, her silence said everything. The truth stung as painfully as if someone had thrust a halberd against his chest.

"I tried to tell you. It was an accident, Arell. I didn't see him in the bushes. I thought the skura…" Tears welled in her eyes. "I can't tell you how guilt stricken I've been. How sorry I am! When I heard that the elders were going to execute the murderer, I feared the worse."

Arell stood motionless—his insides bled as if a double-edge sword had sliced his heart in two. His eyes feasted on her splendor for what might be the last time. He didn't know which cut his soul more deeply—that she had killed his father, or what the elders would do to her.

Time stood still. All that had been beautiful, that had blossomed, that so recently sang a chorus of hope for him, shattered. Like the last sand sifting through the bottleneck of an hourglass, his hopes vanished. Like hail hammering on spring blossoms—tearing delicate petals to shreds and leaving nothing but dull and lifeless browns—withered and faded into a muddy earth.

"I could have loved you," he choked.

He stepped back, repelled by her presence, and with all the strength he had, he pivoted and left her room.

Silas and Kairos

Once on the ship, Kairos embraced Rhea, thankful to see her, yet he pulled away from her kisses. Her passion burned hotter than his, for the terrible fate that awaited Erika distracted him. He backed away and held her at a distance.

"Rhea. Tonight, my love. Yes, tonight I will show you my gratitude. Right now, my mind is spinning in a thousand circles. Think of what's going to happen to your sister." Kairos paced away from her. "We can't leave her. We can't."

"Excuse me, you two, but I need to get home and off this horrid ship." Olinda said as she staggered from the cabin, her face a greenish hue. "My body covets dry ground lest I not have any insides left."

"The boat will launch momentarily," Rhea assured her. "Kairos get a hold of yourself. You're distressed. It must have been miserable for you being a prisoner. We'll be home soon, and then you can forget all about this outlandish episode. It only takes a short while to weigh anchor."

"No!" Kairos said. "No, we can't go. We are not weighing anchor yet. Your sister's life is at stake."

"That's ridiculous. Erika can take care of herself. She's a warrior, remember? She'll be fine," Olinda interjected. "We need to go home."

"She won't be fine. They want to execute her," Kairos argued. "And you, Rhea, helped to put her in that quandary."

"Nonsense." Their eyes locked, and she sobered. "Execute?"

"What did you think, Rhea? She killed their king."

Rhea put her hand over her mouth and stepped back, her face flushed. "I should have kept quiet."

"Yes. You should have. The situation called for diplomacy, my dear."

"What can we do?"

Kairos felt his pocket for the parchment he had penned while in Arell's castle. Troubled over their arrest, and more so over Erika's secret, he gave into his wizardry instincts and wrote the details of the death of the Cho Nisi king. He recorded what Barin and Erika had told him. He considered leaving the memo on the dresser in hopes it would make its way to an elder but brought it with him instead, afraid it would incriminate the princess if they didn't find out otherwise. Now, wisdom told him bringing this missive back to Prasa Potama would be useless. He pulled the letter out of his pocket and slapped it nervously in his hands.

"Someone needs to see this," he muttered. Kairos swept across the deck, looking for any insignificant item that might float. A bottle. If he found a bottle, stuffed the note inside and tossed it toward the beach, they'd find it.

"Kairos, what are you doing?"

He lifted a lid to a crate that held an assortment of articles. No bottles. He picked up a buoy still attached to a line.

"I've got to…" he mumbled, sensing Rhea watching him. "I've got to get this letter to them. Something that floats…"

"What letter?"

He stopped his rummaging and faced her, inhaling deeply to calm himself. "I wrote it all down. Everything that happened. She needs a defense, someone to speak up for her."

"Well then, go take it to them."

"Take it to them?"

"Yes, if you wrote it for their eyes."

Kairos glanced toward shore. Smoke from a small campfire drifted into the air, and the sound of drums beat quietly in rhythm to the rocking surf.

"Yes, of course. I suppose it would make sense to hand it to the chief, wouldn't it?"

"Be brave, Kairos. Please. For me. I would be sincerely grateful if you thought it would ease this trouble. Had I known the seriousness of this situation, I wouldn't have been so vindictive."

"I will relieve you of this burden." He bowed cordially.

"Can you save her?"

"I'll try. For you and for Erika," he said. He might not be good with magic, and sometimes his confidence lacked. Still, Erika's situation called for an immediate response and he took it upon himself to do the right thing. Despite all the wild escapades Erika dragged him through, he held a fondness for her and considered himself her guardian, in a way. He had overheard the natives in their musings. He knew how angry they were over the death of their king, and how they sought retribution. Erika's life hung by a thread. If a measly wizard did anything worthwhile in his life, it would be to save the princess.

If he had mustered any courage at all, Rhea held the blame. He clicked his heels and walked port side.

"You there, you sailors, lower a boat for me. A dinghy. Something I can row ashore. And don't weigh anchor without me. I will be back momentarily. I hope. I just need to talk to someone before we set sail."

The sailors were used to taking orders, especially from royalty. Their respect for a wizard seemed to be one notch higher. They pulled a small rowboat over the guardrail for him and showed how to lower himself on the ladders. A bit nerve-wracking, he found the act more difficult than when he climbed into the boat—balancing himself and trying to keep the rowboat stilled enough to get in. Still, he made it. Nighttime crept over the sea as he rowed toward the fire-lit beach. A few natives lingered, no doubt watching the King's ship, making sure it departed.

Kairos looked up longingly at Rhea, wishing he hadn't left the ship. He jostled the oars until the ends of them splashed in the water and then rowed with urgency, surprising himself that he should be so brave. The Cho Nisi frightened him with their solemn faces and large bodies, but he suffered through the tension. Erika had little chance of survival in their hands, especially if he didn't deliver his message, and so he rowed hard until he worked up a sweat.

Once sand scrapped against the bottom of the boat, Kairos stepped out into the water and pulled it aground. His legs shook, as did his hands. He felt his pocket again to make sure he hadn't lost the letter.

The natives on the beach watched him with those intense expressions. Kairos avoided their eyes as he stumbled clumsily onto shore. "Your leader, Chief Silas. Is he at hand?"

No one responded immediately. The fire crackled, the breakers rolled quietly onto the beach. Finally, one of them pointed to a grove of low-growing trees and a pile of driftwood a few yards up the beach.

"Praying," the man said.

Good, Kairos thought. Perhaps he's praying for the princess. He wiped his hands on his robe, now wet at the hem and weighed down with sand. Stars glimmered in the night sky, and the white beach glowed. When he arrived at the inlet where Chief Silas sat solemnly, beating softly on a drum and chanting, Kairos paused and looked around for a suitable place to sit. In order not to startle Silas, Kairos found a log in sight of the chief, sat, and listened. He cleared his throat twice, but the chief ignored him until he had finished his song. Kairos scratched his chin and peered at him, wondering how to begin.

"You worry?" The chief finally broke the silence.

"Yes…yes," he stuttered. "I am worried. She…Erika didn't mean to kill your king."

Chief Silas grunted.

"I…I don't want to have to tell her father that you…your elders killed her."

"You must tell her father the truth," the man said, and scowled.

"Yes, I'm aware of that. What I mean is, I don't want that to be the truth."

"No one wanted our king brought home to the grave, either."

His words sounded merciless. The chief's tone gave Kairos chills. He hadn't expected Silas to be so cold and not at all conversational. Kairos shifted his weight and looked at the Potamian ship moored near shore, wondering if this plea for mercy would make a difference. Kairos cracked his knuckles and took a deep breath, struggling to form precise words.

"What will your elders do to her?"

Silas shrugged and lifted his head. A proud man, Kairos wondered if that pride came from capturing the princess. The sparkle of starlight glimmered in the chief's dark eyes.

"You want me to tell you how we've executed criminals in the past?"

"Yes. That would help."

"No one has ever murdered our king before. It will be different this time. More brutal."

Kairos cringed. "What happened to your worst offender?"

Silas thought for a while, set his drum aside, and closed his eyes.

"A man killed a child in his anger. He had a history of being enraged. He beat his wife. A Cho Nisi shame-act. It happened a few years ago. I've not seen anything like it since, except for this."

The story seemed to be an unequal comparison, but Kairos nodded. "What did your council do to him?"

"The council strung him up to a tree and lashed him with olive sticks until he bled. After that, the villagers released their anger on him. The men took up rods, and whoever had a grievance struck him. They bruised him badly, his ribs cracked, his bones broken. They hit him on the skull. He died. It took a long time. All day. We buried him in the hills." Silas nodded toward the eastern shore. "No one likes to do those things, but we must uphold justice. It's how we keep our village clean. We have no crime here." He looked Kairos in the eye. "Many of our people despise the killer of our king."

Kairos swallowed. With trembling hands, he pulled the letter from his cloak pocket and held it tight, waiting for an opportune moment. The chief glanced at the letter.

"Silas, I've spent time with Erika. She's remorseful."

"We are all remorseful."

Kairos tried hard not to stutter, for this may be the most important thing he'd ever do in his life. More important than casting a spell or disintegrating a skura.

"Please, just hear me out. She's a young lady who made a terrible mistake. I'm pleading for mercy for her. That's all. I'm not saying she didn't do wrong. She did. She knows it."

The chief picked up his drum, as though he didn't want to hear Kairos' pleas any longer. The drumbeat droned on. When Silas stopped, he looked at the wizard again. "You wield magic?"

"Yes."

"Cho Nisi has greater magic."

"You do. However, if we combined our magic, no telling what would happen."

Silas grunted.

"There's a dark lord that threatens us all," Kairos mentioned.

"This we know." Silas said.

"With your powers and mine combined, we would have more power than he does." Kairos agreed.

"Perhaps. We may have to fight together some day again. Your king and ours," Silas said.

"That's right. Only, I'm not so sure our king will be all that happy with yours if you...if you..." swallowed again, sweat trickled down his temple. "If you torture and kill his daughter." Though his hands still shook, Kairos handed the chief the envelope.

"Give your king this letter at Erika's trial, if you give trials. I hope you do. Maybe King Arell will read it to your elders. Please."

Chief Silas took the sealed letter and tucked it in his belt.

"How much time do we have?"

Silas met his gaze. His dark eyes were stern, intimidating, and mysterious. "We have trials. We are not boors. We will consider all things." He patted his belt where he had secured the letter.

He didn't speak again, nor did they make eye contact after that.. Kairos sighed as the drum sounded. The conversation had ended. The wizard walked back toward the ship, his feet unconsciously stepping in time to Silas' rhythm. He'd done the best he could.

A King's Tears

The castle in Prasa Potama had not been darker. Even in the daytime the sun did not shine through the windows, but fear hovered over the entire Potamian kingdom as some great storm threatening to strike but never shedding its tears. A sadness captured the people as the king mourned for his daughters. Barin paced through the halls, waiting for news from Cho Nisi. No one came. King Tobias' shoulders bent in heaviness. He lingered in silence alone, wandering the gardens or in his study, staring at books but rarely reading them. Often the king would fall into coughing spells, and Barin would have to send a servant with an infusion to comfort him. Barin tried talking to him, but his father only answered his questions with a word or two and often a yawn. The king ate in solitude, which was unlike him, and some days the only ones who saw him were his page and his servants.

Barin worried. Not only about his father's health. A scouting party had come across the remains of several men who it seemed had been attacked by skura in the fields close to Prasa Potama. His father suspected it may have been the fishers whose boat Erika took. No one knew for sure.

Barin also worried about his men sent to Fairmistle and other river towns skura had allegedly raided. No word from them. Rory had been the last messenger who had arrived at the castle—the young soldier who had deserted his army and sailed to Cho Nisi with Erika. When Rory appeared before the throne informing King Tobias that the Cho Nisi demanded a parlay with the king, Barin, in his rage, had him locked away swearing an oath that unless Erika returned unharmed, Rory would never see the light of day.

Now nothing of the outside world but silence lingered within their cold stone walls. Servants moved about religiously, baking, chopping wood, tending to the chickens, swine, and horses. Whether the world around them had vanished, or the dark lord had swallowed it, they had no knowledge.

On a cold and gray day, no brighter than any of the others had been since Princess Erika's departure, a messenger brought word from the valley. Barin greeted him personally and brought him directly into the king's chambers so that his father might hear the news firsthand.

"Your Royal Highness," the young man bowed, his tattered coat touched the floor and clumps of mud fell from its hem. Frost still clung to his cloak and his water-soaked shoes carried mud across the floor. Had he not worn thick leather gloves, he may well have been frostbit.

"I come from over the mountain with news from Lord Garion."

The king raised his head as he looked the young man over. "What is your name, soldier?" An air of hope hung in the king's voice.

"Fermont, Vasil,"

"Fermont, I see that you have traveled hard, and that your journey was not a pleasant one."

"In that you are correct, Vasil."

"Did you cross the path of mountain giants?"

"I did, Vasil. I saw several of them moving in the shadows, however, they didn't notice me. Worse things linger on the mountain though, slowly creeping from their chambers. Dragons."

"Yes, I suspected that. It's only a matter of time before those reptiles join the chorus of the dark lord's forces. And how might Lord Garion be?"

"Sire, he is well as expected, but for the terror that ravages his lands. No longer are skura satisfied with pillaging livestock and destroying gardens. Vasil, the skura have grown stronger and attack children daily now, carrying them away to their nests in the tallest firs. You can hear the little ones scream as the monsters pick them apart and devour them, while parents watch helplessly below. We've hunted, we've struck, we've killed them and still they come too many for us to control. They grow in stature and soon will carry adults away as well. We need your help. Our valley is doomed. Whereas they only attacked livestock in the summer months, the raids have not let up in the snow. Lord Garion asks again for your help. Weapons do little. We need magic."

"And where is my wizard, Barin?" King Tobias lifted his head high and glared at his son. Barin didn't answer. His father knew full well Kairos had left with Erika, along with his daughters. If they didn't return soon, Barin would be the one having to fetch them all. He groaned quietly.

"There are wizard apprentices in the city, Father. We can find Kairos' notes and potions. He's not the only sorcerer."

"It took Kairos a year and a half to find a suitable magic to counter these beasts, and that after being trained by the noblest wizard ever to serve in this kingdom. His father. I would not care to send a school of amateurs to ward off the devil himself." He turned to the messenger. "Fermont, take advantage of our hospitality while I, my son, and our advisors discuss this unfortunate news. Hopefully, within a day or two we can come up with an answer for you. You're weary. Sleep well and eat. Bathe. We'll have some fresh clothes in your quarters."

Fermont bowed low and muttered his appreciation before he left.

Tobias turned to Barin. "Find them."

"Father!"

"I have no one else, Barin. Should I load myself into a ship and sail away as well? We need Kairos here. And I need my daughters here. I want them home. All of them. I am sick from their absence. Do as I say."

Barin bowed low and hurried out of the room, dreading a trip to the island in stormy weather, and with the war so fierce and close to home. He would rather fight the dragons than deal with his sisters.

He met Neal in the courtyard on his way to the stables. His friend had just arrived with his scouts and was unsaddling. Smelling of dust and horse, Neal bowed and then shook hands with Barin.

"I'm glad you're back. I have a new assignment and I'd like your company," Barin said.

"Oh? Where to?"

"Cho Nisi," Barin grumbled as he watched the stable boy tighten the cinch to his favorite mare.

"If you're in pursuit of your sisters, we will cut your trip short."

"How so?"

"Rhea's ships are docking as we speak. I came to fetch a buggy for her highnesses. Perhaps you'd like to come along?"

"I would."

A gentle snowfall dampened the woods, flakes gathered in clusters on his cowl, sticking randomly on Barin's cloak, and blowing on his lashes. Beau's hooves made an occasional squeak as the gelding trudged steadily through the fallen slush behind the carriage. By the time Barin had arrived at the dock, the snowflakes had increased in size and he could barely see the ship. Neal braked the carriage, and bending his head against the wind, walked up to Barin.

"I'll go get your sisters unless you want to come along?"

Barin dismounted and tied Beau to the rear of the carriage and walked with Neal, face buried into his woolen scarf. They did not have to travel all the way to the end of the pier before Rhea appeared with Kairos. A welcomed sight. Weighted down with luggage, the wizard nodded when he saw them. Behind the two, Olinda shuffled, arms tucked tightly in her hand muffs. They exchanged no words. Their faces were too numb from the cold, and the ride back home was slippery and long.

Someone had shoveled the castle courtyard clear, and little sign of snow remained with window washers sweeping ice from the windows and men with shovels freeing sleet off the steps. They stomped their boots clean, entered the castle, and hastened to the nearest fireplace in the hall.

Once Barin warmed himself enough to speak, he inquired of their trip, not ready to ask about Erika. He feared the news would be troublesome. "It took a while!" he said. "But we're glad to have you back, Kairos, Rhea, Olinda."

The three mumbled how they were glad to be home. Barin did not bother with small talk, instead he got right to the matter. "Kairos, my father needs your services immediately. And I'm sure he's going to want to speak with you, Rhea and Olinda."

"He knows Erika ordered me to go with her, doesn't he? I'm not in any kind of …trouble…am I?"

"I'm aware of what happened when you left, Kairos. I would have preferred Erika hadn't left so hastily, and I resented her taking my sorcerer, but at least she had you for protection. I suppose you have word of my sister and why she didn't return with you?"

Guilt paled their faces as the three exchanged glances.

"She's still alive, isn't she?" Barin asked, half-jokingly. But when he saw their reaction, he sobered. "Isn't she?"

"Alive now, yes." Rhea said. "I would really like to have a hot bath and change my clothes, wouldn't you, Olinda?"

Olinda didn't answer but headed for the door before Rhea caught up to her. Neal stood by the fire, warming his hands, and Kairos shuffled nervously where he stood.

"What happened?" Barin asked the wizard.

"Not a lot. Except Rhea...well, I don't like to gossip. I told Rhea I would tell the truth when I saw you. It didn't seem to bother her, so I'll make it short. Rhea told the king of Cho Nisi—that is the new king—you were aware he had an heir, correct?"

"Rory came here and told us King Rolland had an heir. That news surprised us all. Go on with your telling. What did Rhea do?"

"She told the new king who killed his father."

"Rhea did?"

"Yes, Vasil. I guess Rhea held a grudge against Erika for taking me away, and my begging her to keep quiet made her angrier. She accused me of siding with Erika."

"Enough of that chatter! What is the Cho Nisi king going to do with Erika?"

Kairos sighed heavily and looked toward the fire, his face glowing with the red of flame, shadows accenting his strong jawline and high cheekbones.

"That's what took us so long, because after they released me to Rhea, I returned to...to petition the chief. By that time, it was too late to sail back home, so we moored nearer the island. For a couple of days."

Barin shifted his weight and sighed, impatient with all of Kairos' babble.

"Anyway, the council wanted blood for blood."

Barin's heart skipped a beat. He repeated Kairos' words slowly, trying to best comprehend what was about to occur.

"Blood for blood?" He suspected as much, but to hear it coming from the wizard's tongue boiled his blood. Never had he fully realized the gravity of his sister's foolishness.

"I asked him what they'll do to her. He wasn't sure. He told me sometimes their justice demands torture before they kill the criminal, especially if it's an offence like murdering a king."

Barin stared at the wizard, his mouth open, his fists clenched.

"How could you?"

Kairos inched away from the prince.

Barin spun around from Kairos and slapped his fist into the palm of his hand to avoid hitting him. His mind soared with fragmented thoughts.

"You fool!" he growled. "My little sister, Erika! Blood for blood? You let them take her?"

"I asked if they would grant mercy. The chief didn't know if they would. It wasn't solely his decision. He said every council is different," Kairos stuttered, his voice trembled.

Barin whirled back around and grabbed Kairos' collar. With gritted teeth, he shook him. "What kind of wizard are you? Why didn't you bring her home? Why didn't you steal her away out a window or something?"

"I was a prisoner."

"And a wizard! You have spells!"

Kairos pushed Barin's hands off of him, his face fuming red. "Good holy idols, Prince, everyone expects so much out of one measly wizard! I have no magic potions to change people's minds, or hearts. If I did, I would have changed your sister's decision about going there!"

Why bother reprimanding Kairos? Barin turned to his friend. "Neal, we need to go."

"That would be war," Kairos stated.

"Yes! It would."

"Now settle yourself, Vasil," Neal rested his hand on Barin's shoulder. "Let's think this through."

A desperate situation. Still Neal found a way of calming him, though Barin had no desire to be calmed.

"I don't think it's all lost," Kairos assured him. "There are other dynamics at play. We have leverage. Let's go get something warm to eat and I'll tell you all that has happened, and the whole of my conversation with the chief."

Mourning

Long after Kairos left him, and when the night air grew chilly, Silas rose and set his drum on the log, quieted by his prayers. The king left much earlier in the day, storming to the castle on his horse. He would need a confession from the princess, and no doubt he had his answer by now. The elders were in assembly in Nico, waiting for the official accusation. No hurry. Time will bring all truth to the surface. Sentries most likely took the princess to the dungeon and the prince had withdrawn to wrestle with his soul. Silas had a powerful impulse to find him.

He sauntered on his way, contemplating on that morning's events and what might happen in the next few days and how Arell would handle what was to come. Those thoughts were overwhelming, especially since he loved the young king as much as he loved his own children.

Arell possessed no malicious bone in his body and so it would hurt him to see a beautiful young lady executed. Silas did all within his power to caution Arell, and yet Arell ignored the warnings and allowed himself to fall in love with the princess. This would impede justice. As a king, Arell needed backbone—strength to face not only triumph, but disaster. More than ever, Silas sensed the need to talk to Arell and to give him encouragement.

The young king often spent time by his father's side in the graveyard, and Silas assumed the cemetery drew him there tonight. The walk to the eastern shore would take a few hours, but the moon hadn't risen yet, and there were many words to tell the stars. Mourning doves serenaded him as if in answer to his invocations as he strolled along the beaches, maneuvering around the tide pools, the coves, and followed the strings of seaweed left behind as the tide ebbed.

When he reached the sand dunes and climbed the hill, his assumptions proved correct. Arell sat quietly in the graveyard next to his father's grave, hugging his knees. Silas approached him with care, lowered himself next to him, and waited. The sound of the rolling surf was all that interrupted the silence until Arell sighed and acknowledged Silas' presence.

"I could have loved her, Silas," Arell said. He looked up at the trees. The gentle swaying of the branches cast shadows across the graves that resembled ghosts, as if the spirit of his father hovered over them, stirring Arell's angst.

"Right here is where my father is," he patted the ground. "Gone to the Great Eternity, and yet his presence is among us. He loved me and never expressed ill feelings toward me, ever. You know? Even when I showed no interest in his legacy, he still considered me his son." He looked at the chief, his eyes red. "But he's gone, Silas."

The chief nodded.

"And life goes on."

Silas held his breath for what Arell might say to him, hoping his words would not shame the Cho Nisi, nor dishonor their king. He'd seen Arell with the princess. Love was not an emotion one could hide, even if Arell wanted to. Regardless, no affair should discount the gravity of this situation. The woman committed a dire injustice toward their nation, and they must punish her.

"My father lived his life as righteously as any man. I'm sure he made mistakes, but one thing he wanted, and he told me this, he wanted me to be happy. He wanted me to find love and have a family and carry on with life the way he did as a youth, before the rebellion. And when he arrived here."

"I remember those days."

"Yes, I know you do. Silas." Arell looked aside, speaking more to the grave than to Silas. "I lost him. I lost my mother years ago, and now my father lies beneath the earth next to her. Will there never be happiness?" Arell looked at him, pain clearly wrenching his soul.

"Silas, I lost my heart to this woman. But because of her, my father no longer lives. I didn't think love could turn to hate so quickly." His hands shook as he brushed his hair out of his face. "I resent her, yes. I hate what she did, and I don't care if it was an accident." He rubbed his head and covered his face, his words muted. "Silas, I have seen the style of Cho Nisi executions. It would be too much for me." He took a deep breath. "I don't think my father would advocate that sort of revenge either."

King Arell spoke no disrespect with these words. Arell struggled within his soul. This Silas saw through the turmoil, and he accepted that Arell didn't want to see this young woman killed. As chief who also witnessed executions, he, too, despised them. The chief put one hand on Arell's shoulder and the other, with his fist, he tapped his heart. "I will speak these words tomorrow. I cannot promise you what the verdict will be. We must all be strong in life and in death. Justice must prevail."

A Skura Spy

Erika shook from the wet and cold of the mossy walls that enclosed her like a vengeful womb. The king's blood that is on her hands will quickly transform to her blood poured out in vengeance over this isle. She moaned at the thought of death being her solitary friend and so speedily. Never had she thought she would court the end of her life like this. She had assumed, if she were going to die young, it would happen on the battlefield, defending her homelands, or rescuing her brother or her father. Never had she predicted she'd be executed in a foreign land as a reprisal for killing an ally king. How had she come to such a fate?

As she leaned against the stone wall and closed her eyes, she envisioned her bow raised, a noise in the grass, the string releasing, and then her arrow soaring into the brush. She tried to grab it as it flew away from her, to bring it back, but she couldn't catch it, of course. There was no negating what she had done. The man was dead and entombed on a grassy slope on a beautiful reef that had once been his home. Would they bury her in the same graveyard? Or would they toss her corpse out to sea? Or burn it?

Why hadn't she taken time to understand or weigh the circumstances? Why did she forever act on impulse? She'd been a fool. Her ultimate mistake brought her here, in this dungeon, and her life would soon be over.

When the guard locked the cells beyond hers, Erika rose and grasped the iron bars. Already she felt paralyzed and buried with life continuing without her.

Her clothes still harbored the fragrance of the castle. Arell touched the fabric that afternoon and she could even now imagine his softness against her skin, reminding her how gentle he'd been with her—how sweet his kisses were—how lovely his teasing–his warm arms and caresses. He had offered his palace to her, completely unaware of her evil deed. And she let him carry on with his fancies, all the while deceiving him.

Arell had been the closest she'd ever come to loving someone.

She gazed down the dark and empty dungeon, wishing by some slim chance he'd arrive again. Hoping he'd whisper the same words he whispered to her once before. "You don't deserve to be here. Come to the castle with me." Yet she knew he wouldn't. How could he? She killed the most important person he had in his life.

Erika glanced out the small window above her. A full moon had recently risen and the light from it reflected on the cell's embankment, giving the stones a haunting sheen. On the hillside, back-lit by the silvery globe, stood an ancient oak tree. Its branches twisted and gnarly, reached to the sky much like an elderly woman pleading for mercy. A raven sat on one of its limbs and when Erika spotted it, the bird bent his head as if he saw her. They made eye contact, and then the fowl opened its mouth and squawked. The tone that came from the bird didn't sound like any crow she'd ever heard before. It sounded more like a hyena—laughing.

Erika's trial

She'd been watching the window, waiting for dawn, wondering how long after the trial before her execution. Wondering if it will be a civil sort of death. A hanging, or perhaps they'll shoot her with a bow the way she murdered King Rolland. She wondered what her father would think when he got word. For that she felt bad. She didn't mean to hurt Father.

Darkness loomed in the stairwell when they came for her. She could see them on the road coming from the king's stables. Only two soldiers.

She lifted her chin and buried the fear of death. Numb to the world, she regretted her foolishness. Coming to Cho Nisi had, in the end, been a sacrifice. She allowed herself to be in Arell's hands so he could implement reprisal and satisfy his people. Not admitting to guilt earlier had been expedient, for now he did not need to be lenient.

Iron padlocks rattled, and heavy oaken doors creaked. Footsteps sounded hollow as the soldiers neared. One of them opened her cell and handed her a bundle.

"Wear this," he said, his voice gentle. He stepped away.

She pulled a white chiton from the bundle, a dress that resembled the one Serena often wore. A simple smock that wrapped over one shoulder and hung loosely over her body. She left her trousers, chemise, and armor in the cell. Soon, the sound of an iron lock clanked against stone and two men, not natives but Moaton soldiers in uniforms escorted her. One walked in front and one behind. They left the cell door open. Before they unlocked the ingress to the courtyard, one man pointed at her feet. "Take your shoes off," he said. No explanation why. Perhaps so she wouldn't run away. It's an island. Where would she go? She slipped them off.

The sun streaked the horizon, though there were still stars in the sky and crispy cold air that smelled like the frosty dew on a winter's morning. Perhaps the mountains near her home were blanketed with snow already. A sick yearning twisted her gut. How she wished she were home with her father, her brother, and her sisters. How she wished she could relive those moments on the dock when she decided to sail to the island. Better, she wished she could relive the moment she begged her father to let her fight in Tellwater. King Rolland would still be alive.

She waited in the courtyard with the soldiers as a stable boy ran to the barn and brought back three horses. The horse they put her on had a white coat.

Erika had spent all night awake thinking about this hour and decided the state of dissociation would serve her best—to see herself as not in her body because soon she wouldn't be. The men helped her on the white horse, untied her hands so she could balance herself, and took the lead rope, mounting their own steeds. They rode through Moaton where she'd met the old man. The town slept. A small miracle for not being paraded in front of a whole village meant perhaps she'd die with a touch of dignity. At least she hoped so.

They rode past Moaton, through the beautiful highland that overlooked the island and beyond. The peak of Mount Ream in the distance glowed in the sunrise. No cloud bothered the sky. The plateau dropped gently into an olive grove, equally stunning as the sun shone its first rays through trees. After that, they arrived at a grassy hilltop near a secluded Bay.

"Dismount," one soldier ordered after he slid off his own horse. The men were solemn, kind, but stern. One of them guided her down a rocky trail while the other waited with the horses. Once on the beach, he bowed awkwardly.

"Stay here," he said, and scurried back up the path. The two horsemen departed, leading her mount.

They had left her on a quiet beach with only a driftwood bench and a fire pit where hot embers glowed. She sat down and warmed her hands. Soon, above the sound of the gentle surf, she heard a drum beat and several voices. Men chanting. The sounds grew louder until the elders appeared from around the southernmost bulkhead. There were eight of them. Their dark silhouettes trudging through the sand gave her chills. Her executioners.

The drumming stopped when they came to the campfire. Two men followed in white cloaks. They were barefoot, their hoods covering their faces, but Erika suspected the taller one to be Arell.

One of the men put wood on the fire and fanned it with his drum. The others sat in a circle, not in front of her but with her, which surprised her. If she'd been at home on trial, she'd been on her knees in front of the king, and he would have given her a thumb's up or down and would have executed her on the spot.

The men placed their drums on the sand behind them and sat quietly.

The chief stood. "King Rolland. A good man," he began. "He came to our island looking for refuge. He respected our people and learned our ways. He never forgot them." The men uttered unfamiliar words of agreement. "He married a Cho Nisi woman." Again, the men voiced agreement. Erika glanced at Arell. She hadn't known his mother had been an islander, but she could surmise by his dark smooth skin and deep brown eyes that he had Cho Nisi blood.

"He raised one son, Arell, as good a man as his father. King Rolland kept our people out of war, and for the last twenty years we have known peace. Let us give thanks for King Rolland." Some men picked up their drums and chanted. Erika fixed her eyes on the gentle surf while they sang.

When their song was over and the drumming ceased, Chief Silas went on. "King Rolland left his home to fight for people across the sea. That they might have peace as we do. He was struck down, still a father, still a young man by all rights. He was a good ruler and will be missed."

Be brave, Erika told herself, fighting tears.

"We have found the person who killed him. Erika Tobias, stand and identify yourself."

She stood.

"This is the murderer of our king, the one who struck him down in the prime of life and who took away our leadership without thought or care for our people and our ways."

Arell bowed his head, still covered by shadow, but she saw him peeking up at her.

"We are here to pass judgment on this woman. Our laws dictate blood for blood for the offense of murder. Who wants to speak?"

Several men spoke in their native language, and Erika couldn't understand anything that they said. Arell cringed once, but other than that one time he displayed no other emotion. As much as she wanted to go through this whole proceeding unaffected, her heart raced, and sweat dripped down her dress. She had cried her tears in the dungeon and none remained, though. She couldn't have been more remorseful, but there was nothing else to say. To apologize now would sound obligatory, so she remained silent.

All the men spoke, one after another, and for a long time. Some in Erika's tongue. Some talked about their grandparents and their wives and children and how the king had been a friend to everyone. Some commended Arell for the good job he had been doing, having come to the throne so quickly and in duress. No one said anything about her that she could understand.

Mid-morning came. Erika still stood, sunlight shining directly on her. Chief Silas beat on his drum and spoke again.

"We as elders have spoken. We must now listen to our king."

Arell hesitated before he stepped forward. He pulled his hood onto his shoulders and freed his long hair. He held his head up like a king and addressed the men.

"I've heard you all. My heart is with you. I loved my father, as you did. When I heard of his death, I wanted nothing more than to seek vengeance. Even to the point of war. As you have." He pulled a parchment from his belt and stared at it for a long while without unfolding it. Only the sound of the sea and the popping of the fire interrupted the silence. Erika couldn't bear to look at him, knowing his heart grieved for his father. Why did he stop? Surely condemning her couldn't be that difficult.

"I'm...I'm having a hard time doing this," he glanced at the elders as he choked on his words.

"When I didn't know that Erika had murdered my father, I..." He glimpsed at her and then with shaking hands unfolded the letter as he continued, his head bowed. "Please, just remember how kind my father had been and try to..." He choked on his words and regarded the elders sitting around the fire. "Would my father have the daughter of an allied nation executed?" He paused again, glancing at her with eyes that displayed softness and warmth but also a deep sorrow.

"This letter came to us by the wizard while I imprisoned him in our castle. His information comes from soldiers who were there when my father died. I shall read it to you. Perhaps it will move upon your hearts." Arell cleared his throat and read.

"I write this account of what had happened in her defense. Princess Erika had been assigned to a small group of soldiers who were to guard her brother's men-at-arms as they entered a canyon to ambush a flock of skura. When a lone skura circled her brother, she followed it with her arrow, but the beast dove into the bushes near her. Without knowing that King Rolland and his warriors had arrived at the battlefield, and without calling out, without making certain of what she was firing at, she shot…" He looked up. "Our king. My father. An accident. A negligent accident, yes." He folded the parchment, his hands still trembling, and offered it to Chief Silas. He spoke slowly and deliberately.

"One word before I hand this young lady over to you. According to law, the Cho Nisi elder's judgment is final. I cannot intervene and I know you have found her guilty." He glanced at Erika with pain in his eyes. Was the pain on her behalf?

"Before you sentence her, I would have you remember my father, who was a kind man. Even though his people looked down on the Cho Nisi, he took a native for a wife and loved her. He broke the rules, the traditional morals of his people. He thought little of protocol and more of the…" Arell hesitated and stared out at the ocean, lingering on his thoughts. When he spoke, his voice was raspy, and he choked on his words. "He thought more highly of love."

Erika could barely hear his last words.

"As your king, I just ask that you be gentle. Like he was. I have spoken in the way of our people. So be it." He bowed slightly, a formality, and pulled his cowl back over his head. He stepped back and stood next to the other man in a white robe.

She looked away.

"If all have spoken, then we are dismissed. When the sun sets, we will decide." Chief Silas beat his drum.

With that, the men got up. Some walked down to the water to talk, perhaps about her, maybe not. Others went swimming, others jogged down the beach. Chief Silas dipped a chalice into a bucket of fresh water and offered her a drink. She accepted. Arell did not approach her. Eventually everyone went away. Where to, she didn't know.

Alone, just her and the sea, Erika lay in the sand to rest under the warm sun. She had gotten no sleep that night in the dungeon, and so slumber came on her quickly. Perhaps it was the drumming and chanting, or just the stress of being on trial and facing death, but Erika dreamed.

She dreamed she was on the beach and as the sun slowly burned it grew hotter until it scorched her flesh, like a fireball. She sat up, her full armor on, spun around and held her shield to protect herself, wielding a sword at a skura, spitting flames at her, singeing her hair. The dream ended, and she woke.

A high sun toasted her skin. Sweat beaded on her forehead and she smelled. She stood, slightly dizzy from the heat, and walked into the water, diving into the salty breakers as they trundled toward her. The ocean rolled on its never-ending journey to shore. She dove again, deeper, refreshed by the cold water. She surfaced, wiped her wet hair from her face, and walked back to the campfire.

Her long white chiton clung to her body, but Erika gave her appearance little thought until she saw a man in a white robe sitting at the campfire. At first sight she thought it was Arell, but as she drew near she recognized Chief Silas. He stared at the fire. She hesitated to approach him. She really wasn't decent, but he turned his head and held out a blanket, which she immediately took, dried her face, and wrapped it around her body over her wet dress.

"Sit," he instructed, and so she did.

"The elders have made their decision."

That quick? And only Silas here to sentence her?

He looked into her eyes with a long contemplative glare. "The elders have decided the death of our king was an accident, though a careless accident. Because of that, we cannot demand your blood. As you know, the people of Cho Nisi love their king. The one who died, and the one who lives. For that reason, we cannot have you among us. You will return home to your people. You will never step foot on Cho Nisi again. To do so gives us the right to strike you down. Any warrior may kill you in any manner they see fit if you return."

The chief did not cushion his words, but spoke violence with his eyes as well.

"If we make a truce with King Tobias, it will not be regarding you. I as Chief and elder of Cho Nisi have one other demand."

"Yes, sir."

"Never lay eyes on Arell High King of Cho Nisi again, nor talk to him, nor have any communication with him."

She stared at the chief; the pain penetrating deep into her soul, pain that immediately twisted into ire. There had to have been a reason for this added threat. She wanted to snap back at Silas, tell him to make sure Arell never tries to communicate with her, but she didn't. She just nodded.

"The men with the horses will be here soon to take you to the castle. Your clothes have been returned as well. You will change into them and bring nothing from the island back with you. Nothing."

She scowled. What did he mean by that? What would she take?

"After that, this day before the sun sets, you will be on a boat headed to your father." He stood and walked up the hill and out of sight.

Erika spat and threw the cloth he had given her into the fire. Ash flew into the sky as the remnant buried the flames and smoke seeped out from under the wet linen. So too had her life been snuffed out. Perhaps it would have been better if she had been executed.

Erika and Sylvia.

As the ship sailed, clouds dipped low over the sea. A thick fog sealed her vision so that all Erika could see was the wet wood of the deck, and native sailors working the lines. They hardly wore enough clothes to keep them warm. Bare chested, their dark skin contrasted against the gray of the weather. The wind rushed the boat, and the warriors were skillful with the sail, and so they made good time. The nearer to the mainland the boat came, the colder the air until snow fell on her shoulders, her ears and nose, and she stood on deck shivering. No cabin offered shelter on the small dinghies that the Cho Nisi sailed, but they were seaworthy and took on wakes with potency unlike many of her father's ships.

The men taking her home treated her with muteness, as cargo only, saying nothing to her and barely glancing at her unless meal time came, and even then they handed her a bowl of soup from an iron kettle and moved on. Nursing a broken heart, she tried not to think about Arell. She breathed deeply, ready to go on with her life, to start anew.

No blame stained her thoughts, but she owed Rhea a thank you for telling everyone the truth.

The day after they left, the boat arrived in port Prasa Potama at dusk, greeted by a snow-dusted pier. The Cho Nisi sailors assisted her onto the dock, set her baggage in front of her, and then quickly launched again, sailing for their home.

No one greeted her in Prasa Potama, for she had informed no one of her arrival. She considered the hillside surrounding the city. How easy it would be to sneak off into the woods and disappear. A curious idea, except if she vanished her father would probably blame Arell and that never-ending threat of war would rise again. Oh, the eternal and longstanding threat of war! Men always had to blame calamity on someone else!

Once off the dinghy, Erika picked up her bags and marched

down the pier toward the buggy house. No longer a bustling port, winter weather had chased the merchants away save for a few food booths selling grub to hungry sailors. The aroma of their wares set her stomach rolling, excited for the first time that she would soon be in the castle's safety, sitting at a table with a plate of wholesome food before her. The sound of civilization echoed with the clink of coins that jiggled in her purse. Not much, but enough for a carriage home. She assumed her status as a princess remained intact.

The cart-master, Clyde de Munson, sat calmly in his office, wood-burning stove sizzling, the stove pipe red hot, when Erika entered. Absorbing the heat in a matter of seconds, her body relaxed. De Munson immediately dropped his journal and bowed. "Fairest," he said.

"Good morning, Master de Munson. I need a ride home immediately. Have you a cart and driver that could get me to the castle in this snow?"

"Fairest, please warm yourself by the fire and accept my humble hospitality. I can have one readied for you immediately. My sincere apologies that it is not a royal carriage."

"I accept your apologies. Any carriage will do. I just want to go home." *And shed this damp leather and soiled clothing.* The smell of low tide seemed to have clung to her dress, and ice hung from her hem and her shoes. All she wanted anymore was a hot dinner, a warm comfortable bed, and sleep. Much sleep. She thought she might sleep until summer.

She didn't find comfort in the ride home, of course. The carriage hit every rut and bump that the frozen road offered. The jarring brought her back to reality, and she watched the frosty landscape reel by, each rotation of the wheels taking her away from the horror of the island and the love she lost. Once the carriage rolled onto the cobblestones of the courtyard and stopped in front of the stairs, servants hurried out of the castle and immediately assisted her. Pages ran ahead of her through the halls to announce her arrival. The housemaid, Miss Sylvia Prenson, curtsied.

"You Highness, welcome home," Sylvia said. A middle-aged woman, Sylvia had served the family many years. She had tended to Erika's mother before her mother's death while in labor with Erika. Why, of all things, did Erika think of her mother's death now but to add to the guilt that already burdened her. Miss Prenson took her bag and walked ahead of her.

"I still have a room, don't I?" Erika asked.

"Of course, Fairest. You will always have a room. This is your home." She smiled as she held the door open for Erika. "Your father loves you and he will be overjoyed to see you at dinner tonight."

"I hope so. Could you prepare a bath for me? A nice hot one. It's been a long journey."

Sylvia bowed and left the room. Erika immediately pulled off her cloak, her armor and her shoulder guards and rummaged through the closet looking for the most comfortable garment she could find, settling for a cotton chemise and a loose linen surcoat, an outfit she could wear for leisure and still be appropriate for dinner. She set them on the bed, took off her worn dress, and donned her robe.

Servants brought in the warm water as she waited by the hearth. They moved about swiftly and with an air of joy, giving Erika pause. What simple lives they lead. They go about their day obeying instructions, working together for her comfort. Never had she heard a complaint from any of her father's servants. Rarely from a soldier either. Yet she, the king's daughter, the most privileged of all, spent her life complaining and yearning for something she thought she needed and didn't have.

And what is it she wished for?

Erika closed her eyes, and a tear leaked out. She wished for the love that Arell had given her. There had been no sweeter moment in her entire life than the time she spent with him.

"Fairest, the bath is ready." Sylvia spoke softly, as though hesitant to interrupt her thoughts. Erika wiped her eyes and seeing that the other servants had gone, undressed, and stepped into the tub.

Sylvia poured warm water over her shoulders, rubbed oils onto her parched skin and massaged her neck. "You had a hard time on the island?"

"I almost died, Sylvia. I have been a foolish youth, making one mistake after another. Count this the worst of them," Erika leaned back as Sylvia rubbed her temples.

"We are all young once. I have often wondered how any of us survived," she said, her wrinkled smile and bright blue eyes revealed as much wisdom as Chief Silas. More. Sylvia had a kindness about her.

"I'm sorry you had such a rough journey. Your father considered this trip dangerous for you," Sylvia said.

"Dangerous?" Erika sighed. "Is love the most dangerous trial in the world?" Erika breathed deeply. The oils Sylvia used refreshed her spirits and soothed her sorrow.

"I'm not sure what you're asking?"

"Life gives each of us problems to overcome. Purpose, adventure, peril. But the trial of love I find to be the most dangerous."

"Is there someone you fell in love with on Cho Nisi?"

"There is. Forbidden love. And now my heart will be forever broken, all because of my mistakes."

Sylvia frowned and gently nudged Erika's head back, washing her hair with soapwort scented with lavender. "Forever is a long time, Fairest."

"Forever is the time it will take for me to heal."

"You need a mother's love," she said sweetly, kissing her on the forehead. Sylvia had been Erika's nanny when her mother died, and though Erika grew up more with her brother, she remembered the gentle years being rocked in Sylvia's arms by the fire.

"Thank you, Sylvia, but I'm afraid it's not a mother's love my heart pines for." Tears formed in her eyes as she recalled Arell's embrace on the beach.

"Tell me about him, then." Sylvia had Erika sit up in the tub and poured water over her head, rinsing the soap from her hair.

"He is tall, handsome, and has the most beautiful eyes I have ever seen. Dark eyes, but not so dark as a cave. More like chestnuts in autumn."

"His hair is dark as well?"

"Yes, the same color as his eyes. And his skin is as if he lives under the sun perpetually, but not creased or wrinkled like a sailor, instead smooth and luscious."

"And his voice?"

"Soft. He speaks slowly and thoughtfully unless he's being cynical, which he is sometimes. But looking back at his wit, I have to laugh. My words were as scathing as his."

Sylvia grinned. "I can see that. So, you met your match, did you?"

Erika's smile lessened at the words Sylvia used. Yes. She met her match, and she lost him. There could be no other!

"He's gone, Sylvia. Love held us close for a fleeting moment and now it's gone."

"Oh, life might surprise you," the woman tried to comfort her, to no avail.

She might as well have been severed in two by a sword. Her punishment hurt so painfully.

"Love can be as cold as ice when it's annulled," she whispered, her heart becoming stone, tears refusing to fall.

"Perhaps it still lives, my dear."

"They will kill me if I return."

"We cannot tell the future. Besides, you're a beautiful young woman. There are many men who are equally handsome, who are not life threatening. Perhaps your father knows of someone."

Erika shook her head. Sweet loving Sylvia didn't understand. The servant stood and unfolded a soft linen towel.

"There you are. Fresh and clean and smelling like the garden in spring. Hurry now and dry off before you get a chill. Your family is eager to see you and the cook is preparing a meal." Sylvia wrapped her in a towel, and with another dried her hair.

"At this hour?"

"Your father requested it, yes, and he's had everyone in the family paged. They are happy you are safe, my child, as am I."

Sylvia pulled Erika's bloomers out of her drawer and helped her dress. When the servant held up a corset, Erika shook her head. "No, not tonight, please. It's just family and I want to be comfortable for once."

"Very well."

Once dressed, Erika dismissed Sylvia and took a moment to gaze into the polished bronze mirror on her vanity. She had aged. Oh, she still had the smooth skin of a young woman, and strength still coursed through her body, but something inside of her—a sadness—added years she hadn't expected. Her wild drive to fulfill a purpose had faded. Sure, she'd fight again. More so than ever. How could she not with all the perils her people faced? But the hope for happiness remained somewhere in a castle on an island far away.

She turned and faced the ornately hinged door of her room and took a deep breath. She couldn't imagine what sort of reception awaited her.

Homecoming

The family stood behind the solid cherry-wood chairs. Candles lit their faces and glistened in the silver setting. White linen napkins in complicated folds dressed their plates and savory breads peeked out of tightly woven baskets. Father remained at the head of the dinner table, wearing a smile on his face, with Barin beside him. Her brother lifted his chin, his face solemn.

Rhea and Olinda, in clothes as comfortable as her chemise, faced each other at the table. Olinda put her palm over her mouth when she yawned. Rhea refused to meet Erika's eyes, fingering the tip of her chair. That left the seat across from Father vacant, and she ambled silently to her place.

"Greetings, everyone," she said. It wasn't confidence she wielded, but resentment. "It's wonderful to be home."

"Erika! Come give me a greeting!" Her father offered his open arms and after Erika studied her siblings briefly as they remained steadfast like soldiers not budging, nor speaking, she hurried to her father and embraced him. King Tobias stood a good foot taller than her, broad shouldered, with a coarse gray beard that tickled her forehead when she put her head against his chest. He was thinner than she remembered.

"I missed you," she said.

He patted her gently on the back. "I'm glad you're home. You must tell me about your trip to Cho Nisi. How did our neighbors treat you?"

She stepped away and pulled the chair out for him.

"A jarring experience," she mumbled and took her place, eyeing her brother as she passed him. He avoided her glance and seated himself after she sat down. As cold as they were, she wondered if she even wanted to be friends with anyone in the family besides her Father.

"How so?" her father asked, frowning.

"Well, they attacked us with arrows when we first arrived before they knew who we were." She eyed them all. They kept eating. No reaction.

"Rory came back. Why did you not return with him?"

"I...they didn't let me."

Her father looked up, concerned. "Then it's true. You were a prisoner?"

"Of sorts, I guess you could say so."

"Did they know you killed their king?" Barin asked, scooping a portion of turnips onto his plate.

"Not right off, no."

"And still they kept you prisoner, not knowing what you did?"

"Well, yes, I guess."

"And attacked you, threatening to kill you," her father had stopped eating.

"I don't think they were trying to kill me."

"Oh, come now, Erika. If a man is shooting at you, he doesn't do it for the fun of it. You, of all people, should know that." Barin interjected.

"An assault against my family is an attack against our kingdom, Erika," the king reminded her.

Erika bit her tongue. Explaining what had happened would confuse them, and how could she ever rationalize falling in love with the Cho Nisi king? Why should she? Already a rift between Cho Nisi and the Potamian Kingdom had developed because of her. Had the islanders executed her, they would have sealed a declaration of war. Chief Silas had been adamant about her banishment, perhaps to mollify the situation so they wouldn't have to fight her father's army. The death sentence if she stepped foot on the island again justified any future actions. It also kept her away from Arell.

"Kairos is going with Barin to Fairmistle tomorrow," Olinda remarked casually. "No one's going to Tellwater though." She looked up.

"Why do you speak of Tellwater, Olinda?" Barin snapped. "Those are war matters, not for ladies to discuss." He glanced at Erika. She placed several steamed carrots on her plate.

"I must say, I worked up an appetite coming here. Thank you, everyone for leaving the comfort of your soft beds to dine with me. I missed you all." Erika ignored the look Barin gave her.

"Ladies can discuss any matters they choose, Barin," Rhea retorted. "Especially when it concerns a fiancé."

"Fiancé?" Erika asked. "I didn't know. Congratulations."

"Kairos proposed to Rhea, but Father hasn't consented, and Kairos is leaving for war, so we'll see what happens." Olinda said.

"Why do you drone on about Kairos taking up arms?" Rhea asked her twin. "As though you hope ill fate befalls him."

"No, I don't hope for calamity for Kairos. Kairos is a nice man. I just think maybe Erika would like to go off to war with him."

Erika set her cup down and stared at Olinda.

"Erika is not going to take up arms with Kairos, ever again!" Rhea blurted the exact moment Barin bellowed "No!"

The king held up his hand for silence. "Erika is not going to war. She is, in fact, staying home where she belongs, and I'll be arranging some private tutoring for her. I have work in my study she can help me with. Please, let's make this homecoming peaceful. You can work out your differences another time. Preferably when I'm not around."

The king's order quieted them.

"Is Rory going to Fairmistle with you, again Barin?" Erika asked, hoping that wouldn't be a subject too disruptive.

"Rory from Fairmistle is in prison for deserting Barin when he left with you," Olinda announced none too friendly.

"What?" Erika gaped and nearly choked. When no one responded, she took a breath and then picked at her food, fuming inside. That poor boy, he had only been following orders. Deserter?

"Barin, you can't keep him imprisoned."

"It's not up to me," Barin stated.

She peered at her father. What had she expected? Perhaps she needed to atone to Barin, but not to the twins, and she refused to apologize to Barin in front of her sisters. She would do so alone. In the morning.

News of Rory's situation made her stomach upset. She set her napkin down. "I'm extremely tired from the long journey. Father, might I be excused from the table?"

King Tobias nodded and stood when she rose, Barin did so also, as etiquette demanded. Erika curtsied.

"Good night, Father. Everyone."

When she woke, the sun streamed through white curtains gilded with morning golds and pinks. Her window let in the eastern light, and a view of the meadow where horses grazed. Last night's snow had melted, and only a few patches of ice speckled the fields. After donning her robe, she watched the soldiers sparring at dawn, readying themselves for their journey east, a battle she had no regrets missing.

Determined to speak to Barin before he left, she chose a surcoat, as she had no time to tackle a corset. Intent on renewing her relationship with him, she snatched her overcoat from the closet and hurried through the halls, exiting out one of the back doors to the sparring fields.

Barin waited in the courtyard with his men-at-arms as his new squire laced his armor. His gaze followed her as she ran to him. Before she reached him, she slowed. Barin's squire had just finished tying the last knot and bowed with her arrival.

"May I have one moment of your time, Barin? Before you go?"

They locked eyes and stayed fixed for a moment. When the squire had laced his arm-guards, Barin excused him and offered Erika his arm. They meandered away from the busy soldiers to a quiet part of the garden where she took her hand away and he leaned, half-sitting, against a garden wall.

"What, my fair sister, may I do for you?" he asked. "Barin, I wish to ask for your forgiveness."

"Whatever for?" He looked past her at his soldiers sparring in the field, and at the horses being saddled and bags packed.

"For deserting you. And for bringing some of your army and Kairos with me. For giving Rory consent to leave you. I was wrong. Foolish. Reckless."

He glanced at her—his blond lashes half-shielding his blue eyes. "You were. You could have died, Erika. Think how Father would have fallen into despair if that had happened. Far away in a land unknown to him, his youngest most precious daughter slain by allies. As it were, his health has declined with worry over you."

"I'm sorry." Erika looked away. "Could you forgive Rory, also?"

"Rory has probationary work. In the garden. He's not imprisoned any longer. Olinda exaggerated, making things sound worse than they are. Father said he would release Rory as soon as you returned, and so he did."

"And you?"

"What about me?"

"I want to be on good terms with you before you leave." Erika's heart beat hard. He hadn't been this kind to her since that fateful day in Tellwater. She didn't want to waste the opportunity. The sun beat on her brother's fair hair, his shining armor almost too bright to look at.

"Ah! So, you think I will meet my end this time, do you?"

"No! I mean, I hope not! Why?"

"Usually, people want forgiveness when they assume the other person will die. It's a way of shirking the guilt they've buried without adding more."

She crossed her arms and shook her head. "I don't know about other people, Barin, but I want forgiveness because you're my brother and I love you."

He only stared at her, but she detected a slight smile.

"Barin, please just say you forgive me."

His stance softened, and with it his eyes. "Erika, Erika—" He wore dark leather gloves that were warm and smooth when he touched her hand. "You're my baby sister and will always have a place in my heart. When Kairos came home without you, I wanted to hurt him. You play with our emotions as if you were skipping rocks in the river, tossing our hearts as far as you can throw to see if we sink or not."

His words struck a painful chord inside of her. She bowed her head and fidgeted with a pleat in her dress.

He lifted her chin.

"I've considered all that has happened, and confess I bear some responsibility. When Father told me you were in Cho Nisi I worried. When I heard you came home last night, a tremendous burden dropped off my shoulders. Those people could have killed you. You are family and no matter what odds we're at, I still love you." He looked away again, watching his troops make ready for travel.

"I had a hand in King Rolland's death. I knew the Cho Nisi must have been hiding nearby, but I failed to warn you. I should have been more careful as I know those warriors can sneak about in the brush like a fox. I blame myself for his death as well."

Erika exhaled, comforted by his words.

"I also haven't told you, but what you did in Canyon Gia made me proud."

"Proud?"

"Yes. You didn't panic, you were brave, clever, and showed your compassion. All the signs of a good soldier. Being the youngest sibling, you were the spoiled one, but I think I spoiled you as much as Father did. I only wanted for you to be happy. Fulfilled. I wished to see you meet your goals. But you're not ready yet, Erika. You aren't ready to be a hero. Stay with Father. He's not doing well. He's going blind and may be dying. Be the daughter he wants you to be. Be his hero. For now. Until you get old enough to fulfill your dreams." He took her hands and squeezed them affectionately.

"I love you, Barin. I'll take care of our father. You just come home soon and safely."

"I plan on it. Now let me get to my men. We have a long journey ahead of us and some terrible demons to face. We may be gone all winter."

"Be careful!"

"Always. And you study hard. Keep up your sword training. Someday we may need you back on the battlefield when you have a bit more of your senses about you." He smiled at her, touched her nose, and pinched her ear.

She watched him walk away. Kairos lingered in the fields with the others with Rhea on his arm. They kissed, such a long passionate kiss that Barin had to break them up. Rhea stepped back and the troops, now ready to depart, mounted their steeds.

Her father emerged from the castle, and with his guards, and his scepter, said a blessing over them. And then the hundreds of troops headed into the forest. Many horses and carts followed. Such a long line of travelers! Erika didn't think she'd see the end. Civilian merchants and their wares, cook's carts covered and filled with grain. Carts carrying livestock, geese and chickens and a herd of goats. Soldiers leading horses trailed behind them all. The size of the army, and how well armed they were traveling indicated they expected to be away a long while. She worried for them and whispered a prayer to the gods in her father's hall for their safe return.

Captured

Barin rode a bit taller in the saddle as he watched the company go before him. Four hundred soldiers, six hundred horses, sixty-four civilian carts, a wizard and sixteen apprentice wizards. Neal pulled his horse next to Beau.

"Lord Garion will be pleased. Extremely pleased," the commander said, confidently.

Carts passed them carrying barrels of food, water, goats, chickens, fodder, and dried firewood, weapons, and a blacksmith's wagon. The assembly was to split once it came to Ream River. Neal would take a third of the company into the Tellwater Valley and meet up with Felix and his men. They would divide the troops, horses, and food. All but the sheep, for Lord Garion had his own if the skura hadn't pillaged the rest of his livestock. From the foothills Barin would march his men into Fairmistle and the river basin, stationing men in intervals, around towns and villages, bringing them much needed supplies and protecting the country people. He'd teach them the tricks to kill mountain giants too. There, the men-at-arms would stay until springtime, or until the enemy threat had lessened, whichever came first.

They traveled slowly.

Leaving while still winter had been a change in plans and found Barin's company nearer to Mount Ream than initially intended. A blizzard had slowed the company's travels, and because the passage down the canyon was next to impossible in the snowstorm, the weather forced them to make camp in the highlands before they reached the junction along Ream River.

Barin patrolled the campsite as the tents were raised, and

campfires built. He trudged through the icy snow with his head bowed to ward off the cold. Traveling had gone smoothly up to this point. If he were superstitious, he would be wrapped in dread as well as in his wool cloak and scarves. Whispers of impending ill fate seemed to ride on the winter chill, though the voices were discreet, and he could have been imagining them. Perhaps the wind played with his mind.

He nodded a greeting to those setting up camp, lending a hand with a tent when needed and checking to make certain everyone had ample provisions.

"Evening, Vasil," Madeline, one of the camp cooks, greeted him as Barin walked up to her cart. "We're brewing up a chicken broth for the soldiers they can mix in with their stews. We'll have it ready soon." Hens squawked as her husband and two other men pulled pullets from a cage in their wagon and took them out to the woods, hatchets in hand.

"Thank you," Barin said, his breath like steam. "I'll let the soldiers know. Ask those men to bury what you don't use. There are scavengers in these parts that would do more damage than just cleaning up after a butchering. We don't want to leave the scent of blood."

"Of course, Vasil."

"I'll let the men know to expect some broth tonight," he said.

"Expecting trouble?" Talos asked as Barin passed his campfire. A large man, Talos had several years on Barin. Fair-haired, bearded, and mild-mannered Barin enjoyed spending time with him. A good leader, having fought by Barin's side in many battles, Talos had been assigned a company of soldiers to oversee. He offered Barin a mug of mulled wine, and Barin gladly accepted. Even though the prince wore thick leather gloves, the heat from the cup sent warmth through his body. He sat on a log next to Talos and enjoyed the fire.

"Two days out of Prasa Potama and we've had no incidents. With this large of a company, we've been fortunate. We're on the mountain now, though, Talos. I don't know what to expect."

"Been watching those hills," Talos nodded, holding his cup close to his lips. The steam of the hot wine merged with his foggy breath. "Sometimes I don't know if it's the wind picking up the snow, or that devil-wizard's mountain giants creeping about."

"Fear will play tricks with our minds, Talos, but in a place like Mount Ream, we can't be too cautious." Barin gazed into the dull gray woods. Only the trunks of the trees offered contrast against the snow.

"Have your men keep vigil tonight. I want the livestock and horses guarded with an extra patrol."

"Yes, sire. I don't suppose anyone is going to sleep much, anyway."

Barin finished his wine and handed the mug back to Talos as he stood. "Keep hot coals in your fire pit just in case."

By the time Barin had made his rounds, most of the soldiers had already cleaned up after their meal and retired. Their campfires dwindled to hot embers and fading streams of smoke.

The prince returned to his tent, where Neal stirred a pot of soup made from dried vegetables and rutabagas, a broth which warmed his insides and renewed his strength. But nothing would calm his nerves. The sooner the expedition reached the valley, the better he'd feel.

"I think if the snow subsides tomorrow, we can move on down the ravine. Once off the mountain, the trail to Tellwater follows the river. My party will head south from there into the plains." Barin suggested, warming his hands over the coals. Snowflakes sizzled on the embers and steam twirled into the sky.

"And I travel with whom?" Kairos asked. "You never quite made that clear."

"That's because we were feeling things out, Kairos," Barin blew into his gloves to warm them. "Wherever the threat is the greatest. Father says you've become a champion against our enemy now."

"Did he? Well, that's good to know I have your father's faith. I have plenty of vials with me, but I'm not sure how it reacts should it freeze. For now, they're tucked under my chemise. But if you could get me to a warmer climate, I'm sure they'd function much better."

Barin shook his head and smiled. "Kairos, Kairos, when are you going to take this war seriously? We need you where the threat is greatest. Not where you'll be the most comfortable."

"Yes, I know," the wizard mumbled, brushing his long locks behind his ears and wrapping his cloak tighter around himself. "But you can't blame a fellow for trying. I'm serious about the frozen vials, though. If we have to wait for them to thaw…" his voice tapered when Barin stood, staring up into the hills.

"I'll try to persuade our prince to allow you to come to Tellwater with me. The concentration of Skura there, and this news of them stealing children seems to warrant your services." Neal said.

Kairos's eyes lit up. "Ah! The vineyards!"

Barin grinned and winked at Neal. He had already considered

sending Kairos to the valley. His smile faded, though, while observing the slopes above them.

"What? What do you see?" Neal asked, rising next to him.

"Tell me that's just snow up there," Barin whispered over the subtle sound of a crackling of the fire and his heart hammering.

"Snow. Or mist." Neal said.

The sun had already fallen below the horizon, leaving a dark but brilliant blue sky. Ice on the mountain accented its hues and a thin wisp of snow still floated in the air, preventing Barin from seeing further than his immediate camp. He had been on this mountain before, and his experience had not been a happy one. If the giants were creeping toward him, he wanted to know before he woke up to the sound of bones crushing.

"Build this fire up," Neal suggested as he pulled wood from out of the tent.

Barin signaled for a sentry who'd been patrolling nearby. The man jogged to meet him. "Send word to the men to stay alert. Campfires should burn visibly all night. Also, no one may wander away from camp."

"Yes, sir."

Within minutes, the men-at-arms and civilians both had been alerted and dozens of fires ignited again so that smoke filled the basin.

"Is it our job to keep them away? Or to destroy them?" Kairos asked. "I mean, just out of curiosity."

"Right now, our job is to get to our destinations. If that means killing mountain giants, that's what we do. However, my dear sorcerer, we have not yet found the secret to destroying these devils. We can make them less harmful with fire, but a flame will merely drive them away, not extinguish them from existence."

"Ah! I see," Kairos lifted a finger and looked Barin in the eye. "Which will be your father's next project for me, I assume."

"Yes, you can rightfully make that assumption. And if you can devise some sort of magic tonight, we'll gladly test it for you."

"For me to do that, I must know more about these creatures."

Barin watched the mist for a while longer, but already the smell of smoke traveled up the mountainside. If there were giants approaching, they would sense the fire. Fortunately, the heavy fog he'd seen before had dissipated.

"Relax, Barin," Neal suggested. "I see nothing. If there's a threat, we can make torches like Erika and Rory did in Canyon Gia."

Funny that Neal should mention Erika regarding mountain giants. Barin considered their parting words and how pardoning her had freed him of a burden he'd been carrying. He sat on a log next to Neal and confronted the wizard.

"We don't know a lot about them. Anyone from Fairmistle can tell you the rumors and legends. How much truth they hold, I don't know. What I know is that they live as a mist on the mountain and are drawn to flesh. Like any predator, they kill, and as their victims die, the mist manifests into giants made of stone, and then they become harder still, like iron."

"And how do they kill if they're only a fog to begin with?"

"They hunt in packs. When they snare their prey, they gather until they become a dense fog. The denser the fog, the more they weigh until their weight crushes their victim." Neal explained. "It's almost as if the act of killing is what they feed on—what gives them their bodies."

Kairos shuddered and moved closer to the fire. "You'd think their victims would squirm away before it came to that."

"There's no time. Had it not been for Rory, Samuel and Erika, Neal and I would be nothing but a pile of bones left to rot in Canyon Gia." Barin said. "Let's stoke that fire and let it burn through the night. Get some sleep, we'll need it. We have a long day tomorrow, snow or no snow."

Eager to get the company moving, Barin slept little and rose before sunrise. Bundled in his cloak, he stepped outside of his tent, puffed a cloud of steam in the night air, and marched through the camp, waking the men.

"Pack up. We're leaving," he ordered.

The word rippled through the campsite. Soon horses were saddled, tents folded and packed away, and campfires put out. The sunrise brought a cloudless sky, and a deep freeze. Barin shuddered from the cold. The sooner they were off the mountain, the better.

The narrow road to the ravine allowed the carts passage but barely. Travel would be slow and might take an entire day to get the last of their company to the flatlands. Having come this far with no mishaps, Barin considered their fortune good, but such good fortune comes with a price. The stillness of the mountain made him tense. This country belonged to the Mountain giants, and they were trespassing.

Barin divided the company so that well-armed men rode alongside the livestock, and armed men surrounded the civilians. Neal would lead with a portion of his troops, and Kairos would ride with him, so if skura attacked as they entered the ravine, Kairos would be up front. Barin and the best of his men, and several apprentice magicians would bring up the rear, the magicians riding in a cart directly in front of him. Stationing spotters along the way allowed for word to travel through the caravan easily and without error.

Neal left before dawn. The carts followed. By the time the last of the horses entered the gorge, the sun had already risen. Aside from what snow blanketed the trail head, most of the powder had either been packed down, or melted as the sun hit the canyon walls. Small streams trickled in crevices along the buttes. Barin allowed his men to ride first and followed last, Talos at his side.

With some difficulty, two horses could walk side by side on the trail, but because of the steep banks and icy surface, Barin let Talos ride in front of him. The line of travelers was visible as far as the next switchback and they were not moving as quickly as he would like, often coming to a complete halt.

One such delay for an especially long interval brought a spotter to them. Barin could still see the trailhead above when they stopped.

"There's a cart up ahead that's broken an axle," the young man's horse wheezed, its sweat foamed on its chest as the spotter tried to calm the animal.

"How far down?"

"Midway."

"Do you need me?" Barin asked.

"No, sir. It's taken care of. We're unloading the cargo into another cart and will roll the vehicle over the side of the cliff to get it out of the way. We're not in a place to fix an axle. No one wants to stay in this canyon. We have spotted skura nesting in the oaks."

"How far from here did you see the skura?"

"Two switchbacks down, Vasil. The horses are nervous, so be careful." He patted his mount and spoke calmly to the animal. "We're hoping to reach bottom before sunset."

"How far has Neal gotten?"

"He's made camp already. Someone said he's down there fishing." The scout laughed. "They told me to let you know."

"Yes, thanks I appreciate that. I expect fish for dinner! And you're right, the sooner we're out of this gorge, the better we'll all be." Barin snickered. "Fishing, eh?"

The man saluted and rode away, disappearing around a switchback.

"No sense sitting on this animal longer than I need to," Barin told Talos as he dismounted and took a drink of water from his gourd. "Take a break, Talos."

Talos remained saddled, eyeing the cliffs above him. "I don't know, Vasil, I don't enjoy lingering on this mountain. The hair on my arms' standing straight up."

"I'm not too fond of this ledge either."

"Keep thinking we're being followed." Talos' voice trembled.

Barin glanced up at the cliffs that surrounded them and pulled his cloak tighter around his shoulders. White stone bluffs towered over the trail—icy, rocky, and desolate—absorbing the residues of the sun's warmth. Straggly half-formed firs reached out in space, their roots spreading like fingers grasping for illusory soil. Boulders balanced precariously over them, threatening to tumble.

"Keep a sharp eye out, then Talos. I never discount a soldier's intuition."

"Yes, sir. I don't see why we don't just move everyone from Tellwater to Prasa Potama. It'd be much easier protecting folks there."

"It would seem. Except not everyone would live in the city, nor could they adapt. Country folk have their own lifestyle. Besides, we need farmers to till the soil. Not much farming goes on in the city."

"No, but not much farming in mid-winter. Should bring them all home with us. At least while the dark lord is sending his army out to kill people. It makes it extra hard for us to keep them safe."

Barin laughed to himself. Talos had little knowledge of how populated the Potamian farming regions were. "You're talking about hundreds of serfs, Talos. Prasa Potama couldn't hold that many people."

"You know best, Vasil. Just a thought."

The sun had risen to its zenith, and still the company hadn't advanced. Rolling a cart off the side of the cliff must be harder than it seemed. Barin mounted Beau again. "I'm going to check on this obstruction. We should be moving by now."

Before he passed the magicians' wagon, dust and flying snow shot out onto the road ahead of him. The neigh of terrified horses echoed up the canyon. The scream of skura followed. Winged creatures filled the gorge and attacked the livestock.

Barin and Talos drew their crossbows, but the horse pulling the cart with the magicians spooked and bolted forward. Talos took off after it. His mount stumbled over the rocks and then slipped and skidded off the road. Talos rolled with his horse as it tumbled down the side of the bank. Before his horse slammed into a rock, Talos went spinning from his saddle onto the craggy cliff below. Barin watched helplessly.

Someone had calmed the magicians' horses, and the apprentices had already shot streams of lightning at the skura, annihilating them with bursts of explosions. Further down the gorge men still shouted orders, and an occasional bolt flew from a crossbow. But they had killed the skura.

Barin jumped off Beau and skidded over to the bank. Talos had fallen into a ravine where the slopes were steep and slippery. One wave from Talos showed the soldier was alive. He held his leg, and attempted to stand, but instead fell again.

"I'm coming," Barin told him, and slid further down the mountain, losing his balance as he hit a bank of mud and ice. When he finally reached the man, Talos groaned.

"I think I broke my hip. I can't move my leg at all."

Barin glanced at the dead horse and wondered how he'd get Talos back up the hill. Or down the hill.

"Looks like they're moving again," Talos said between groans of pain.

"That they are," Barin agreed as he watched the caravan. From where they were in the ravine, the company appeared no larger than a parade of ants. He hadn't realized how far down the mountain Talos had fallen.

"Blazing varmints devouring whatever isn't theirs!"

"It appears the magicians have rid us of them all."

The caravan moved on, soon disappearing out of sight. No one seemed to notice that Barin and Talos weren't with them. The Magicians were fighting skura, and everyone else had already moved ahead. Barin pushed his cloak off his shoulders and wiped his hands on his pants, regarding how he might lift Talos. "Guess I carry you."

"They'll discover their prince missing soon enough, won't they?"

"Possibly, but what can they do? Pulling you up over those boulders will be impossible and the sun will be down soon. Sending out a search party for us will be dangerous. I hope they don't. I'll carry you down this mountainside and meet them at the river."

"Blazing idols, Vasil, you can't carry me I'm twice your weight. And we have to climb out of this ravine before we can descend the mountain."

"I'm not leaving you here."

"Let me lean on you, then."

Barin supported Talos as the man stood, even though the older man's height and weight exceeded Barin's, making it harder for Barin to prop him upright. They took a step, and then another. Slowly the two inched across the steep and rocky terrain, resting frequently whenever they came to level ground or a boulder to sit on. The sun set quicker than they moved, and they could see the river far below them, campfires being lit, tents being pitched, but at their pace, they would not reach the river until well into the night. They heard scouts calling for them once and answered. The men must not have heard them, for the search party's calls subsided and the dark of night crept over them and silence returned. They were so far from the road and hidden in the gorge, Barin doubted anyone would find them that night.

As the hour grew late, fog rose from the river, a natural occurrence that happened as a chill swept over the flowing waters. Yet Barin couldn't help but remember the misty manifestation of mountain giants the last time he crossed this mountain range. He seldom gave into fear, but the pain of being crushed by the beasts still haunted him.

"You're trembling, Vasil. I know that feeling. You should just set me down and get to your men. I'm not worth the blood of a prince."

"Nonsense, Talos, I'm not abandoning you," Barin insisted.

Fog grew thicker and soon he could see nothing in the distance, not the river, nor the sycamore trees that grew in the basin, nor the fires of the campsites. Talos collapsed again. "Let me just rest here, Vasil. I can't move any more. Pain's too great. Maybe we could sleep a bit before we go any further."

Barin stood up straight. His back hurt from supporting Talos, and so he took a drink of water and stretched. When the fog which hovered around their feet materialized, he jumped away.

"Talos, look out," Barin warned and drew his sword, but misty fingers immediately flicked away his blade. Barin froze, stunned, watching a mountain giant take shape. The ogre's body appeared moss covered, hard and cold. He had huge shoulders and a beard and hair made of lichen. Barin staggered backward, tripping over his cloak. The giant's hands blocked any means of escape and closed in around him, making a rock wall Barin could neither penetrate nor climb over.

He faced the giant, surprised that he wasn't being crushed.

"Who are you?" The mountain giant asked.

Barin's heart raced, yet he stood tall. "I am Barin, son of King Tobias, Lord of this land."

The giant shook his head slowly. "Well greetings Barin, I'm Sol. Prince of the mountain giants. I come and go as I please, for I'm the personal assistant of your Lord Skotádi. King Tobias is not lord of this land. There is another greater than any man." His mouth turned upward into a smile, though a toothless one. Where his eyes should have been, mist swirled in the sockets instead. The mountain giant folded his hands tighter, pressing against Barin's body. "My liege will be happy to see that I've caught me a prince. Extremely happy."

Barin made one last attempt to climb out of the giant's grasp, but the giant's stony fingers pinched him tightly. Talos lay on the ground, eyes wide in shock, unable to move. The giant lifted Barin higher, so he was level with his wicked toothless smile. His breath smelled like the air in a musty cave.

"Lord Skotádi is going to love you, yes indeed," he said as he poked against Barin's chest, knocking the wind out of the prince. "You're coming with me."

Osage

Arell stood on his favorite hillside overlooking the northern shore. He could hear the drums of the warriors on the beaches below. They'd been on guard ever since Erika left, worried that King Tobias would send his soldiers to the island, or that more skura would appear. Despite Cho Nisi having been at peace with all of its neighbors for more than half a century, the people expected trouble now. Even Chief Silas had suggested Arell pick up a sword and learn to fight like his ancestors, the Casdamians.

"You never know if someone greater than the king's daughter will challenge you. They know our magic. Maybe they have spells to counter our charms. They know about you, that an heir sits on the throne. You must protect yourself. Our magic cannot be everywhere."

With the trial and banishment of the murderer of his father, came a sense of urgency. Silas called it "maturity". Arell spent more time at the library in Moaton learning his people's history and their war strategies, talking to the immigrants who lived there, learning their names and who his father's people were. He tired of emotional pain and had grown weary of wrestling with his sentiments. He spent less time on the beaches, having less desire to flirt with Silas' daughters and her friends. Erika had done something to him, planted a distrust for women in his heart. Either that or a distrust of falling in love. He missed her terribly, but whenever he thought of her, he trained himself to think of his father, instead. The struggle proved difficult, but to survive the emotional whirlwind of passion, he had to nullify his love for her. So far with little success.

He tired, also, of depending on the Cho Nisi to be the sole protectors of the island. Their magic hinged on whether they believed in their cause. What if in the future there was a disagreement? Had the elders executed Erika—and that had been a decision they had wavered on—he'd have been devastated. Even that they had considered her death caused him to mistrust them and made him question his allegiance to the tribe. Was he really more a Cho Nisi than a Casdamian? Or was he influenced by neither, ready to take the Crown into his own hands and challenge the islanders?

He still respected the Cho Nisi, yet he needed to defend himself against predators, be they of the devil, or Potamian, or female.

He sighted no ships in the distance that morning, and so Arell walked into the village. Robed in his regal cloak and gold embroidered blue doublet, he marched the streets as a king, his boots tapping softly on the cobblestone road.

He nodded to an elderly woman sweeping leaves from her doorstep. She bowed and whispered as he passed. "Vasil. May your passage be safe and your life long," she added. Chills ran up his spine, as if her prayers were an augury, words that needed utterance to avoid some tragic fate.

"Thank you," he breathed.

The heavy smell of metal melting drew him to the blacksmith's tent, and a man named Osage. A muscular fellow, in his middle years. He wore only a vest on his upper body, his biceps sweating from the heat of the forge. With thick leather gloves protecting his forearms, he maneuvered the forceps artfully. Arell watched him move the block of glowing metal back and forth between an anvil and a hot coal furnace, pumping the bellows alternately. When Osage finished, he lay the blade back in the coals, wiped his head with a rag and nodded to Arell.

"Vasil."

"I've come to learn from you," Arell said.

"What? Blacksmithing?"

"The long sword, sir. And quarter-staffing. Defense."

Osage pulled off his gloves, wiped his face again, and then his hands, stepping away from the fire. "I'm not a master, but I can show you some technique. We have had no one interested in sword fighting since we left Casdamia. I build these mostly for collectors. But, as a king, if you feel it is necessary...."

"It is necessary. And I would have you come to the castle if you please. We'll work in private."

"All right, Vasil. I will oblige. When?"

"As soon as possible. In the morning?"

"That's possible."

"Perfect. And please, bring a couple of your best weapons. I will purchase them from you."

Osage bowed and Arell acknowledged the honor with a cordial nod, moving on. He would visit the library again. Books pertaining to Casdamian's history lined the shelves, and he hadn't had the time to indulge before this, being preoccupied with lesser matters. Erika, for one.

He had questions about his heritage and suspected he could find the answers in those tomes. Questions such as why his grandfather left the region in such haste with hundreds of other immigrants. Had he been part of the insurrection? And why had they traveled as far as they did to an island, when they could have migrated a short distance to the Potamian province? Who drove them away? Perhaps he would discover the reason his father fought alongside King Tobias in those books.

Moaton was a tightly built and tightly knit settlement with narrow streets and tall flats constructed of cut stone built one upon the other. So tall were the apartments that three or four families lived in them comfortably. The residents seldom wandered past their yards and rarely traveled to the beaches. Seclusive by nature, and unlike his mother's people, Moatons kept to their own, which is why he rarely saw the residents on the streets. They gardened from their windows with large pots on hangers supporting both flowers and vegetables. They kept a pasture on the slopes of the castle for sheep and goat. Young men from the village enlisted in the king's guard and supported their families with their wages. Moaton, however, did not depend solely on coins for their economy but worked in the barter system. Moaton merchants were the only class of their people who reached out to the Cho Nisi, bringing carts to the beaches to trade fabric for seafood. That so many Moatons had showed up at his father's grave to feast had been a surprise, for the two ethnic groups got along hollowly at best.

The narrow door to the library creaked when he opened it, and the ring of a bell disturbed the silence. Immediately the smell of books filled his senses. All shapes and sizes of leather journals tied shut with lacing lined the walls. Trunks of scrolls stood upright against them. Some writings were carried by mule over the plains and shipped to their new home on sailing vessels half a century ago. The immigrants had been on the island fifty to seventy-five years, arriving the year that Arell's grandfather fled the war. He'd been a leader of some sort of rebellion, Arell didn't know the particulars, his father never told him. Now would be a good time for him to discover his roots.

"Vasil," a boy no older than thirteen years bowed cordially, feather duster in his hand, his doublet a fine garment of red linen, not the quality of royalty, but handsome none the less. "May I help you, sire?"

"Yes, I think so. I've come to research, and I believe there's a master librarian who works here who can help me. Do you know where he might be?"

"Yes, Master Oliver. I'll fetch him for you." The boy disappeared through another small door beyond the many aisles of books and documents. Arell browsed through the shelves, looking for titles or indications that would suggest history, hesitant to touch the fragile parchments for fear they'd crumble and turn to dust.

"Some of those journals are older than your grandfather would be if he had lived to this day," a feeble voice informed him. A small man, Master Oliver barely reached above the top of the desk, his face wrinkled, white hair thinning on the sides of his head, yet thick as a cap on the top. He wore spectacles that balanced on the tip of his nose, and he had a cleft in his chin that several whiskers tried to hide. "Vasil," he added. "I wondered when you would come to talk about him. Better that you inquire of these things before they carry me to my grave. Least wise there are few who can tell you all there is to know."

"You knew my grandfather?"

"I didn't just know him, I fled the country with him. Crossed the plains of Casdamia and boarded that old merchant ship *The Rendezvous* with him."

"Why hadn't Father told me?" Arell questioned, fascinated that all this time someone in Moaton had known his grandfather personally. Surely his father would have introduced friends from the old country to him. That Oliver had never been to the castle to tell his stories puzzled him.

"Could be your father wanted to forget his roots. Don't blame him. It's a dark past, and he and your grandfather never got along since they arrived on the island. Oh, for the public's benefit they were cordial with each other, but your granddaddy he told me some things about that relationship you might not want to know! He didn't want rumors to spread, so he hid away after he relinquished the throne to your father."

"Grandfather gave up the throne?" Arell had thought his father had inherited the Crown when his grandfather died. "May we talk? I mean, some place more comfortable?"

Master Oliver chuckled. "You're a lot like him, you know, Old Win, your granddad. From what I've heard of you. Come on, I have a study in the back room." He waved Arell to follow and, with a cane and a limp, led the young king into a dark but cozy flat. A cook stove heated the room, and an iron kettle steamed. One small window let a hint of light inside, hindered by a dirty blue curtain. The boy who had greeted Arell had just finished eating cake when Arell entered.

"Jamie, watch the library, will you?" Oliver asked.

"Yes sir," the boy bowed to Arell on his way out.

"I came looking for books that might tell me what happened in Casdamia that drove my family away. Why did they immigrate to Cho Nisi of all places?"

"There are some books out there. Diaries and journals. Most of them slanted, written by people who'd rather change history than record it. All but one that I keep locked away."

"I see." Disappointed, Arell glanced through the open door into the library. "May I see that one?"

The old man shook his head. "Too dangerous. If you want to know what happened, I'll tell you. I've been writing a book about it myself, though I'm not sure I can get it all down before I die."

"That would be fascinating, sir. Perhaps I could have a scribe sent to help you."

He waved the notion away. "I'll tell you and you tell your children and grandchildren."

Arell shifted in the rickety chair at the mention of a legacy. One must be married to have children, and his romantic life had taken a fall off the highest cliff on the island. His wounds were far from healed, so much so he had sworn to stay away from women altogether.

"Your granddad was nephew to the late emperor of Casdamia. His father's brother. Wouldn't know it by the way they acted. I think there's a story in that too, but I don't know enough to tell it. Rumor is all. Nothing you want to know about if you're edgy." He looked Arell up and down.

Arell immediately positioned himself against the chair, hoping he didn't look uneasy. Being a king, now, he should be able to handle any truth thrust at him, especially if it were about his family.

"When Win's uncle Bahldi took the throne, he started making a lot of changes in the kingdom. Dangerous changes like taxing the people for more than they had. I remember my mother complaining about a bushel of millet once and the tax she had to pay for it—more tax than the ear-worms that came with the grain were worth. Poor farmers didn't see any of that money. Never satisfied, old Bahldi. The man turned on his family. Had his sister's son executed for a remedial offence. Too close to home for Win, being a nephew himself. We figured something underhanded was going on. No emperor in his right mind executes family. Win, he came to me, of course being his best friend, we confided in each other, so he came to me through all of this. He suspected an outside influence. I told him not to do anything until we knew for sure. You don't accuse an emperor of wrongdoing."

Oliver shook his head and scratched his whiskers as a distant look glazed his eyes. He nodded and mumbled and then continued.

"So, me and Win went sneaking around late one night and watched your granddad's uncle take off on horseback to Casda de Moor. You know what's up, there don't you?"

Arell shook his head. He knew little about the continent. He'd seen the mountain from the distance—knew its name and that the valley bordered by Casda de Moor and Mount Ream was where his father lost his life.

"Lord Skotádi," the man said.

"The dark lord?"

"Some people call him a dark lord. He's a wild man, I can tell you that. Once was a Casdamian wizard, but his magic got the best of him. Only certain kinds of people should be wizards. Ones that can contain themselves. Unfortunately, that's not how life works, though. Old Skotádi graduated to Vouchsaver and made a vow, blood sealed with the emperor. Called the demons to serve him. Made him close to immortal, some say. No one knows, but he hasn't died yet. Anyway, it became pretty apparent that his uncle had made a pact with the devil up there on Casda de Moor. You won't find that information in any of those books. They blamed the battle on your grandfather."

"Battle? My grandfather fought against the Emperor of Casdamia?"

"Not only fought against his uncle but killed him dead. That's what got him run out of the country. It wasn't safe to go the Potamian nation either. They were allies at the time. Those treaties are gone, but they held weight back then."

"My grandfather killed an emperor. His uncle?" Arell asked, his voice a bit louder and more emotional than he would have liked. The shock overwhelmed him, though. Here he had just finished banishing a woman for killing his father, a king, only to find out his grandfather had done something similar.

"Had to, son. Someone had to stop the insanity." The old man gave Arell a sympathetic frown and shook his head.

"I know, it's hard to take. Your dad was ashamed of it too." Oliver stood, shuffled to the cook stove, and poured himself a cup of granatus. "Want some?"

Arell shook his head.

"That's why you never met me, or some of the other old folks that live in Moaton. Your father stayed clear of us who knew the story, and us? Well, we didn't want to shake things up either. Let bygones be, we'd say. Folks got used to staying to themselves in this village. Not one of us who came over on the ship were proud of what your granddad done, but we supported Win. Had a temper, but that didn't mess with his standards. In the end, he did the country a favor. Just wished it were the old wizard he'd killed instead."

The room grew silent. Arell couldn't meet the man's eye. Too much raced through his mind. Kings and emperors getting killed, rebellions, dark lords. Arell could hardly believe his own flesh and blood took part in an assassination.

"Did the Cho Nisi know?"

Oliver shook his head. "They're good folk. We told them we needed a place to live, and they gave us this hill up here. We worked out a trade with them. Built them some roads, made some carts for their goats, traded them linen for their baskets—things like that. They never asked questions. No one ever offered the information either."

Arell leaned back in his chair and closed his eyes.

"Shouldn't make any difference to your rule here on the island. Most people have forgotten those days or tucked them away in their closets and threw away the keys. You'll be a righteous king. We'll support you just like we did your granddad. That's how we see it, anyway."

"What about Casdamia? Who sits on the throne now?"

"His grandson. Barte. Your cousin."

Arell's eyes popped open. "Does he have a vendetta against his grandfather's murderer?"

Oliver swished his brew around, either contemplating the answer, or contemplating on whether he should tell Arell the answer.

He took a drink and looked Arell in the eye. "Don't know."

Arell had Osage demonstrate the moves before he himself picked up a sword, circling around the man, watching his feet, his arms, his rhythm. Like a dance, Osage called out the footwork, the stance, the way he held his weapon and Arell listened. Arell learned rapidly. The best of lessons Arell remembered when he was younger were the ones that taught him how to learn—to free his mind of anything he already thought, and to open it to new ideas. This skill kept Arell dexterous and attracted him to mentors such as Chief Silas and the elders. His regard for Osage heightened as he watched the man. Dressed in the plain Moaton garb, a loose-fitting shirt, cuffs clinging to his large wrists, his knee pants buckled over wool stockings and pointed shoes, Osage handled his sword competently.

When Osage finished his demonstration, he bowed to Arell, catching his breath. "Vasil, there you have the foundation. All others are based on these moves. Learn these and you have the fundamentals of swordplay."

"Thank you. And I shall learn them hopefully as well as you have exhibited them."

"Better, perhaps. You're much younger, and more agile than I."

Arell laughed, "But you, sir, are the epitome of strength."

"Strength gives in to speed and flexibility. You'd be surprised. Let me show you."

Osage tossed him a practice sword and wrapped Arell's fingers around the hilt in the proper position. "Lightly," he said. "Don't grasp it tight unless you're expecting to decapitate your foe."

Arell cringed. He may be young and agile, but he had never killed a man before. The idea of severing a head from a body made him shudder. If Osage sensed his hesitation, he didn't say. He merely assisted Arell in finding the proper handhold and then had him position his feet for maximum balance.

"Always be aware of your feet. Attack first with your lunge and let your body carry your sword forward. Keep your balance. Your enemy's goal is to make you stumble. A man is much easier slain on the ground than on his feet."

"You've seen battle?" Arell asked as Osage instructed him.

"Many."

"In Casdamia?"

"Yes, Vasil."

"Did you fight alongside my grandfather?"

Osage paused and met his eyes. His were brown, deep, and troubled. "I fought alongside your father, Vasil."

Arell saw clearly that the man didn't care to elaborate.

A sweat trickled down Osage's forehead. He looked away and closed his eyes. "There are many things you don't know about your family. I should not be the one to tell you."

"My dear man, you are the only one I have. Who's left? My father's gone. My mother was an islander, she'd never been to the mainland. Only you and a few people in Moaton know what happened. Shouldn't I know as well?"

The man sighed and bowed in obedience. The sort of bow that agrees without really wanting to. Arell met his sigh and resigned to his wishes. "Teach me to fight today, and then we will dine together this eve, and you can tell me all you know"

Osage returned from Moaton that evening, dressed in what were probably the best clothes he had. A dark tunic with his grandfather's insignia. Perhaps the same outfit he'd worn in battle when the Emperor of Casdamia fell. Serena introduced his arrival and showed him to the hall which had been set with their finest silver, and hand-woven napkins her sisters had made. Clay bowls with fruit and fish as well as petite sandwiches, olives and pomegranates were spread out before them.

Arell followed Serena and Osage into the hall.

"I must admit, Vasil, I'm not used to dining in such elegance."

"I'm not either, Osage," Arell nodded at Serena as she bowed and left the room. "I spent little time in the castle, I prefer the beaches, walking barefoot in the sand and paddling a canoe. Spear fishing, clamming." He picked up a decanter of wine, and Osage lifted his flask. Arell poured.

"It's true, the villagers speak of how much time you spent away from the palace." Osage admitted.

"In criticism?" Arell led his guest to the table.

"No, Vasil. In amusement. Until your father's death, you were a youngster and thought of affectionately. We wished the best for you and still do."

"Yes, well, I have to admit, inheriting a kingdom is difficult. I had no preparation for this," he held out his arms, signifying the castle, and the responsibility. "It might not be wise to be so candid, but Father ruled in a time of peace on a beautiful island with little to no worries. He died, and now it's as if the world itself wreaks havoc on us. I'm not prepared, and I don't want to see you, the Moatons, or the Cho Nisi suffer because of my lack of ability. Please be seated," he offered.

"I will do all I can to help, Vasil." Osage sat across from Arell.

"I must learn sword fighting so that if the time should come when I need to use a weapon, I'll know how. However, should there be a battle, I'll need more than just …me."

"You need an army, Vasil."

"Help me build one, Osage."

The man met his gaze. Arell leaned over the table, his dark eyes wide. Not fearful, but excited.

"The world darkens. I'm afraid my father's death is only the beginning. I don't know who we must fight, or what. The Cho Nisi protect our coasts with their magic, but the dark lord's underlings swarm in the skies. What with King Tobias' daughter, the murderer of my father, the mainland's allegiance remains a mystery. Chief Silas suggested I learn to fight, but I don't want to brawl alone."

"I understand your concern, sire. But what of the natives? They do well to take care of their own."

"The natives are archers, and they fight with magic, but they cannot be everywhere, nor can they drum forever. I want swordsmen."

Osage nodded, "I will help you build your army."

Arell sat back, took a sip of wine, and put the cup down. "How many can you muster?"

Osage shrugged and scratched his beard in thought. "Several hundred young men live in the village. Some more seasoned men would be willing, as well, I'm sure."

Arell let the conversation die as Serena and her sisters brought in a hot platter of crab cakes smothered in wild mushroom sauce. He thanked Serena when she scooped a serving onto his plate. She had such a natural island beauty. Arell must heal from the loss of his father, wipe his mind free from the red-haired princess, and settle in his position as king before he can spend more time with her. She gave him a dimpled smile, teeth white against her golden skin, her dark eyes glistening. Yes, he would make more time for her, despite having sworn from romance.

"Osage, have you met Serena?"

Osage nodded to her.

"Chief Silas' daughter."

"I'm pleased." Osage stood and bowed politely. Serena curtsied in return. When she left, the man took his chair and gave Arell a puzzled look. "You treat your servants as equals. That's unlike your father."

"She has volunteered to assist me. A friend. I offered her a place here in the castle under Silas' suggestion. He insists I have support. Close friends, Serena, her sisters, and other members of the tribe. They like it here. It's their home. I do not treat them as servants. They come and go as they please."

Osage nodded with a peculiar smile on his face. "One can never have too many…friends."

"It seems odd to you?" Arell asked.

"Your affairs are your own."

Arell offered the platter of fruit to Osage and then helped himself.

"So now we come to the questions. What battles did you fight with my father?"

"What do you know already?"

"Only what Oliver told me. That my grandfather killed the emperor of Casdamia."

"Your father fought in that battle as well. He was a junior commander, your age, and I fought alongside him. You have a cousin who's inherited the throne, you know?"

"So, I've been told. Do you…" Arell sat back in his chair.

"Does anyone from Moaton have any correspondence with anyone in Casdamia?" Arell referred to the merchant and fisher ships that crossed the sea from the mainland to the island, carrying letters back and forth and tradable wares. Even his father sent such correspondence by boat, though Arell never felt the need, nor did he really have anyone to write. In fact, he hadn't visited Northport in years, and then only at his father's bidding. To him, a few ships coming and going seemed disruptive to the peace of the island. Coming to the throne showed him just how isolated he'd been.

"There may be some people who send letters. Many of the Moatons have relatives, grandparents in Casdamia."

"What do you think of my cousin? Has anyone mentioned what sort of emperor he is?"

Osage shook his head. "Either the reign of Barte son of Moshere is uninspiring, or he keeps such restraint on his people they are afraid to speak. I've heard no news."

"And yet King Tobias is legendary, and he's been on the throne for how long?"

"He took the crown a year before Barte's father took the Casdamia's throne."

"Casdamia, according to my father's maps, covers more territory than the Potamian dominion. More cities, more villages. More farmland, nobles and serfs."

"Yes, Vasil."

"Why?" Arell asked.

"Vasil?"

"Why is the reputation of King Tobias more highly regarded than this incredibly extensive empire?"

"I don't know the answer to that. Perhaps King Tobias has done greater things for the people."

"And perhaps Casdamian's emperors have been tyrants."

"It would seem so, according to your grandfather."

Arell set his knife down. "I would think that Barte son of Moshere would be more of a threat to Cho Nisi than Tobias. And yet Tobias' daughter came here to conquer the island. Were it not for our drums and the Cho Nisi supernatural protection, there would have been a fleet of ships arrive from the Potamian kingdom."

"All nations that are not allies are potential enemies, my King."

"And my father had aligned himself to King Tobias and still

lost his life to a Potamian arrow."

Osage shook his head slowly, his eyes sympathetic. "I am sorry, Vasil."

"So am I. Such a short time wearing the Crown, and already I find the world is against us. We have so many enemies, and potential enemies."

"Yes."

"Several hundred soldiers will not be enough."

"We're a small island. The potential of being invaded and conquered is ever present. I'm surprised we've held out as long as we have. Casdamian armies could easily have followed our people here."

"And yet they didn't. Do you think Lord Skotádi had something to do with that?"

"Of course, he did. Casdamia may be larger, but the region is closer to Casda de Moor, and hence more open to invasion by the dark lord's monsters. They fight continually against the evil that comes from that mountain, that is, if they don't give in to his wishes. Attacks were common. But then you have heard the rumors of the uncle your grandfather killed and his dealings with the demons."

"Could they have carried those treaties with Skotádi down from one generation to the next? To Barte, son of Moshere?"

Osage shrugged and studied his chalice. "All things are possible."

Arell stood and walked to the alcove, a concave window overlooking the sea. He knew so little about the world, and about the people who lived in other lands. He had missed so much while being carefree and blithe—to the point of foolishness. No wonder Chief Silas corrected him constantly. No wonder he needed an adviser like Silas. Arell felt inadequate, and unprepared to confront Skotádi's armies, those winged beasts, and those unknown kingdoms?

Despondency

As days passed, the snowfall continued. One morning after an exceptionally bleak blizzard, Erika woke having dreamed of fighting the fire-breathing skura again. Staring at the ceiling, she lay in bed, recollecting the first time that dream had come to her, when she'd been waiting for sentencing on that warm beach on Cho Nisi. To even think of Arell brought on a heartache, and so she tried to shut off those memories, to set them aside somehow. But the wounds would not close, they would always torment her, she loved him that much.

Nothing but her father's health mattered to her at the moment, not even returning to the battlefield. Erika would don her armor and pick up a sword if she needed to, yet, for her father's sake, she stayed in dresses and did her assignments on history and literature, resisting her desire to spar with the soldiers.

There'd be no sparring today, though. When Erika pulled back the curtains, tiny crystals in magnificent patterns clung to the stained glass. Frozen spikes of icicles hung down from the sills, and a soft blanket of white covered the entire courtyard. The only tracks were those of field mice, a rabbit, and a deer. The snow had stopped, but dark clouds hung low.

A tap on her door drew her attention. The breakfast call, she thought as she put on her robe and opened the door. A frail maid, Reena by name, no older than eighteen years and who had been working in the castle less than six months, curtsied.

"Fairest, the king would like your presence at breakfast this morning."

"Yes, thank you. Tell him I'll be down shortly."

"Fairest, he says he has urgent news and would like you to come as quickly as possible."

"Yes, Reena, I will." Erika was about to shut the door when the maid spoke again.

"Fairest,"

Erika scowled and sighed. Couldn't she give all her messages at once? "What?"

"You father looks ill, Fairest. I think it's from the news he has for you."

"Thank you. I'll hurry." Erika dressed and raced down the stairs to the dining hall. The doors were open and her father, bent over holding his stomach, sat on a chair. Both Rhea and Olinda were with him.

"Father, are you ill?" Erika asked, rushing to him. He looked up at her, his flesh pale, his eyes red, and a sorrowful expression soured his face.

"What ails you, Father?" she asked. "Is it your heart?"

He shook his head and handed her a letter.

My dear Lord and King,

It is with great regret I must inform you that your son, our loving prince, and dear friend, Barin, has disappeared during the trek to Tellwater Valley. A search party has labored fruitlessly day and night, hoping for a word or a sign, but to no avail. And now the snow is so thick, and the hillsides too dangerous, I fear we must call off the quest, though many men are willing to still risk their lives to find him.

I am so sorry to have to send you this news.

There is one man who claims he saw Prince Barin the day he disappeared, but the man had a serious head wound and broken bones. It is amazing that he made it to camp in the condition he was in. We considered his report with some skepticism, as his story is rather absurd. My experience with mountain giants is that they kill on sight. Never have I heard of a man being imprisoned by one, but so you have all the information we do I am including his note.

I promise you, as soon as the weather lets up, we will resume our search.

Our deepest regrets and heartfelt sorrow.

Note: despite his majesty's disappearance, I have sent his troops on to Fairmistle to carry out orders as you had

commanded while I continue to Tellwater.
Commander of the King's Army, Neal of Failsworth.

Erika took her father's hand and squeezed it. She leaned over and kissed his tears. "I'm so sorry, Father, you didn't need to hear this. Not now."

"We were going to take Father to his room, but he wanted to see you first," Rhea said.

"Do you have the other man's note?"

"It's fodder," Olinda said. "That soldier suffered from delirium."

"May I read it?"

Olinda shrugged and pulled a wrinkled parchment from her skirt pocket.

"You were going to toss it?"

"It has upset Father more than the letter from Neal. Only you would want to read something like this. Come Rhea, let's walk Father to his room. He really needs his rest. Reena, would you serve his breakfast in his quarters please?"

Olinda and Rhea helped the king to stand, each holding him with his arms around them, and walked him slowly down the hall. Erika followed, pressing out the wrinkles in the parchment and setting it on top of Neal's letter. Both had suffered damage on the long trip to them with a date showing a week and a half had passed. The other 'note', scribbled in another hand, had ink smeared where rain or snow had leaked through.

Vasil
The commander asked me to write my witness of the disappearance of Prince Barin. Pardon my penmanship, I'm not much of a scholar. Been a soldier most of my life, and I've fought alongside the prince more often than not.

Commander Neal asked me to tell you what I saw. He claims I acted a little lightheaded, having had to stumble with a broken hip down the side of a mountain by myself after they took Prince Barin away. He's probably right, but I can tell anyone reading this, this my account of the way I saw it happen as I swear on Vasil the Crown of Tobias.

The prince and I were riding tail while coming down the mountain to River Ream. Skura attacked, horses and men panicked. When we tried to get to the trouble, my horse slipped down the hillside, throwing me and breaking some bones. The horse died. Prince Barin, with his good heart, didn't want to leave me alone, so he climbed down to where I fell to help me. Well, by that time the rest of the company defeated the skura they moved on before the prince and I could even start down the hill. Sun set. Mist started forming. This is where everyone says I went a little daft, but I swear on the King's Throne itself I speak the truth. A mountain giant took him. The thing came out of the mist and turned into a tremendous rock who talked. His hands were stone, and he took Prince Barin in his fist and asked him his name and title. Barin, gallant soldier that he is told that giant his name and his royal affiliation and that mountain giant laughed and told him he was taking him to the devil, Lord Skotádi himself. I'm not lying. I've been in these mountains before. I know this sorcery. Only way to get him back is to chase down that devil Skotádi.

Your loyal soldier Talos Del Monroe.

Erika's heart raced, and her hand grew damp with sweat. Her sisters had hurried well ahead of her and so she ran to keep up, following them into her father's room. They helped him gown, Erika brought his night cap and cool rag.

"You may leave me, girls," Tobias said, his voice soft, mournful.

Both Olinda and Rhea curtsied. "Erika, are you coming?"

"In a moment," Erika said, busying herself with the curtains. Once they closed the door, Erika put a chair next to her father's bedside and took his hand.

"Father, did you read the note from Talos?"

He patted her hand and sighed. "War is a dreadful thing, Erika. We lose many good men to it," tears welled in his eyes and instead of crying he coughed.

"Father, Barin isn't dead. It doesn't say here that he's dead. Did you read Talos' letter?"

Tobias nodded, "Even if this man's words are true, how would we find your brother? If Neal could, he would." Her father sniveled.

Erika gave him a hankie, and he blew his nose. "I will not give up. Not until spring will we announce this tragedy. We may yet find him."

"Talos said they captured Barin. They didn't kill him. When Barin and I came home from Mount Ream, mountain giants attacked us. I know personally how horrible they can be. They almost crushed Rory in a matter of minutes. If they wanted to kill Barin, they would have. They're horrible, but we can easily defeat them. I know how. Let me go find Barin."

"Don't be ridiculous."

"Where is Rory?" Erika asked.

"I signed his release last week. He's training again. Why?"

"I want to show him this letter."

"Girl, what are you planning?"

"Nothing, Father. I just want to show him the letter and talk to him. I promise I won't do anything to upset you."

Her father took her hand in his. His face had been pale before, but now he flushed. The whites of his eyes were yellow. "My dear daughter, so long as I live, promise me you will not go chasing delusions. I need you near me. There are letters to write. You do that much for me. Do not pick up a sword unless the devil storms our keep."

Skotádi may just do that, now that he had Barin in his clutches, she thought. She didn't repeat her concerns to her father. The king's health was marginal, and she worried about him, but she also frowned because of the promise she had to make.

"I promise I won't leave you. Just let me take this letter to Rory and talk to him about it."

"You won't go away?"

"I won't leave you, Father. I know you need me."

He patted her hand again. "I don't want to send your sisters to spy on you."

Erika laughed, "Neither do I," she said, drawing a grin out of him.

He ceased smiling immediately and whispered her brother's name as, with a blank stare, he gazed out the window. "My dear son, Barin."

She wanted to tell him she'd find him, but he wouldn't hear it. Perhaps there's another way. Perhaps she would send someone like.... Rory.

Rory

King Tobias had failed to tell Erika the details of Rory's "training". She wore her fighting clothes when she went to look for him. It had, after all, been snowing and she couldn't see soiling her gowns and making undue work for her servants, so she wore the trousers she used to wear when on campaigns with her brother, and her boots. The snow had turned to ice and crunched under her feet as she trudged through the courtyard. She asked a sentry by the gates if he knew Rory.

The man glanced at his fellow sentry and nodded. "Yes, Fairest. We are familiar with this man."

"Can you tell me where he's stationed?" She thought he looked after one of the many gates, or the keep.

Instead, they pointed her to the stables.

"Thank you," she said.

She found him there, digging manure from a stall. Before she got his attention, he set his shovel down and filled a bucket with oats from a grain bin. She hurried into the barn and followed him. Horses poked their heads out from their stalls, blowing and stomping restlessly. They hated winter, penned up on cold dreary days. They got exercise in the afternoons, but the days were too short and their spirits too free, like hers. She reached over to rub a mare's nose.

"I know what you're feeling, lady," she said. "All penned up but wanting to run. I feel the same way."

"Fairest, Erika? That is you!" Rory set the bucket on a bench and hurried toward her. He didn't wear a soldier's uniform, but clothes of a stable boy, tall boots up to his knees, a loose-fitting shirt tucked into his trousers and only a sheepskin vest to keep him warm. He smiled warmly and his blue eyes sparkled.

"I sure did worry about you after they sent me off the island."

He stood in front of her, his face red with delight. She could do nothing else but hug him, though he shuffled a bit. He hesitantly put his arm around her and gave her a squeeze.

"Don't know if this is proper, Fairest," he whispered in her ear. "I smell terrible. It might rub off on you."

"I don't care if it's proper or not, Rory, nor do I care what you smell like. I missed you and I'm so happy to see you again!"

"Fine to see you as well, Fairest."

She stepped back and held onto his shoulders, looking at him, tickled to see him, yet hurt inside for what he went through on account of her.

"I'm so sorry they put you in prison, Rory."

He looked at his feet and shrugged. His smile vanished for a moment. "They called me a deserter. Never meant to desert. I thought being by your side and protecting you was the right thing at the time. You needed someone. Me and Kairos, I thought. I guess the prince saw things differently."

"You did the right thing. I wish I had been here to defend you."

"It's over now, though. I served my time, I guess."

"More than you should have. Are you still a soldier? Or just a stable boy?"

"They said I can serve again come spring. They thought I should do some hard work before that, so they have me here. Taking care of the horses is a joy, though. I don't mind. Fairest, may I ask you something?"

"Of course."

"I've been hearing gossip about Fairmistle. That frightening things happened. I've got a brother there, his name's Stormy, and my mother. Do you know anything?"

She sighed. She'd have to tell Rory all that's been happening, including Barin's disappearance.

"Let me help you with your chores and we can talk." She grabbed another oat bucket and followed Rory. He shoveled each stall while Erika led the horses to another corner and fed them oats.

"What rumors did you hear, Rory?"

"Heard that the mountain giants stormed through Fairmistle. Tore down buildings and took some prisoners." Rory kept shoveling straw out of the stall, into the aisle, and then lifted it into a cart.

"Where did you hear that?" Erika asked.

"At the pub."

"The pub?"

He laughed. "They made me a stable boy, but that doesn't take away my manhood. I enjoy a brew once in a while."

"The rumor came from the pub, then?"

"It's not just a rumor, though. The men who told the story rode this way from Fairmistle. I didn't know them well, but I knew them all the same. It had me thinking. Prince Barin rode to Fairmistle, didn't he? That's what the soldiers said early part of this year."

"Rory, I need to tell you something. Mountain giants kidnapped Barin."

He looked up, and when their eyes locked, he leaned on his shovel, his smile gone. "Your brother Barin? Our Prince?"

"Yes, according to the men that traveled with him. They sent us a letter." She took the note from her vest and unfolded it, handing it to him. He shook his head.

"I'm sorry, but I cannot read."

Erika sighed and walked to a bench and sat down with him, reading the letter slowly, stopping at the important parts and letting him digest all that Talos had relayed.

"My father doesn't believe this, and I think Neal didn't either. But I do."

Rory nodded. "It's true sure as the cow gives milk. If the men travelin' with him seen it, then best ought to believe it's true. Same as the snatchin's in Fairmistle. But what do you think that devil means to do with your brother and the other men he's been stealin'?"

I don't know. Perhaps…" She gasped, just now thinking about the possibilities. "I don't want to think about it. Barin is in danger, and so might we all be!"

Rory patted her shoulder sympathetically. "Don't fear, Fairest." He squeezed her hand and stood. "We be rescuin' him."

"My thoughts exactly. But how?"

Rory picked up his shovel again, moved more hay, more manure. Erika filled more oat buckets and fed more horses. Neither spoke. Her thoughts rambled through all the possibilities. They'd come up with something.

Though the sun never peeked through the clouds, the day faded into an evening just as gray. Rory lit a torch and walked Erika as close to the castle that would be proper and turned to her.

"I've got my thinking cap on, Fairest. Give it a night for an idea to work its way into my head."

She smiled, relieved that she had shared her news, and her day with someone she could trust. Someone who respected her. "Thank you, Rory. Between the two of us, I know we'll find him."

Come morning, Erika could not wait to step away from the dismal atmosphere of the castle and meet up with Rory. He was the only person with any hope in his heart, even after all he's gone through on account of her. He might be able to rescue Barin.

Before looking for Rory, Erika first went to visit her ailing father. King Tobias had his eyes closed when she entered his room, so she settled by his bedside and watched over him. His skin had a yellow hue, and he took quick short breaths in his sleep. His eyes twitched, as if dreaming, and he woke with a gasp.

"Barin!"

"Father," Erika cooled his head with a damp rag that had been in a basin on a nightstand. "You were dreaming."

He blinked and sat up. "Yes. A dream. That's all. Is Barin here?"

"No. Not yet."

A tea kettle steamed on the coals in the fireplace and so she poured a cup of soothwort infusion and mixed a dollop of honey into his cup. He looked around the room, blinking, and then he took a deep breath.

"I'm fine now, Erika." He took the cup and nodded toward the night table where a journal and quill sat waiting. "We need to write a letter."

"Right now?"

"Yes. The sooner the better. I meant to have you do it yesterday. I had Olinda bring me the tools, but I fell asleep."

"Very well," Erika picked up the writing quill and the parchment and waited for her father to form the letter in his mind.

"Say this," he cleared his throat and looked up, not at her but at the ceiling, deep in thought. He seemed desperate, eager to have the letter written. "My dearest friend and ally." He looked at her. "How does that sound?"

"Formal, if that's what you want."

"I'm not sure. I'm the king here, so maybe I shouldn't be so formal."

"Who are we writing to, Father?"

"Who? You know his name. You must. I don't know his name. A king. He's a king. A young king."

Erika gave her father a puzzled look. "What young king, Father?"

"The one on the island."

Heat rushed through her, though she didn't know why. Surely she had burned away all those feelings she had harbored. "You're talking about Arell? I mean King Arell of Cho Nisi?"

"Yes. That's the one. Arell. Is that his name? How should I address him? You know about these matters."

"I think I would just address him as King Arell of Cho Nisi?"

"Yes, good write that down. And then this," he waited, sipping his tea and watching her. "I know that we have had conflicts. Misunderstandings." He grimaced at her and she avoided his stare. "However, I am asking for your allegiance once again. The allegiance that your father so kindly offered." He cleared his throat again and paused, thinking.

Erika read what she had written. This letter would go to Arell. The man whom she loved. Whose heart she had broken and who allowed his elders to banish her with a threat of death should she return. What is Father doing? He dared not ask him to come here!

"Your father fought bravely. Write that." He looked Erika in the eyes. "He knows, doesn't he?"

"He knows," she answered.

"Well then, we should apologize. Did you apologize when you were there?"

"Father, they imprisoned, sentenced and banished me."

Her father nodded and grunted a bit, pushing himself up against a myriad of pillows. "That's not what I asked. I asked if you apologized."

"Well, yes, besides all that, of course I did."

"Good. Then we have to approach this a bit more diplomatically. Say this. My kingdom offers you our deepest sympathy in the death of your most noble father and our ally. If there is recompense we can offer you, please make us aware of what it is. I would like…no I very much desire that our nations set aside the past and reach across our borders, and the sea, to join hands in unity. We face one of the most dreadful opponents this world has ever known. It is imperative that we stay as allies in this broken world."

A tear welled in his eye. "Erika, I want to tell him about Barin. I want him to come and help us. Somehow. I will not live much longer. I have no heir but Barin. If I die, who will reign? Who will fight against this foe?"

"What can Arell…" she caught herself. "What can King Arell do about Barin?"

"Cho Nisi has a most incredible magic, Erika. Those native people can control the elements. Just think. They could melt the snow and destroy the mountain giants. They can find my son. Or, if not, perhaps our nations can just become as one."

"How?"

He shrugged and looked at her. "In the old days, for nations to unite, they joined in matrimony. I have three daughters. You say this young man is single?"

Blood rush to her head. "You wouldn't suggest that? Not in a letter. You hardly know this man."

"I'm dying, Erika. My pride is fading away with me. I only want what's best for our kingdom. It will not survive without me or Barin. Your sisters have no idea how to rule a nation, and you are too…young. One of you girls must marry and carry on our legacy. The throne will go to your husband. I dread the thought of Kairos on the throne. But there is Felix. Unless this young man on the island should marry Rhea or Olinda—or you?"

Erika took a deep breath and dipped the quill in the ink. "How do you want me to finish this letter, Father?"

"Ask him for help. You'll think of something."

Their eyes met. His were shallow, as if his life were fading as they spoke. Erika set the quill in the well, stood, and covered him. "Rest, Father. You don't have to worry about this now. Get strong." She kissed him on the forehead, and he took her hand with a firm grasp. He wouldn't die. Not now.

"Finish the letter, Erika. Send it soon. Today if you can."

Erika took the letter and the inkwell and slipped out of the room. The halls were cold this morning, empty and cold. Even the servants grieved for Barin. She could tell by the way they refused to meet her eyes and kept themselves scarce until they were called upon for service. Her father's condition made it worse. He couldn't die.

All her life Erika assumed her father would forever be on the throne, and everyone else in the kingdom did as well. The lands were named after him. Diplomats and merchants from other nations had come to the palace, giving the prince his due respect, but they came to see King Tobias, no matter if their affairs were officially with Barin or not. Even Moshere, the late emperor of Casdamia, bowed before her father, though his ill-mannered son Barte refused to speak to any Potamians to their face. The two rulers were not at odds, but they were not on good terms either.

More urgently, she needed to address the Cho Nisi and plead for their magic to save her brother. Surely their chants could find him, but would they come? If the letter had Father's signature and they didn't suspect she had written the request.

She would finish this letter, minus the implications of marriage. Marriage! If only! She shook her head and walked the halls of the castle, recollecting the good times she had with Arell. But those memories ended abruptly, as did their relationship. She will never forget his face when he stormed into her quarters and announced that she had killed his father.

No. There would be no matrimony with Arell the High King of Cho Nisi, sadly.

Erika sat on the garden patio that morning, trying to finish the letter. Without her father's exact words, how could she sound like him? So far, she scribbled nonsense that only a broken heart would utter. Oh, how she wished she could simply sail to the island and steal away into Arell's closet with no one else knowing. There she would live in secret and visit him in his bedchamber like a ghost who haunts her lover in the deep of night. She tore up another parchment just as Rory tapped on the door.

When she answered, he bowed.

"Fairest!"

"Rory come in and sit with me."

"Fairest, I think I've thought of something. A way to save your brother."

"Tell me!" Erika set the quill down and offered him a seat. "Would you like a bite to eat? Some rose water?"

"No, Fairest. Thank you." He seemed anxious and refused a

chair. "If the giant imprisons your brother, that's one thing. We have men that could find him and kill those monsters. You and I know the secret to destroying them."

"Fire."

"Exactly. However, if he's in the clutches of that evil Vouchsaver Skotádi, there's not much a common man can do but say a few prayers."

Erika's shoulders slumped. She had thought, by the excitement in his voice, Rory had found a solution. "I will not give up. I can't."

"That's what I'm saying. There's not much a common man can do, but there're men who aren't common who are walkin' the earth!"

She looked up. His eyes were as wide as his smile. "Rory, my dear fellow, please tell me what you're thinking."

"The Cho Nisi. They're as common as a horse that flies, and no one's seen a flyin' horse. It's the Cho Nisi we should be askin' for help."

"Yes, Rory. Funny that you should suggest the Cho Nisi. My father is having me write a letter to them now." She gazed at the crumbled leaflets on the table.

"Then why the long face, if I might be so bold?"

"It has to be from the king, Rory. If the elders suspected I wrote the missive, Arell would never see it. Father started dictating a letter but told me to finish it. I'm afraid I don't sound like a king in my writing, much less a man. Could you help me?"

"Fairest, I don't know how to read or write."

"Well, perhaps when I get it finished, I could read it to you, and you could tell me if it sounds like a king's letter."

"I could. If you finish soon. I have permission to go home for a spell. Goin' to visit my brother in Fairmistle to see what damage the giant did. Someone at home might know where they took the Prince."

"I will have this finished by noon today."

"I'll be back this eve."

He turned to leave, but she touched his arm. "Rory, please..." she hesitated. She'd been seeing too much sorrow lately, losing too many people who were dear to her.

"Please, Rory, when you return to the south, don't put yourself in danger. I need you to come back."

"Yes. Thank you, Fairest." He bowed, his face blushing red.

The Dark Lord's Prisoner

Barin gasped for breath. He closed his eyes, trying to calm his racing heart. Sweat trickled down his brow—his entire body wet from fear and perspiration, his lungs hot from lack of oxygen. He fought to stay awake and alert as he rumbled in the giant's fist, tumbling against the rock walls that made up the giant's hands.

His journey would end at the foot of the Skotádi himself. And then what? Barin had no weapon that could match the magic of a sorcerer, nor could he outrun a giant. Could he outwit an evil wizard? Doubtful, he thought. A genius created these beasts. They were formed from bones, air, stones—with powers that exceeded anything in the natural world—sorcery used for vengeance and spite. Hardly an empire, kingdom or township had not been affected by this deviltry. And yet, if this wicked lord wanted to kill him, why hadn't he already?

The rocking stopped. Barin's cloak fell over him as a blanket covering a dead man. The walls opened slowly as the mountain giant exposed him to a deep and wet chamber. Barin lay prone, afraid to move less he be trampled, or kicked, or grasped again by the giant.

The cave, only an overhang of obsidian the size of a small horse stall, faced another peak. Unprotected from rain and snow, an icy wind whistled against its interior. Barin slowly looked up at the snowcapped peak of Mount Ream in the distance. That would put him on the western ridge of Casda de Moor—a long course from where he had been, a longer way from any help. The distance didn't surprise him. A giant could cover much ground in little time.

Sol pushed him under the overhang and dragged an iron portcullis down. Snow flew from the rocks as it slammed into place, and then the giant walked away. Barin looked out at his surroundings through the grille. Precipices and crags of the steep mountain on which they had caged him glared back. He shivered and drew his cloak closed, creeping into the rear-most part of the overhang as far away from the chilly wind as he could. He rubbed his arms in an attempt to get warm. The gash on his head had scabbed over but fatigue overtook him and Barin collapsed to the ground, drifting off to a state of unconsciousness.

If he had slept, he may have dreamed, but instead the numbness of the cold, snowy mountain took his mind and played games with it. Voices rang in his ears—a pleasantly familiar drinking song popular in Prasa Potama. Men's voices rang out so distinctly he could almost see them lifting their mugs and toasting to the king.

When he opened his eyes, he listened to the wind. He perked up, sure that something more than the sound of a storm whistled in the gusts. He heard people!

"Hey, up there! Can you hear us?"

Barin crawled to the gate. He couldn't stretch his neck between the grilles. But the voices were clear.

"Who's there? Who did the evil devil catch this time?" a man called.

"Hallo!" Barin answered. "Prince Barin of Tobias. Who are you?"

He heard men talking. Someone whistled. "Vasil. We're from Kevshire and some of us are from Fairmistle. Caught up in a raid. We've been here a week."

"How many of you?"

He waited for an answer. Either they were counting, or they didn't want to say. "There are twenty-two of us now. One death, Vasil."

"Are you well?"

Another silence. "Mostly," came the reply not as eagerly. "We'd be better if we were off this mountain in the warm of day. Never see much of the sun in these shadows. Some pretty remarkable sunsets beyond, though, if your eyes don't freeze shut."

"Are they feeding you?" Barin asked.

"They give us food. We don't know what it is, but it's kept most of us alive, those of us who can stomach it. Some of us are fasting."

"Is there any way to escape?" Barin asked, knowing full well if there were, they'd be gone already.

"Vasil, we'll do whatever you ask."

"Vasil," an unfamiliar voice yelled out and echoed over the canyon. "Is it true, about your father?"

"What about my father?"

"That the Casdamians overthrew him and killed him?"

"No." Barin answered as a chill rushed up his spine. "Who told you that?"

"The man who died...he'd been summoned. He came back ill, Vasil. Told us they killed your father and then he died. The demons poisoned him, we'll wager. Be careful."

"Lies!" he called to them. "He said nothing else?"

"No, Vasil. The poison took him pretty quick-like."

Barin sank back into his corner.

There were other creatures besides the mountain giant who visited Barin. Strange human-like individuals. Hairless, who didn't seem to have much bone structure, nor any gender. They had eyes the color of their flesh, a reddish tan hue, and did not wear clothing. They moved on rubbery legs and could change shapes to pass through the small openings in the gate. In the evening, five of them congregated outside Barin's cell and gazed at him. One squeezed through the grille, carrying a clay pot in an indentation in its arm. It set the bowl in front of Barin and hurried to join the others. They left after that.

Barin took one look at the contents of the bowl—oily green chunks of unidentified meat, He refused to taste it, especially after being told Skotádi had poisoned a man. The pot sat in the middle of his cave and slowly the frosty night seized the steam away. He didn't hear from his friends below the rest of the evening.

The other prisoners might have kept themselves warm huddling together. Barin had only his cloak to keep from freezing to death that night. He shivered—his body cramped. He had nowhere to bed but on the hard, icy surface. His teeth chattered as he trembled. Occasionally a burst of energy rushed through him and he stretched, jumped, and trotted in place, but exercise caused hunger pains. The bowl of stew sat in the middle of the cave, now with a thin layer of ice over it. He resisted the temptation.

Counting helped him to stay alert, for if he handed himself over to fatigue, he'd never wake. He stared out through the portcullis, regarding the countless stars, wishing he were with his men fighting these demons on the outside, rather than being imprisoned by them.

Before dawn, the hairless creature climbed again into his prison to take his bowl away. The contents had turned to solid ice. The creature shook its head but said nothing, glancing at him several times as it yanked the bowl from the rock. Barin wondered if the creature could talk or communicate at all. The thing climbed through the grille and disappeared.

Dawn had come, and the sun rose onto the landscape of another dismal day. A slow change of dark gray to blue gray and then to gray. Aside from the slimy creature who visited Barin's cage, the world lacked color. The clouds, however, seemed to keep the heat close to the earth. Fog filled the valley. Fog evaporating into the atmosphere, or mountain giants seeking prey. Perhaps both. The mist came and went, taking on the dull glow of sunrise and sunset. Wind swept snow off Mount Ream and clouds hovered on top of it, sealing off the uttermost peak. A flock of skura flew from the valley and landed near the cave, squawking, fighting over scraps of meat they'd brought with them. Barin noted their habits. He could hear them talking but couldn't hear them well enough to know what they said. When not riled, they hid their human faces under a furry head appearing more like owls than monsters, but their scaly wings looked like those of giant bats.

Days passed, and Barin lost count of them. Flurries of snow came and went, yet the cold remained. Barin paced across his cell, flexing all his muscles from his head to his toes. Each morning the strange shapeless creature crawled through the bars and delivered to Barin the same grotesque bowl of stew. Three days Barin refused to eat. He peeled ice from the rocks for water. By the fourth day, he held the bowl in his hands to absorb its warmth. On the fifth day, the stew smelled more appetizing to him and so he took a taste of it to see if it would curl his tongue or upset his stomach. Tasteless, he had no reaction to the broth. He put the bowl down where it had been placed, giving the appearance that he hadn't touched it. The creature took it away again that night. Before it left, it looked at him, its flesh-toned eyes somber. It reached out its hand and a piece of parchment paper floated to the ground in front of him. Barin waited for the creature to leave before he took the letter and read it.

Once you eat, we'll bargain for your freedom.

Barin fumed. The devil had a plan, then—to starve him until he hands over his soul. He wrinkled the paper and threw it on the ground. It rolled and curled in a corner, a bright white parchment against the cold slate tempting him, beckoning him. Barin looked away and shivered. The lack of food depleted his body. Over time, his fatigue would overwhelm him. Then he would die.

Barin had seen people starve. Three years ago, in the lower plains of his father's kingdom, there were villages where drought had hit, caused by crop-devouring demons. Before his father could send food to the serfs, several hundred people had died, not just of undernourishment, but of the diseases that came with it. Even when he and his soldiers brought wagons of supplies, some of those who were stricken never outlived the illnesses. He glanced at the note with disdain.

Each day after that, Barin tasted a little more of the stew. Sufficient to offer his body a touch of nutrition, but not enough to make a difference in the amount left in the bowl. Every evening the stew froze, and the pot stuck to the ground. The creature came and yanked it free and shook its head. Barin said nothing.

By the seventh day, Barin's insides contracted in unbearable anguish. Hunger, combined with the freezing weather, had taken hold. His shirt fell loose over his shoulders, and he had to buckle his trousers tighter to keep them up. Even his cloak seemed too heavy to bear. The icy temperature crept into his bones and his hands had a blue hue to them. He exercised less simply because exhaustion consumed him. By the end of the seventh day of his incarceration, Barin called out to the men below, but no one answered. Had his voice grown too weak for them to hear? Or had the men been moved? Or had they died? The loneliness added to his suffering. He picked up the note and read it again.

When you eat, we'll bargain for your freedom.

Barin had given all the fight he could. He relented. Should he be poisoned, death would come quickly, and he would welcome it. When the creature came with the bowl, Barin waited for it to leave, and then he ate. The tastelessness of the substance mattered not. It warmed his belly and satisfied his hunger.

Barin and Skotádi

After the strange creature fetched his empty bowl that evening, Sol came to lift the portcullis. He did so with little strain and his breath filled the cave with hot musty air. He gave Barin a dagger's look.

"My Liege is ready for you." The giant unfolded his fist and nodded for him to get in.

"No thank you, I can walk," Barin said, lifting his chin.

A low growl came from the giant. "The only way down for you is by me. Get in." He lay his hand on the ground again. Barin wrapped his cloak around him and stalled. Perhaps he shouldn't do this after all. "I got sick last time I rode in there," he stated bluntly, although his stomach already turned, and he shivered. Barin did not look forward to facing a demon.

"I'll let some air in this time," the giant retorted.

Barin looked him in the eye, and in that horrendous smile he saw nothing but sadism.

"I promise."

"Mountain giants make promises?" Barin snickered.

"As good as a man's."

Barin, weak and disoriented, sauntered toward the giant and climbed into Sol's palm. "Keep your hand open, please."

The giant grunted, but instead of encasing Barin within his stony fist, he held his palm flat as he carried the prince down the steep incline to Skotádi's chambers.

"Why night?" Barin asked the giant, staring out at the starry sky.

"Master always works at night. Sleeps during the day. Wizard hours. Better for spells he says."

"Is he planning to cast a spell on me?" The question barely passed Barin's lips. A drowsiness overtook him, and he closed his eyes.

"You'll find out." The giant chuckled to himself and as he did, his body shook so violently that Barin awoke and, glimpsing the bottomless chasm, clung to Sol's thumb to keep from falling.

Sol scaled a vertical cliff downward, huffing with exertion. When he came to a level ridge, the giant chuckled again and tilted his hand as if to drop Barin. The prince clung tighter and then glared at into Sol's laughing eyes.

"Scared you?" Sol said.

"You would have to answer to your master why you killed his prisoner," Barin reminded him as he tried to calm his racing heartbeat.

"Right." The giant leveled his palm and continued his downward trek with no other mishap. When they came to the mouth of a cave, Sol lay his hand flat on the ground and Barin slid off onto the slate surface, glassy from melting snow. The side of the cliff in front of him shielded him from any starlight. Wind howled in the abyss below, and a skura screeched somewhere in the pinnacles above. Sol bowed, his stony form dissolving into the rocky exterior of the cavern as Skotádi emerged from shadows. The scaly demon stared at Barin—his vaporous eyes glowed in the moonlight.

"Bow, peasant," he told the prince in a voice that made the mountainside tremble.

"I bow to my king, only." Barin swallowed and stood taller.

"I will break you from that. Follow me."

The Vouchsaver pivoted, his cape wafting in a draft that his presence alone made. The wind blew Barin's hair and sent a chill to his bones.

Skotádi drew a torch and led Barin into a chamber where a smokeless fire burned, a fire fueled not with wood or kindling but sweltered by magic. A throne of obsidian faced the fires, and across from it a bench of granite. Skotádi waved for him to sit on the stone bench as he returned his torch to the wall and stepped on his throne. On a round table to Barin's left lay a map of the world, sketched with an artist's hand, and to the right a cast-iron kettle filled with steaming brew. Barin sat next to a small dining table and a plate of food—some sort of meat, assorted vegetables, and a sweet cake.

"Eat," the Vouchsaver insisted.

Barin fought back his hunger and gazed at the Vouchsaver suspiciously. "And if I do, what am I consenting to?"

"We haven't made a bargain yet. I don't take advantage of your weakness, Prince of Tobias. I care to negotiate like two sensible adults."

Barin frowned. Though the fire between them flamed, casting gold hue on him and deepening the shadows on the Vouchsaver's face, Barin could not see his eyes. Skotádi's cowl hung low over his head. Only the vibration of his voice gave Barin any indication to his temperament.

"Eat," the wizard repeated.

Barin picked up the meat and sniffed it, glancing at the Vouchsaver.

"Sheep. Good meat. Raised by Lord Garion's serfs."

Barin set it down. "Stolen."

"Of course. Do you think the man would take coin from a devil?"

"Have you ever bothered to ask?"

Skotádi laughed and then he frowned. "Eat before you die of starvation. I can very easily bring Sol in here to take you back to your…'room'. What are a few more bones to my collection but fodder for my darlings?'"

Barin hesitated.

"What good is pride at a time like this, Prince? You're hungry. Eat."

Barin took a bite. The juices from the lamb dripped down his chin, the flavor unlike anything he'd ever tasted. Of course, the emptiness of his body craved every last morsel. He gnawed the meat to the bone, stripping it of tender sinew, sucking the marrow. When he realized how ravenous he'd been, he set the bone down, wiped his chin with his sleeve and locked eyes with the Vouchsaver who'd been watching him with a cruel smile on his face.

"You eat like a skura," he snickered. "Finish your meal."

Barin sat up straight, embarrassed to have displayed such predatory manners, and ate the vegetables with all the manners of a noble.

"Tea?" the Vouchsaver offered.

Barin noticed one of Skotádi's creatures standing near the cast-iron pot, holding a flask. When the Vouchsaver spoke, the thing brought the cup to him and set it on the bench at his side.

True, the chamber had the fragrance of freshly cooked meat.

But an underlying smell reminded Barin of Kairos' study in the tower—a smell of herbs, potions, and magic. It didn't appear the Vouchsaver had poisoned the food. Barin had eaten it and still lived. But this after dinner tea—could this be poison?

"Surely you want to wash all that food down with something warm and liquid," the Vouchsaver suggested. Barin took the cup, but he didn't drink. He warmed his hands.

"Now with essentials out of our way, let's talk," Skotádi rose and approached the fire. "There's a reason I've kept you alive. You and your father have a large army and much land."

"Land that you would have destroyed half a decade ago if my grandfather had not rescued it."

"We see things differently," the Vouchsaver said. "What I see are men no better than cockroaches hoarding something that never belonged to them. But regardless, you will help me get it back."

"Ludicrous," Barin spat.

"Did I feed you too soon?" the Vouchsaver asked, his temperament unchanged. "You have no choice." His eyes went to the cup that Barin held. The prince set it down, and then the Vouchsaver laughed, but he did not say why.

"Sol!" Skotádi called.

Sol's movements resonated through the cave. The giant crawled into the chamber, his huge body too large to stand upright. "Yes, My Liege," he said.

"Bring in the others."

Barin stood, reaching for a sword out of habit, a sword that didn't exist. Twenty men shuffled into the cave with their hands tied to one another. Tattered clothing, downcast faces, beaten, pale from the cold, and half starved. The remnants of their clothing bore the markings of Fairmistle villagers, the red vests now faded and torn. Others wore Kevshire tunics. They were young men, all of them.

"Vasil," several of the men whispered when they saw Barin.

"They call you king! This is your army, Prince," Skotádi told him. "What would you do? Have them starved? Frozen to death? Crushed by mountain giants as you look on? Watch as I suck their souls out of them?"

Barin drew a heated breath and flexed his hands. Looking for a way of rescue, but the only means of escape for these men was by negotiation. The prince contained the flood of rage beating against his chest... for their sakes.

"Decide, son of Tobias. Freedom for you and your men to return to Prasa Potama? Or stay here and die. All of you, one by one."

Barin studied the Vouchsaver, waiting for him to say more, but Skotádi remained silent.

"What must I do?" Barin asked.

"Be my pawn. Help me in my goal."

"What goal?"

"Two things. There's a journal I must find, and then I need men. Humans to make a way for me to the caves of Mount Ream."

"There are Dragons in the caves."

Skotádi laughed. "Surely your army isn't afraid of a few reptiles. Join me in a toast. I am tired of taking care of you. I want to get off this mountain. I don't particularly like the thought of having you tag along, so I'm setting you free. If you agree, that is. So?" He nodded to the creature who ladled tea into twenty-one cups and set them on the table.

"Join me?"

Skotádi drew his dagger and walked to the men, slashing their leather bonds, ushering them to the table. Barin watched, questions racing through his mind. The firelight cast eerie shadows on the wall, or perhaps those ominous figures weren't shadows? They could have been demons for all he knew. The drowsiness he experienced earlier returned. He took a deep breath, hoping for air, but the flames from the torches swallowed the oxygen. The fragrance of mint and ginger—infusions his sisters sometimes served—now filled his lungs.

The men were so weak that they collapsed on the ground when Skotádi cut their ropes. Their moans wrenched at Barin's heart. Those who hadn't fallen on the ground accepted the cup Skotádi handed them, thanking the Vouchsaver.

Thanking him! Barin frowned.

They held their flasks with two hands, absorbing the warmth like he had done with the stew. It must have been pleasing to them, for they had not been warm for weeks, having been here longer than he had.

"Why?" Barin asked Skotádi, his voice barely audible, not wanting to discourage the men. They were suffering. "Why should we fight the dragon for you?"

"I will tell you, but this isn't for them to hear."

Skotádi shrugged, and with a whisk of his hand sent a flame that seared every man's ears. They groaned and fell over, spilling their cups. Barin jolted toward them, but Skotádi jetted the flame not at his ears, but at his torso, searing his shirt and scorching his chest. Barin fell to his knees as the heat traveled through his body.

The cavern imploded.

The prisoners disappeared.

On the stone bench sat a middle-aged man. Not an ugly man by any means, with a neatly trimmed beard speckled with gray. Dark eyes peered out at him, tinted by the red of the firelight. He wore skins of beaver and wolf and smelled like wild game, but he had a pleasant smile, and a full set of teeth. He spoke as though Barin had known him for many years, though the prince had never seen him before.

"It hurts?" the man asked Barin.

When Barin touched the burn on his chest, the blister disappeared, and the pain faded.

"No need for injuries." The man spat. "Get up."

Barin rose from his knees and sat on the bench facing him.

"I once lived in a castle like you do, Prince Barin. A beloved wizard, was I serving the Crown of Casdamia." He held his thumb under his belt, showing off the insignia of the empire he spoke of. "Best of my field in all the land. You believe that?"

"Indeed," Barin said, wary of this man who appeared through some sort of deviltry.

"As I experimented with magic, I discovered greater powers than that of kings, armies, or the force of a man's sword. I used my powers for the benefit of the kingdom until I realized everything the emperor had was because of me, and yet he gave me no credit. None! So, I allowed myself a little more power. Why should someone else sit on the throne and have me do the work for him, eh?" He winked at Barin. "I kept my secrets so well concealed, and so inaccessible, no one could ever steal them from me."

"Why are you telling me this?" Barin asked.

The man nodded with a smile, but without answering his question went on. "I murdered men. Peasants mostly and took their blood to make demons out of them. Their souls I learned to drink."

He chuckled when Barin sat erect.

"Needless to say, the more I consumed a man's spirit, the more effect my own spells had over me. Granted, those spells made me greedy and before I realized it, I had already become addicted to the taste." He licked his lips and looked Barin up and down. "I can no longer kill on my own, the creatures I make do that for me. But...." He stopped, picked up a cup and tossed the contents into fire. Flame burst at them and they both jolted back.

"But what?" Barin asked.

"But my days are numbered. I need to reach the caves."

"For what?"

He smiled again. "I said my days are numbered. I must go back to where I began."

"Why the caves of Mount Ream?"

"The spell to free me lies beneath the mountain. I need an army to help me."

"That's where I come in?"

"You've seen me in Canyon Gia. Either you help me, or my creatures' bellies will be satisfied with the flesh of those men over there. We'll kill you all, and it will be sport for us when we do."

Barin glowered at the man.

"You contest my power?"

Barin had never seen such power, such augury. He had nothing to counter it with, but perhaps if he got away, Kairos could help. He had to buy time.

"It's a pact?"

Barin hesitated. Oh, for the sake of his father's holy idols, he didn't want to agree. But if he didn't give in, these men would die. He was responsible for them. He was their king.

"Yes." Barin said, his body heating with dread.

"Good. You speak for your people, Barin, son of Tobias. Let it be known that the Potamian kingdom and I are allies. Then it's sealed."

The man patted him on the shoulder and then touched the prince's eyes.

A sharp pain pierced through Barin's head and for a moment he saw fire and his eyes burned just as his chest had burned earlier. The pain quickly subsided. The man no longer sat next to him. Nor were Skotádi nor Sol nor any of the other demons in the cave, only the poor souls who had been imprisoned. They were seated by him, sharing what few morsels had been left from his plate.

"Are you well, Vasil?" one red-haired young man asked.

Barin blinked and looked around. No sign of any magic. The

fire burned wood and the smoke smelled of cedar.

"Did you see him?" Barin asked.

"Who?" The young man leaned over closer, looked at him, and gasped. "Vasil! Your eyes!"

"The man. The man in furs." Barin explained.

"Weren't no one here after Skotádi and his giant left, Vasil," one man interjected.

"No, no, maybe not," Barin said. The memory of the man quickly faded away. Perhaps he had imagined it.

"Your eyes are red, Vasil."

"Yes," Barin said and blinked again. Fatigue had taken over his body, and now he had a grueling headache. Still, his hope had returned. The portcullis no longer blocked the entrance to the cave, and they were free to leave. If they could make it off this mountain, get back to the valley, and join with Neal's men, they'd be able to fight against Skotádi.

Barin stood amazed that he had his balance.

"And you are well?" he asked them.

"We're weak, and still cold to the bone, but we would give anything to be home again."

"Thank you for saving us," another man said.

Barin frowned at him and hesitated. Did he save them?

"Yes," he answered. "Of course."

Freed

They were free from the vile claws of the giants, but that didn't change their circumstances. They'd been no better off if the devil turned them loose in a pit of fire. Aside from the mountain being steep and treacherous, Barin didn't know the trails. He set his compass on the descent, assuming he'd get his bearings once he reached the plains. He hadn't seen the route which Sol had carried him, having been encased in his stony hand. With Sol's enormous body, the giant could have leapt cross-country up the mountain for all he knew. So, Barin and his men hurried out of the cave they followed a slippery trail downhill and paused at the first level clearing they came to.

He turned to his weary comrades, his heart aching because of them. They shivered for want of clothing. A few had worn shoes, and the others were barefoot. Were they healthy enough to make the trek down the mountain?

"What's your name?" Barin asked a red-haired youth who stood nearest to him.

"Stormy. My brother's in your army, sir."

"Your brother's name?"

"Rory, Vasil."

"Rory?"

"You know him?"

Barin nodded but said nothing more. Of course, he remembered Rory, the soldier whom he had confined for desertion because of his sister's insolence. Stormy bore a family resemblance to Rory, though the lad wasn't even a man yet. To look at the dark under his eyes, and the grime and filth on his face broke Barin's heart. Boys his age should be home with their fathers, learning a trade, fishing, enjoying their youth, not imprisoned in an icy cave by a demented wizard. The experience had been too much for any man. They were all frayed. Not only worn by the lack of clothing, and the overall gauntness of their bodies, but tattered on the inside. They had lost hope despite being free men.

"It's been hard for all of you. I know. You've been prisoners for longer than I." No one responded. They looked at him with eyes of distress. These were men from the country, Fairmistle and the river towns. Poor fellows. None of them had ever had much wealth. A few cows. Chickens. Heat from a hearth in their modest homes. Could he, as a prince, offer them solace for what they had suffered? If he could give them a horse and carriage to carry them home, he'd do it. But a long and treacherous journey awaited them. Barin sighed, lost for words.

"We'll first need some clothing for you." Barin removed his cloak and wrapped it around a man who was so cold his teeth were clattering. "What's your name?"

"Effie," the man said. "From Fairmistle, Vasil."

"Effie, I want you to wear this until your body warms and then pass it to the next man. Moving will generate heat, and we need to move as a unit."

"Yes, sire," he said.

"Let me see your feet," he instructed the men. They exchanged glances, puzzled, but sat at Barin's biding. Despite the dark night, Barin stooped and inspected their feet. Too many swelled with sores and frostbite. Three of the men wore boots and warm stockings, though torn and threadbare. The others had long since worn the soles out of their footwear. Barin tore strips of cloth from his tunic and wrapped each of their feet.

"We can't have your toes turning to icicles, now can we?" he asked, patting the shoulder of the last man he cared for.

"Thank you, Vasil."

"Do you remember what route the giant took?" Barin asked.

The men glanced among themselves, and finally one of them answered.

"Don't remember as some of us were unconscious when we arrived, taken up by the giants. We'll trust you to get us home, sire. We'll obey anything you say, Vasil. You are our king."

"Prince. I am not a king, merely a servant for my father. King Tobias still sits on the throne."

"That's odd," another man spoke up. "The dark lord said your father died. Said the armies from Casdamia killed him."

"When?"

"The day you arrived."

Barin laughed, "The dark lord lies."

"It happened after you left home. We swear it's true. Even the skura spies brought word. They had proof."

"What sort of proof?"

"A lock of your sister's hair, Vasil."

Barin stared at them as they relayed their story. What they said seemed, at first, plausible, and then as the tale progressed, probable. His hands shook, and so he put them behind his back to appear calm. He mustn't overreact. They could be wrong.

"Red as the bark of a cedar tree, Vasil. We don't know what she looked like, so you'd have to tell us if it's a lie. All we know is what they said. The skura said she succumbed to Barte of Moshere before she died. Robin grabbed the token through the bars after they tossed it on the ground. Show him, Robin."

Barin held his breath as the man named Robin pulled a lock of auburn hair from his pocket and handed it to the prince. A long curl, soft and silky, lay in Barin's hand. He swallowed and closed his fist over it. He didn't want to believe he held a lock of Erika's hair, but where would skura have gotten this token? His nostrils flared, and he set his jaw, swearing revenge. He must contain himself outwardly. Use this anger to lead these men off the mountain. There would be time to explode once he finds Barte son of Moshere. For now, his men needed him.

"We'll hear no more of this for now," Barin ordered as he wrapped his sister's curl in a kerchief and tucked it in his pocket, sealing his heartbreak and wrath along with it.

While leading the men down the slopes of the mountain, he anguished over the possibility of having lost his family and struggled to stay in the present. He scratched his hands from bramble bushes and sharp rocks he had grabbed onto to keep from tripping. Still, he led the men through the steepest cliffs. Every man took care and watched their footing.

Effie removed Barin's cloak and gave it to a friend, and he, once warmed, passed it to another. In that way they passed Barin's shroud from person to person. Stormy stayed near Barin. The boy showed unusual strength for his age, his bright red hair telltale to his kinship with Rory. Stormy whispered to the prince.

"Back at the caves, did you eat the food?"

"I did, Stormy. I tried not to, but I couldn't hold off any longer. They might have given me poison, but it seemed an easier death than freezing or starving." He didn't focus on their conversation, but on finding a straightforward way down one particularly rocky incline, so Stormy's words did not register right away.

"The dark lord force-feeds his skura, mountain giants, and his shapeless creatures the same food. I believe it's how he gets them to obey."

The young man's voice quaked. Barin paused and glanced up at him. They had imprisoned Stormy on a cold mountain top for two weeks. It had been rough on Barin, how much more so on a lad Stormy's age? Barin put his hand on the young man's shoulder and squeezed it.

"We're free of that devil, now. We're leaving this mountain. Once we join up with Neal and his troops, we'll be a unit again. You needn't fear Skotádi and his creatures any longer."

"I know that, Vasil, but the food on the mountain! You ate it?"

Stormy didn't have the expression of a madman, nor did his countenance reflect on the suffering he had endured, but deep concern darkened his grimace. Barin paused, searching the boy's eyes.

"What are you telling me, Stormy? You didn't eat?"

"Not the demon's platter, Vasil. Moss that grew on the rocks kept me alive. Nibbled on mushrooms. I tried to tell the others, but they wanted the stew. Said it warmed their insides."

Barin released Stormy's shoulder, contemplating his words. His stomach felt fine. If Skotádi had poisoned the stew, Barin and his men would be sick by now. Or dead. But they were healthy, considering the circumstances.

"Let's get off the mountain, lad," he said. "There are pressing matters at home. Look, there's a trail below. Once we reach it, traveling will be much safer."

Neal had assigned three quarters of the troops that had continued with him to Tellwater, to stay with Lord Garion's estate. With them he left instructions and plans for the king's fortification—a unique structure that would protect against skura, giants, and any other known beasts Skotádi created. He stationed the merchant civilians who had come with them with Felix, ready to begin a new life. All the apprentice wizards also stayed with Lord Garion.

The morning sun promised a good traveling day, and so Neal and the rest of his men headed south. Once at the junction, Neal would send another search party for the prince and take the rest of the men to Fairmistle. He would meet the scouts on his return to Prasa Potama.

The morning of the ride had been pleasant as they traveled through the vineyards now leafless and pruned. The weather had turned for the better recently, and the fields were richly green under the melting snow. Sun warmed his back, and billowing clouds floated through the blue skies.

Without warning, a skura burst out of a tree and dove into the valley, snatching a boy from the fields in the distance.

Neal whipped his horse to chase, aimed his crossbow, and fired. The skura fell, the boy with him, and one of Neal's men loped out to retrieve the lad.

Alerted of danger, the other men spread out across the fields. Kairos rode his horse ahead of them, dusting the air with a potion his mother used to use, a liquid spell that drew animals out of their cover, much like wood rises after falling into a body of water. The potion misted the air, sucking a horde of skura into the open. Caught unprepared, the flock swarmed, flapping their ghastly wings as the magic lifted them into the sky. The soldiers fired, and a cluster of skura plummeted. The rest of the flock continued to fly and then in one menacing mass, turned around and dove toward the soldiers.

"Take cover!" Neal ordered.

The soldiers dismounted and pulled their horses to the ground. Where there were no gullies or ditches to hide in, they crouched next to their mounts. Kairos threw his spells and many of the skura vanished in explosions, but the skura were too spread out for him to kill them all.

Bolts soared through the morning sky and struck the diving beasts. Blood splattered across the fields. Wounded skura landed and limped toward their prey while men beat them off with swords.

Neal could no longer supervise the battle. The skura were as thick as tar, flying from above and crawling over the land. His ears throbbed from the screams of men, horses, and demons. He swung his sword at the screeching half-man, half-beast monstrosity that lunged at him, slicing into its scaly wing. It jumped back, favoring its wounded limb, but pressed on snarling, its nose wrinkling like a rabid bat. Neal dodged the teeth that snapped at him and swung again, severing a portion of its other wing. The skura leapt and came at him with its razor-sharp talons. Neal slid low, the skura's talon cutting his forehead as it touched ground. Neal rammed his sword through the skura's heart and quickly pulled it out of the monster, jumping out of the way before the beast collapsed. He swung at another beast that had been clawing at his horse and severed the fiend's head from its body, saving the shaken equine.

Three more skura dove at him, but they were slow and sleepy. Had it been nighttime, Neal might not have been so lucky. The gash across his forehead dripped blood, as did his armor..

When the last skura on the ground died, a hush fell over the fields. The remaining skura vanished into the clouds, leaving a thick blanket of dead animals spread out across the valley. Neal counted his men as they rose. None had fallen to death, but he counted five men wounded. Several horses had died.

Kairos rode up to Neal on his horse, a buckskin mare splattered with mud and blood. The rescued boy sat in front of him, a fair-haired young man, small in stature and perhaps thirteen years young. He had a torn coat, and scruffs on his face and neck, but he seemed unharmed otherwise.

"You all right, lad?" Neal asked.

"My arm hurts, I might have broken something, but I'll live. I owe you my life, sir," he answered.

A proud young man, perhaps too haughty, he sat tall in the saddle and held his head high.

"Your name?"

"Clay from Tellwater. How many horses did you lose?"

Neal looked to a soldier next to him, an older man by the name of Papett. "How many?"

"We lost six. One we had to put down," Papett said.

"I'll tell my master what's happened. He'll send you horses to replace the ones you've lost. At my request."

Neal raised a brow and glanced at Kairos.

"I'll bring him home," the wizard offered. "We're not far. Maybe his master will hold to this young man's promise."

Still in Lord Garion's fields, and only a short gallop away from the manor, Neal consented.

"Tell Felix what happened. He'll want to burn these bodies before any more predators catch the scent."

Kairos nodded and Neal let him go while he saw to the wounded. There was no reason not to head further south before sundown should they replace their horses. The soldiers retrieved their belongings from the fallen steeds, stacked them near the river, and waited.

Kairos returned midday with Felix and a group of serfs driving a cart full of kindling and a barrel of oil. They led six horses. Felix hurried to Neal, jumped from his horse, and handed Kairos the reins. He surveyed the damage and waved to his serfs to begin their work. "My apologies, Neal. If I had seen the trouble, I would have sent troops to your aide."

"It happened rather quickly, and all because of one nasty skura attempting to steal a young man." Neal replied.

"Clay. He's my cousin. Someday he'll be the owner of this manor. We've told him before to not wander alone, but he's headstrong and does what he wants. What happened today might change his mind. I hope so. Did you need to return to the house and spend another night?"

Neal watched his men in the field saddling the new mounts, packing their bags. He had already decided. With the warmer weather, it'd be wise to continue.

"The day's still young. We'll be leaving within the hour." Neal assured him.

The serfs had already started a bonfire, dragging the skura carcasses and tossing them into the flames. They buried the slain horses.

"You lost no men, then?" Felix asked.

"Not a one, and those wounded are more willing to leave this valley. Everyone wants to go home. We're fine. Take care of Talos for me. Tell him we'll come back for him in the spring, but he needs to get walking again before he can make the trip home."

"I will. Thank you again," Felix patted Neal's horse. "May the Creator give you safe travels." He frowned as he looked Neal in the eye.

"And may you find our Majesty Prince Barin on your way home."

"Thanks, Felix. That's my prayer as well."

Journey Home

Smoke from the pyres in Tellwater followed Neal and his men as they rode along the river basin. The cultivated fields ended where wild clover began. As the elevation lowered, signs of winter lessened, and the terrain leveled to a shallow bank that led to the river. Known to be a flood plain when the snow melted, their departure proved timely. Another month and this entire area could be under water. When they reached the junction where Prince Barin had disappeared, Neal stopped the company and took his men aside. He appointed as lead a man named Terrance, a strong and able-bodied scout with excellent tracking skills.

"There's no sense taking the entire company up that trail. Enough snow has melted on this side of the mountain that you might find signs of the prince. Tracks, perchance. Perhaps there are... remains." It hurt him to think of Barin as deceased, but he had a duty, and a passion to discover what happened to the prince.

"We'll leave immediately," Terrance agreed.

"The company will camp along the river. You'll see our fires. Bring word if you find any sign of him. Tomorrow we'll ride into Fairmistle and check on the men there. We'll be back here in three days. That should give you time to uncover any leads."

"Yes, sir."

The five men, their horses heavily packed, rode up the hilly trail. Terrance was as good a scout as any, and his dedication to Barin was as passionate as the commander's. Neil trusted him to follow whatever lead he came across. No one wanted to lose hope. Neal would go himself if he didn't have the company to command. Even now, as he watched them disappear among the rocks, he imagined turning over every stone and following every broken branch. He didn't want to lose his prince. Barin had been his best friend ever since they were small lads.

He watched the men until they receded into the hills, vowing to return after his troops were home safe. He would search these hills for the rest of his days if he had to.

When Neal could no longer see the scouts, he gave his men the order to make camp. The soldiers dismounted and filled their canteens. The river here flowed as a vast watercourse, no longer confined by the bluffs of the majestic mountains and icy boulders. Neal stood at the bank of the river and let the sound of rushing water soothe his weariness. This had not been the best of mutations. They had fulfilled the mission of bringing troops, supplies and settlers into the valley. They would build new homes and a fort that will secure Tellwater for the kingdom. Lord Garion and Felix had the labor force and new weapons now to hold off further skura attacks. But unless matters changed, and by some miracle they found Barin, Neal considered all was in vain. For this he grieved.

Kairos walked up to him and stood by his side, perhaps wanting to talk, but the wizard kept his thoughts to himself.

"We will follow the river into the plains, toward Fairmistle before we come back this way and meet our scouts. Then we'll head home to Prasa Potama." His voice was low and melancholy. "We'll trade for fresh horses in Fairmistle. I'll be riding to the villages along the river to see how our troops fared, if there were any attacks during their stay, and if they need more men. You may remain in Fairmistle and rest if you wish."

Kairos nodded. He was no soldier, and he knew nothing about scouting. Neal smiled to himself. Of all the people to be telling his plans to, Kairos should be the last.

"How are you holding up, Wizard?" Neal knew Kairos, but not personally before this trip. Now, because of what they'd experienced together, Kairos seemed like family. "I have never been in battle, but I've grown because of all of this, and maybe I've stepped into my father's shoes. A little. But..." he shook his head and gazed at the river. "But I am a friend of the king. I am close to his daughters, and I know his son. I know that the darkness in those halls will be great." He sighed. "It will be good to be home. But the palace will not be an auspicious place to return to."

"No. You're right. And it will be up to us to hold it together." Neal placed his hand on Kairos' shoulder. "They need us more than ever."

Warm air turned to cool as the sun fell below the horizon, though the temperature lacked the icy cold they experienced on the mountain. The vast landscape of blue grasslands stretched as far as the distant hills, and beyond a dark ribbon against the night sky which marked the greenbelt. The men's spirits picked up as they unsaddled their mounts and made their beds. They would sleep well with a measure of comfort here in the warmer climate under the stars. Some men made lean-tos with their blankets, others, like Neal, made their beds in open air. They must take turns keeping vigil through the night.

Neal—tired yet his mind too restless to sleep—stared at the heavens. His thoughts wandered to the day Talos stumbled into camp muttering he had lost the prince to the mountain giants. Those thoughts kept him awake.

Legends told of the giants guarding Mount Ream and even that there lived a dragon deep in the mountain's cave. Neal was skeptical of folklore, so he paid it little mind, but not even in the ballads sung by bards did mountain giants venture off the pinnacle. Yet they were in Canyon Gia, and now Talos swore they captured Barin on the trail into the valley. How? Are the giants really leaving the highlands? If so, why?

Months ago, when Neal and Barin were attacked by mountain giants, he hadn't seen their physical form until after Erika and Rory chased them away with fire. And then, only fleetingly, as they vanished. That experience was so different from the story Talos gave. He drilled the soldier, asking him if the giants were as mist and if they were, how was it that they took Barin? That the giant could talk left him critical of the confrontation. And why wasn't Barin killed? Clearly, Talos had a horrible experience, but Neal made little sense out of his story.

When Neal spied movement in the distance coming from the mountain—long shadows in the moonlight—he jumped up, grabbed his bow, and rustled Kairos awake.

"Wizard, wake. Grab your potion. We have visitors."

Kairos sat up, as did other men who heard him, each with their weapons in hand.

"Stand guard. Don't shoot but stoke the fires," Neal

commanded.

Soldiers woke, quietly rustling to action. They gathered dry grass and driftwood from the riverbank, placing them on the hot coals in their fire pits, fanning the embers until they burst into flame. Neal lit a torch from one fire and clinched it, a cold sweat creeping down his temple as the shapes slowly approached. Kairos took a vial from his pouch.

While Barin led the men down the mountain, the stronger of them foraged for huckleberries, chanterelles, and wild spinach buried under the snow. These provisions gave the travelers enough nutrition to keep them moving. They quenched their thirst from pools of melting snow but once in the foothills those pools were not as abundant. The men were so worn and fatigued that Barin pushed them on. Had they fallen asleep as dehydrated as they were, they might have died. Barin was exhausted, lips parched, and his body numb stumbled on. His shoes were worn thin and rocks bit through the leather, scraping the soles of his feet, now bruised and bloody. Those who were able carried the weakest, supporting more than half the weight of men who were not able to walk. When Effie fell in the grassland, Barin pulled him to his feet. "Just a little longer. Listen. You can hear the river now. You can make it." The young man shook his head and leaned on the prince.

"Fire, Vasil," one man said, his voice raspy, his body shaking in excitement. "There are people over there. At the river."

Barin blinked, his eyes still watery from pain. He lit up at the soldier's announcement. Those weren't just reflections of stars in the river. They were campfires. He smelled the smoke. He wanted to run to them, but his body wouldn't let him. His legs were too heavy to lift, and the men too weary to follow. "Keep walking, men. There is hope in sight." He saw a horse, and as he neared, he saw the king's banner on a pole near the river.

And then he heard someone yell out. "Hold your fire!"

Barin recognized that voice. Neal! His pulse quickened. He laughed and cried a flood of joy and relief poured out as tears.

"Vasil!" came the call, and Neal ran toward him.

Neil's men escorted Barin, and the freed captives to the camp. Neal's soldiers carried those too weak to walk and gave them blankets and coat once they arrived at the camp. Their feet were bandaged, their bodies nurtured. Barin enjoyed a warm bowl of stew, and soft grass to lie on. Fires burned throughout the night and so with the countless stars and Neal's army watching over him, Barin, for the first time in a long while, slept like a baby.

Barin woke at dawn, earlier than Stormy and the other Fairmistle boys. The river sparkled with the colors of sunrise—golds and pinks and a soft valley fog. So tempting was the water that Barin stripped naked and dove in. The cold shocked him awake. He scrubbed his face when he came up for air and swam back to shore, shaking droplets out of his hair. He dried with a cloth, which Neal tossed him.

"Well, that was refreshing!" Barin remarked, slipping into his stockings and trousers. While still shirtless, he eyed the camp, the horses, and the sleeping soldiers. "Your men aren't up yet?" he asked.

Neal simply shook his head. "Tell me, Vasil, what's it like to be imprisoned by a mountain giant." Neal poured him a mug of hot wine.

Barin accepted the cup, took a drink, and then set it down.

"Completely senseless and horrific, Neal. The giant's fist bore a resemblance to a tomb in which he carted me to the top of a mountain." Barin nodded toward the distant peak of Casda de Moor. "He then threw me into a cave with an iron gate and left me alone to freeze, starve and dehydrate. After Skotádi decided he had tortured me enough, he took me into his cave, and then released me with these men to find our way back."

Neal stared at him as Barin dried his hair by the fire. Barin tossed Neal the towel and slipped on his shirt, and then his doublet. He slung his cloak over his shoulders, wondering why Neal hadn't shaken his soldiers awake.

"Your men will be ready to ride soon? What are you staring at?"

"Talos told the truth, then?"

"Good man, if he told you the mountain giants had me, you'd best believe him. Talos is an honest man. He wouldn't lie about his prince. Where is he?"

"He stayed with Lord Garion, too weak for the trip home.

Why, in the king's name, were you tortured if only to be released?"

"I don't know, Neal"

"Did you see him?"

"Who?"

"The phantom. Skotádi? The one who they say controls these demons."

Barin paused for a moment, trying to remember. All that came to mind were the icy caves, the giant, and a dark night inside a different cavern. "No. I thought maybe… no, I didn't. Only the giant named Sol, and a slimy sort of monster who brought food into my cage in the morning and took it out at night. And then these good men who had also been taken captive from Fairmistle." He looked around, anxiously. "Neal, we shouldn't delay. We need to return to the castle."

Neal shook his head, a look of disbelief in his eyes.

"Vasil, may I?" Stormy asked, nodding toward a cup of wine. Neal handed the cup to him. "A good biddin' to you. Everything is well with you?"

"I'm fine, Stormy," Barin snickered slightly, wondering why the boy still worried about his health. Bothered by Neal's stare, Barin waved the comment off. "Stormy thinks I should be ill, or out of my mind, perhaps."

Neal glanced at the boy who looked away, blushing.

"Why?" Neal asked.

"It's nothing." Barin answered. Don't start a panic in the camp, he thought as he glared at Stormy. The young man didn't see his expression though or paid no attention to it if he did.

"Sir, His Highness Prince Barin and the men—they ate food prepared by the demon. Folks in Fairmistle say Lord Skotádi controls his beasts with tainted food."

"And yet we're fine. No one is ill. It's a fable, Stormy. A folktale. Pay it no mind."

Stormy bowed. "My apologies, meanin' no harm to you."

"Of course, you didn't mean any harm. Just don't worry so much over me. Please." Barin said and turned his back to the young man who glanced at Neal and then stepped back to his bedroll.

"So, you're ready to ride on, Vasil?" Neal asked.

"Immediately. You and your men are headed for Prasa Potama?"

"Our plans have changed since you're here. We were going to take a side trip to Fairmistle to get fresh horses and check on your men in the river towns. I also have a search party in the hills looking for you. But yes, we were riding to Prasa Potama after that."

"I will ride there directly."

"Your father will be euphoric to see you, Barin. We sent word that you had disappeared. I can only imagine the suffering he's been going through."

"If my father still lives." Barin said as he laced his boots. Not a minute could be spared. If Barte indeed invaded his father's land, Barin would have to drive him out. His stomach sickened at the thought of what he might find. If indeed his family had been slain, Barin would retaliate. He pulled tight the knot of his laces with a quick yank, wishing it were a rope around Barte's neck he was constricting instead. He leapt to his feet.

"Pardon?" Neil asked.

"My men tell me that my father's castle has been invaded," Barin met Neal's surprise. "They presented proof. If that's so, we can't waste time. I fear for my sisters."

"I didn't hear any such rumor."

Barin glanced at Stormy. "Tell him, Stormy."

Stormy hesitated, so Effie interjected. "We overheard the skura talking,"

"What exactly did they say?" Neal asked.

"They said they had it easy now that Barte son of Moshere has invaded our kingdom. They were laughing about it."

"And the proof?"

Effie shuffled nervously.

Barin stood, dressed, and paced around the fire. "Stormy, wake the men, let's get them moving."

"Yes, sir."

He turned to Neal, his temper flaring as he repeated what his men told him.

"The skura possessed something that belonged to Erika. Something... personal. The men saw it."

Neal shot Barin a concerned grimace. The soldiers woke, shuffling out of their blankets, getting ready for the day. They gathered around Barin, telling Neal their side of the story.

"We thought they were tricking us, but they didn't know we were listening."

"Said that Barte is sitting on the throne and securing the palace with his own guards. Said he's dressing them like Potamian guards so if Prince Barin returns, he'll be lured into the castle."

"They're fixing on killing you, Vasil. And any men you bring with you."

"And the King?" Neal asked.

"Said he died, sir. Said Barte son of Moshere drove a sword right through his heart. We don't know if that's true, but that's what they said."

"You believe this, Barin?"

"Yes, Neal." The remnant became too personal for Barin to mention. He fingered the kerchief in his pocket. "With the illness of my father, think of how easy it would be for Barte to come and invade us. Even more so if he knew I was gone. You have a horse for me?"

"Yours," Neal nodded toward his destrier in the field with the others. "The men led Beau all the way to the valley and back, hoping we'd find you. He's fresh and ready to go."

Barin's spirits lifted when he saw his horse. He picked up his blanket and threw it over his shoulder.

"Good. We have no time to dally. Take what men would go to Fairmistle with you, Neal, and assemble our men who are there. Recruit others if you can. Gather weapons in the village, horses. We'll need a large army to defeat Moshere."

Neal bowed cordially. "Of course, Vasil."

"That's an order!" The look on Neal's face expressed doubt, but this was not the time for his commander to balk, nor could he waste these moments explaining. The men Barin rescued on the mountain were energetic this morning, and instead of riding with Neal to their homes in Fairmistle, they chose to rally around him.

"We're with you, Vasil," they agreed. "May the gods save the King."

Barin nodded and gathered the things that Neal salvaged and saddled and packed his horse. He mounted, rode to the banner that sailed in the breeze near the river, and pulled it out of the sand. Holding the standard high, he circled the camp.

"You who are loyal to King Tobias take heed. When we left the king to aid Lord Garion and fight against the devil, to our ignorance we left the Crown city Prasa Potama vulnerable to the wiles of a foreign invader. Barte son of Moshere has assaulted the throne of King Tobias. Our enemies have conspired against us. Who is there to join me and drive this trespasser from our kingdom?"

Barin pointed to Kairos. "Wizard! Come with me."

The wizard bowed low and then mounted a horse.

Soldiers raised their fists and saddled their mounts, leaving Neal with but a few weary men desiring to return to Fairmistle. Stormy included. It was just as well. Barin's men believed in him. Proud of his new militia, he led his soldiers, fully armed now, refreshed from their quiet sleep by the river, canteens filled, and a day's ride to Prasa Potama.

The once-imprisoned men rode by his side in solidarity. They had suffered together and overcame adversity as a unit. They were of one mind now invigorated by conquering inconceivable obstacles. Barin eyed them with a steaming pride. His body flamed with anger as he visualized a skura in possession of a lock of his sister's hair. He will kill whoever is responsible. If Barte son of Moshere is working with the devil, he will put an end to the man. He prodded his horse faster.

Invasion of Cho Nisi

Mist had covered the island overnight, and when Arell awoke, he could see nothing of the landscape when he stepped onto the terrace. A shrill fog whistle from a caravel at Northport wailed, and the sound of drums in the distance answered the call. Something felt wrong. Arell rushed into his street clothes, his gold trimmed red doublet, his cloak, his boots, and hurried down the corridor to the Hall.

Serena and her sisters were by a window when he entered.

"Those are the drums of war," Serena told him.

Arell seized the sword Osage had made for him off the mount on the wall. He had never used it. A weapon decorated with a pommel shaped like an osprey—Cho Nisi's insignia—while its wings spanned the recurved quillons and a freshly sharpened two-edged blade.

"Serena, have a page summons Osage and his men."

The girls hurried out the door. His palms sweated as he sheathed the weapon and fastened it onto his baldric. He took a moment to calm himself before he stepped into the courtyard. He was the King, he must suppress his fear for the sake of the inhabitants of the island.

Grooms and sentries lingered in groups, talking among themselves. When they saw Arell, a sentry ran up to him.

"What is it, Vasil? What's happening?"

"I'm not sure."

With such thick fog, there'd be no way to tell if invaders had come from the sea, not without going to the docks, and that would be a foolish thing to do without advice from the council. "Have you seen Chief Silas?"

"No, Vasil, no one from the tribe has been up here."

"This came for you this morning, though." The page handed him a letter.

"From King Tobias?" Dread paled his face as the drums of war beat louder. He regarded the sentries standing in the courtyard.

"Prepare yourselves for battle," he told them. They left his side hurriedly.

What was this note? Not a declaration of war, he hoped. Not from King Tobias. Hadn't they left that riff behind? He tore the letter open.

> *King Arell of Cho Nisi, my dearest friend and Ally,*
> *My kingdom offers you our deepest sympathy in the death of your most noble father and our ally. If there is recompense we can offer you, please make us aware of what it is.*

Arell looked up from the parchment. The page and stable boys stared at him as if waiting for a response.

"Please! Privacy," he turned his back to his audience and walked away. This letter had King Tobias' signature. Whether the king wrote this, or a servant did he couldn't tell but the letter came from the castle where Erika lived. And fortunately, it brought tidings of good will.

> *I very much desire that our nations set aside the past and reach across our borders, and the sea, to join hands in unity. We face a most dreadful opponent. It is imperative that we stay as allies in this broken world.*
> *You may not be aware, but the evil demons that live on the mountains abducted my son Barin. I am an old man. I need help. We have no magic that can fight the dark wizard. We beseech you please send your drummers to our land to help us free the Prince.*

They must be in dire circumstances if they're asking him for help.

> *And Arell, if you see them in the mist, prepare yourselves. They are giants and they are evil, but you can win. Fight them with fire.*

Arell's heart skipped a beat. Was that Erika's voice? The king would never call him by his first name. For an instant, Arell imagined her beautiful red hair and fiery blue eyes. He felt her kiss.

> *Your strongest ally, King Tobias.*

Arell folded the letter and tucked it in his pocket just as Osage and several hundred men from Moaton rode through the gate. So prepared were they as a mounted cavalry, that they caught Arell off guard.

"Get my horse Honor," he requested of a stable boy nearby.

"Who is the enemy we're fighting, Vasil?" Osage asked.

"I'm not sure, but..." Arell touched the pocket where he had secured the letter, grateful it had arrived at the same time as the mist. "What knowledge do you have of mountain giants?"

Osage's eyes grew wide. "Only that they appear as vapor before they manifest."

"That's what I've been told."

The stable boy brought Arell's horse and held him while Arell mounted, while the courtyard now buzzed with men-at-arms, servants, and horses and still the drums beat. The spell of the drums was effective against skura, but considering the thickness of the fog, they seemed not to have any defense against mountain giants.

"You there," Arell called to one servant. "Light torches for as many men here as you can. Quickly. Bring me one!" Arell mounted.

"I need to contact Silas," Arell said, accepting the torch handed to him. Osage looked puzzled but received his torch, as did several other soldiers. Honor tossed his head and stepped in circles. Osage and the other soldiers also had difficulty keeping their mounts calm. "We'll ride to Nico."

Seeing the open road ahead, Honor ambled energetically through the gate. They rode single file over the spit and into Moaton. The beat of a hundred steeds clapping over cobblestone drew the attention of the town, and soon people congregated in the street as the soldiers passed. "What's happening, Vasil?"

"Stay inside until you don't hear drums any longer and until the sky clears. Burn a candle in your window."

If this white mist proved to be a horde of mountain giants, flaming candles would protect the villagers. "Go quickly inside your homes! Keep weapons near you. Do not open your doors or shutters." Frustrated that only a few people were hearing his instructions, he called for two of the pages who had been following.

"Go door to door. Tell them their king commands every man, woman and child to remain in their homes and keep their doors bolted.

Someone will announce when it is clear. And you two," he stopped the boys before they were out of hearing range. "When you've knocked on every door, get yourselves inside the last house."

"Yes, Vasil," they answered.

Arell left the city with a hundred soldiers following. With fog so impenetrable he couldn't see the trail but depended on his horse's instinct to find its way. Osage rode next to him, sitting tall in the saddle, his eyes fixed ahead of him, but Arell paid attention to his surroundings. He kept his torch held high. There's an enemy here, but not knowing exactly where it would strike unnerved him.

"You've done well with your sword, Vasil. You've learned what you needed to."

Arell glanced at him and wondered how he could remain so calm.

"Stay sharp, keen-eyed. Listen," Osage advised.

"If I knew what to listen for, I'd be more at ease. Knowing who our enemy is has its advantages. Are they men, monsters, or spirits?"

"We'll find out soon enough. And then we'll know what to do."

After an hour of riding at a brisk trot, the trail descended toward the cliffs near Nico. Arell slowed the company to a walk. "When we get to the village, I must dismount and go there on foot, alone. Stay with the soldiers and wait on the hill."

"Yes, Vasil," Osage said. "Let's hope someone is there you can talk to."

"Chief Silas never leaves the village without drummers and an elder," Arell assured him. When Arell reached the overlook, he dismounted and handed his reins and his torch to Osage. "I'll be back soon," he said.

"The men will be on guard, Vasil."

Arell stumbled over the rocks, his thick boots clumsy and hard to manage down the steep grade, but it wasn't a long trail. The pathway ended at the beach where the elders recently held Erika's trial. He paused for a moment as the memory of her flashed through his mind. That very log was where she waited for her sentence, not knowing whether she would live or die. She had held her head high though and had showed courage as the elders announced her fate. She never meant to kill his father, that much she had proven to him.

Justice was complete, though he wondered who it hurt the most for the pain of losing her riveted inside him. He breathed deeply and moved on.

The drums were louder here and blended with the sound of the surf. He could see people congregated around a campfire on the beach singing, and natives of the village were dancing. Chief Silas waved to Arell.

"We need to talk," Arell said.

"Follow me."

Silas led Arell past the village homes and along the beach, pale and white as the mist. Salty air tingled when it hit his cheeks as they walked, and breakers pounded on the sand at their feet. Steps made from driftwood the color of the mist transported them to a stony hillside and to a simple shelter camouflaged by the rocky. Silas opened the door and ushered Arell inside. A woman sat on the floor at a low standing table. She wore the purple robe of a Seer, one of the few mages of the island. Arell had heard of her, a friend of his mother's, but he had never met her. A middle-aged woman with an uncanny beauty, slim of build, she looked frail, and yet her dark brown eyes sparkled with life.

"Sit," Chief Silas offered him a mat on the floor so Arell sat cross-legged at the table opposite the woman. A low ambient light lit the Seer's face. She had watched him come in and stayed focused on him while he took a seat, as if she'd been waiting for him.

She nodded a greeting.

"The drums are warding off the attack," she explained. "There are ten thousand skura hovering over the island. Were we to stop beating the drums, everyone on Cho Nisi would die. There is no other magic to save us. Your sword, your soldiers, they cannot save us."

Arell nodded and swallowed. The scent of sandalwood calmed his nerves. Chief Silas sat down on the woven mat next to him and kept a solemn stare on the woman as she spoke.

"The mists are demons from the mountains. We aren't sure if the drums are preventing them from forming into giants or if they haven't gathered their full army yet, and that's why they haven't attacked. They are still coming. I'm sorry, but we practice no other magic except our chants and our drums and our herbs. They are useless against this threat."

Arell wet his lips as sweat formed on his forehead. Ten

thousand skura. He wondered how many giants were settling in on the island. He had only two hundred readied soldiers to fight them.

"The world of Cho Nisi waits for you, King Arell," she continued, her voice monotone. "Forever is a long time to beat a drum."

Arell bit his lip and looked at Silas, who avoided his gaze.

"Women, children, your loved ones. The immigrants in Moaton. Your soldiers, our tribe. Chief Silas. Me. You. We will all die."

He needed to take charge, and yet he did not know what to do. All he had... "Wait," he said and pulled Erika's letter out of his doublet. He read slowly, softly.

"... if you see them in the mist, prepare yourselves. They are giants and they are evil, but you can win. Fight them with fire."

The room fell silent, and they could hear the drums on the beach. Finally, Silas cleared his throat.

"Who wrote to you?" Silas glared at the parchment in Arell's hands.

"I think this is from Erika. King Tobias asked us to help them. They too are experiencing an attack."

"I told her never to write..."

The Seer held her hand up to quiet Chief Silas, and he stopped.

"Do what you must, King Arell. Anything will help. Now go."

Arell stood, and despite his status he felt he should bow to the woman. Silas nudged him out the door. The fog had grown thicker and darker. The drums louder, the breakers stronger. They returned the way they had come; the dancers had gone, and the men had rotated their vigil.

"Forever is a long time to beat a drum," the Seer's voice droned in his mind.

"How long, Silas?" Arell jogged to keep up to the chief. "How long can they keep this vigil?"

Silas shook his head. "I don't know. The need for survival will keep us going. Our love for our families will keep us drumming. But I don't know how long. There are many men all over the island. They will need to return to their families sometimes. They will need to eat and rest. There are not a lot of us."

"Maybe you can teach some Moatons to drum also?" Arell asked.

The chief shrugged.

"I can send them to you."

"Wait and see. I'll send messages." Silas stopped at the trail and turned to Arell, laying his hand on the king's chest. "Did you write her back?"

"Who?"

"The assassin."

A wave of heat rushed through Arell. Erika the Assassin? "No, I haven't."

"Do not."

Arell straightened. Chief Silas had been a father to him, but Arell resented this invasive order. Not that he had considered writing Erika. Yes, she killed his father and changed his life. Broke his heart. But the Cho Nisi had served justice, hadn't they? He fingered the letter in his pocket. She had given him a clue to overcoming this threat, saving the lives of many. That had to account for something.

"I will do as I see fit as king, Silas," he said, and with a nod, pivoted around and walked up the trail to his men.

Rory Visits Fairmistle

After traveling all day, Rory rode into Fairmistle in the dark of night, certain he'd been on the right road. It had been four and a half years since he'd been back home. The oak grove where he used to play as a youth still stood, but he saw no other sign he had reached the village. As if a disc had floated from the heavens and planted itself on the earth where he stood, a sterile landscape surrounded him. No white stone walls of the portico glowed in the moonlight, nor did candles shine through shutters, nor smoke twirl out of chimneys. He listened for dogs barking and heard none. As his horse's hooves clipped on the cobblestone that used to be a courtyard, his heart beat hard. He had either been transported into a dream, or something tragic had happened.

There were no homes. No shops. No dance hall. Something had leveled Fairmistle to a pile of rubble.

Rory dismounted and walked his horse through what once had been the town square. The entire village gone! Bricks that had once been homes scattered, lumber, thatching, rubble spread in piles around him. Numb, he dropped the reins, his eyes wide, his heart throbbing. Blood had risen to his cheeks. Hurrying from one pile of remnants to another, he tore through broken tables, chairs, and pottery, hoping to find a clue where his people were.

Not until he eyed a faint light flickering in the distance at the home of the innkeeper by the river did he walk quicker,. He lead his horse past the rubble, down a trail bordered with sagebrush and tumbleweed and into the sandy river basin sheltered with cottonwoods and mesquite. When he neared the inn, he heard voices. People mingled outside and more people lingered in the drawing room of the Sheepsgate Inn. Light glinted in through the bone panels upstairs and below. Eager to discover what had happened, he ran.

"Rory!"

Rory spun around, gratified to see his brother. Stormy raced to him and flung his arms around him. "By the goodwill of the king, Rory, I thought I'd never see you again." "Stormy, what happened?"

Stormy had lost weight. Bruises darkened his flesh, and he had aged with creases around his eyes and his mouth. He wore tattered clothing and there were holes in his shoes. He looked like a scarecrow might if it were picked apart by a flock of ravens. Rory touched his face.

"What happened?"

"Mountain giants attacked Fairmistle."

"When?"

"A few days ago, maybe a week, I'm not sure. I've lost track of time. I just arrived myself. Neal brought some of us home. We're going to rebuild this place, Rory. We lost a lot." He wiped his eyes and clung onto Rory's arm. "I worried about you too."

"Arrived from where?"

"Casda de Moor."

"The devil's mountain? You were a captive?" Rory's eyes widened.

"You wouldn't believe it, Rory. This giant carried me in his hand. Like a tomb, it was. I hit my head so hard rollin' from side to side I passed out. Woke up in a cave with some other neighbors from here and downriver from us. They'd been defendin' the villages from giants. We lost a lot of folk, Rory. Made me sick. I was one of the lucky ones. Come get some food and we'll talk. Commander Neal is here recruitin' more soldiers. We're ridin' first light."

"Where to?"

Noise inside the Inn drowned Rory's questions. Men, women, and children crowded the rooms. The hearth harbored a roaring fire, and breads, shepherd pies and sweet cakes were on the table. Friends he grew up with took his hands and welcomed him, slapping him on the back, handing him a flask of wine. The villagers were tearful, but they seemed to have a sense of hope about them. They talked of building what the beasts had torn down. For as many folks who crowded into the inn, the numbers weren't a fraction of the population that once made up Fairmistle.

"Is this it, Stormy?" Rory took his brother aside. "Are these the only people left? Is mother... Don't tell me she's...?"

Stormy turned his head and watched the crowd in the room,

biting his lip. His voice broke when he spoke again.

"There's a list posted on the Inn keepers board. The mayor wrote the names of the poor souls who perished. The dead's been buried. Mom died, crushed by a beam when the roof caved in. Least the giants' vile hands didn't get at her. We've got that to be thankful for." His eyes had already told the story. He'd already cried his tears. Rory pulled his brother close and embraced him, his own heart breaking. "I'm sorry, Stormy. "His voice cracked as he fought to stay strong for his younger brother's sake.

Stormy squeezed him. "She's at peace now. Devil can't hurt her anymore. We fought 'em, Rory. Best we could. But they're big and ruthless and we don't have any weapons that can kill 'em."

Rory sighed, despondent. "If we'd only got to you sooner. You do have what it takes to rid them, Stormy. You just didn't know it." He took his brother's shoulders and faced him eye to eye. "Fire will send them away, sure as a log burns it'll make them turn to vapor again. They shy from it. If you'd only known."

"Fire?"

"It'll melt them dead. Swear to the Potamian Throne." Rory hugged him again. The crowd of people didn't let him linger in his remorse. They pushed by and interrupted him with bits of conversations that weren't meant for him or Stormy. Rory looked over their heads at the tall dark-haired commander in his royal uniform talking to a group of soldiers. Commander Neal stood out among the others. Not only because the commander stood taller than most of the people in Fairmistle, but no matter how hard he rode, or fought, he always looked cleaner and more important than anyone else. Maybe because he stood so straight-backed, proud, and calm.

Rory made his way through the crowd with Stormy at his heels, saluting the officer once he stood in front of him. Commander Neal turned from the soldiers and returned the salute. Afterward he looked Rory up and down, a disapproving sneer crept over his face. "You! You're the soldier whom we imprisoned for deserting."

"Yes, sir. I served my time though, sir."

"And now you're here. That surprises me!" he snickered. "Or perhaps it's no surprise."

"They gave me leave, sir." Rory took to defending himself. He'd gotten used to being reprimanded. Just something about being simple and too apologetic that made him the scapegoat, he assumed.

Neal scowled. "Why would they give you leave at a time like this? Who gave you leave?"

"Officer Lennon."

"At the palace during a time of siege? Why are you here and not protecting the castle, soldier?" The commander straightened his back.

"Siege?" Perhaps Rory misunderstood what the commander had said. He frowned and shook his head. "Wasn't much to protect the castle from, sir. The king's in mourning for the prince, true, but I couldn't do much for him."

"Who? King Tobias?" Neal looked confused, which puzzled Rory more. "You came directly from the palace? The palace isn't under attack?"

"Attack?" Rory shook his head, confused. "By whom? Skura? Or mountain giants? I saw no attack. The king mourns the loss of the prince. He's not feeling well. Her highness Erika…"

"Princess Erika is alive? The Casdamians didn't abduct her?"

Rory frowned. "Quite alive, sir. No one took the princess."

"You saw no signs of soldiers, no foreign militia?"

Rory shook his head, scratching his flaming red hair.

"Sir," Stormy's eyes widened. "It's just as I said. There's no army. It's the devil's lies. His Majesty Prince Barin, has taken the bitters of the dark lord, he went…"

"What?" Rory asked. "The prince lives?"

"We were in the dark lord's caves. Like animals, they had us. The others ate the food, not I. Prince Barin must have been poisoned with the devil's bitters along with the others. Our prince believes the castle is under siege, so he's leading his soldiers to defend his father's throne."

"This is true?" Rory asked.

Commander Neal flushed, tongue-tied. "They had me believing Barte son of Moshere came to conquer the Potamian kingdom. My orders were to gather a militia and join Barin. He swears we're under attack, but now you say you were just there—?"

"This morning. It's all well in the castle, sir. Fairest is taking charge of the men-at-arms. Once the prince sees our soldiers, he'll know all is well."

"I'm afraid not, Rory. He believes Moshere's troops are putting on our uniforms to disguise themselves. His mind is taken, sure as the fire spits."

Rory looked at the Commander for instructions.

"It seems this news is correct. I'm not sure what Barin will do when he gets to the palace. I wonder if Kairos could perform some magic to stop him."

"With your permission, let me ride and warn the princess and King Tobias," Rory offered.

"You can get there before the prince?"

"I can ride like the wind, if I say so myself."

"I can trust you?"

Offended by the commander's question, Rory accepted the rebuff with a graceful bow. "Let this be my test, sir. I give my allegiance to the Crown and to you. Never did I wish to desert, but only to protect Her Highness Princess Erika who was going to be sailin' on her own with no sense of the sea—with or without a guide."

The commander paused, studied him for a moment, and then nodded. "Go then. Hurry."

Rory took Stormy's arm. "If it is your will, sire, please let my brother stay with you."

"Very well. He can ride with us. Hurry now. I'll muster the recruits. We'll be right behind you," Commander Neal made his way through the inn, giving orders to his men and his recruits to prepare to leave. Rory raced out the door.

Torches lit the garden beds, and the many assemblies of people outside. In the shadows Rory eyed the soldiers highline where mounts waited. He untied his horse and hurried to them.

"Lend me a fresh horse," he said.

"These are for Commander Neal's recruits, lad," the man said.

"And that I am. Take my horse," Rory handed him his reins. "He's just as sturdy, but I'll be running like the devil in chase tonight. Don't want to be running my horse to the ground. He carried me all the way from Prasa Potama this morn."

"Do you have the captain's permission?"

"I do."

"Very well. Take that one." He nodded to a chestnut stallion saddled and readied.

"Is this one of the King's horses?" Rory asked of the chestnut.

"Yes, it is."

"Good. Take care of mine if you would. He's got his own stall in the castle stable." Rory jumped on his new mount, spun the animal around, and trotted away from the Inn. Once in the open plains, he clicked his tongue and the horse shot into a gallop. How quickly the steed dashed! Smooth like a gazelle, outrunning a cougar—and sure-footed! The cold air on his face and the horse's swift gait awakened him to the urgency of his mission.

Not a cloud tarnished the sky, and a thousand stars lit the plains.

Barin lived! News of the prince's survival will be well received—that is, if Neal can keep him from storming his father's palace. How tragic that Prince Barin is under Lord Skotádi's spell. What other deviltry is at work in this? Stormy may not have convinced Commander Neal of the phantom, but Rory knew Skotádi's ways. He and Erika saw the devil. And if the ghost can suck a soul from a dying body, he can kidnap a mind from a living one. If Barin spent time in the devil's lair, and Skotádi released him unharmed, then there's something sinister brewing.

Rory nudged his horse faster, and the animal beneath him flew. The mountain tops glowed blue in the night sky. Snow dotted the landscape as he rushed by, but the plains of Kevshire were grassy and green still. The air had the crispness of winter, but a warm breeze beat against his cheeks.

He should have asked more questions. The wizard was with him, but how many other men did Barin have? When did they leave? The princess would need to know those things. But judging by Commander Neal's reaction toward him, the prince may have a grievance against him as well. The last time he saw Barin, the prince threw him in the dungeon. In Barin's eyes, Rory had been a traitor and a deserter.

Rory wouldn't try to find Barin. He'll ride to the castle and find the princess. She'll know what to do.

He galloped his horse all night over the plains, the nocturnal sky his shield.

Siege

Erika woke with a start and sat up quickly in her bed. Something's wrong. She pulled her satin covers back and hurried to her patio, pushing open the doors. A red sun climbed over the hillside, illuminating the sky with a bright magenta glow. Below her, a thin stream of gray laced the forest surrounding the castle and the fragrance of burning evergreen filled her lungs. Smoke? There were no flames, only smoke. She threw her surcoat over her chemise, slipped into her shoes, and hurried to her father's study, a room whose stained glass faced another section of the castle grounds. Her father slept, and careful not to wake him, she opened the thick oak door to his terrace. A small fire burned in the distance, beyond the lake. Erika let her father sleep and ran down the corridor, seeking a guard.

"Find out who is camped out there," she ordered. The sentry bowed, "Already Captain Lennon has ordered men to investigate."

"Well, what news?"

"None yet. It seems the fires are unattended."

"Unattended?"

"They surround the castle. But no one is near them. Our men are snuffing them as we speak."

No one lights fires around a castle without intending to do something pervasive. But who and what? She met Olinda and Rhea at their door, still in their nightclothes.

"I smell smoke. What's happening?" Rhea asked.

"Someone is burning the castle grounds."

"Who?"

"How should I know?" Erika asked. "Get dressed!"

They slipped back into their rooms and closed the doors. Erika hurried through the palace. Whatever the threat, she shouldn't confront it in her nightclothes. She pushed the door to her room open and startled Sylvia, who'd been preparing her wardrobe for the day.

"My armor," Erika commanded none too pleasantly.

Sylvia sighed. "Fairest, we have soldiers?"

Erika scowled, and immediately Sylvia bowed. "Pardon my boldness." Sylvia wasted no time gathering Erika's gambeson, her trousers which had been washed and put away in the cedar chest, her pauldrons and gorget. "Did you want the gauntlets as well, Fairest?"

"We're fighting men this time, Sylvia. I will need whatever is in that chest, and my father's sword and my bow. And a shield if you can find one for me."

"As you wish."

"We must move Father to the keep."

"I will send guards to take him."

"Send guards but I will lead them."

"Perhaps you should stay with him," she suggested. She spoke kindly, like a mother. Erika sighed as the woman tied her gambeson taut.

"Thank you, Sylvia, I know you're concerned for my safety, but my brother isn't here, and my father isn't able to fight. Someone from our family needs to lead the soldiers. There's no question it should be me. My sisters should stay in the keep with Father."

Sylvia bowed and picked up the breastplate. "As you wish, child."

"Sylvia! Please. I'm no longer a child."

"Of course, you aren't, Fairest. You are a strong and brave woman, and you will defend your palace and be victorious." Their eyes met.

"Thank you."

"Fairest!" A soldier stopped at the door, breathless. He bowed. "The fires were a trap. Our men are being ambushed as they put them out"

"Who is doing this?" Erika gasped, tying her cuisses, and buckling her baldric. "Fetch the sword, Sylvia." The maid slipped out the door in a rush.

"They wear masks and heavy cloaks. No insignia that we've seen. They hide in the bushes."

"How many soldiers have we lost?"

"Three were wounded, but we've brought them to safety. These revolutionaries have surrounded the castle, They're everywhere."

"Pull your soldiers back and regroup. Have the hoplite soldiers guard the entries. Let the fires burn for now. We can't lose men like this. No attack until we find out who this is and what their intentions are."

"Yes, Fairest." He saluted Erika, sending a warmth throughout her body. She returned his salute as Sylvia stepped past him with her father's weapons. The soldier left.

Erika sheathed her sword, attached her daggers to the baldric and stormed into the hall as the guards carried King Tobias on a stretcher.

"Take the tunnel," Erika ordered, and shadowed them as they opened the walls to the secret passageway.

"What's going on?" King Tobias asked, waking. He shuffled on his stretcher as they lowered him down the circular stairwell. "Let me up. Where are you taking me?"

"You're fine, Father, we're taking you to the keep. The castle is under attack."

He tried sitting up, so Erika rushed to his side. "Just lay quiet."

"Give me my sword, young lady."

"No! Father! You're in no shape to fight. I'll wield it for you."

The soldier at the foot of the stretcher adjusted his weight. "Please, Vasil, we could move you more easily if you lie still."

Tobias sighed heavily and shrunk back down onto his pillow. Erika adjusted his robe as they walked and then held his hand. Olinda and Rhea came down the stairs behind them.

"Who in God's name is attacking us?" the king asked.

"We don't know." Olinda answered. "But we've brought breakfast. When we get to the tower, we'll make you all comfy and feed you. Rhea's got broth."

"I don't want broth! I want to defend my throne. Where is Barin?"

"He's not come home yet," Erika whispered. She wished they were at the keep already. The soldiers needed a commander. "Can we hurry?" she asked the guards.

"Erika, you're making matters worse. Go do whatever you need to do. We'll take care of Father," Rhea suggested.

The tunnel had already narrowed too much for Erika to walk alongside the stretcher and trailing behind made no sense. "I will return," she promised and ran back the way she had come.

Rory's horse had slowed to a canter once he came to the forest that bounded Castle Prasa Potama. A welcome sight with the rising sun. What he didn't find welcoming was the smoke floating downwind toward him. Had someone set fire to the palace? He veered east, intending to ride to higher ground where he could see the landscape and determine if Barin and his men were inside the castle spread. On a road often used by merchants and their wagons, he prodded his horse to a trot along the hillside and where several bends leveled to viewpoints that looked out over the castle and all the valley. When he rounded the first bend, he pulled his horse to a quick halt. Soldiers occupied the overlook. They crouched behind brush and bramble directly in front of him, bolts nocked and pointed at the castle.

Barin leapt onto the road. His sudden presence startled Rory.

"Vasil!"

"You! The Deserter! What are you doing here? Spying?" Barin pointed at him. "Shoot this man!"

Rory's horse reared. He swung the steed around and galloped down the hill; the stallion kicking up a tail of dust and stones. Bolts shot out at him. Within minutes a cavalry pursued him. Rory whispered in the stallion's ears and the horse leapt off the hilly trail, changed course, and galloped cross-country toward the castle. The horse stretched his head and flew, clearing gullies and soaring over logs and garden walls. A volley of projectiles soared at him. Like a lightning strike, an unexpected pain hit Rory. An arrow burrowed deep into his shoulder. He bent over as tears flew from his face.

Thank God this horse belonged to the king, for the stallion raced for his grain. Blood leached down Rory's back and sprayed across his arm. The arrow caught the wind and jiggled inside his flesh, tearing open the wound. Rory fought to stay conscious. He had to get to the king. He had to find Erika if only he could stay mounted, he'd make it. His arm grew numb. The grasp on his reins loosened and his vision narrowed as the world went black around him. His horse slowed and stopped.

He fell.

"Fairest, a rider. Someone's fallen off a horse just outside the castle ingress."

Erika had no sooner appeared out from the passageway to the keep and closed the door when a guard came running.

"Where?" she asked.

"The Eastern entrance. He's been wounded, but I believe he's still alive." The guard raced alongside her, their boots echoing on the hardwood floors. "They're bringing him in. We wanted you to see, though, in case he's a spy, or…"

"Why would they shoot their own spy?"

"For precaution? It's a thought."

When she neared the ingress to the eastern entrance, she broke into a run. The man lay on the ground, face down, his red hair a sure sign of his identity.

"Rory!" she cried and knelt next to him. The arrow shaft protruded out of his back. She slid her hand under his arm to see if it had gone through him, and, feeling no point, she called to the soldiers who had surrounded her. "Bring me cloths, a lot of them, and warm water. Tell Sylvia to come here. Get a stretcher ready." Her hand shook as she untied his cowl and removed her armguards. Blood oozed from the wound, staining the floor. "And a jug of wine. This is going to hurt." She leaned low over Rory and whispered. "Rory, it's Erika. You're safe in the castle. Can you hear me?"

He gasped with shallow breath and flinched when she touched the arrow. "I need…"

"You need to be quiet. I'm going to get this arrow out of you, but first I have to dig into the wound and find the head."

Sylvia came with a tray of folded linen and knelt next to Erika, offering a flask of red wine to the princess. When Erika took a drink, the alcohol warmed her insides and calmed her nerves. She knew what had to be done, her brother taught her about arrow wounds, and she had helped him on the field before, but never had she performed this maneuver on her own. She thanked the maid and rolled up her sleeves, poured wine over her hands to sterilize them, and drew her dagger. Rory's cloak had bunched up near the arrow, and so she rent it and then cut Rory's shirt around the shaft. Peeling his clothes from the wet blood that they adhered to, she pushed the frayed fabric away to expose his back. She closed her eyes for a moment and said a prayer to the healing goddess Ygeía, knowing how badly this would hurt. With both hands, she carefully twisted the arrow. Rory's wail pierced not only her ears, but her heart.

"The arrowhead is not lodged in a bone," she whispered to Sylvia after making a complete rotation. Slowly Erika worked her fingers into the wound alongside the shaft and inched them through his flesh. Her clothes absorbed his blood. She pushed gently, carefully. Rory moaned and kicked.

"Hold him down," Erika told a sentry and two men quickly knelt by her and held Rory's legs steady.

"Soak a rag in wine and put it in his mouth," she instructed Sylvia, tears forming in her own eyes, but keeping her hand immersed inside the wound. When Rory's cries were muffled and he sucked on the wine, she continued digging into the lesion until she felt a large, sharp object.

"There!" she said. "I have it now, Rory," she said, clutching the arrowhead. She closed her fingers around it, lifted herself on her knees to get traction, took the shaft with her free hand and gently pulled. Rory screamed. As much as Erika wanted this to be over for his sake, she had to keep pulling. The shaft and stone finally came free with a gush of blood. Erika moved away, and Sylvia immediately packed the wound with multiple folds of cloth. Rory panted, his face red and soaked with tears. Erika leaned over him and kissed his cheek.

"I'm sorry, Rory. I didn't mean to hurt you." To the sentries who had brought a stretcher, she said, "Take him to a room once Sylvia has the dressing wrapped tight. Give him water. Give him whatever he wants whenever he wants it." She rose as the soldiers lifted him carefully onto a stretcher. "Sylvia?"

"I'll tend to him," her servant answered.

"Fairest!" Rory called out as they lifted the stretcher. "I must talk to you."

She'd rather he had time to heal before they talked, but she returned to his side.

"It's Barin."

"What's Barin?"

"Outside. Attacking the castle."

Erika gawked at him. Was Rory daft?

Rory took long breaths between his sentences. "He thinks

Moshere has invaded us."

She waited. Unbelieving. Barin had died, hadn't he?

"He's under a spell."

"Barin, my brother?"

"Barin the Prince. Yes. Your brother. Skotádi captured him and gave him a brew… or something. The demon has control of his mind. He's part of the devil's plan."

Erika pushed Rory's hair back from his face and touched his burning cheeks.

"Thank you, Rory."

"You don't believe me, do you?" he asked.

"I find it hard."

"I rode all the way from Fairmistle. All night. I stumbled on his troops this morning. Neal is coming with more troops. He knows what Barin is planning. Fairest, we must stop your brother. Neal will kill him. I fear…" he swallowed, biting his lip. "I fear for your brother."

"Where is Kairos?"

Rory squeezed his eyes shut. The pain must be unbearable, she thought.

"He's with Barin."

Erika took his hand and whispered. "I'll think of something."

But could she?

Kairos' escape

Erika ordered her soldiers to withdraw. She'd rather be under siege than fight her brother. She had to believe Rory. What other explanation had she? If Barte son of Moshere had attacked the castle, he'd have brought an enormous army and would have broken into the keep in the dark of night. Casdamians were famous for their aggressive fronts.

Setting brush fires and ambushing men as they doused them seemed odd, and not in Casdamian's character. She hadn't known it to be Barin's style either, though the strategy was clever. Because Skotádi had taken control of her brother's mind, she needed Kairos. Or one of the lesser magicians, but most of them were wintering in Tellwater Valley.

The fires died down on their own, and no more violence occurred that morning. In the late afternoon, Erika went to visit her father in the keep and to relieve her sisters. They were reading to the king, and when Erika walked into the quiet stone sanctuary, she couldn't tell who yawned the widest.

"Oh, good!" King Tobias greeted her with a smile.

Rhea stretched. "I'm hungry. I'll have the cooks make something up for you, Father," she said. Olinda closed her book.

"What are you reading?" Erika asked, wondering why all the sleepy eyes.

"Bronstein's Theory and Strategy of World Power Domination," Olinda answered, looking at the cover.

"I didn't know you were interested in stratagem," Erika commented.

"I'm not. I just pulled a book off the shelf in the library."

"It's dry," the king commented, catching Rhea's yawn.

"Well, I can sit with you for a bit, but I need to be back in the castle before dark."

Olinda set the book down next to the king, but he waved at her. "Take it."

"When I get back…"

"Take it. I'm not the least interested in world dominance, my dear daughter. Look at me. I can't even dominate my own palace."

Olinda curtsied, book in hand, and nodded for Rhea to follow her out the door. When they no longer heard their footsteps, the king fixed his eyes on Erika.

"Tell me what's going on out there."

"It's a siege." Erika answered. She didn't have the heart to tell her father that his own son had attacked the castle. It didn't matter if the devil had the prince's mind or not. The news would be heartbreaking. Father may still have his sense of humor, but his color had paled and there were circles around his eyes. Thinking his son had turned against him would kill the man.

"You have blood on your clothes." King Tobias said. "Did you fight someone?"

"No, Father, I healed someone."

He eyed her sleeve again. "Why aren't you telling me everything?"

"Because I don't understand it myself."

"Well, good, then. Talk to me and I'll help you sort through it. That's what I'm here for. A guide, aren't I? A king? A father?"

A father, yes, and just to hear him say that brought tears to her eyes. A father to her, and her sisters, and to Barin. How could she not tell him the truth? He needs to know.

"He's in trouble Father," Erika melted and fell on her knees at his bedside. "I didn't want you to know. It breaks my heart."

King Tobias combed her hair with his hand. His face sorrowful. "My son has come to kill me."

"The devil has Barin's mind, Father. He thinks Barte is in here, not you. He's defending you, so he thinks."

"Then someone has to tell him. Take me out there. Let him see me."

"It's not safe. They almost killed Rory."

"If it's a curse, where is my magician?"

"Rory says he's with Barin."

"Curses," King Tobias sat up in his bed, his face flushed.

"Don't, Father. I'm sure Kairos is only there because he's

under orders. He's not against you. No one is."

The anger had been too much for him. The king wheezed as he tried to take a breath. A coughing fit followed. "Erika, make this right before I die. I want to see my son."

Erika bit her lip, tears streaming down her cheeks. "I will, Father."

Kairos did not doubt that Prince Barin was mistaken about a Casdamian invasion. If the foreign king had been here, the grounds would crawl with soldiers.

The wizard kept to the shadows, avoiding attention. Barin's men were spouting off in fits of rage, cursing Casdamia and making threats that seemed vicious. Barin encouraged it. He laughed with them, raised his fist in anger with them. His eyes had grown wild ever since he ordered the men to shoot at Rory. Kairos feared them all, for the king's sake and for his own life. He avoided Barin for fear the prince might ask him to use his magic, and he worried about Rory. He'd seen the young man hit—a trail of blood spewed after the soldier all the way to the eastern gate. The young man was a gentle sort, he didn't deserve to die, not by the prince he loved. Such injustice turned his stomach.

When twilight faded into night, and Barin and his men sat by their fires, Kairos lingered in the shadows, chewing on a blade of grass, listening to Barin's conversation with his new officers, Fergus, George, and Daniel.

"When Neal gets here, that's when we storm the gates. Barte is a coward, so I'm assuming he'll be hiding in the keep. I'll bring three men with me and we'll take the tunnel. Fergus, you lead your men into the main gate. Let Neal think he's leading the charge, but I want you to climb the stairs to the towers. George, you find my sisters and get them into the woods. I don't want any of them to be in harm's way. That includes Erika if she's still alive. Erika! The fool woman will get herself killed if we don't look out for her."

"You think she still lives, then?" Daniel asked.

Barin fixed his gaze on the fire and his hand slipped into his pocket and he fingered the lock of hair. He didn't answer the man but continued relaying his plan. "Daniel, you'll come with me to the eastern gate. They took the traitor into the ingress, so we know there are soldiers guarding the great hall. They know we're here now, so we must be sly. The rest of our men will kill as many guards as they can and imprison the others."

"What about the servants, Vasil?"

"Shut them in the cellar until the fighting is over. If there are spies among them, we'll deal with them later."

The trees behind Barin rustled. Not enough to garner Barin's attention. He kept his focus on the fire, but Kairos could see the disturbance and something of a form. It wasn't a man. Men don't climb olive trees, their branches are too weak, too flimsy, but what moved was too large and bulky to be a bird. Kairos watched with a keen eye.

"There's a chance that Barte's men are wearing our uniforms—an old war trick. Barte is witty. He'll want us to think it's our people in the castle to lure us in. Don't believe it for a minute. It's a trap and they will slaughter you. Barte son of Moshere would love to wipe out the blood of Potamian kings, and I, being the last of the heirs, would be his grand finale."

"Then maybe you shouldn't go in," Daniel suggested. "Maybe that's too risky."

"Let us protect you," Fergus offered.

Barin shook his head. "My sword screams for Barte's blood. I will be his end."

Barin put another log on the fire. Flames shot up and then Kairos saw the face in the trees. It wasn't a face of a man. If he guessed right, a skura spy lurked in the brush.

The wizard bowed back into the bushes as quietly as he could, hoping the snapping of the fire would keep Barin from hearing him. Apparently, it did, because no one pursued him.

He would have ridden a horse to the castle, but that would be too risky. Better to walk. If he crossed the field before the moon rose, he'd be safe. He'd stay in the shadows. He had a dark enough robe, save for the gold threads, so he took it off and put it on inside out. Kairos walked to the north gate garden and approached the castle from the orchard where he'd be out of sight of Barin's soldiers. The servants kept the northern ingress bolted. No one frequented that entry, but he had a chance of climbing up to Rhea's window without making a disturbance.

    The castle walls were built from cut stone, large and jagged with corners that jutted outward and could be used as steppingstones. A man with climbing skills could find his way to the window on the second story with no difficulty. Kairos did not have climbing skills, but he had agility, having performed various physical maneuvers to retrieve herbs and minerals for his potions—or bats from hoardings. So, using the stone wall to procure entry into Rhea's rooms wouldn't be too difficult, he presumed. Aside from wanting to warn the king, he had a strong desire to see his sweetheart again. He also wanted to be rid of Barin's insanities.

    His cloak almost became the death of him as he tripped on it twice climbing the wall. He grabbed onto the rock above him, and kicked the hem from under his feet, muttering a profanity. He bit his tongue, for he spat the words a bit too loud.

    Sure enough, Rhea's shutters flew open, and then he heard a gasp.

    "Kairos!" she whispered. "What are you doing?"

    "I'm climbing this wall trying to get to you," Kairos answered. "Are you going to help me or just shout at me until Barin's soldiers shoot me down like a trapped turkey?"

    She surveyed the steep castle wall and then stepped back inside. She peeked out again, this time with Olinda by her side. Olinda laughed.

    There were no more jagged corners to use as steps, and so Kairos could climb no higher.

    "Jump," Olinda told him.

    "No!" Rhea argued. "We can send him a rope."

    "Do you have a rope?" Kairos asked.

    Again, Rhea disappeared back into the room. When she reappeared dangling a curtain line, he sighed. "Open the door for me."

    And then he jumped.

    He scrambled to his feet as the door beneath Rhea's room opened. She reached out and pulled him inside. He would have told her what he'd been through, he would have poured out his fears and misgivings, but she kissed him. He forgot all of that. His lover had him in her arms. Kairos shut the door with his foot and drew her close, pressing his lips against hers.

    "You two, get up here," Olinda ordered in a hushed voice.

"Erika is going to want to hear everything you have to tell her, Kairos!"

"Come," she whispered and grabbed Kairos' hand. She didn't have to pull him—he went voluntarily to her chambers. The fragrance of lavender teased his senses once they'd topped the stairs and entered her room. With Olinda gone, Kairos no longer had reason to restrain himself. They sat at the end of her bed, her soft hands stroking his face where a beard should be. He held her hands and kissed her fingers, her soft arms. She giggled, and it made him laugh.

"I thought I had lost you forever," she said, stroking his cheek again. Such a soft touch. He fingered her blond curls, wondering why he had left, and then remembered the king had ordered him to go.

"What's happening outside?" she asked.

"That's Barin out there, you know."

"Erika told us."

"How did Erika know?"

"Rory. Poor fellow. Erika removed the arrow. But he's in a bad way. I nearly retched to see him. I hope he survives."

Kairos frowned. "It's a shame they injured him. He never should have been punished as a deserter either or locked in prison. Why was he the only one who got in trouble over that escapade? I was there too, and no one accused me of desertion."

"Neither the king nor Barin would lift a finger against you, Kairos. You're the king's magician!"

"How is the lad? Is Rory recovering?"

"I don't know. Erika said if we see you, we're to tell her. She's taken charge of the men-at-arms. Father is in the keep and he's not doing well."

"Who's with him?"

"Sylvia. Erika is too frantic to be of help to him. She roams the castle like a cheetah ready to pounce."

"The woman is fire."

"She needs you, Kairos. We all do."

He kissed Rhea again, loving those words coming from her.

Erika burst into the room. "Kairos!" Her voice so startling, Kairos jumped off the bed.

"Tell me what you know."

"Fairest," Kairos said with a cordial bow.

"What is going on with Barin? Has he gone mad?"

"No, Erika, he's not mad, he's misinformed."

"Misinformed?"

"He believes what the devil is telling him. Everything he's doing would make perfect sense if indeed Barte had conquered the castle. Barin's method is curiously clever."

"Reverse the spell," Erika commanded.

Kairos shook his head. "If I could keep Barin from hearing the lies he's being told, I would have done it already."

Rhea sulked, her stare burning a hole in his heart. "You're our only hope, Kairos."

"I'm sorry." He took Rhea's hand with both of his. "I'm sorry. I hate seeing our prince like this as much as you do. But to undo a curse by a Vouchsaver is against convention. It cannot be done. Or undone, I mean. Especially if the Vouchsaver is a demon. Certainly not if he were the Devil himself. It's not in the books."

Erika threw her hands up in the air and paced. She had boots on, tall shiny boots that drummed on the wooden floor in a nervous beat, the sound unsettling. Rhea walked to the window. "What's going to happen?"

"That I can help you with." He turned to Erika. "Barin is waiting for Neal and his men to show up. They'll be here before morning. Then, with Neal's help, he plans on storming the castle."

"That's absurd. Won't he see that it's us? There doesn't need to be any bloodshed," Rhea said.

Kairos held up a finger. "It would appear so. However, before I left, I heard him warning his officers that Barte will disguise his men as Potamian soldiers. He has given the order to kill on sight."

"That's ludicrous!" Erika blurted. "He'll kill us all!"

"No. He won't."

"Why do you say that?"

"Rory's brother Stormy told Neal that Skotádi has control of Barin's thoughts and Stormy went with Neal to Fairmistle. Did Rory tell you where he had been riding from?"

"Rory went to Fairmistle." Erika said.

"Ah! You see. My suspicions are they all met in Fairmistle and through their conversation, perceived the truth. Hence, Rory was sent, or volunteered, to warn you."

"Where is Neal?"

"Most likely arriving soon. What is the protocol for an officer whose prince betrays a king?"

"The commander is to stand for the king."

"So, you see? Neal's army will slaughter Barin and his men before they step foot on palace grounds."

Erika's mouth flew open. Rhea gasped.

"Yes," Kairos said. "They will murder the prince while he is attacking his own kingdom. The thought is preposterous. There is no rhyme nor reason, and the devil has the upper hand."

"I'll just go out there and meet him."

"That might not be wise, Fairest. Barin would think it a trap. In his state of mind, he cannot listen to reason. He's possessed, Erika."

"Abduct him, then." Erika whispered.

"What?"

"Sneak into his camp and kidnap Barin. Render him unconscious, somehow. If he's in the castle, you could work your magic. Surely you have some kind of potion that will subdue him. Without Barin leading the troops, Neal, as commanding officer, could restrain the others."

"It could work, I suppose." Kairos juggled that idea in his mind. "I'm not, however, the sort to do any kidnapping. I may have something that will put him to sleep once you have abducted him, though. Ah!" He held up his finger again. "There's one other thing."

The women's eyes were on him.

"When at camp tonight, I spotted a skura listening in on them. Skotádi's spies are near."

Erika breathed in deeply. "Skotádi is behind all of this, isn't he? Looking for souls to rob."

The girl knows more than she lets on, Kairos thought.

Arell's letter

Erika had gone to her terrace to look out over the grounds once more. Though night still held the dark, she thought she'd see activity. Campfires glowed in the hills, but she had seen no sign of Neal's men.

"Before morning," Erika whispered to herself. "We have to get Barin before morning. She waited for word from the two soldiers she sent to abduct Barin. With Kairos' directions, her brother shouldn't be too hard to find.

A slight knock on the door interrupted her thoughts. Her servants had all gone to bed at her orders. There was no reason for them to stay awake just because she couldn't sleep. She cracked the door open and found a page with a sealed envelope.

"Where did this come from?"

"Cho Nisi, we believe."

"How did it come here?" Erika asked, taking the parchment from the young man.

"A runner from the port, Fairest," he said.

"How did they get by the soldiers?"

The boy shrugged. "Cephas lives near the docks. He'll do anything for a coin, just about, and he's fast. He's not much bigger than I am, and some people call him a scalawag. Cephas'd do nothing... immoral, but he *is* sneaky. We're best friends."

Erika smiled at the boy. "What's your name?"

"Donald. But you can call me Donny."

"Donny, stay close. I may need you."

"Yes, Fairest."

Erika dismissed the boy, shut the door, and then strolled back to the patio. Cho Nisi? Her hands trembled in anticipation as she opened the letter. Written in a shaky pen, she would have guessed the author had been under duress.

My dear Noble King Tobias,

I am deeply grateful for your most sincere apology and have taken it to heart. There is nothing more I would like but to resume being allies with you. Our differences have been realized, a debt has been paid, and I hope to visit with you some day.

That day, however, cannot be soon. I regret most wholeheartedly that the entire island of Cho Nisi is under attack. If this letter finds you, it would surprise me, as our port is under the watchful eye of ten thousand skura.

I am thankful for your counsel, however. When I read your letter, the mist of Casda de Moor had already swooped in upon us. After taking heed of your advice, I had the entire population of our island make fires, carry torches, and burn candles. I am pleased to say not one mountain giant ever manifested and the skies are clear of fog, making it easier to see the black demonic cloud of skura. If you have a remedy for them as well, please be quick as I'm not sure how long our drummers can endure.

I wish I could come and help you find your son.

Your friend and ally,
Arell King of Cho Nisi

She read the letter again, focusing on phrases that stood out, that pulled her heartstrings, that ignited the yearning to see him again.

Our differences have been realized, a debt has been paid, and I hope to visit with you some day.

He couldn't come here without seeing her. Is that what he's saying? Stop reading what's not there!

She read the last line, slowly.

I am pleased to say not one mountain giant ever manifested and the skies are clear of fog, making it easier to see the black demonic cloud of skura. If you have a remedy for them as well, please be quick as I'm not sure how long our drummers can endure.

Ten thousand? He must be exaggerating.

Even a thousand skura would destroy that island. The only weapon those people have is the magic crafted through their chants and drumming. What if they did tire?

Erika opened the door to the terrace and looked out into the dark. Arell's in peril, Barin's cursed, and her father is dying. Even Rory is near death with a hole in his body.

She breathed in the nocturnal air, absorbing the magnificence of the galaxies. "Why? Why do we suffer so? What can we do to set the world right again?" If a voice had spoken to her from out of the heavens and instructed her on what course to take, she would have bowed in worship and obeyed. But no voice responded to her plea—only her heart pounding faster than it should. "It's on my shoulders, isn't it? There isn't anyone else to fix things, is there? The men I love are falling with no one to save them."

She tucked the letter in her gambeson pocket. "Love can't fail them, nor will I fail them. I'm stronger than that. I've made mistakes, but my mistakes are not what's made this world evil. It's you Devil that makes the world evil and I'm coming for you." She set her jaw. She can't keep death away, but life has to be at least as strong as death.

She paced back and forth on the patio, listening for the bird call that would tell her they had captured Barin. She heard horses in the distance. That must be Neal!

She hurried to the door. "Donny," she called. "Are you still there?"

"Yes."

"Get your friend Cephas. I need you to deliver a message. It'll be dangerous, but it's important."

The boy's eyes lit up. "I've been waiting for an errand, Fairest. We're not afraid of danger."

Erika let the boy back into her room and sat at her vanity, penning a message to Neal. She sealed it and handed it to him.

"Beyond the soldier's camps there will be horses. Men who just arrived. They'll be dirty and tired. Those are the men I want you to go to, not the men who have been here."

"Yes, we've seen the men who've been here. We'll find these newcomers."

"Good. Deliver this to their leader. Commander Neal is his name. Don't let anyone else read it. He must read it tonight, well before dawn, do you understand?"

"Yes."

She ruffled his hair, and he ran out the door on quiet feet. He'll get the job done. After the boy disappeared, Erika removed her armor piece by piece, and set it on the bed. She changed into her chemise and surcoat, brushed her hair, and let it fall over her shoulders. Then slipped out into the hall.

Rory lay quietly in a small room that had nothing more than a chair and an end table beside his bed—a servant's quarter. Damp and musty, Erika kept the door open to let in fresh air. She stood there, not wanting to bother him, but his eyes were open, staring out the panes of the tiny window. They had wrapped his shoulder in bandages. Sylvia must have changed the dressing recently because it looked clean and tight.

"Thank you," he whispered as she stood at the doorway. "For saving my life."

He didn't move. She imagined it would have been too painful. She came and sat on the end of his bed. "I'm sorry it hurt so bad."

"Not your fault."

"We'll fix things, Rory."

He smiled. "I know you will. Sure as the sheep give wool, you'll be fixing things."

She touched his swollen hand. Too warm. His body fought that wound. It would be a long struggle for him and she wanted him to win that struggle, just like she wanted her father to keep living, the demons to leave Barin, and for Arell to survive the skura.

"I'm sorry things have been going so roughly for you. You don't deserve any of what's happened to you."

He was quiet for a moment, his eyes still fixed on the window.

"They make those panes out of bone, you know. They take an antler from one of those pretty deer that run wild. Flatten it with a hammer till the light comes through. Put them all together in panels like that."

Erika stared at him until his eyes met hers.

"No one deserves anything, Fairest. Life just happens. One day you're a deer in the woods, the next day you're a window letting the light in."

Erika fought tears.

"You're the one that shines through the window, Fairest. The light is what you are. No matter what your battle is, you're going to win."

She bit her lip and wiped her cheeks with her hand. "Rory, I'm so blessed to have you for a friend."

"The blessing's mine, Fairest."

A Wounded King

While on watch, Arell left the castle on horseback and traveled north. By mid-morning he came to Northport, a small, uninhabited dockside where merchant ships and fishing boats berthed occasionally. Foreigners made the stop over during extended fishing excursions, or merchants from nations far to the north used the island as a midway point to the mainland. Few seafarers had any interest in Cho Nisi, the natives, or the king, but used the pier as a safe place to wait out a storm, or to make repairs. Occasionally someone would request a meeting with the king concerning trade, but those visits were few.

Arell employed boys from Moaton as letter carriers to meet ships from the mainland whenever he spied one from his watch point. However, the last ship seen in Northport had been the one that took Arell's letter to King Tobias. The threat of the skura and the constant beating of the drums had frightened away seafarers aside from a few fishers who happened to drift by. Arell had little hope of any nation coming to his aide. A little island out in the middle of the sea? Why would anyone risk their lives to help?

He lost any hope of victory. Silas and his warriors still took turns chanting and drumming all day and all night, still the best they could do with such a multitude of skura hovering over the island was to conjure enough wind to keep them in the air. The men in Northport grew tired and less energetic, and so that's where Arell traveled the most. He led a pack horse every other day carrying fresh-water, smoked clams, oyster rolls, and any other treats the women from Nico made up for them. Women from Moaton contributed yeast breads and mutton pies.

There were five men and two women keeping vigil in the Northport area. They drummed on a lonely jetty weathered by ocean wind and turbulent surf. The skura flew lower here than other parts of the island, a sign of the drummer's fatigue. Arell's horse refused to venture on the rocky pier, and so Arell had to walk. Warm from the ride and the muggy weather, he took off his doublet, tied it to the saddle and left his horse on the sand dunes to graze near the native's lean-to, while he packed in on foot.

Especially rough winds blew this morning. Abenda, the elder, stood when he saw Arell approach. All but one drum had been silenced, and so Arell kept a cautious eye on the sky.

"Good morning, Abenda." Arell gave him a cheerful greeting. Abenda did not return his smile.

"King Arell, have you found a solution?" he asked, his voice more accusing than inquisitive. Abenda and Arell hadn't gotten along since Erika's trial. The elder had voted to execute the princess, and for that Arell found it difficult to talk to him.

"There is no solution but to fight these beasts, or continue what we're doing," Arell answered as he set the pack down. "I've brought some nutritious food this time."

"We don't want your nutritious food," Abenda said. The surrounding men grunted in agreement. The last drum stopped beating and Arell looked up at the circulating skura, placing a readied hand on his sword as Abenda continued.

"We want a solution. We're tired of being here when there is no end in sight. If fighting these beasts is the only other option than let us fight."

Arell looked at him in surprise. "How can you make that decision without consulting the rest of the tribe?"

"The tribe is on the other side of the island, a full day away. We have no communication with them."

"Then let me find replacements for you so you can go home." Arell's breath quickened as he found himself on the verge of panic. Abenda clearly didn't realize the danger of halting the drums. Warm wind from the skura's wings brushed against his face. He could smell the stench of their wickedness as they orbited even lower than they had.

"We're not staying here another day. If you want replacements, get them." Abenda signaled to the others to rise. "We're done. Today. We'll go back home with you, maybe ride your horses."

Arell spoke quickly. The skura would be on them in a matter of moments.

"You have no weapons besides clubs and sticks. How are you

going to fight them?"

Abenda didn't glance at the sky but kept walking off the jetty. "We're not afraid."

Arell drew his sword, his eyes fixed on the skura now breaking formation and diving toward them.

"Fear would do you well. If that's your decision, I suggest you move quickly toward the horses. Now!"

He lifted his sword in the guarded position that Osage had taught. The skura dipped lower as Arell stepped backward. Abenda must have looked over his shoulder because he picked up a club of driftwood and hurried the men and women to their lean-to. Arell followed them, walking rearward, sword raised. The natives' steps hastened.

"Find shelter in the trees," Arell called to them.

No sooner had he uttered those words than the first skura attacked. Arell swung, a single stroke severed the beast's head from its body. Another came and Arell sliced a wing. It fell.

"Remember to keep your balance," Osage had told him during training.

Walking backwards didn't help.

The beasts were angry, having been beat about in the wind for days, without rest or food. Their revenge would be brutal.

Another skura dove at him. Arell cut upward, ripping the ogre's belly open. Then face to face with the next, stabbing the monster in the heart. Blood spewed across the quay. No longer did they attack one by one. They stormed him as one mass of yelping varmints. One grabbed his shoulders with its thick pointed talons, lifting him off the ground, Arell sliced himself free. Wings beat against his head blinding him, he staggered. Teeth bit into his chest and ripped his flesh as Arell drove him away with the hilt of his sword. Blood gushed, the beast's blood and his. Now, from behind a skura rammed into him and knocked him down, pounced on him, and as Arell rolled over it pinned him to the ground preparing for the kill.

Defeated, Arell lifted his sword, but he had no strength left. Certain this was the end. As he looked into the monster's ravenous eyes, the creature unexpectedly fell to the side as Abenda hit it with a driftwood rod. Drums and chanting began and soon all the warriors sang, once again creating a wind that blew the skura back into the sky. Arell closed his eyes, his life bleeding out of him on the stony ground.

They lifted him on to his horse. He could see Abenda ahead of him, riding the pack animal. Blood soaked his torn shirt as he bent over in the saddle, numb and dizzy—too weak to feel the pain, to even sit up. Men-at-arms came for him once they reached the castle, and Serena wept over him as they carried him to his room.

"I will speak to Silas and the elders," he heard Abenda say.

Serena and other maids quickly took off his bloodied cloak and peeled away the remnants of his shirt and trousers. They washed him, cleaned, and bandaged his wounds. They mopped the trail of blood on the floor.

"Burn these," Serena told her helpers, holding up his clothes.

"What about his cloak, Serena?" a maid asked.

"We'll take it to the sea and scrub it with sand. It's too beautiful a garment, and too wonderful a king not to spend the energy to get it clean." She pushed a lock of hair from off his forehead and applied a cool rag to a gash on his head. Their eyes met, and she smiled at him.

"We'll make you well," she said. "I will send Osage to guard the castle and keep a night vigil, with your permission," she asked. Arell could do nothing more than nod.

When Arell woke, he did not know how long he'd been unconscious. They had opened his shutters, letting in a moist breeze. The sun warmed him as he lay in bed. He tried to remember what had happened and why the bandages.

His door cracked, and then closed again, followed by a quiet knock. Arell smiled. Why did she bother knocking if she were going to peek in?

"Please, enter, Serena." He hadn't much of a voice, and it hurt to talk. They had wrapped his entire torso in linen so that he could hardly move, and still blood seeped through a portion of the bandages.

Serena stepped inside and bowed. "Chief Silas and Abenda would like to speak to you."

Arell motioned for them to come in. They wore ceremonial clothes, turtle shells strapped on their legs, woven loincloths and feathers and beads around their necks. The scent of sandalwood followed them in. They both bowed. Formal. Sometimes Arell didn't understand the chief. Silas could be a close and intimate friend, or be stiff, stern, and severe like this. Today Silas stood in the middle of the room in his somber mood, his head held high, his dark skin contrasting behind the white feathers and reed-woven breastplate. Abenda stepped forward and bowed, and then he got on one knee.

"I ask forgiveness, Your Lordship."

Arell frowned. "For what?"

"I was foolish to contest you. Foolish to stop the drums and put you in danger. I could have killed you."

Ah yes. A skura attack. How could he have forgotten? Arell swallowed and looked aside. He must not have fought them well, considering his condition.

"I have nothing to forgive you for."

"Chief Silas said you might not remember."

"I remember. A skura attack."

"They wouldn't have attacked if I had been obedient. Instead, I acted on my own and commanded my men to stop beating the drum. You put yourself in between the Cho Nisi and the enemy. You saved our lives by risking yours. I owe you honor." He beat his hand over his heart and then held it there.

They had raised Arell as a Cho Nisi. He knew well what Abenda implied by owing him honor. If he refused the man, it would be both offensive and disheartening. "Very well," Arell whispered. "I will give you a task when the need arises."

Abenda stood, kissed his hand, and stepped back to Chief Silas.

"I too owe you an apology, King Arell," Silas said. Arell just stared at him.

How could Silas owe me an apology?

"When I saw you in your bed, wounded, I asked myself where would we be without a king?"

"The Cho Nisi people survived many years without a king before my father's people came, Silas." Arell reminded him.

"Regardless, that's the past. I have denied you to continue your heritage."

"What do you mean?"

Silas turned to Abenda and spoke in their language. Abenda nodded, turned to Arell, bowed, and left the room. Silas walked up to Arell's bedside, and, removing his somber self, he sat next to the bed. "I have had a hard hand in what is natural for you. You meant to be merciful. I fought that."

"Explain yourself."

"I encouraged the elders to pressure you. To go the course of revenge and not forgiveness. I was wrong. You had in your heart to be kind, and we fought against you. When the princess left, I told her never to write you. I threatened her with death. For that I've wronged you."

Arell stared at him. This he didn't know.

"I was angry when I heard she wrote to you."

"Her father wrote to me."

"As you say. Still, I owe you honor." He stood erect and held his fist to his heart.

"Oh, holy idols, Silas, you owe me nothing."

"You risked your life for my people. You could have died."

"I was trying to save myself!"

Silas grimaced, so Arell raised his hand. "Very well. You owe me honor. The time will come for me to place a bidding on you. I accept your honor."

Silas bowed, and with no further words, left the room. Serena came in smiling.

"Beautiful Serena. How may I serve you?"

She blushed. "You are the king. It is I who serve you, Vasil. We have your breakfast ready. I will bring it in. Your wounds are too tender for you to move."

Arell tried sitting to prove her wrong, but a sharp pain raced through him and he could barely swing his legs over the bed. "Very well," he flinched. "You can bring it in. Thank you, Serena."

She bowed and hurried away, leaving Arell to think on what Silas had said.

His body hurt, but the Cho Nisi healers had fine herbs that took some pain away. Judging from the wraps, and his overall weakness, he had bled profusely, and from the ceremony Silas and Abenda performed just now, he may have been near death. He seemed to have given the elders a scare.

The note from King Tobias nested in his doublet. Silas also suspected the king hadn't written the letter. Why did they both suspect Erika penned the warning?

Arell bore the pain and slowly rose from bed, finding his

equilibrium first, and then he staggered to the armoire and found the doublet he wore the day he received the letter. The day he discovered that there were ten thousand skura hovering over the island. Arell felt for the pocket and pulled out the parchment. Taking the letter to his bed, he read every word again. There was no change in the handwriting from one paragraph to the next.

He sniffed the parchment. A sweet floral fragrance—rose or lilac. A king would not send a perfumed letter to another king. He ran his fingers over the ink marks, the color of her hair clear in his memory.

"I could have loved her," he whispered. The last paragraph was a word of warning, and of encouragement which, if he hadn't received the counsel when he did, the entire island might have been destroyed. "She killed my father, but she saved my people."

Witnesses

Ferdinand and Peroy rowed their fishing boat over the quiet waters of the sea. They had just left the Potamian docks that morning, having heard rumors about a school of whiting running off the shore of Cho Nisi.

"I told you before, Peroy, those are dangerous waters," Ferdinand mumbled, pulling hard on the oars. He was a well-built middle-aged man, his bare chest a journal for the life at sea he lived, and the hard work he completed, having once sailed with King Tobias' navy, now taking a well-earned retreat from battle. He wore his work pants and a belt with two daggers sheathed to it. His short hair curled around his ears and over his forehead. He didn't wear a hat like Peroy. He liked to see all around him, the sky, the waters. Hats got in the way. If Peroy didn't wear a hat, he'd be burned to a crisp, fair skinned and all. Peroy, three years older than Ferdinand, lived on the coast town of Melrose, province of Prasa Potama. Ferdinand was married to Peroy's sister.

Peroy squinted, looking at the dark clouds that hung over the island. "If a squall arises, we'll just beach at Northport. We're safe." He took his hat off and wiped his brow. "Can't really give up an opportunity to catch some whiting, Ferdinand. What with the economy like it is right now in Prasa Potama, the prince being gone and everyone all panicky about those winged beasts coming from the mountain, our families could use a little bounty, don't you think?"

"Hear tell the skura are stealing fish from the fishers," Ferdinand complained. "Be just my ill fortune if they stole from us before we ever get back to the mainland."

"Anything else you want to fret over?"

"Sometimes worry does a man right. I've heard many a tale come true in these waters."

"Let's just catch us some fish and forget about gossip today,"

They neared the shoreline of the island cautiously. Despite speculations, they both knew the Cho Nisi could cast spells and sink ships a hundred times larger than their dory. It's one reason King Tobias never thought to conquer the island.

"We're just a couple of lowly fisher people," Ferdinand whispered. "Not meaning any harm."

"Who you talking to?"

"Those natives. They say if you talk to them, they won't curse you." Peroy snickered and tossed floats into the water. Ferdinand lay down his oars and kept a leery eye on the sky.

They hadn't released half their nets when they heard a deafening scream up on the hills of the island. They looked wide eyed at each other.

"Let's get out of here." Peroy said, pulling back the nets.

"Sounds like someone up there's in trouble."

"What does it matter. That's their affair."

"You pull the nets in, then. I'm swimming ashore to see who needs help."

"You're a fool."

"A fool raised as a soldier. If you're any kind of man, you don't run from danger, you run to it, Peroy."

Ferdinand jumped in the water and swam whole-heartedly toward the beach, while Peroy pulled in the nets.

The bank towered high above, and only a small portion of sand made up a beach, but enough to wrap around the cliffs in and out of coves and finally come out at Northport. Ferdinand hurried up the shoreline, and when he rounded the last bend, he stopped and gasped at what he saw. Hundreds of skura dove from the sky, sweeping toward the ground like a tornado where a lone man with a sword fought them. His blade flashed in the sunlight, cutting at the beasts one at a time. When he fell, Ferdinand panicked for the beast covered him with their wings. If Ferdinand had a sword on him, he'd run to help, but with a small dagger, what could he do? Before he decided, he heard drums beating and suddenly the wind picked up. The skura could not fight the gusts of wind and so were blown high into the sky. There they rotated as a thick black cloud.

A group of natives bent over the man who'd been fighting. Natives dressed in colorful garb lifted the swordsman onto a horse.

One of them rode another mount and led the wounded man's horse away.

Ferdinand watched, mesmerized by what he saw. He'd been rowing all day and he was tired, but this could not be a hallucination. Ferdinand ran back the way he came, waded out to the boat, and joined Peroy.

"You won't believe what I saw. Let's get some fish and go home."

"What'd you see?"

"Skura, Peroy. Hundreds of them. Closer to home than they'd

ever been. King Tobias needs to hear about this."

The King's Son

Plenty of stars adorned the sky, and the moon would come up soon. Stormy brought his and Neal's horse to the highline and tied them with the others. It'd been a long and hard ride from Fairmistle, and exhaustion had the best of him. He'd love to sit down, have a bite to eat and sleep. He hadn't fully recovered from his trek off Casda de Moor, nor had he time to quiet himself from the trauma of being starved, frozen and in the enemy's clutches. Nor of seeing his homeland destroyed. Nor of chasing a prince to prevent him from attacking his own castle. Confusing days, these were. Ever since his youth he dreamed of visiting Prasa Potama, but not like this. Not as an enemy. He loved his king and his prince. But from what he knew of the circumstances, he'd be fighting one or the other. He wondered if Neal's men were as nervous about the morrow as he.

"Tell me what you're thinking," Stormy's friend Leo asked in a whisper as they pulled blankets off the horses and brushed their sweaty coats. Leo and Stormy were the same age. Leo's folks offered to take Stormy in when his mother died during the mountain giant attack, and Stormy was still giving it some thought. They'd grown up together and now joined the king's forces together. Neal had reservations enlisting the two because they were so young. Sixteen, but with Rory pleading for his brother, Leo came with the package. Friends needed to be together.

"Could be a lot of killing, Leo. Could be we kill the prince if there's no Casdamians, and the prince storms the castle, anyway. He's under a curse, you know. The devil makes madmen out of the best of us. Part of me is scared out of my trousers and the other part so curious what's going to happen, you couldn't drag me away."

"Same here," Leo said. They left their horses and walked up the trail. Stormy still had a wrap of sweet cake left from the gathering at the inn. He pulled it from his belt and handed a piece to Leo. Leo traded him some smoked beef.

"Neal has cheese and pickled fish in his saddlebags he got from the innkeeper. He said he'll hand it out later tonight after he talks to the prince," Leo said.

"My stomach shrank at the caves, Leo. Don't feel much like eatin'." Stormy eyed Neal farther up the hill, standing alone by his campfire, and nodded toward him as he chewed off a bite of beef. "Wonder what he's thinkin'."

"I wouldn't want to be him right now, that's for sure. Whatever's in his mind, we won't know til sunrise when we get our orders."

Stormy jumped when he heard something in the bushes behind him. He pivoted. Leo had his dagger out. They stood hunched, holding their breath.

"Psst," the sound came again. This time it sounded like a person. A child, actually.

"Yer about you get yerself killed," Stormy said to the bushes.

"Don't tell!" the voice ordered, and two young people emerged from the brush. One wore peasants' clothes, his shirt dusty with a hole in his sleeve. Sitting crooked on his head balanced a sailor's cap. The other boy wore proper attire, as if he worked in a castle.

"Who are you?" Stormy asked.

"My name's Donald and this is Cephas. We've come by order of Princess Erika to deliver a message to your commanding officer," the taller of the two answered.

"Princess Erika?" Stormy asked and exchanged a long look with Leo. That meant she was alive and Barin was wrong. That meant things could go nasty come sunup.

"Which Commander are you lookin' for?" Leo asked.

"Don't know his name," Cephas said.

"Commander Neal," Donald interrupted.

"I don't think I should take you to him. Could be dangerous," Stormy said.

"I'm not afraid!" Cephas said.

"Dangerous for the commander!" Stormy squinted at the two.

"Please sir, it's urgent. Lady Erika says this message has to get to him before morning. It's a life or death message," Donald pleaded.

"Let's see it," Stormy held out his hand, still suspicious of two young rascals.

"Could be horse thieves," Leo mumbled quietly.

"We're not thieves. We had to sneak to get here so the other men didn't see us."

That made sense. Stormy wiggled his fingers, prodding the boy to give him the message.

"It's sealed. I can't give it to you. Lady Erika says no one opens it but Commander Neal."

If they were going to get the message to the commander before the sun comes up, and before he takes off to see the prince, they'd better go now. Leo stashed his dagger in his belt.

"Follow me," Stormy said.

Neal finished his stew, brooding over the task before him. In a quiet nook in the woods, away from the soldiers and away from Barin, he stood by his campfire warming his hands, contemplating on confronting the prince before sunrise. A difficult task, Barin was royalty, he only a servant. Friends all their lives, Neal had been Barin's confidant. Whether he could get Barin to listen to him would depend on how he delivered his advice.

Perhaps the answer to the situation would come from the castle. He hoped Rory delivered the warning. So far, no sign.

He heard a disturbance further down the hill at Barin's camp. Someone shouted, men scuffled, and then all went quiet. Neal didn't think too much on it. Soldiers sometimes fought amongst themselves before a battle, and this would be an edgy situation for anyone.

From where Neal stood, he could see both his own horse-bowmen and a little further down the hill Barin's crossbowmen, soldiers that Neal once led, but who now rode with Barin. They were dangerous men, each one skilled with their weapons. As a unit, these seasoned fighters could do a lot of damage. Would they believe Barin and attack King Tobias and the castle guards? Or would they be willing to follow Neal should he put a stop to this insanity?

Neal kicked a half-burnt log into the fire pit. He didn't want to fight Barin. They'd been friends for many years. Good friends. This whole situation turned his stomach. Every one of these men were faithful Potamians—every one! Loyal to the Crown. Good, faithful soldiers. And the men from Fairmistle were devoted subjects.

In his right mind, Barin would never kill his own men. He loved his father. His intentions were honorable, even if what he's doing is appalling.

Neal was allowed to discuss battle plans, but he should not argue with the Prince. By the grace of King Tobias, he swore to push his boundaries tonight. He might be court-martialed. Contesting a decision by a royal during a time of warfare could bring a charge of high treason. Even arguing with an heir to the throne could be an offense worthy of the guardhouse. But he'd risk it. Tonight!

His only other option, if the prince murders Potamians, would be to kill him.

Neal spat and threw the rest of his soup in the fire.

"Commander Neal, sir! A note from the princess!" Stormy and his friend appeared from out of the woods, catching him off guard. His heart skipped a beat! He should be more alert and not so engulfed in his own thoughts that the enemy could ambush him. He sighed when he saw who they were. They had with them two boys who were much too young to be in a war camp.

Neal regarded each of them quietly before he responded. A note from Erika?

"Very well," he said, and took the letter. He reached in his pocket for a coin or two and offered them to Cephas first, who grabbed the shillings out of his hand. Neal handed Donald a coin as well.

"Thank you, sir, you can give my portion to Cephas. He lives on the streets. Princess Erika, she takes fine care of me in the castle. I do not need coin."

Neal nodded and gave Cephas the other two schillings. Sure proof who is occupying the castle, he thought. "What are your plans? Are you going back to the castle now?"

They looked at each other.

"It's not safe. There are men up here who will shoot if they see anyone move toward the palace." Neal explained.

"We know, sir. We watched a man get shot yesterday," Donald said.

Neal frowned. "Who? Do you know?"

"I don't know him personal. Fiery hair, he had. Kind of like yours," he pointed at Stormy. "He came from Fairmistle with a message to Erika. Rode one of the king's horses. I know the horse. Sometimes I work in the stables."

Stormy gasped. "Rory?"

"I don't know his name. Got shot bad though. Lady Erika pulled the arrow out and he's recovering, but lady Sylvia says if he gets an infection he'll die. Hope no one else gets shot. It's not pretty."

It had to be Rory, but for Stormy's sake Neal said nothing. Still, he moaned to himself for another young ally sacrificed. This has to end! At least Erika got their message.

"Why are you folks here? Isn't that Prince Barin? Why is he...?" Donald brushed his hair out of his eyes and looked around. "What's he doing? What are you doing?"

"War maneuvers, son. Classified information." Neal glanced at Barin's camp again as the prince's fire seemed to have grown.

"You two stay here until this conflict is over. Going back to the castle now is dangerous."

"Yes, sir."

"We'll pay you a soldier's wage," Neal told Cephas.

The boy stood straight and saluted. "Yes, sir!"

"Your job will be to watch my campfire. Stay here and get warm. Make yourselves comfortable. There's soup in the pot. Help yourselves."

"Thank you, sir, but aren't you going to read your letter?" Donald asked. "Princess Erika wanted me to promise I'd have you read it before dawn."

"I'll read it in private, thank you." Neal excused himself from the boys after offering them a stick of smoked beef and showed them where the cups were. He walked a way toward Barin's camp and then broke King Tobias' seal on the letter.

Dear Neal

The only thing I can think to do is capture Barin and bring him here. I sent two men to do so, but I don't think they succeeded. It's up to you! Kairos has a potion to put him to sleep until a more appropriate time.

Please don't hurt him.

Erika.

"So! Kairos got away! Good for him. But capturing Barin might be a little harder than it sounds," Neal whispered to himself. The scheme made sense. With the prince indisposed, Neal would then be in command of the troops. But how do we do such a thing? Neal had only an hour before sunrise.

He tucked the letter in his coat and ambled to Barin's camp, passing his troops. The men following Barin had come from Tellwater with Neal, but the few others who had walked off the mountain with Barin had been half starved and traveling for days. Their clothes were ragged, they were thin, and they had a wild and confused look about them. Their minds half gone and in the hands of Skotádi, Neal would have to watch them closely.

Prince Barin stood by his campfire, hands behind his back, head held proudly. He faced two soldiers tied with rope, their mouths gagged. Men stoked an already raging fire, adding large chunks of cedar wood. No one spoke, but the anger fuming from Barin could have burned more logs than the flames in his campfire.

"What's happening. Why the massive fire?" Neal asked.

Barin glanced at him, a brief, angry glare. "We're about to teach our soldiers a lesson," he said, nodding to the two captives. Neal recognized the men that were tied. They were sentries from King Tobias' guardhouse. "Soon as everyone gets here."

"What happened?" Neal asked cautiously, noticing how Barin's wild eyes glowered.

"I caught these men in the act of treason. An attempted assassination."

Neal raised his brow and made eye contact with the men. They were sweating, their eyes unusually wide and fearful.

"And what kind of lesson are you going to teach them?" Neal asked.

"One that all our soldiers should learn, Commander Neal. These men came from the castle, sent by Moshere. Traitors! They have committed high treason, punishable by death." He nodded to the fire. "Which will be carried out immediately."

"You're going to burn them alive? Without a trial?"

Barin glared at him and lifted his chin. "And send their bones back to the emperor with a message. We will not surrender the Tobian kingdom to him."

"Have they defended themselves?"

"Lies, Neal. I have no time to listen to lies."

Neal's heart stopped. "These men are Potamian. You can't do this without a trial!"

"And you're going to stop me? This is war, Neal."

The crowd congregated around them, men who were being forced to witness this horrendous act. Apparently Barin had summoned everyone in camp to watch. Some of them wore terror on their faces, some confused, some merely following orders. A few looked at Neal with pleading eyes. They knew their prince had stumbled into the hornet's nest and feared he would do them more harm than any battle would. Neal must rescue them.

And he must rescue Barin, as well.

He set his jaw. Prince or not. Duty or not, he refused to allow Barin this savagery. Neal turned his back to the prince. He clenched his fist and allowed the rage inside of him to swell.

With no warning, he whirled around and with the full force of his angst, hit Barin in the face so hard that the prince fell in the fire. Neal quickly drew his sword and pointed it at the soldiers, some ready to pounce, but most of them simply gawked. Barin scooted out of the flames and bounced back, drawing his sword yet disoriented. Neal quickly sheathed his weapon and grabbed Barin's cloak collar, pulled him close and hit him again. This time Barin fell unconscious.

Neal's entire body shook, his fist throbbing from the impact. He pointed at two men who stood next to the prisoners

"You two, cut those men lose."

They obeyed hesitantly. Several soldiers drew their swords. Neal glared at them, daring them.

"I am your commanding officer," he said. "You," he spoke to the two Potamian sentries who had moments ago faced execution but were now rubbing the rope burns on their wrists.

"Yes sir," they said.

"Take your prince to the castle."

The men immediately lifted Barin, one at his shoulders, one at his feet and proceeded down the trail with him.

"These men did not commit treason," he told the assembly, pointing at the sentries. His body shook from having hit the prince, but he contained himself.

"Princess Erika sent them to take Barin to safety. The prince has been under the influence of a demon." The men gasped. "That's right. The princess lives, and so does King Tobias. Your prince might have gotten himself killed tonight. Would you have wanted that?"

He searched the crowd for the men he'd seen earlier, the thin ones that Barin had come down from the mountain with.

"You! You were up on Casda de Moor with the prince, were you not?"

"Yes, sir," someone in the group answered.

"You all are also affected by a demon. Hear me. Emperor Barte son of Moshere has not invaded our land, nor has he overthrown your King. Princess Erika has been holding the keep. There are no foreign invaders. There will be no attack. No siege. We're home. Before we go on to the castle, I want every man who has been on Casda de Moor to stand before me." He looked at the men who had swords in their hands. "Starting with you two."

"What are you going to do to us, sir?" one of them asked meekly.

"I'm going to keep you under careful watch."

The Curse

Having kept watch, when Erika saw the soldiers carrying a body, she ordered the guards to open the ingress, and the castle soon thundered with activity. Soldiers met the sentries with a stretcher, and they carried the unconscious prince into the castle, through the dark hall, and up the spiral stairwell to Barin's room. Following them were chamberlains and physickers. Criers raced to Olinda, and Rhea's rooms to announce the prince. A page summoned Kairos. Servants rushed to bring linen, water, and food.

Get my father from the keep," Erika ordered two guards as she passed them. Breathless from the excitement, she hurried behind her soldiers carrying her brother.

"Bring Father to Barin's room." She stopped the chamberlain. "We need another bed made up. One for my father. Hurry."

"Do you think that wise? To have your father in the same room with the prince in the state he's in?" Kairos asked as he trotted down the stairs and caught up to her.

"You're going to put him to sleep, are you not? Isn't that what you said?"

"I did."

"Then he'll be fine. Father will watch over him. He'll be ecstatic. He's been despondent over Barin and he wants out of that dark prison of a tower, anyway."

Erika and Kairos hurried to Barin's room and arrived just as the sentries lay the prince on his bed. Erika immediately unstrapped Barin's weapons and handed them to a page.

"Take these to my room," she ordered. "Oh, my heavens, look at him!"

The bruise on Barin's head had blackened and soot covered his topaz hair.

"How we missed you, Barin!" she whispered and kissed his cheek. "What do you need, Kairos? What kind of potion? Do you have everything?"

"Yes. It's right here in my vial," he patted his robe. "We don't want him to wake up."

She felt the bruises on Barin's face. "I told them not to hurt him." She looked up at the soldiers.

"Commander Neal hit him. I don't think there'd been any other way. If it hadn't been for the commander, we'd be dead men."

"They caught you?"

"We were hiding, waiting for him to step off alone when he saw us. It didn't take long before he had us tied and bound with the rope we were going to use on him. Next thing you know he had his men start a bonfire and..." the other man nudged him. "He was going to punish us."

Erika shuddered. That her brother would turn on his own men made her stomach upset. It was up to her to convince the soldiers that Barin was as much a victim as they were.

"Commander Neal saved you? He's a good man. My brother has been under a spell. He's disoriented, confused. Please don't hold it against him, no matter how much he's threatened you. He's a good man too."

"Yes, Fairest. We respect the Prince and have fought for him through many battles. He hasn't been himself, and it's because of his imprisonment. We're all worried for him. It grieves us he's in such a state as this."

"We're glad you have him, now," the other sentry said.

"Well, he's going to get better now." Erika took a rag from the basin a servant brought her, and sponged Barin's face, picking charcoal and ash out of his hair. "Neal can certainly throw a punch, can't he?" she whispered. For a moment, Barin's eyes opened, and he blinked. "Erika?"

"Shh,"

"Get me up!" Barin tried to sit.

"Quick, Kairos!"

Kairos rummaged through the pockets of his cloak for his vial. Barin would have sprung forth if Erika hadn't stepped away and let the soldiers hold him down. The more forceful his restraint, the harder Barin fought. Like a rabid dog he drooled, and his pupils had a faint red tint to them, as if his soul were on fire.

"Where is my sword? You! What have you done with my sister?" Barin's eyes were wild as he tried to lunge at Erika.

"What did they do to him?" Erika gasped as she stepped back.

"You killed her, you deceiver!" Barin choked as Kairos poured the contents of his vial down his throat. Barin had to swallow and within moments the prince relaxed and fell against the pillows with his eyes closed.

"Poor, Barin." Erika whispered as she wiped the drool from his mouth. "My poor brother." She threw the rag into the wash pan and buried her head in her hands.

"I will fight this, Kairos," she whispered to the wizard. "No matter the cost I will fight Skotádi." She looked Kairos in the eye. The wizard nodded.

"Give this tincture to him every morning. He needs to be awake in order to eat. Perhaps we should strap him down." Kairos looked up at Erika. "Someone strong will have to feed him. One of your sentries, I would think."

Erika nodded, still shaking. "Guards, bring in restrainers and keep him in them until I give the word to release him."

The men left and her sisters flowed into the room gracefully, bringing food and a kettle.

"Barin's not eating right now."

"This is for Father."

"Father can't stay here." Erika stood, preventing the men from bringing in the king. "Take him to his own chambers."

"Let me see him!" King Tobias demanded.

"Father, you can't stay here."

"Just let me see him."

Erika nodded to the men who bore her father, and they brought the king by Barin's bed. The room fell silent as King Tobias gazed on his sleeping son. Erika could not decipher her father's thoughts, but he had a sorrowful expression, and his shoulders sank. He merely nodded.

"Very well," he breathed. "He's home now. That's good."

The men took King Tobias out of the room with Olinda and Rhea hurrying behind

Erika went to Rory's room before she retired for the night. He deserved to know what had happened. He had risked his life for Barin's sake. Worse, he had been treated as a criminal ever since he came back from Cho Nisi, and she blamed herself for that.

Rory had been sleeping when she opened the door, but he raised his head as soon as she stepped inside.

"I didn't mean to wake you."

"I've been restin', Fairest."

She regarded the small room, one bed and a bone lit window. "It's more like a prison, isn't it?" she asked. "I'm sorry. We should get you into someplace better come morning."

"I don't much care."

"I do." She sat on the foot of his bed and felt his head for fever. Warm, but not hot.

"We have Barin," she said.

"Good!" he answered and then frowned. "What do you mean you 'have' him?"

"We've taken him into the castle, away from the troops. So, there will not be any siege by our own men. No one's going to get killed."

Rory sighed in relief. "Oh, Fairest, that warms my heart. We didn't want to see the prince carry through with the dark lord's plans."

She nodded and folded her hands. "He's ill. Kairos can't cure him, you know. But the wizard has a tonic that puts him to sleep and aside from having to strap him down to feed him, he'll be sleeping until we find a way to get the curse out of him."

Rory frowned. "You'll find a way."

"I think we will. We love him too much to let him stay in Skotádi's hands."

She patted his leg and then stood. "I mean what I said about getting you someplace nicer than this. I want you to get well and no one can heal in a cell."

"I won't be arguin' with you."

"There's a guest room upstairs with a terrace and curtains and all the niceties. I'm reserving that for you. I'll send for someone tonight to take you there."

"You're special, fairest princess."

"No. You are."

Father's Wisdom

Barin's drug wore off early in the morning, and then the servants administered food to him. With the prince strapped to his bed, despite how hard he fought to be free and the profanities he uttered, the terror and carrying on, the men managed to feed him.

Erika missed her brother. She kept vigil by his side every night when he slept, held his hand, spoke to him, cooled his head with a rag. But during his waking hours, she dreaded seeing him struggle and often stole off to her father's room during his feeding. Her brother's screams echoed through the halls and could be heard as far as in the king's chambers.

Three days after they had rescued Prince Barin, Cephas came to Erika's door.

"You have a note for me?" she asked the lad. With Barin's condition, a cloud of depression hung over the castle as if Skotádi had cursed the entire kingdom. Good news would be a healthy reprieve.

"No note. Just words," the boy replied. His eyes were open wide, as if what he had to say would terrify her.

"And those words are?" she asked.

"There's a rumor the sailors wanted you to know."

"A rumor? Why do you worry me with rumors?" she asked.

"They told me you would want to know. Two anglers who were fishing near the island heard a great noise and threw down their nets. One of them hurried along the beach to see who had called out for help. He said he saw a man up on a hill wielding a great sword about as big as this room fighting those winged beasts. The flock became a black cloud and came at him like a twister swallows a farmhouse. The man didn't win. The anglers saw him fall."

She stared at the boy, not sure if the reason he came to her was because the rumor was about Arell. Her skin grew cold as her heart slowed. This is only a rumor, she told herself. It couldn't be Arell. Odd how he was the first person who came to mind, as if the man were continually in her thoughts. She caught herself from falling by leaning against the door frame.

"Are you all right?" Cephas asked. She nodded.

"After the man fell, chanting began, and the skura were taken up into the sky. The men saw natives put the man on a horse and rode off. The fishers thought you and the king should know."

Erika reached in the purse strapped around her waist and pulled out a few coins.

"Is that all?" she said, breathless, afraid she would faint in front of the lad if he didn't leave soon.

"That's all. Just that the anglers were sure this man was important. Maybe a king or someone. Just bringing the message. That's what they told me to say. Only they didn't say the sword was as big as this room, I said that because it had to be if he were fighting those monsters three at a time like they said he was."

Erika listened intently, her heart sinking.

"Thank you, Cephas," she said as she dropped the silver pieces in his hand.

"Much obliged!" He grinned just before a blood-curdling scream came from Barin's room. Cephas jumped and looked down the hall. Feeding time.

"Go now," she told him. He mustn't know the condition of the prince. No one in Prasa Potama should know. After Cephas raced away down the corridor, Erika felt her head for fever, collected her balance, and left for father's chambers.

"Is he going to get better, Erika?" the king asked as soon as she stepped into his room. "I don't know, Father. Kairos says he can't undo a curse."

"I bet those Cho Nisi can. Didn't your Arell fellow write a letter telling us they wanted to be friends?"

"He did."

"Why don't you write him back and ask him to bring some of their healing ministers here?"

"Father, I don't think they can."

"It won't hurt to ask."

"I just got word that the skura have surrounded the island and that maybe...," she breathed deeply. It was just a rumor, she told herself again. "They said that maybe it had involved the king."

King Tobias frowned. "When did you hear this?"

315

Erika bowed her head. There was a tremor in her voice when she spoke of the news. "Cephas was just here, only a moment ago. He said a fisher saw someone mauled by the demons. The man didn't know who, but they thought it was King Arell. No one has said whether he lived or died." She turned away from her father, afraid that she'd break down. Her father sighed, exhaled, and patted her hand.

"You should go see."

"Me? Father, they banished me from the island." She wiped her eyes with her sleeve.

"Who did?"

"The elders. They have orders to kill me on sight."

"Nonsense. You can't banish an ally from your homeland. Either you're friends, or you aren't."

"Well, they did."

"Go anyway. Take an army."

"Father!"

"Since when has the threat of death ever stopped you?" He took her chin and lifted her head. "My daughter, you've fought against being a princess since you were small, you defied your brother and took off to conquer a nation, you adorned yourself with armor when all odds were against you. Who's stopping you now?"

His eyes filled with love, his words were like a waterfall to her soul. She'd been a goose flying against the skein all her life. She never regretted soaring against the wind. Passion had always been her motive.

"It's not death I'm afraid of."

"Then what is it?"

She swallowed her tears. She couldn't see Arell again. It would break her heart. What would she do if he told her to leave? To be in his presence again was more than a dream, more than a hunger, more than impossible.

"Love."

Her father raised his brow and gave her a contemplative frown. "Then I shouldn't ask such a thing of my daughter. There's no need for you to be involved in politics. Perhaps we can send someone else. Kairos. They didn't banish him, did they?"

"No! I mean, no he wasn't banished but… it's not that I don't want to go. I do."

Her father raised his brow. "You do?"

She swallowed and composed herself. "Of course, I want to help in any way I can."

"You can help with Barin."

"Father."

Wisdom beamed on his face. "What Erika?"

"You're teasing me. You tell me to go to the island and now you tell me no. Which is it?"

"Do what is in your heart."

She looked deep into her father's eyes. Had he known all along her feelings for Arell? She had contested Rhea at one time, challenging her to tell Father that she loved Kairos. Now it was her turn to speak the truth to her father.

"Arell is in my heart," she whispered.

"Just as I suspected," he said, and a smile slowly crept over his countenance. His smile turned to a soft chuckle, and he nodded. "That sounds more like the Erika I know." He patted her hand.

Life had come back to him. If that were a sign, she could defeat the devil. Yes. She would go.

"Thank you, Father."

Kairos had been at the door watching them with his arms folded. The king waved him inside. "Ah! The wizard! Just in time. See that, Erika? Take Kairos with you. And some of his apprentices. They can help with Cho Nisi's skura problem."

"Excellent. Did you hear that, Kairos?" she asked the wizard. He observed Erika and her father for a moment.

"What? Go to Cho Nisi with you? Again?"

Erika nodded.

"To do what?"

"To fight skura."

Kairos breathed in deeply.

"You do a marvelous job."

"Yes, well, we need to talk about that. You see my heart—" his voice tapered, and he rolled his eyes and sighed again. "I will be strong," he muttered and then smiled. "So long as I'm not taken prisoner, I suppose I could oversee it. Can Rhea come?"

"No," Tobias said bluntly. "Rhea stays here. That way I know you'll come back."

Kairos frowned. "Well, then if I must."

Truth

A veiled horizon wavered between the sea and the leaden clouds of the afternoon the Potamians drew near to Northport. Despite the flurrying skura that hovered above the island, Erika's ship glided to the pier without incident. Kairos' apprentices and archers stood along the gunwale, assessing their enemy and readying their munitions until the ship docked and sailors lowered the gangplank to an equally damp wharf. Drums on shore beat like an excited heart of a dying man, the charm keeping the beasts in the air, though it resonated more like a death chant than a vigil. Erika said nothing, but she and the wizard kept their eyes to the sky. She could see them in the clouds, black wings whipping furiously as the beasts struggled for control, and every so often a glower of a skura's eye scowled down at her.

"Send only a few soldiers with me, have the rest stay here," she told the shipmaster. "I and the wizards need go right now. I'll leave two of the apprentices with you, just in case," she added. "Better not to offer more bait than necessary."

The shipmaster bowed. "Thank you, Fairest."

Erika wore her silver armor, her breastplate, shoulder guards and arm braces over her dresses. She buckled her father's sword to her belt and adjusted it to her side. The cloak she wore, as green as the pine on Mount Ream, with the Potamian coat of arms on its lower front emphasized her royalty. Her red hair trundled over her shoulders, braided at the sides and down the back tied with a leather lace. She stepped off the boat and a small regiment of soldiers followed her.

Kairos took her hand and helped her down the gangplank. "Where to?"

She looked around and glanced again at the dark cloud of skura. "We could start right now ridding the island of those horrid creatures."

"We could. Didn't you want to see the king first, though? Shouldn't you—I don't know, ask permission?"

She shot him a grimace. "I'm sure the king won't mind if we kill skura on his island. He did request help in his most recent letter. Why waste time, Kairos? There are thousands of the brutes up there and you do so well at annihilating them."

Kairos waved for his apprentices. "As you wish, Fairest."

Seven wizards, all in cloaks of dark silk and gold embroidery, pointed cowls and poulaine shoes, followed them down the pier and onto shore. King Tobias had chosen well in his selection of apprentices. They were a graceful group. Young men and women, frail in stature, but strong in spirit and extremely talented.

"Follow me," Erika said and headed toward the sound of the drums. Oddly, she had no fear. Her confidence in Kairos had grown and being on the island with an army of support gave her buoyancy.

By the sound of the drumming that resonated over the waters, there was an army of natives chanting. However, only six men and two women kept vigil here. She recognized one of them. An elder. Abenda by name and she held her breath as she drew near, not certain what to do. Before she came close to the man, Kairos moved in front of her and he and the wizards approached first. The drums didn't stop beating, but Abenda stepped forward in his ceremonial garb. He also had a sword, drew it, and with two hands, held it in front of him. The blade shone, catching rays of sunlight, a threatening glow. His focus rested on Erika, and he lifted his head. The grimace and steel eyes seized her. Abenda's desire to see her dead radiated in his eyes. Indeed, he was the reason the Cho Nisi had issued a death warrant against her.

"You defy our law," he said.

Erika kept her fear contained. Her father reigned as king of a great nation. This man meant nothing to her, and she already paid her debt to the island more than they would ever realize. Her intentions for coming here were for their benefit. She should have nothing to fear.

"Law or no law, my wizards can take this curse away," she said confidently, though her heart thumped.

The soldiers behind Erika also drew their swords, but it was Kairos who moved closer to her. He fidgeted with something under his cloak.

Erika gave the soldiers a hand signal to stand down.

"There is a death warrant for you. I have legal right to take your life." Abenda lifted his weapon, but Erika stood her ground.

Kairos pulled a vial from his belt, dropped a potion on his hands, and rubbed his fingertips together, his dark eyes fixed on Abenda. He made no secret of his actions.

"And there is a death warrant for those skura you wrestle with. Let go of your hostilities and let us help."

The moment froze, the elder ready to strike, Erika poised, daring him. The sound of drums and the low groaning of the ship broke the silence as the world held its breath. Abenda did not move his head, but he eyed the wizard, the apprentices, and the soldiers.

After Kairos flicked a spark of magic into the air that popped and sizzled, Abenda took a step back, his hands still grasping his sword upright. He wouldn't dare try to kill her now with so much at stake and Kairos' magic hot in the wizard's hand, would he? Perchance his thoughts mirrored hers, for his eyes darted between her and Kairos. Anger burned in his cheeks, but finally he withdrew and pushed his sword back into its sheath.

When Abenda exhaled, he bowed—slightly—with no expression on his face, but he *did* bow. Erika swallowed, glad Kairos didn't have to bluster him. She would help Cho Nisi, despite the elders.

"Where is King Arell?" she asked, holding her breath, dreading the news. If he died, she would shatter into tiny fragments and sail on a gust of sorrow to the depths of the sea.

"In the castle."

Erika nodded a thank you without revealing her relief.

"The wizards will take care of the winged demons. Please, just let them do their work."

She wet her lips and looked up at the terror in the sky. A mass of evil, black as night, the skura flew against the wind in circles, squawking. Their horrid human faces contorted, their mouths open wide, fangs showing. She despised them and despised the one who created them.

She turned to Abenda. "You must stop drumming."

That brought a disturbed countenance, and a worried glance. He looked at his drummers, she at her wizards. Kairos stood more confident than she'd ever seen him, and he had a look of pride. She smiled and spoke to Abenda.

"Never fear. They know what they're doing. And there's an army here to oversee any strays that might slip by Kairos."

She nodded to the soldiers and stepped away toward the castle.

Before she got up the rise, though, she looked back. Already Kairos had taken over, ushering the drummers to a safe overhang on the beach. He silenced their drums by laying his hand on one and holding his finger to his lips. The drumbeat stopped.

The apprentices formed a circle under the ring of skura, rolled up their sleeves and pulled their vials from their robes. Kairos rushed back to them and snapped his wrist at the sky. The skura dove, and then the explosions began.

Sudden puffs of black smoke dotted the atmosphere as one by one the skura burst. The individual eruptions multiplied until the entire sky filled with sparks while thunder shook the earth. Smoke mingled in the clouds, and red ash fell. There were many more skura to contend with, but Kairos seemed to enjoy himself. He dared the beasts, waved at them, while sporting that grand smile of his.

Pleased and proud of her wizards, Erika continued her trek. The narrow path wound up a rolling hill and, in the distance, through a mist, she could see the towers of the castle.

As she moved away from Kairos and the wizards, an eerie chill rushed through her. More than skura hovering over the island, this odd sensation reminded her of the trip from Tellwater Valley. The same premonition she had in the forest when she saw the misty fingers of a mountain giant for the first time plagued her now. The same heavy ambiance she experienced in Canyon Gia. That couldn't be right, though. In his letter, Arell said they had chased all the mountain giants away. Maybe they did, but tonight there were no fires along the hillside as there should be. The Cho Nisi had become too engaged in keeping ten thousand skura from attacking to worry about tending fires.

A grey sky and low clouds drifted over her head. She could see the palace now, its ashen walls covered with moss, and the towers lost like islands in the mist. The dankness sent a chill through her. The troublesome odor of discord lit her senses. She tightened her grip on her sword and hurried to the gates. A Moaton sentry greeted her.

"Fairest," he bowed.

"I'm here to see the king," she told him.

"And you are?"

"Princess Erika, daughter of King Tobias."

"Fairest," he bowed and when he rose, he looked over her shoulder. "I've heard your name on the lips of the elders. And you escaped the native's death sentence? Did you have any trouble on the beach?"

"We took care of the trouble at the beach."

He took an on-guard stance and his hand went to his sword, though his expression showed confusion. "You threaten our king?"

"No, soldier, I come in peace."

He relaxed as he studied her. "The king has mentioned your name and always with compassion."

"I'm no threat, I promise."

"King Arell is in his quarters. He's not expecting visitors. On the contrary, he has ordered everyone except the warriors to shelter in Moaton? There are only a few of us keeping watch on his behalf."

"Shelters? I don't understand?"

"The skura! Haven't you seen? They overrun the island. We're defeated. The Cho Nisi grow tired, and it is only a matter of time before the drumming ceases. Osage leads an army along our shores, but we are small in force. The homes in Moaton have cellars, and that's where most everyone is. I suggest you take refuge there as well. We're hoping Skotádi will have mercy on the common folk."

"If you're hoping for mercy, why isn't the king in a shelter?"

"King Arell has accepted death. He asked us to let him pass this life while in his chambers. It is his intent to slay as many skura as he can before he dies."

Erika's heart skipped a beat. Death? "King Arell is dying?"

"He's in a bad way, having been ravaged a few days ago by the skura. They say he will die the moment the drums cease. With so many skura, and with the mist hovering over the island, there is little hope for any of us. When the attack comes, Osage will return here with his troops and King Arell will raise his sword in the castle's defense. A ceremonious end, for I don't believe he's extraordinarily strong."

"Let me see him."

He hesitated for a moment and then stepped aside. "As you wish. No more ill could come to him than what we've already expected."

The sentry opened the door to an unusually dark and empty palace. The stone walls were lit by torches, rays of gold light reflected on the polished floor, beckoning her inward. She took a torch from its bracket. The hollowness of the fortress made her edgy, so she hurried.

Erika followed the hall past closed doors to the servant's

quarters and the pantry. Several women worked near the hearth, but they didn't see her, and she didn't recognize them, and so Erika moved on. She hurried up the spiral staircase to the second floor where Arell's chambers were. The doors to the grand hall were open, the room empty but for the dining table, now unadorned.

A shape outside the window caught her eye. A figure in a dark cloak. At first, she thought a wizard had followed her, but when she saw the mist swirling around his feet, and hollow darkness under his cowl, she panicked.

"No," she gasped and then ran. Her feet were silent on the wooden floors, but her heartbeat loudly. Each room she passed she looked out the sheer bone panels to see the mist outside coagulating, thicker and thicker, and it rose, as if traveling up to Arell's room with her.

She sped faster, out of breath, her lungs hurting as she flew up the spiral staircase, down another hall until she came to his room. She hesitated for only a fleeting moment and then drove the door open.

Shutters rattled. Mist filled the room, nebulous fingers stretched to the bed and coiled around Arell, seizing him from the covers and thrusting him up against a wall. The mist pressed the king. He woke, his eyes wide. His arms bound in vaporous rope tightening around him.

Erika held out her torch, and the mist sizzled away but then resurfaced. The cloaked figure materialized, his face shadowed under his hood. Darkness menaced the room, as if she'd been transported to some sort of chasm and now faced the devil. The sickly sweet smell of death pervaded the air. The mist strengthened its grasp around Arell, the mountain giant's shoulders slowly manifested with his gritty arms clutching the king. Arell gasped for breath. Erika lunged forward with her torch, but the robed figure held out a hand and a flame of heat shot at her. She recoiled in pain.

"Skotádi!"

The phantom held his other hand up toward the giant, and the mass of vapor loosened its hold enough for Arell to breathe. The king wheezed.

"Leave him alone," Erika cried.

Skotádi strolled up to Arell, grabbed his chin and inhaled deeply next to his mouth. Arell rolled his eyes back, breathless. The phantom turned to Erika and released a hollow laugh. When Arell looked at Erika, he wrestled against the phantom's hold, too weak to free himself. But how could he against a stony giant? His old wounds bled as he fought.

"What do you want with us?" Erika asked.

The phantom turned to Arell, his face hidden under his cowl, but a glimmer from his teeth revealed a snarl. "Where is it?" he asked, and when he spoke the room vibrated like pools of water.

Erika shuddered.

Skotádi stretched out his hand and pointed his scrawny thumb downward, a signal to the giant to kill, all the while watching Erika. Arell moaned. The tighter the misty form gripped Arell, the more the giant became visible. He was huge! His head bent under the ceiling and his shoulders were as wide as the bed. Dwarfed by the ogre, Arell had no chance of escape.

"Tell me where it is!"

The giant grunted as he squeezed. Erika heard bones snap. Arell cried out and blood drained from his wounds. Sickened and furious, Erika lunged again with her torch, screaming as Skotádi's flame burned her. The wind from his blaze pushed her back. She fought against it, coming near enough that she caught the giant's elbow and then seared his arm. The giant's limbs vaporized, and Sol disappeared. Arell fell to the floor.

Skotádi raged when his giant vanished into vapor, and the phantom's flame grew fiercer. He stood over Erika, scorching the hand that held the torch, and then the hand that held her sword. She dropped both. Skotádi stomped out the fire she held while pinning her to the ground with his blaze. He whistled loudly, and a skura flew to the windowsill—its hyena howl vibrated the room. It opened its mouth and spat fire.

"Demetri, kill!" Skotádi commanded and stepped back as the skura, a smile on its dreadful face, dove for Erika, giant talons extended, mouth open wide. Flames scorched her face and her hair. Fangs came at her throat. She screamed.

Its talons grasped her armor, its body pinned her to the floor. But before it could sink its teeth into her throat, its head sailed across the room, severed from its body like a cannon ball, crashing into Arell's vanity and breaking a mirror, a stream of smoke and embers trailed from it into the room. Skotádi vanished instantly.

Erika gasped. The dead skura's headless body lay at her feet, and Arell—propped up against the wall, pale, barely breathing—held her bloody sword in his hands.

She settled where she had fallen, exhausted, her heart racing. Arell sunk to the floor. Erika listened to his gasping as she, herself, recovered. Her hands still burned, leaving red marks that blistered.

"Why is he doing this?" Her voice trembled. "What is he looking for?"

Only forced breathing from Arell answered. She crawled next to the pale and bloody king. He'd been staring at her. Despite his wheezing and his wounds, he pulled himself to his feet while leaning on the wall, and offered her his hand, though he seemed not to have enough strength to help her up. She accepted but used her own weight to stand.

He drew her close to him and then, as if it should have been happening all along, their mouths sealed together. Their tongues spoke a language there were no words for. She heard the sword drop. He caressed her hair as they kissed—massaged her head and rubbed her neck—she, his back. If she hadn't armor on, they would be closer still.

She pulled away. "You're bleeding."

Arell squinted as she helped him to his bed.

"They need to be wrapped again. Let me dress your wounds."

"Why did you come back? They elders want to kill you."

When she unwrapped his lesions, she moaned in sympathy. He'd been pulverized. "Those skura really did a number on you."

"I got a few in return. Not enough."

"One man cannot kill ten thousand demons. Someone should have helped you."

"They did, eventually. Serena keeps the dressings in the vanity."

"Serena's in a shelter?"

"I made her go. She wanted to stay, but I wouldn't have it."

"What's this I hear about you dying?"

"I'm a king. I must take a stand, even if it's my last one. We don't have a chance. You shouldn't have come. You should go to the cellars. Find safety there."

She pulled the soiled bandages back and got him fresh ones, poured water from the pitcher into a basin, and returned to the bed. He winced, though she washed his wounds as gently as she could.

"Why did you come back?" Sweat beaded on Arell's face, and

Erika could see the pain in his eyes, and hear it in his voice.

"I heard rumors you were hurt, and your island invaded." She smiled at him and wiped his hair out of his face. Death had been too close. If he had died, she may have given up on life herself. Her passion for Arell far surpassed her love for her family. This is where she longed to be—by his side. "Besides, I missed you."

He only stared at her. Perhaps she had no right to confess her feelings for him, but she didn't care. She nursed his wound tenderly as she spoke.

"I couldn't get you out of my thoughts. Remember that day on the beach? How we laughed together. How gentle you were, and kind. At home I thought of you every morning and in the evenings, I would lie on my bed and wish…" She shook her head and he frowned. "I wished I had not shot that arrow that killed your father." She wrapped the last of the surrounding dressing.

His hands were warm and gentle when he touched her cheek, and his eyes searched her soul, making her heart race. He moved toward the center of the bed and she found a place next to him.

"I wished things had been different as well. But they aren't," he whispered. "I wrestled with my feelings toward you after I found out what had happened. I didn't want to love you, Princess Erika."

The look in his eye melted her.

"I thought it more appropriate to hate you. You had ripped my heart in two. I tried to despise you, but I couldn't. So, I hid my feelings from the elders, too ashamed to love you for my father's sake." He sat upright on his pillow and reached out to her. She tingled at his touch, his fingers so gentle as they ran along the side of her face, behind her ear. He brushed her hair over her shoulder. "Take your armor off," he whispered.

As she unlaced her breastplate, he continued.

"When Silas told me not to write to you after you sent that warning—which saved the entire island—then I knew I'd have to yield to the truth."

"The truth?" She set her armor on the floor and loosened the ties to her bodice. He moved further to the center of the bed and she lay in his arms, careful to avoid his wound. He lifted her chin.

"The truth is, I care for you."

She shared the same air with him as they sealed their mouths together—warm and sweet—a delicious salty dampness. His tongue set her heart on fire and she pressed against it with hers. He moaned, a deep and resonant sound that vibrated through her body. He moved to his side and then groaned. Their lips parted, and he fell back on the pillows.

"You're in much pain. Lay down. Heal," she said and sat up again, her heart beating rapidly.

"How can I feel this way about you? You killed my father," he murmured. The elders will speak against it."

Her head flamed. She stood and pulled herself away from the bed. There were ethics to adhere to, moralities, protocol. She'd forgotten herself. Being this close to him felt both wrong and necessary. She tied her bodice with trembling hands.

"I came to save your island. That will help to make amends for your father's death. War is raging. You must get well. This evil Vouchsaver sees the union of our nations as a potent force against him. We can do him damage if we treaty with one another."

"Did you find your brother?"

"Yes. He's home now, but not well. The mountain giants imprisoned Barin and some of my father's soldiers. Skotádi is manipulating Barin's thoughts and had him lead a siege against my father's castle. We stopped him by kidnapping him. He is no better off than a madman right now. Kairos subdued him, but the wizard can't remove the curse, he says." She glanced at him to see his reaction.

"Perhaps the chief and his elders could have helped," he said.

"Could have?"

"Things have changed, princess." Arell sighed. "We cannot send anyone to Prasa Potama. We can't leave this island unprotected. The Cho Nisi will end the vigil soon. They grow weary and won't continue forever. We're hanging on to life by a thread until our drummers weaken and they release the skura. You received my letter?"

"There are ten thousand skura circling your island?"

He nodded, despair in his red and weary eyes.

"Kairos and his apprentices are ridding your island of the skura as we speak. He's found the spell to obliterate them and it works well. I think that's one reason Skotádi is so angry at us."

"Kairos? You're ridding the island of skura? Completely? Now?"

Erika nodded.

He sighed as he stared at her, disbelief in his eyes.

"It's true. Can you hear the explosions?"

She stood by the window and fell silent. The thunder of the battle came into his chamber.

"I hear it. We'll survive after all. You are a remarkable woman, Erika Tobias." When she returned to his bedside, he touched her face again, his voice affectionate. "Such a beautiful lady, and warrior. Strong, clever, loving, and full of fire. If only you—"

"Yes. I know. If only I hadn't killed your father. I'll never live it down. It is the shipwreck of my soul."

Return

Erika napped in the same room when she first came to Cho Nisi and washed up for the elegant dinner the scullions prepared. She didn't refuse a bath this time, familiar enough with the staff that she had no inhibitions. Serena proved herself a skilled domestic.

Erika often wondered about the girl's place in the castle, though. She knew Serena to be Chief Silas' daughter and assumed Arell loved her, surmising the chief would be more than delighted if his daughter married a king. Perhaps that was why Chief Silas added his own measures to her deportation. Had he been saving Arell's affection for his daughter?

Jealousy claimed her whenever Serena came into the room. Arell often smiled at the servant flirtatiously while Serena spent her days serving him. Erika must return to Prasa Potama tomorrow and Serena would still be here living in the castle with him. Who was Erika to Arell that she ask about these concerns? Arell had made no promises to her, no confessions of love either. As far as she knew, he was satisfied keeping his distance.

Serena poured water into the tub and felt the temperature making ripples with her delicate fingers. She smiled at Erika. "I think it's just right for you."

The servant's hands were warm, and her silky black hair tickled when it brushed Erika's shoulders as the servant slipped off Erika's robe. A sweet fragrance emitted from the woman, as though she'd been bathing in lilacs. Serena had a sensuous presence which might very well lure Arell into her bedchamber. But alas, Erika blocked such thoughts from her mind. What affair was it of hers?

As she slid into the bath, the warm water soothed her tired muscles. How sweet it would be if the bath could wash away the memory of Arell being crushed by that mountain giant, or the horrid look on the skura's face as it attacked her.

"I wish my thoughts were happier ones, right now Serena."

"You've been through a lot, Fairest. But there are pure and beautiful things you can wash your mind with."

"Such as?" Erika asked.

"Well," Serena said as she poured warm water over Erika's shoulders. "For one, you are lucky to have the attention of King Arell. He is a merciful man."

"Yes," Erika slid further down into the tub, letting the water cover her shoulders, and closed her eyes, enjoying the heat. "Merciful."

"I hope that you'll come back to our island and marry him."

What an odd thought. Erika sat back up.

"There was a time when my sisters and I flirted with Arell, we were carefree back then. Now he is a king and deserves a queen."

Erika looked at Serena, searching the girl for sincerity. Serena poured water over her shoulders again.

"So, you were interested in Arell as well?"

"Oh yes. All the girls on the island are. But my admiration was as a child who loved to look at sea glass. He is handsome and has a wonderful smile. He is gentle, kind, and loving. I enjoy being with him. But there's a Cho Nisi warrior who is making eyes at me of late. It's him I will marry."

Erika laughed to herself. What does all this mean? Falling in love with a young king whose father she killed and whose life she saved now to return home empty of spirit and alone.

"Those are pleasing thoughts, Serena. However, I doubt that would ever happen. Arell despises me for killing his father. I don't think we will marry. How can we? His grief is deep."

The servant didn't answer.

When Erika finished her bath, she dismissed Serena and dried off. Her clothes were laid out on the bed, and though blood stained Erika's armor, her dresses had been spared. With her gown on, and her hair now neatly brushed and flowing off her shoulders again, she considered her reflection in the brass mirror, hoping she looked as handsome to Arell as he appeared to her.

She needn't have worried. When she entered the dining hall, Arell stood. He wore his leather breastplate to help keep his torso steady and to relieve the pain of his broken ribs. Still weak, he held the back of his chair to balance himself, but he wore a smile. Both Chief Silas and Abenda sat close to Arell, who took the seat at the head of the table.

"You look lovely tonight, Erika," Arell whispered as he pulled her chair out.

"You needn't help me, Arell," she said. "Please. Don't strain yourself and open those wounds again."

Arell ignored her request and waited until she took her seat. She flushed and avoided looking at all the eyes studying her.

Serena and the servants brought food for them—shellfish and salmon, trays of different olives and berries. Bread and tiny petite cakes made from bakers in Moaton, and of course more wine from Tellwater Valley.

"My people are thankful for your help in eliminating the skura, Kairos," Arell opened the conversation as he offered Erika a basket of bread.

"The pleasure was mine." Kairos commented between bites.

"Abenda told me that the powers you possess, and those of the Cho Nisi work well together."

Kairos shrugged.

"Erika and I were confronted by Skotádi this afternoon. He tried to kill both of us."

None of these people were aware of what happened in Arell's chambers earlier. Only the servants and soldiers who discarded the dead skura understood, and so this announcement brought gasps of surprise. Chief Silas stopped eating, as did Abenda.

"Vasil, you were attacked by Skotádi himself?" Kairos asked, dumbfounded. "Erika, you as well? He is real, then? Did you kill him?"

"He exists—still. No, we didn't kill him and I'm not sure if we can. Whether he has an earthy body to destroy or if he is an apparition that is immortal, we don't know. He appeared in the mist and simply vanished with it. I fear the legends about him consuming souls are true. He almost consumed mine."

Silence.

Erika's stomach churned at the thought of Skotádi taking Arell's soul.

Arell went on, ignoring the food on his plate, and not touching his wine.

"You see, no matter how hard my soldiers, and my servants and the elders attempt to watch over me, this creature can slip in at the most unfortunate moments. I'm convinced, though, that I'm not his only target."

Though he hid it from the others and spoke calmly, Erika noticed his body tremble. He'd been hurt. He almost died. "I believe the threat that faces us, and faces King Tobias, and men in other parts of the world where we've never been can only be addressed by our union, not our divide."

She wasn't sure what Arell was getting at, but the word union filled her with a certain joy. Their nations would be allies again. How happy that would make her father! She peered at the two elders. They sat emotionless. They were always so hard to read, yet Abenda loathed her, this she knew.

Arell fixed his gaze on Abenda. The elder looked up at him.

"Please. Soften your heart toward this woman. She saved my life. There will be no peace with the kingdom of Tobias unless you do."

Abenda and Silas exchanged glances but again said nothing, showed nothing. Erika's blood rush to her head. She wanted to cry or run, aware that the elders were resisting his request. Short of slaying her, the elders did everything possible to keep her away from the island.

"Let us enjoy our meal. I for one am thankful for Erika that I have another day to live."

After another stiff silence, Kairos cleared his throat and stood, lifting his chalice. "To Your Royal Highnesses King Arell of Cho Nisi, and to our beautiful Princess Erika. May our nations know peace through you both."

His toast coaxed a smile out of her. Everyone but the elders raised cups.

They ate their meal and indulged in friendly conversation. When Serena cleared the table, Arell set his napkin down and tapped his chalice. "Please, hear me out." He waited for quiet. Erika watched him curiously.

"Chief Silas and Abenda have offered their honor to me."

The elders sat up straight and looked at each other.

"And tonight, I am going to make my request in front of these witnesses."

"Ask, Vasil," Silas said. It seemed ceremonious to Erika, and she wondered how it came to be that the two most important elders of the island had offered 'honor' to him. She remained quiet.

"This woman killed my father, and for that our island banished her and put a death warrant on her. She risked her life to return and to save not only our people, but my life. I ask that you return to King Tobias with the princess tomorrow and use your healing powers so that her brother be rid of the Skotádi curse and be made whole. Please."

A reverent stillness infused the room until the chief cleared his throat. "We will do as you ask, my king." Silas answered quietly. Abenda nodded, though a hint of resistance ignited his eyes.

Arell took a moment to compose himself and then looked at her. She mouthed the words "thank you."

"Good. Then we should waste no time, less we suffer another attack. The ship will leave in the morning for the Potamian mainland."

A sick feeling came over Erika. The news should be joyous, but dread and remorse stirred inside of her. She trembled as Kairos called for another toast and the wizards held their cups up. Of course, he and the sorcerers were happy, for they had completed their mission successfully. Through Kairos' hard work, the Cho Nisi were free of the skura. The wizard and his apprentices were heroes, and King Tobias would reward them.

But Erika would return home without the man she loved. She won his favor to the degree that he would ally with her father's kingdom, and that should satisfy her. Should, but didn't. Would she ever know a personal happiness, or would her only joy be in political achievements?

Her musings were selfish. Arell must guard over his kingdom, this entire island was under his charge. She would leave some wizards here to help him.

Erika woke just before dawn, slipped on the robe Serena had given her, and went outside on the terrace to watch the sunrise. She enjoyed the peace and beauty of the island, regardless of her experience here. The place had its charm—unusually warm weather compared to Prasa Potama, and rich in greenery with an abundance of fruit and colorful birds. So much of the heavens could be seen here, like a jeweled globe blanketing over this faraway world. The sun peeked into the dawn, illuminating the tips of mountain peaks on the mainland, spreading colors all over the sky and on the ocean. Birds sang. She would live here forever if Arell asked her to, but what a foolish fancy!

She must go home. Her father's kingdom needed her, the only royal child capable of leading her father's soldiers right now. The elders never ascertained whether their spells would heal Barin. They promised to do their best, and that was all she could ask. But she needed to be with them and make certain they did all that they had promised. Would their charms work? What if they found out they, like Kairos, had no power to remove a Vouchsaver's curse? Would Barin be bound as a madman for the rest of his life and Father die of a broken heart? Yes, she must go home and oversee the healing. There was much work to do.

She dressed slowly—solemnly. She approached this farewell nobly. First her gowns, and then her armor. Serena came and helped her.

"I'm sorry to see you go, princess," she whispered.

If Erika responded, she'd break down in tears and so she kept silent.

Arell came to her door. His chamberlain gathered her packs while Arell escorted Erika through the castle. He walked stiffly, wrapped in bandages under his doublet, but the Cho Nisi had herbs for pain and she hoped they'd given him ample to see him through the day. A groom waited for them with their horses and assisted Arell onto his. They rode horseback and said nothing on the way.

Grooms led the company through Moaton. The wizards followed, marching gallantly on the cobblestone road and carts with supplies for their trip and gifts for King Tobias rolled over the lane behind them and then onto the trail. Arell and Erika followed.

When they arrived at Northport, the servants helped the wounded king dismount. Erika slid off her horse gracefully. Having already arrived, Kairos and the apprentices waited for them on the beach and walked behind them. The wizards stepped lively, and Kairos hummed a pleasant song. Other Cho Nisi tribesmen came along also, but only Chief Silas and Abenda were going to make the trip with their drums strapped securely on their backs. Erika had chosen two of her wizard apprentices to stay behind in case Skotádi attacked Arell again.

Arell drew her aside as the entourage continued down the wharf and boarded the ship, saying nothing, he simply waited. He turned away from the docks and gazed at the white shores and olive groves that grew on the side of the hill. Erika enjoyed the view as well, in a yearning sort of way. Cho Nisi was a beautiful island. The sea shimmered turquoise, and sometimes she could see colorful fish under the water. Plants she'd never seen before grew wild and bore fruit she'd yet to eat. The island was indeed a paradise, too lovely for times like these. A utopia that she could fancy returning to someday, just as loving Arell had been a marvel too good to be real. He was someone she would lie on her bed and dream about.

Erika enjoyed walking close to him, his warmth, his strength, the fragrance of his sandalwood scented doublet. Her heart ached, wishing she didn't have to leave him. They could grow closer had they a few more weeks together. Unfortunately, the time came too soon for departure. The grooms finished unloading their wares and rolled the cart back down the pier. The helmsman called out, and a whistle blew.

"Come," Arell said.

Each step to the ship seemed like a funeral march to her, the brutal outcome to another hope lost. When they came to the gangplank, Arell walked up with her and escorted her to the prow. He looked out over the sea.

"Weigh anchor, loose for the sea!" the shipmaster called out, and the ship creaked and moaned as the sound of men's boots pattered on its decks.

Erika looked up at Arell.

Sailors heaved lines, and the vessel slid away from the dock. Once in open waters, the sheets were pulled, and the sails set. Arell, steadfast, faced the wind.

"There is much to do, Fairest," he said to her. "A brother to heal. Demons to destroy. Treaties to make, and contracts to fill." He looked at her. "I want to meet this father of yours. Perhaps he can give me advice on ruling a kingdom. Osage is watching the castle. He will protect Cho Nisi until I return."

Tears of joy welled in her eyes, and then the tears turned to agony, for Arell nodded. It was a gentle nod, but the closeness she wanted wasn't there. She reached for his hand but instead of taking it, he turned and walked to the elders.

She breathed in the cool ocean breeze and let the salty air dry her eyes. At least she'd be home with her family soon.

The End

Acknowledgments

Writing a novel is never a one person project. Granted the author takes the initiative, creates the characters, the story, the world. But until readers and editors survey it with a critical eye, it can never be assumed finished.

For that reason I want to thank two of my dearest friends, critique partners, and third eyes on this story, Gwen Whiting and Kim Mutch Emerson who helped me tear this work apart and put it back together again! I have a special thank you for Amy Ross Jolly and Toni Glitz who did my last round of edits. As always I want to thank my husband for supporting me during my intense hours at the computer If he weren't there to help the family, and make sure the house was in order, I may not have been able to write this work.

Sword of Cho Nisi is a new adventure for me and I hope you enjoyed book 1. The series continues, books 2 and 3 are all but complete and if, while reading this, they haven't been published yet they will be soon.

In April of 2021 I did a Kickstarter campaign for the series and one of the rewards was a personal thank you to those who offered the highest pledge titled "Lester's Revenge".

I want to thank **Cynthia Billodeaux** for her endearing support of this series and toward all my work!

Watch for

Sword of Cho Nisi Book 1 Rise of the Tobian Princess
Sword of Cho Nisi Book 2 Fall of a King
Sword of Cho Nisi Book 3 Curse of Mount Ream
Silver Threads: 5 companion stories to the Cho Nisi Saga

Other novels by D.L. Gardner
Ian's Realm Saga (seven book series)
Dylan
Where the Yellow Violets Grow
Thread of a Spider
An Unconventional Mr. Peadlebody
Pouraka
Hoarfrost to Roses

Novellas and short Stories
Tale of the Four Wizards
Lost on Taikus
The Far Side of Heaven

To subscribe to my newsletter and learn more, visit my website https://gardnersart.com

CPSIA information can be obtained
at www.ICGtesting.com
Printed in the USA
JSHW021020161222
34938JS00002B/76